He balled his fists, the
Because he didn't **much.**

And he certainly didn't need the distractions; this was one mission he couldn't afford to fail. He sighed and Ashli flinched. Máax lifted his head, ready to make a mad dash from the room if she woke up, but found himself entranced. Her plump lips and golden skin; her dark lashes, fanning along the crease of her catlike eyes; her hair a wild mass of thick black curls. He had no idea of her heritage, but never had there been a more seductive female in existence.

His eyes swept down the length of her small athletic frame covered only in a flimsy white sundress. Next to his large body, Ashli appeared more petite than she really was. An urge to dominate her, to take her right there, sparked.

Hell, man. That's enough, you horny bastard.

He slipped quickly from the bed before he did something he regretted. Like kiss her.

Or motorboat her.

You randy bastard.

He needed to go for a swim. Yes, the ocean water would cool him down. The ocean always made him feel better, like being home.

PRAISE FOR MIMI JEAN PAMFILOFF'S ACCIDENTALLY YOURS SERIES

"The story really made an impression and she definitely makes me want to continue on with her series...witty and catchy."

> —BookMaven623.wordpress.com on
> *Accidentally In Love With...A God?*

"Pamfiloff's knack for deeply engaging and funny story-telling is on clear display...The intense, fiery attraction between the two main characters, along with their crackling yet comfortable banter, will leave readers riveted...One truly delicious tale, which you'll savor with the turn of each page. 4½ stars, Top Pick!"

> —*RT Book Reviews* on
> *Accidentally In Love With...A God?*

"*Accidentally Married to...A Vampire?* remains one of the funniest paranormal novels I've read in a long time."

> —IndieBookSpot.com

"It was fun, the pace was fast, there were laugh-out-loud funny lines, plenty of pop-culture references, and lots of very sexy moments. I am *definitely* going to be reading the author's other books!"

> —SarahsBookshelves.blogspot.com on
> *Accidentally Married to...A Vampire?*

"Hot sex, a big misunderstanding, and a shocker of an ending that made me want the next book in the series now! I can't wait to go back and read the other books in the series."

> —Romancing-the-Book.com on *Accidentally...Evil?*

ACCIDENTALLY... OVER?

MIMI JEAN PAMFILOFF

FOREVER

NEW YORK   BOSTON

Copyright © 2014 by Mimi Jean Pamfiloff
Excerpt from *Vampires Need Not…Apply?* copyright © 2013 by Mimi Jean Pamfiloff

Forever
Hachette Book Group
237 Park Avenue
New York, NY 10017

www.HachetteBookGroup.com

Printed in the United States of America

First Edition: August 2014
10 9 8 7 6 5 4 3 2 1

OPM

Forever is an imprint of Grand Central Publishing.
The Forever name and logo are trademarks of Hachette Book Group, Inc.

The Hachette Speakers Bureau provides a wide range of authors for speaking events. To find out more, go to www.hachettespeakersbureau.com or call (866) 376-6591.

The publisher is not responsible for websites (or their content) that are not owned by the publisher.

To my family. Thank you.

Humble Groveling
Goes Out To

Thank you again to Beta Team Accidental (Kim, Vicki, Karen, Ashlee, and Nana). Your LOLs, Whats?, and Huhs? always make these books far more coherent for the general public.

Mimi Jean Street Team: many grovels for so many fun discussions and contributions to the man-parts vocabulary! You're like my coffee break of laughter every day!

As always, thank you to my editor, Latoya Smith, and the entire team at Hachette! Many grovels for your hard work!

Elise H.: thank you for bringing the word *hangry* to my vocabulary. It just so perfectly describes how I feel at 11:00 a.m.

Cassie: I can always count on you for naughty brainstorming! *Privie* goes on the list of world's best new words.

Warning

This book contains excessive use of the f-word by an overly cocky deity, corny references to sitcoms, a unicorn, the answer to life's questions, some very steamy jungle sex, inappropriate use of caramel topping, and poorly phrased Latin curses. In other words, Cimil approves.

Final Accidental Note from Cimil, Goddess of the Underworld

Well, my little people-pets, I must say that this journey has been a fun one. However, all things must come to an end, even for us fabulous deities. And though I know not (yes, I do; that's a lie!) where this last leg of our voyage will take us, I have a few guesses. Would you like to hear them? But of course you would! Because I'm awesome, and you love hearing anything I have to say.

A. Minky, my unicorn, finds the light of Eärendil, learns to mass-produce it, and saves the planet with green energy. (And she marries Legolas. Their children have pointy ears and a uni-fang.)
B. Clowns all around the world rise up from centuries of oppression by my hand and take the gods out with their horrifying, unnatural smiles.
C. I save the day by winning a mean game of Hungry Hungry Hippos, thereby restoring the Universe's faith in the power of the gods.
D. My stupid jokes finally catch up with me, and I am sent to live on another planet occupied by outrageously tiny, furry men with minuscule ding dongs.

Well, there you have it, my fun little humans. I hope you enjoy. And just remember, YOLO!

Mine Forever,
Cimil (Just . . . Cimil)

ACCIDENTALLY... OVER?

Prologue

Death is trying to seduce me.

I always suspected he would come for me after I survived the accident, and now there's no doubt. And death isn't some ominous creature that carries a bloody scythe, his face obscured by a black cloak, his spindly fingers protruding from the cuff of his dripping sleeve as he enters your dinner party, points to your plates, and declares in a gravelly voice, "You're all dead. It was the canned salmon." Oh no. This is no snarky Brit skit, and he's no monster.

Death is a sex god.

He's tall, built from indestructible solid bricks of muscle. His cheekbones are chiseled works of art, and his full, sensual lips are meant for doing anything but killing. Like I said, sex god.

How do I know this? He's been watching me, whispering in my ear while I sleep, quietly hiding in the shadows while I eat, while I work, while I shower.

So for once, I'm turning the tables.

I follow the sound of his footsteps through my beach cottage, out my back porch, and then pick up his large footprints in the sand. I crouch behind the tall, dry grass blanketing the massive sand dune. The crashing waves mask the sound of my thumping heart and heavy, frantic breaths. I'm sweating like mad as the tropical morning sun beats down on my back, and I spot my stalker splashing in the waves.

He stands, and I can barely breathe when I look at him.

Though he's nearly transparent, the outline of his naked body glistens with drops of ocean water reflected by the sun. I've never seen a more beautiful man. Shoulders that span the width of two normal-sized men, powerful arms and legs that make me wonder if he's not actually carved from rock or molded from steel, and incredibly sculpted...jeez, everything. There's not an inch on this beast—not a neck, an ab, not a pec or a thigh—that isn't constructed from potent, lethal-looking muscle. Well, except his hair. Though I can't see the color, it's beautifully thick and falls to his shoulders. I imagine it's a warm shade of brown, streaked with reds and golds. Because he's utterly beautiful and that's the kind of hair a beautiful man would have. Yes, he's a god, not the bringer of death. And I can't help but wonder why he's made that way. Is it so that when he comes for me, there'll be some sort of consolation—getting to see his face? I don't know, but I'm not ready to see it yet. I want to live. I want to grow old. I want to fall in love. Just once before my time is up.

Yet somehow, I want him, too. Why? That's gotta mean I'm *loca*, right?

My eyes study every poetic detail of this "man," hoping to find answers. But there's nothing. Nothing that will help save me from him.

Suddenly, I see his chin lift and his head turns in my direction.

Can he see me? *Oh my God. He's coming right for me.*

I bolt from my hiding place and make a run for it. I know if I make it to my house I'll manage to lock the doors, but that won't stop him. There is nowhere to hide from death, but I run anyway.

I make it to my back porch and reach for the door, but I slip on something. *Shit. Really? A banana peel?*

My body crashes to the hard cement. My head cracks on the sharp edge of the porch's step, and I can't move. All I feel is my beating heart and heaving lungs, burning with fear.

"Dammit, woman. Why the hell do you always run from me?" His deep, melodic voice washes over me, and I love how it soothes my soul.

I look up and try to focus my eyes, but he's difficult to make out. His dripping hair catches only a few rays of morning sunlight.

"You're so beautiful," I croak. "But I changed my mind; I don't want to die. Please don't take me away."

I feel his warm hand brush against my cheek. "I am trying to save you, Ashli. Why won't you let me?"

Why does he say that? Why is he lying to me? It doesn't matter now, because I'm already dying. The darkness begins to swallow me.

"Shit!" I roll from my bed and fall to the floor with a thump.

Sonofabitch! Why do I keep having these dreams?

One

‿

Camp Uchben. Sedona, Arizona. Near the Estate of Kinich Ahau, ex–God of the Sun. February 1

Eenie, meenie, miney, mo. Catch an invisible deity by the toe. If he hollers, don't let go. Just give him Ashli and watch him—oh, dammit, what rhymes with go? Ho? Crow? Potatoooo?

"Cimiiil? Are you listening? Cimil!" Roberto the Ancient One rapped his pale knuckles on the thick glass of the holding cell. "Have you not heard a word I said, woman?"

From her cot, Cimil looked at the very large, very angry vampire standing outside her cell and wiggled her fingers. "Howdy, Bob!"

Dark, lethal eyes gazed back with frustration. Or was it lust? Maybe both? *Yes! It's lustfration! My fave!*

"I sincerely hope," he said, "that you were not in the

midst of devising yet another escape from your cell. It would foil everything."

Escape? Not even a magical flea—Minky, her unicorn, hated those—could escape this three-story underground prison built to contain the most powerful of creatures alive: the gods themselves. Now, as for the foiling? *Well*...

"How did you know?" she asked.

"Because I am your mate," he said. "And you are the Goddess of the Underworld; you cannot help your evil ways."

"Good point." She sat up and sighed happily, tugging at the hem of her fuzzy pink tank dress. "So wassup?"

"I am here to tell you the first task is complete. And now we will have sex. Hard. Hot. Savage immortal sex."

"Sex? What? And why are you speaking? You vowed not to speak until this was over. It's not over." Cimil feigned a sudden interest in her jail cell, twisting a long lock of hair around her finger. She knew how that drove him crazy. Her long red hair was his fave. Or was it her ass? Or perhaps both?

Thank the gods I don't have a hairy ass. Then he'd never leave me alone.

Carnal eagerness twinkled in Roberto's ancient eyes. "I have captured the gods. Something you wagered to be impossible. In fact, I want to hear you say it. Say I am this thing you call awesomesalsa. Because that is what I am."

"Awesomesauce," she corrected.

"Yes. That," he agreed.

She stared.

"Cimiiiil?" Roberto's eyes bored into her, cautioning not to push him. "Say. It."

"Nope."

"Do it or no *Love Boat* for you tonight."

Dammit! Why are vampires so cruel?

"Okay." She stomped her foot. "I'll say it: You rock. You're the most awesome vampire ever to walk the planet."

Roberto crossed his powerful arms over his broad chest. "Aaaand?"

Cimil huffed like a crabby four-year-old. "And if the apocalypse is halted, I vow to have your love child." *Maybe.* "And I will keep my vow to marry you." *Maybe.*

He displayed a set of gleaming white fangs, grinning from ear to ear. "And we will not fail, Cimil. Just as you are predisposed for destruction, I am predisposed for victory. Don't ever doubt that."

It was true. Although Roberto was a vampire, really the king and father of all vampires, he truly was an unrelenting force for good. Yes, yes, and victory. The damn man never failed at anything. She, on the other hand? It was a little known fact that the Universe had wired her to be the bringer of destruction—aka the apocalypse—but that didn't mean she wasn't good. Right? For thousands of years, she fought her nature, always doing the exact opposite of what her instincts dictated. Okay. Didn't work out so great; they were all going to die in seven months. But still, she'd tried. And now, Roberto insisted if they worked together, they could turn everything around.

Pfff ... Yeah. Right. They had a ninety-nine point nine-nine-nine-nine-nine-nine-nine ... nine percent chance of failing. In fact, she was ready to throw in the towel and party, enjoy these final months of existence. But she did love Roberto. And she did want to make him happy. Letting him have this one last battle meant a lot to her crusty, old ex-pharaoh. Okay, she had other reasons, too. But those were not for sharing aloud. Not even with herself. After all, she was evil and not to be trusted.

"Ah! And here comes my first step toward victory now." Roberto glimpsed at the prison entrance.

One by one, Roberto's vampire soldiers dragged the unconscious deities and several of their mates inside the surrounding glass-walled holding cells. Why? Well, she'd told Roberto about the visions she'd had: The gods finally lose their marbles—damned marbles, always getting lost like a rabid flock of zombie sheep!—and end up fighting each other. Then boom! Over! Done! Planet bye-bye.

Solution? They'd subdued the gods right in the middle of a summit meeting by filling the room with a harmless yet powerful gas made especially for the occasion. Not such a bad plan except, well, imprisoning the gods to keep them from going to battle with each other was a Band-Aid. They needed to permanently alter the trajectory of their paths. That's where Máax, the God of Truth, would come in.

She hoped. Or maybe she didn't. Who knew?

Damn, I love being me. Especially right now.

"Boy, are they going to be peeved when they wake up." *How fun!*

Roberto flicked his wrist in a casual kingly sort of way. "I care not if your brethren feel angry. I simply want sex, as you prom—"

"Cimil! What is the meaning of this?" Máax's deep voice boomed inside the institutional-style structure.

Ah! Right on schedule.

"Showtime," Cimil whispered under her breath. "Hey, Máax baby! Now, before you get your mankini in a bunch—you are wearing underwear, aren't you? It's kinda hard to tell, with you being invisible and all."

Poor guy. He'd had his mortal shell confiscated oodles of moons ago as part of a major deity spanking (aka punishment). He'd violated several divine laws, including repeatedly breaking the ban on time travel. All for good reasons, but still, he'd landed himself the precarious title of the El Gran Bad Boy.

"Cimil! Why have you betrayed us?" Máax's voice radiated just to Roberto's left, outside her cell.

Because you're about to have your world rocked, and I'm so gonna enjoy watching?

Cimil cleared her throat. "There is a perfectly good explanation. And you will notice that I, too, am caged! So, it's not like I'm—"

"You are exactly where you should be, Cimil," Máax growled. "You will release the others immediately, or I will remove your mate's pinkies. With a rusty nail. Or perhaps, a power washer—"

"Yikes! Okay. I get the point Dr. Franken-ewww. But I can't release them." She smiled sweetly, hoping to win points.

"I've already alerted the Uchben army; you will not get away with this," Máax warned.

"Ha! You think we didn't expect that?" Roberto had seen to it that nothing, *nothing* would get in the way of this plan. In fact, Cimil had to hand it to him; Roberto was more impressive than the new unicorn tat on her bum. "Why do you think we rounded up the entire vampire army for this occasion? They're right outside."

"You lie," Máax said. "The vampire army is on mandatory furlough at Euro Disney. I can't believe I just said that. Sounds so fucking ridiculous."

But it was true. On both counts. In accordance with

ancient law, all vampires had been sent away on an oblig-
atory, one-year vacation in celebration of the recent exter-
mination of all evil vampires. Obviously, they chose the
happiest place on earth for this vacation. After thousands
of years battling evil, who wouldn't? Of course, no one
knew that Roberto had made up this ridiculous "ancient"
law in an effort to gather them up in one place without
rousing suspicion, only to redeploy them here for today's
special event.

Cimil gloated. "What can I say? Roberto's the man.
And by man, I mean he's really awesome. 'Cause he's not
a man, but a vampire—my vampire. Did I tell you how he
rocks my world? Did I? Huh? Huh? Hu—"

Roberto hit the floor with a thud. He clawed at his
neck, gasping for air.

"Máax! No! Let him go!" Cimil wailed. "Dammit, you
overly spunky, nudist deity! Let me explain."

Roberto grunted when something punched his nose.
Máax's fist? Blood trickled from Roberto's face, and he
winced in pain.

"You have exactly three seconds, Cimil, or I will
remove his head," Máax roared.

"Wait!" Cimil pleaded. "How did we go from pinkies
to heads? You skipped arms and kidneys. What about
earlobes?"

"Speak, you batshit crazy wench!"

Roberto's vampire soldiers gathered around, but Cimil
waved them back. They knew to obey her, no matter what,
despite who wore the kingly britches.

"All right, but you're not going to like this." She
cracked her knuckles. "Truth is, in about seven months,
the gods destroy the planet. We get into some war with

each other. I have done everything possible to change course, but I failed. Miserably. Locking *us* up is the only way to make sure that doesn't happen."

Máax released Roberto, and her beloved vampire sat up rubbing his neck, grumbling profanities in his native Egyptian tongue.

"This must be some sort of mistake," Máax said.

I don't make mistakes.

Yes, you do. Just this morning you lit your cell on fire while trying to make a grilled cheese with a flamethrower.

Fine ... guilty as charged.

"Brother," she said, "I've been dealing with end-of-the-world crappity doo for thousands of years, and I know when a dead end has been hit. The gods must be jailed until things are set right again."

A long stretch of silence didn't fill the air. *Because silence can't fill the air, now can it? That would be weird. Like saying—*

Cimil! Focus. Get Máax on his way. He has work to do. "Look at me, Máax," Cimil said. "You're the God of Truth. You can smell a lie from a mile away."

Another long, silent stretch.

"Truthfully," Máax grumbled, "I find it difficult to know when you are telling the truth anymore. You're so full of shit, even your aura is brown."

Damn. He can see that? "That's because I've been lying for so long, lies layered up layers of lies, that even when I tell the truth, I'm not really sure I am." She shrugged. "Makes life kinda fun! Dontcha think?"

"No."

Such a stick-in-the-godly-mud. "Okay, okay. I swear to you, on Roberto's life—"

"Cimiiil? Do not tempt fate in such a manner," Roberto objected.

Fate? Pfff…Tempt her all you like. Ain't gonna make a sea turtle's ass of a difference.

"Fine," Cimil grumbled. "I swear on my own life that this time I'm telling the tru—"

The ground rumbled beneath their feet and the angry sound of grinding bedrock filled the cavernous room. Everyone in the prison stilled for three long seconds.

"What the fuck was that?" Máax asked as the emergency lights flickered on along with an ear-piercing siren.

"Oh, boy. That came a lot sooner than I thought," Cimil yelled, cupping her hands over her ears.

"What came sooner?" Máax screamed.

"That's the planet! She's very attuned to the Universe and senses the end is near. She's not happy!" Cimil pointed toward the ground. "According to my sources, there will be ten global earthquakes, none of them catastrophic until the final one right before the big un–Super Bowl event. After that, the shit hits the fan. Cities topple. We go to war. Our allies and humans take sides. Everything is destroyed."

"That's impossible," Máax yelled over the noise.

"Oh no. Not impossible! Worst of all, pigs are finally gonna fly! It won't be pretty. Have you ever seen one crap?" The screeching siren stopped. "Ah! That's better. So what was I saying? Oh yeah. We're screwed."

"Cimil, please tell me this is a joke."

"Okay. I made up the part about the pigs, but not the rest. So now do you see why I had to lock everyone up?"

Máax grumbled several unhappy thoughts in the key of F—effing, eff, eff, eff, and effing hell. "If the gods should be locked up to prevent this war, then why are you allowing me to remain free?" Máax asked.

Here came the hard part. She needed to convince Máax to once again break the sacred law banning time travel. It was expressly prohibited, not to mention difficult and extremely risky. However, Máax had already broken the rule a thousand times, landing him in hot water. Not that he cared. *Bad boy alert!* Sure, he'd had a perfectly good reason for each offense, but that didn't mean there weren't consequences. The last time he'd been caught, he'd been banished, stripped of his powers, and left without a human shell. Yep... powerless and invisible for ten thousand years. Again, not that he cared.

'Cause bad boys rule!

That said, he'd broken the law once again (*so, so bad!*) to save his sister, Ixtab (*so, so thoughtful!*), and if they managed to stop the apocalypse, he'd be tried again. This time, he'd be entombed for eternity. *So, so sad.* On the other hand, he was going down anyway, so...

Cimil cleared her throat. "I had another vision. I believe it's the precise moment in time where everything *could* be put back on course."

"Do you truly expect me to believe that?" Máax scoffed.

Yes! No. Maybe? "Okay. Technically, you'd be a baboon's ass. A stinky one at that."

Máax's laugh was laced with sinister arrogance and just a smidgen of "you fucking amuse me."

"Let us pretend for a moment that I believed you," he said. "Then why do I have the feeling you're going to ask me to do something unlawful?"

Cimil clapped. "Ding, ding, ding! I need you to go back

a few teeny tiny decades, to 1993, find a certain chicky-boo, and make sure she doesn't croak prematurely."

"Why?"

Oh. There was no good way to explain it so she'd have to make something up. *Hmmm... what story would make him believe?* She tapped the side of her mouth.

"You are getting ready to lie. Aren't you?" Máax asked.

Dammit! She sucked at lying. "Yes. But only so you'll do what I want."

"Try telling the truth, Cimil," Máax growled.

But I suck at that, too.

Okay. Deep breath. Sell the story. Be the story.

Right.

"At some point in the future, the woman will act as a neutral party and defuse the tension between us. If she dies, no neutral party. And what's a party without Switzerland? They make awesome cheese. Minky loves eating the holes."

"I'm not going to risk my ass to save some woman simply because we had a little earthquake."

"I'm telling you, Máax, it's the apocalypse. And... make that two earthquakes," Cimil said cheerfully just as the ground rumbled like a ravenous, subterranean beast. Once again, sirens blasted through the prison.

"I don't give a shit!" Máax bellowed over the noise. "I refuse to do any more of your bidding. It always leads to trouble."

True. Máax had, in fact, been doing a lot of bidding for her lately, but he had to attempt this one final task. Not only did her latest vision reveal that saving the woman was their last chance to put things back on course and avoid the apocalypse, but it was also Máax's one shot at happiness. Why? Well, that was something he'd soon find out.

Okay, time for a new tactic. Speak to his extreme horniness. Poor guy is 70K and has never been kissed. Kind of like Drew Barrymore, but seven feet tall. And invisible. And naked. And a dude. Okay. Nothing like Drew Barrymore. Dammit, I can't hear myself think!

"Roberto!" Cimil yelled. "Have someone turn that crap off, or I'll start turning vampires into insects! And they won't be cool ones, either! I'm talking pill bugs!"

Roberto signaled one of his men to the caged guard booth to address the noise, which he did by punching the communication console.

"Thank you, baby." She blew a kiss to Roberto. "Máax, I'm telling the truth. You must go back and save this beautiful, smokin' hot, young woman so she can fulfill her destiny. She *needs* you. *You.* You are the only one who can pull this off. So I'm asking, please save her? And hurry up with the answer because Roberto is about to bust a triple-stitch zipper if I don't give him his Cimi-treat."

Roberto crossed his arms and nodded with a pissed-off expression. "She hasn't put out in months. I am so aroused that even you look enticing, Máax."

Cimil burst with laughter. Roberto had made a joke. Not so easy for a five-thousand-year-old ex-pharaoh vampire. "Good one, honey. I'd high-five you, but that would be hard to do through the glass."

"Perhaps we can have sex instead," Roberto stated dryly.

"Through the glass?" she asked. That would be even more difficult, but if he was game to try, then so was she.

"I am able to open your cell, Cimil," Roberto clarified.

"Not so kinky, but okay." She winked. "Just as soon as Máax makes up that empty head of his." Cimil held out both palms, mimicking a scale. "Save hot chick and humanity? Or be a sucky coward, and let us all die. Hmmm...decisions, decisions."

"Precisely how does the pathetic mortal woman die, and how do I save her?" he asked.

Pathetic? Emotionally, he was a pre-Cretaceous amoeba compared to the woman. "Have no clue and ummm...no clue."

"Why not? And why the fuck not?"

"They're called visions," she whispered, "not detailed instruction manuals to thwarting apocalyptic events." Of course, even if she did know, she would never tell. Kinda ruins the challenge. But not like Máax could resist helping his brethren, or anyone for that matter. Helping others was his Achilles' heel. Throw a little danger, risk, and rule breaking in there, and he was happier than an evil vampire with an ice-cream truck.

Máax chuckled like a chump. "Fuck it. I don't have anything better to do."

Ha! Knew it! Sucka!

"I assume you have another tablet?" he asked. "I will need two in order to travel there and back." She knew Máax already possessed one tablet, which he'd snagged from that Spanish vampire slash incubus, Antonio, whom their sister Ixtab had hooked up with. As for the other he required, Cimil had a couple stashed away for this very occasion. The tablets were the size of small headstones, a few inches thick, and made of black jade—a rare material mined from caverns beneath the River of Tlaloc, a powerful river of energy that flowed between the human world and the deity realm. In short, a group of evil Mayan priests, known as the Maaskab, had discovered the supernatural material ages ago and learned to manipulate energy with it, mostly dark energy. It did all sorts of wonderful things such as blunt or neutralize a deity's power or open portals to just about anywhere on Earth at any point in time.

Oh! I should go visit the dinosaurs again!

Really? Did you not learn your lesson last time? Poor, poor dinosaurs. All your fault...

Don't cry. Don't cry.

And clearing throat... "Of course I have a tablet! Roberto's men will give it to you. Oh! And Máax?"

Get ready for one hell of a ride, my dear brother. The SS Ashli is about to disembark, and this voyage is going to make your bad boy, overbloated deity ego whimper like a sissy.

"Yes, Cimil?" Máax rumbled.

"Whatever you do, do not, and I repeat, *do not*, take the woman from her time. Do you understand? The woman *must* remain where she is and be allowed to age the old-fashioned way. No exceptions."

"Do I want to ask why?" he asked.

"No, you do not, but I will tell you anyway. I'm in a gracious mood." She took a deep, happy breath. "In order for events to play out precisely and stop us from going to war, the woman must remain where she is in 1993. Alive. Any shortcuts or additional changes to the past would create a different outcome."

"Not following."

"In other words, the *only* variable we can impact is

her living. Everything else must remain constant or you will create an entirely new future—a new version of our messed-up one. And I do not believe the Universe will throw us another vision bone in time to course correct. Consider this our last tango at the Oh No Corral. *Comprende?*"

"Sure. Whatever. Not like I give a crap where the woman ends up," Máax grumbled on his way out the door.

Oh. But soon, he would care. Very, very much. In the meantime...

"Roberto, baby, open this cell and get your ass inside. We only have a few moments before my brethren wake up."

Estate of Kinich Ahau, the ex–God of the Sun. (A few miles from the prison.)

Máax repeated the year in his head as he stood in a large bedroom of the sprawling southwestern-style home, preparing himself for the journey back in time: *1993, 1993...* His brain itched with suspicion. Was this really the end? And was saving some mortal female, who died decades ago, really their last hope? Or was this simply another one of Cimil's mind games well-timed to a few tremors? He didn't know.

On the other hand... *What else do you have on your plate, asshole?*

Nothing. Besides, either way he was fucked, his days numbered. He'd broken the gods' sacred laws so many times that if he went on trial again, which he certainly would if he managed to stop doomsday, then he'd spend eternity in some godsdamned tomb. If he didn't succeed, well...that would be that.

Wait. What the hell am I godsdamned doing? Sanctis infernus! He was screwed either way, so why wasn't he off enjoying his final days as a free—albeit, invisible—deity? He could be surfing in Australia or diving off the coast of Belize. He could be wrestling great white sharks in South Africa or playing tic-tac-toe with Minky—one of his favorite pastimes.

But nooo. He was a god, bonded to the Universe herself. A slave to his godsdamned honor and his godsdamned need to do right. That was the very reason he was in this fucked up mess; he never turned down a plea for help. Not even from his godsdamned, ungrateful, childish brethren. "Just ask Máax. He'll do it. He's the loyal one, the honorable one," they'd say, knowing that he was the God of Truth. Those responsibilities also included justice and protection. He simply couldn't say no even when it required him to stick out his neck and break a few sacred laws. *A few thousand times.*

All right. It was true; a tiny part of him reveled in taking risks. He enjoyed it immensely. But that didn't mean he wanted to be on call every godsdamned time they needed help. What was he? Fucking Superman?

No, he was no superhero. More like an idiot. In fact, his need to protect everyone else—and keep their dark secrets—was the one reason he'd never pushed back when punishments were handed out. He would never betray one of his own simply to save his skin.

You're a lost cause, so let's get this over with. He glanced at the two black tablets laid out on the bed and gave his neck a little crack. *Go save the human, Máax,* he bitterly mocked Cimil. *Stop the apocalypse, Máax. Máax, help us*...

He picked up one tablet and stared at the hieroglyphs on the surface, rubbing his callused fingertips over the indentations. He knew what the symbols meant, and he knew the key to opening the portal on demand. His little secret.

He grumbled a few more profanities and shoved one tablet under his arm—his return ticket. He then focused his thoughts on the tablet still lying on the floor: *1993, 1993*...

The tablet on the floor began to vibrate and hiss. The sound was deafening. *Stay focused, stay focused.*

Máax's gaze shifted to the slip of paper in his hand. Roberto had handed it to him before Máax left the prison. On it, Máax knew there was a location and a name.

He opened it. "Ashli Rosewood. Tulum, Mexico."

"Ashli." Máax stepped through.

Two

⌒

February 1, 1993. Tulum, Mexico

At 7:00 a.m. sharp, Ashli Rosewood dug the keys from
her bag and unlocked the front door to her quaint little
café. It was still pitch-black out—normal for this time
of year—but as soon as sunrise hit, the caffeine fiends
from the eco-resort next door would start trickling in for
their fix. Tourists from all over the world came to enjoy
the morning view at her rustic beachside establishment.
Thatched roof over the patio out back, a trinket section in
the front, reggae or salsa music generally playing in the
background (though at cleanup time, Nirvana or Smashing Pumpkins fit the bill), and all the sand you could ever
dream of sweeping (the tourists usually carried it in on
their feet), it was her little slice of paradise, too.

She flipped on the lights, set down her keys, and quickly
inspected the six tables and chairs and the polished cement

counter that ran the length of the room to the side. Fernando, who she'd hired three months ago, had done a nice job cleaning up last night. He was a local guy, nineteen, studying to be an English teacher. Ashli knew he also had a little crush on her, but she was twenty-five now—a little too old to be dating nineteen-year-olds. In any case, the last thing she needed was a boyfriend. She lived alone. She took care of herself and her café, the only thing she had left of her parents, and she liked it that way. Alone meant safe. Alone meant not having to lose anyone. Alone was . . . good.

Ashli slipped an apron over her white tank and shorts, unlocked the back patio door that led straight to the beach, and dragged a few sets of tables and chairs outside.

Ashli took a deep breath and gazed out across the ocean, toward the horizon and its first rays of light. The sound of crashing waves and the stillness in the air, right before the sun broke ground, was always her favorite time of day. It reminded her of getting up with her mother to do yoga before opening time.

But instead of that awe-inspiring peace she normally experienced, there was a nagging feeling, the one that had been her constant companion since the day she lost her parents. *Death isn't done with you yet.* The dark thought had grown more persistent lately.

No, Ashli. Don't think about it.

She sighed and returned inside to set up the register and get the drip coffee going. She crouched behind the counter and opened the small refrigerator. "Dang it." She'd forgotten to tell Fernando they needed low-fat milk. She looked at her watch. He'd be there any minute with fresh pastries so he could cover while she ran to the mom-and-pop store a few kilometers away in town.

She started up the coffee machine, poured in fresh grounds, and prayed the thing didn't crap out on her again. The bell on the front door chimed. "Hey, Fernando. Guess what I forgot—" She turned her head, but there was no one there.

She froze.

Had she just imagined that? Her eyes moved to the small swaying bell. *Shit.* She held her breath. Okay. Maybe someone walked by and pushed the door, but didn't come in.

You're such a scaredy-cat!

The door flew open and in waltzed Fernando, carrying a box of pastries. His short brown hair was its usual mess, but at least he'd managed to put on a clean T-shirt today. "*Buenos días*, Ashli," he said, his voice groggy with sleep.

Ashli instantly felt calmer. "*Buenos días.* Hey, I forgot to put milk on the list. Can you set up the Illy while I make a quick run?"

"*Por supuesto, jefa.*"

"English. You need to practice your English." Fernando was never going to become an English teacher if he didn't try harder.

He reached for an apron hanging on a hook behind the register. "Yes, boss."

"Good boy." She winked. He was always such a grump before his first cup of coffee, which was why she needed to hurry. No customer would want to be greeted by that sad face in the morning. "Be right back."

She grabbed her purse and headed out the front door to her VW Bug, which was practically new, by the way. It still amazed her how they manufactured them in Mexico just like they had in the seventies. Even their odd, sticky-sweet smell hadn't changed. But they were cheap, good on gas, and easy to fix.

She dug for her keys, but remembered she'd left them inside the café on the counter. "Jeez." *I'm forgetting everything today.*

She turned and walked right into a wall. Only there was no wall. It was an empty, dark parking lot. "What the f—"

"Hello, Ashli," said the deep male voice.

She shrieked.

Máax stared down at the hysterical, screaming woman. He was about to offer a few calming words, such as "Shut the hell up," but then something peculiar happened.

What the fuu...? He stumbled to the side but caught himself. He'd never experienced anything so unusual, so potent. But what was it? It didn't hurt. No, quite the opposite. It felt like a sack of fucking wonderful dropped on his head.

Máax looked at the woman once more, and it hit him again.

Click.

He gasped. *She* was doing this to him? How? There was no logical explanation, other than...

He lost his train of thought. *Gods, she is magnificent.*

Holy Christ! He stepped back and stared at Ashli. *Is that...Am I...?* He was drooling! Like a hungry dog!

The odd, euphoric sensation hit him again, nearly tumbling him over. Nothing in his seventy thousand years of existence could help him articulate the sensation. It was as if the damned woman had jumped inside his body, soldered herself to every molecule of his light, and then sucked away any rational thought. The hollow pit in his chest, one he hadn't known existed, felt instantly placated. That spot now felt warm and mushy. The center of gravity shifted from beneath his feet toward the direction of the woman and began pulling him to her like a shooting star.

Oh, shit. She's my mate? He took two more steps back. *No. No. Hell no! But how?* And why now? He'd never asked the Universe for a mate. He didn't want this. He didn't want to be tethered to some...some *weak mortal* woman, or any woman for that matter. Where was the godsdamned logic in that? For fuck sake, he was a lone wolf—answered to no one and nothing. And he was invisible, went where he liked when he liked. (For the time being, anyway.) After he went on trial for his recent multitude of offenses, he'd be entombed for a very, very, very... yes, *very* fucking long time! And now this, this...*woman* had messed it all up! *Filii canis!* Now he was truly going to suffer. He'd have something to miss!

Then another truth dawned on him. *Cimil set me up! Again!* He was going to kill her. And, gods fucking dammit, did the woman—this, this, Ashli—have to be so godsdamned hot?

Infernum. Her beauty was beyond that of any deity. Dark golden-brown skin, hair like black-licorice ribbons wild about her face and trailing down her back, and exotic eyes, turning up in the corners like a feline's. And her lips...Her lips were plump and full, just the sort a man longs to feel sliding over every inch of his—

Get a hold of yourself, man! But holy saints she was hot. What was he going to do?

Why don't you start by saving her, asshole?

Right. First things first, though; he had to get her to stop screaming. "Ashli, I command you to stop screaming."

Her beautiful hazel eyes widened, and she bolted toward the dusty, narrow road that ran along the beachfront.

Sanguine ad infernum! She's running away? "Ashli, I command you to stop. I won't hurt—" A large silver bus came out of nowhere. "No!"

Three

⌒

"Cimiiil," Máax roared.

"Máax, honey." Cimil pulled down the front of her dress and Roberto dropped his hands. "I didn't expect to see you back so soon!" Cimil snorted. "Get it? See you? Damn, I'm funny."

"Have you completed the task?" Roberto asked. "You've only been gone for one minute."

Máax tried to speak, but his red-hot anger and desire to punch something got in the way.

Cimil waved her hands in the air. "Máax? You still here?"

Máax cleared the rage-coated lump in his throat. "Yeah. I'm here."

"What's wrong?" Cimil placed her palms against the glass.

What was wrong? What was wrong? She had the impudence to ask what was wrong? "You set me up, Cimil! That's what's fucking wrong!"

Cimil began chewing her index finger. "Why, Máax," she said in an exaggerated southern belle accent, "I do believe you're vexed. But I assure you, sir, I don't have the slightest clue what's gotten your man-fritters in a pickle." She fanned her face.

"Don't start your bullshit, Cimil. You knew who she was, didn't you? And you sent me to her! What the *sanguine ad infernum* were you thinking?" he roared.

"I was *thinking*," Cimil replied, "that the doom clock is ticking, and it's about time you met your *media naranja*, the other half of your orange, the hop in your scotch, the ohhhhh in your oh, baby. And don't you speak Latin to me! I hate Latin. It reminds me of the time a bunch of witches threw me in a pot and cooked me! With carrots and onions, no less. Can you believe that? Not everything tastes like chicken."

"I'm going to kill you, Cimil." What had she gotten him into?

A mate? A mate? He didn't want a damned mate!

"Now, now, brother—"

"You know I face entombment. For eternity! *If* we survive this!"

Cimil sighed. "Máax, I'm sorry—not really—but the woman must be saved regardless, and you're truly the only god for the job. Besides, who's to say you wouldn't have met her anyway? She is your destiny, your fate—the good kind. And you're right, who's to say we all get out of this apocalypse alive? Don't you want to experience true love just once before your time is up?"

True love? Being mated wasn't true love. It was being shackled against one's will. It was cosmic brainwashing. "So I may act like a pathetic, lovesick idiot, unable to control his physical desires even when in public? No, thank you."

"Don't know what you're missin'." Cimil sang her words and then did her strange little jazz hands move. "It's magical. Besides, if you really, really don't want her, you can always have what's-her-face erase Ashli from your memory."

What's-her-face was their sister, the Goddess of Forgetfulness. Actually, that was a pretty good idea.

Roberto pulled Cimil close. "You are so sexy when you're thoughtful, my love. I am going to bone you until your head spins." The two began mauling each other with hands and tongues.

Love was so degrading. Why would he want that?

"Guys," Máax said.

They ignored him as they grunted, ground, moaned, and slurped. Máax felt his immortal skin crawl.

"Guys!" he yelled.

The two paused and sneered in his general direction.

"I need to—"

"Máax," Cimil said. "Yes. You still have to save her—"

"But—"

"Okay!" she barked. "I'm sorry for introducing you to the one woman in the world who has any chance in hell of making you happy. And perhaps less bitter. And prickish. But what's done is done and—"

"I killed her," he blurted out.

Fuck. How had it gone so wrong? He was there with her one moment, the next she was gone.

"You killed her?" Roberto stifled a snicker.

"I did not mean to," Máax explained. "Irrational, crazy woman. She ran out in front of a bus. There wasn't even any fucking traffic. It was seven in the godsdamned morning. She just"—he let out an anguished sigh—"ran away."

Cimil burst with laughter.

"This is not funny." Perhaps this woman was not really his mate, he thought. Perhaps the Universe and Cimil simply wanted to have a little fun with him. Because he'd never heard of one's mate fleeing in terror.

But why did it chafe him?

Cimil continued to giggle. "Like hell it's not funny. I sent you back to save someone, and you get her killed in what—sixty seconds? Nice job, Buck Rogers. Biddy, biddy!" Cimil elbowed Roberto. "Get it? Get it? Biddy, biddy. Like the little robot who always caused problems." Her laughter died with a sad, little sputter when she noticed Roberto's cold stare. "Oh, never mind. Listen, Máax, glad you came back to report on the fine work you just did. But—and I mean this with all of the hate in my cold, twisted heart—what the hell are you doing here? We've already had two earthquakes. Two! Get your ass back to 1993 and fix it. You still have to save her."

Hmmm. Good point. What *was* he doing there? He guessed he had been so shocked by what happened to Ashli that he hadn't quite known what to do. Thankfully, the bus had been going so fast that she'd not suffered, but that did not make the event any less traumatic. She died. She'd run away from him and died.

"I'm leaving," he grumbled.

"Thatta boy! And next time, could you come back ten minutes later? Roberto and I need a chance to play hokey-pokey." She winked.

"Two minutes. Make it two mind-blowing minutes." Roberto began unzipping his leather pants.

Máax grimaced. Had they no shame? Were they really going to have sex in a cell with a glass wall, with Roberto's men milling about, and the other gods and their mates drugged, moments from waking up?

"As you wish." Máax took the tablet—the other had been left behind in 1993—and headed to the conference room in the back of the prison. This time, he would play this out differently. Perhaps save Ashli without revealing his presence. Completely incognito.

Aren't you forgetting something?

Infernum. Yes, he was. He'd have to rethink the plan. He needed to return to the past. Return to her. Which meant if he wasn't careful, he might bump into himself. That couldn't happen. Allowing oneself to overlap, being in the same place at the same time, started a feedback loop similar to reverb on a guitar. It fed off itself, creating a chain reaction of dark, nasty, evil energy that circled the globe, raining down hate and destruction for centuries.

How'd he know? Two words: *Cimil* and *dinosaurs.* Oh yes. Humans liked to believe that those giant beasts died when an asteroid crashed to Earth, but nothing could be further from the truth. It was all Cimil. Cimil and her destructive curiosity: "I wonder what it would be like to go back in time and ride a velociraptor?" Apparently, she'd had that thought more than twice and bumped into herself. It wasn't until the gods started to experience violent episodes of seizures, followed by decades of amnesia and sugar cravings, that they realized what Cimil had done. Not only had she wiped out the creatures and drastically altered the future, but she could've destroyed humanity, too.

From that day forward, time travel was banned—no exceptions—and there was a damned good reason for it.

So now what? Not only did a past version of him exist in 1993, the version actually alive at that time, but now there was another version of himself from moments ago.

The ground rumbled violently beneath his feet, causing him to stumble to one side. The dangling overhead lamps swung like a recently vacated trapeze.

Shit... Was this really happening? He scratched his overly scruffy chin. Apparently, it was.

All right. Perhaps if he returned one week earlier than he'd originally encountered Ashli, that would resolve the issue. Yes. That would work. And how hard would it be to ensure they were nowhere near her café on the day of his original visit? He'd figure something out. *There's always a solution.*

Is there now?

Yes.

Are you so foolish as to believe that your sister, the Goddess of Forgetfulness, can truly make you forget your mate if we manage to survive this?

What's-her-face can make anyone forget anything.

He sighed. He hoped he was right about that. Eternal entombment would be bad enough without having to pine away for some female. It would be too much pain and suffering for any being to bear.

Four

⌒

January 25, 1993. Save Ashli. Take Two

A day off! A day off! Ashli stretched in her warm bed, savoring her soft, velvety pink sheets. The morning sunlight sieved through her wispy white curtains. It was heavenly to get up after the sunrise for once. Granted, Mexican winters were pretty nice compared to most places, but the shorter days and rising before dawn took its toll on her spirits.

She rolled over and looked at the clock—8:00 a.m. She reached for her phone on the nightstand and stared at the thing. *No, Ashli. You promised. Fernando can handle one day by himself. It's just making coffee, not performing brain surgery.*

She blew out a steady breath, knowing how badly she needed this. She hadn't had a day off in over a year, and that day didn't really count. She'd been in bed with the flu and simply hadn't opened the café.

Fortunately, however, her workaholic tendencies had little to do with money. Her parents' insurance had seen to the basics, but keeping that café alive felt like keeping them alive.

She and her parents had come to Tulum for a family vacation when she was eighteen. They lived in Miami for years and the beach had always been a part of their lives—playtime, summertime, exercise time. But her parents instantly fell in love with Tulum's rustic charm and virgin white beaches. Then her parents did the unthinkable. They quit their high-paying jobs as lawyers, moved to Tulum, and opened a café. Café Cielito Lindo or "Beautiful Little Sky." Ashli had gone off to college that year at the University of Michigan to study marketing, but she came for visits every chance she got, and the café became her second home. When she graduated, she planned to spend the summer there, then return to the States where she'd already landed a job in Chicago. That was three years ago. Three long years ago when everything changed in a heartbeat. Her life, her future, everything.

Tulum was her home now. Always would be.

Ashli slipped from bed and pulled back the curtains, gazing appreciatively at the view of the tropical turquoise waves and soft, powdery white sand. No. She'd never leave. Not for anything.

A jog sounds wonderful.

Máax arrived at Ashli's café to inconveniently discover she was off for the day. Seemed many of her regulars were also disappointed by the news. Nearly every godsdamned male who passed through the door asked for her.

Máax stomped out his spark of jealousy. *You idiot. You do not want her. Even if you want her. That's the bond speaking.*

Máax waited until the young man working the counter went outside to deliver a cappuccino. He slipped behind the register and dug around, quickly finding Ashli's home address on a sheet of emergency contacts, along with her phone number. *Bingo.*

Máax silently made his way out the door and started down the palm tree–lined, dusty, narrow road that ran for miles along the beach. Yeah, that road. The one where Ashli was to die in about a week. Of course, he would change all that today. Just as soon as he found her. Not that it should be hard. There wasn't much to this tiny beach community except for a few small—

"Ya viene el fin del mundo! Arrepiéntanse ahora! Ya viene el fin del mundo! Arrepiéntanse ahora!" A small, beat-up truck with a megaphone strapped to the roof sped down the dirt road, blaring, "The end of the world is coming. Repent now!"

Thanks, assholes. Like I needed the reminder.

Anyway, where was he? Oh yeah. There wasn't much to the tiny community apart from a few eco-resorts, the kind with huts instead of hotels, and—

"Ya viene el fin del mundo! Arrepiéntanse ahora! Ya viene el fin del mundo! Arrepiéntanse ahora!" The truck had made a U-turn.

"Oh. Come on!" Máax yelled. "I'm on it, okay?" *Motherfuckers.*

So instead of hotels, there were several small communities of private vacation homes on the beach. How'd he know? Let's just say, he'd been suckered into "helping"

Cimil with another one of her little schemes. One that took him to these parts, and one that he now questioned having participated in.

A little too late now.

Máax was almost to the first house along the road when he spotted a young woman with *café con leche* skin wearing the tiniest pair of shorts and an even tinier little top, running down the beach.

Ashli…

His body began to heat immediately, and it wasn't due to the searing morning sun beating down on his naked body or the balmy tropical air lacking even the slightest breeze. It was her large, plump breasts and small, athletic body. It was her wild, dark hair whipping against her back as her aggressive stride carried her down the shore. He couldn't help but hunger for her. Even if he didn't. But he did. Wait. No, he didn't.

Sonofabitch! Get yourself together, man. You. Do not. Want her. You do not want a mate. There was no reason in the world for him to get sucked into some ridiculous, sappy, tragic love story. Romeo and Juliet. Lancelot and Guinevere. Tristan and Isolde. Those were stories written by fools about fools. Those stories were for humans, weak and driven by impracticality. He was a god. Strong. Defiant. Loyal. And very practical, he might add. Most certainly, he would not allow himself to suffer for an eternity simply because the Universe—cruel-hearted bitch that she was—decided to create an ideal female. One specifically designed to make him feel complete. One that would give him the most euphoric pleasure a male could ever know—

Idiot. You're not helping yourself here.

With Ashli out on a jog, Máax decided this was the perfect opportunity to explore her home. If he were to protect her, he'd have to learn her surroundings, her routine, and he'd need to prevent her from getting in a car, where it would be difficult for him to follow.

He walked along the road until he came across a house with a gated driveway and tall stucco walls. He peered through the bars and spotted her little red car parked on the gravel driveway. A lush, tropical garden obscured most of the Spanish-style bungalow, and impressively tall palm trees shaded the roof. It was a charming, cozy home, but it irritated him to see her in such a modest dwelling. She was his mate. She deserved a grand, modern house with—

Sonofabitch. She is not yours. You must resist the urge to shelter and care for her.

Snarling at himself, he made his way around her property via a small trail that led to the sloped beach. He found the back entrance to her yard—a tiny patio with a low wall that butted against the beach without much protection from intruders. He hopped over the wall and tried the back door.

Unlocked.

"Damned woman is asking for trouble." He'd have to talk to her about that later. If he talked to her. At this point, he didn't know if he'd ever speak with her.

He entered the kitchen and was hit with a delicious scent—sweet, floral, and fresh.

Ashli.

Must ignore how good she smells. It is simply chemistry. A physiological reaction. Are you weaker than chemistry? No! You are not. You are a god. Chemistry is your bitch.

He looked around the kitchen, inspecting for any obvious dangers. It was cheerful and tidy with white-and-blue Mexican tiled counters. A bowl of mangos and papayas topped the little wooden table in the center of the room.

Nothing overtly perilous.

Máax continued to the living room. Typical for these parts, the floors had that reddish-brown tile and the walls were made of rough plaster. On the coffee table, a bright blue, hand-painted ceramic water pitcher sat next to a small potted plant and a little Mayan statue of his sister Akna, the Goddess of Fertility. The statue depicted her with a giant round belly, gritting her teeth as she prepared to give birth. Máax instantly found himself imagining Ashli with a big round belly, carrying his bab—

Sonofabitch! No. You will not have babies with her. You are going to be entombed. Forever. And if that doesn't happen, it's because there's an apocalypse. There is no future for you and her.

Grumbling profanities at himself, he finished inspecting the room. Beautiful black-and-white photographs of the ruins of Tulum hung on the wall. He leaned in toward one of the frames to inspect the signature. "Ashli Rosewood." She'd taken the pictures. He didn't know why, but imagining her traipsing about in the ruins with her camera made him smile. Then there were her stunning photos of the beach. She seemed to love the ocean as much as he did.

Not that it mattered.

That's right. Means nothing. Millions of people love the ocean. It's not like she's a fucking unicorn.

He continued down a long hallway and found a study

without much to see: desk, chair, bookshelves filled with those god-awful romance novels. The next room was a dusty guest quarters with a private, enclosed patio.

He pushed the last door open and saw the large unmade bed. Her sweet, tropical scent filled the air.

Her room.

He inhaled deeply. A wave of heat flooded his groin, triggering his male anatomy to thicken. *Exactly how fucking old are you, man? Pathetic.*

But he could no more stop his arousal than he could that sliver of satisfaction he felt from finding no trace of any male. None at all. But why was a woman of such beauty, who clearly had a rabid following of eligible men as he'd seen when he went to her café, without a man?

Perhaps she has been waiting for you. That thought pleased him.

Why? She is not yours. In fact, you should be hoping and praying she moves on. Finds a male worthy of her.

Ignore vicious pangs of jealousy. Must ignore.

Máax completed his inspection of the entire home—bathroom, laundry room, closets. It was clean, well cared for, and had no obvious dangers about with the exception of the easy access to the beach. He'd have to make sure her doors were always locked.

Now for the next task. He grabbed Ashli's car keys from a clay dish by the front door, went outside, and ripped out her battery cables.

That should prevent her from driving for a while. She could walk to work, and he would follow closely behind to protect her.

Yes, but not too close.

Ashli panted hard, her sweaty body burning with heat while she stretched. The run had felt amazing, and her muscles now trembled from the exertion. She hiked up the steep, sandy embankment to the back of her home, but as she was about to enter the enclosed patio, she noticed large footprints in the sand, disappearing where the cement slab started a few feet from her back door.

She froze. Someone was inside. She and her neighbors paid for a security service to patrol the beach, but that didn't mean someone couldn't sneak by.

She backed away from the door and sprinted toward the shoreline for a better view of the beach.

There he is. "*Oye! Oye, Señor Luis!*" She waved at the short, older man wearing Bermudas and carrying a baton. He waved back, and she pointed at her house. He immediately understood and charged toward her back porch, disappearing inside her house.

Ten minutes later, Luis emerged. "*Nadie. No hay nadie. Qué pasó?*"

She explained about the footprints, but Luis swore he'd checked every inch of her house and found no one. Nothing missing. Nothing disturbed.

She thanked him and went inside, but the moment she crossed the threshold, an eerie sensation nearly sacked her. "Hello? Is anyone here?"

Dammit, Ash. Luis told you the place is empty. But what was that strange scent? It was faint, but she did smell it. Like a sweet, exotic spice of some sort. Not Luis. Luis smelled more like last night's tequila and rancid ocean.

She grabbed a large knife from her kitchen drawer

and tiptoed into her living room. Although her home had those natural clay tile floors (kept things cooler), the rest of the house was bright and cheery with lots of windows and light, tons of fun Mexican *artesania*—little clay statues, handwoven tapestries, and hand-stitched pillows with bright red flowers.

But not one single item had been disturbed. Nothing.

Quietly she tiptoed down the hallway. When she got to her room, she pushed open the door and held out her knife, quickly releasing a breath. "No one's here. And you're an idiot." Why was she so determined to spoil this wonderful day? Her first day off in a year.

She would take a shower, put on her favorite little hang-out dress, make poached eggs with the handmade tortillas she'd bought yesterday, and sit out on her patio reading a book. She'd ordered five new historical romance novels, the ones with the hunky kilted guys, and had yet to dig into any of them.

Shaking her head, she placed the knife on the dresser and began shedding her sweaty clothes. Naked, she trotted down the hallway to her bathroom. She reached inside the shower stall to turn on the water and heard a crash. Her head flipped in the direction of the sink where her perfume bottle lay.

That's funny, she thought. Hadn't she left the perfume on the other side of the sink?

You're imagining things. Stop. Trying. To ruin. This day!

Ashli slipped inside and took the longest shower of her life, carefully shaving all of those places that needed shaving since she planned to go swimming later, and then wrapped herself in her robe. She went into the kitchen, turned on the kettle and music—salsa always put her in a good mood—and began heating her frying pan to warm up her tortillas.

"My day. It's my day," she sang over the peppy Celia Cruz tune. "Nothing's going to ruin it. Nothing's going to—ouch!" She slapped her neck. A burning sensation spread through her shoulder and down her arm.

She glanced down at the twitching bee next to her bare foot. "Crap, crap, crap."

She leaped to her refrigerator and dug through the top shelf. Dammit! Her syringe! Where the hell was it? It didn't require refrigeration, but it was where she always left it. Maribel, her cleaning lady, must've moved it.

"No. No. No." Ashli rushed to her purse on the kitchen table, but when she opened the hard plastic case containing her epinephrine pen, it was cracked.

Empty. But how? She'd just checked the damned thing a few days ago.

She gripped her throat and began wheezing. Her head began to spin.

Car! She kept an extra epinephrine shot in her glove box.

She stumbled through her living room and fell to her knees only a foot from her front door. She could make it. She knew she could.

"Holy fuck, woman!" The heavenly deep, masculine voice filled her ears. "I only left you alone for three minutes."

Her brain couldn't process where the sound had come from or who spoke, but she suddenly felt grateful for another person's presence. She pointed toward her car. "I...need...my shot," she said, gasping her words.

"*Sanguine ad infernum,*" said the voice.

She felt her body lift into the air and float outside. Head spinning, the air to her lungs becoming shorter and shorter, she tried to focus on his face. Who was carrying her? And had he just spoken Latin? She hated Latin. *It sounds so weird.*

"Sonofabitch!" the deep voice screamed. "Where the hell did I leave her keys?"

Her body was suddenly on the gravel next to her car. The rocks were warm on her back and bare calves. Was she imagining all this? There was no one there. No one at all.

She watched a large rock float from the edge of her driveway and smash into her car window. The driver's side door flew open.

She must be losing her mind, she thought as she blacked out completely.

Five

⌒

"You have *got* to be joking Máax!" Cimil barked. "That was, what, fifteen seconds?"

Roberto removed his hands from Cimil's waist. "It was twelve seconds. Twelve. What exactly is your brother's problem?"

Cimil sighed. "Please don't tell me she died again. 'Cause this time, I might not laugh, and then where would you be? Huh? It would be just plain sad without my laughter."

Máax pressed his palms to his temples and paced the floor in front of Cimil's cell. "I left her alone for two minutes!" He didn't think that a few fucking minutes would be a problem, but the moment he'd seen her strip off her clothes—those perfectly shaped golden-brown breasts and rosy nipples; the firm, smooth ass; and lean, long legs—well, he'd never seen a more delicious woman. He'd nearly given himself away when he turned and knocked her perfume bottle clear across the counter with his erection. *Christ,* he'd thought, *I can't very well spend the day like this, bumping my cock into everything.* After all, he wore no clothes. (What was the point? So humans could watch them miraculously float through the air?) So as soon as Ashli had left the bathroom, he decided he'd take care of business. Two minutes tops, he was ready to go off like a bolt of lightning. But before he knew it, he'd heard a strange sound coming from Ashli's living room.

"What was it this time?" Roberto asked with a bored tone. "Did she fall off a cliff, trying to escape you?"

"No. A fucking bee. I gave her medicine, but it was too late. She never woke up." If only he hadn't had to waste time smashing the window, he probably could have saved her. Where the hell had he left her car keys?

"Dammit, Cimil," Máax groaned. "What aren't you telling me about this woman?" He could swear the Universe wanted to snub her out, which seriously pissed him off. Ashli belonged to him in theory, and it was his job to protect her. His.

Then there was the tiny detail of the Universe trying to take something that theoretically belonged to him. Not that he wanted Ashli. But nevertheless, where the hell did that bitch of a Universe get off trying to take something that belonged to him? Not that he would keep Ashli. Because he was a god. And didn't need a mate. Especially when his destiny was carved in stone, because he was a man of honor and would never betray one of his brethren only to save himself. Even though they should never have put him in such a position to begin with. Not that he cared. He was tough. Tougher than all of them. Usually.

Cimil shrugged. "There's not much to tell. Ashli

dies—I can't tell you how, because I don't really know—
and if you save her, she saves us all. Our pathway to peace.
Wow!" She elbowed Roberto. "I sound like a poet."

"Your voice"—Roberto gripped her chin and applied a
long, wet kiss—"is always like poetry to me."

The two began to maul each other again, tearing away
their clothing.

Oh, sweet gods, make them stop! "Eh-hem. I hate to
interrupt, but I cannot save a woman who is destined
to die."

Without detaching her lips, Cimil shooed Máax away.

"Cimil! In your own words, the clock is ticking! You
must tell me what you know," he demanded.

"She's destined to live! Now go! You're a deity. Figure
it out!"

Máax groused profanities under his breath and returned
to the conference room. What the hell was going on?
Something strange, that was certain.

And how many times could he return to her and risk
bumping into himself? Máax had always been cautious,
never chancing overlaps, and careful not to alter the future
in any detrimental way. But this was really pushing it.

He took a deep breath.

Options. Think options. Okay. She seemed to be
accident-prone. So perhaps he could take her somewhere
safe, somewhere with around-the-clock security. And
medical supplies. And no traffic. Or bees. *Hmmm...that
might work.*

He could have the Uchben watch over her business and
home. But dammit, how would he convince her to go anywhere with him? He terrified her.

Dammit. Why was this getting so complicated?

Getting?

He gave it another moment of thought, scratching the whiskers on his chin. *I will go back another week earlier—prior to her latest death. I will stay close to her, guard her at every moment, and learn more about her. Then, the night before she is to die from the bee sting, I will reveal myself and take her away.*

But this time, he'd stay close, and never leave her for a moment.

January 18, 1993. Save Ashli. Take Three

Wearing her favorite yellow ducky pajamas, sipping a hot cup of coffee, Ashli stared at the calendar pinned to her kitchen wall. It had a photo of a chocolate lab puppy with a bow around its neck, sitting inside a basket. She'd always wanted a dog, but her hours at the café would leave the poor animal home alone all day.

Well, maybe after things settle into a quieter routine. Which is exactly what she hoped for.

Lately, she'd been feeling the effects of years of stressful living. Long workdays, not enough sleep, and little exercise were finally catching up, and she knew it. It was definitely time for a change, and she'd already taken the first step by hiring Fernando, but it wasn't enough. That feeling, the sensation of dread, was growing stronger with each passing day. *Has to be the stress. I need a day off.*

Then there were the dreams. Vivid, disturbing, wild dreams. Some were of a faceless man and too erotic to admit she had. Then there were the ones of death hunting her, watching her. She'd been stung by a bee, hit by a bus, slipped on a banana peel—the list went on and on. Each time she'd wake up right at the point of dying, covered in sweat, the dream having felt so real that her body throbbed with pain and tingled with adrenaline.

Maybe it was time to start seeing that therapist again to address her lingering guilt; she'd never quite come to terms with being the only one who'd survived the accident. Yes, she thanked heaven or the universe or whomever had been watching over her that day for letting her live, but that didn't mean she was without baggage. And working fourteen-hour days, seven days a week wasn't helping.

There. It was decided: once Fernando got the hang of things, she would cut down her hours. Who knew, maybe she'd take up photography again. Until then, however, it was business as usual.

She glanced at her watch. "Oh no." She needed to open the café in ten minutes. She scrambled to her bedroom, stripped off her pj's, and threw on a pink tee, jean shorts, and her favorite little leather belt with the pink flowers. She slipped on her sandals and dashed to the bathroom.

When she flipped on the light, she immediately noticed the bags under her eyes. The bloodshot whites made their greenish-hazel color look more like sad, drab army green.

"You'll get through this," she said to herself and began brushing her teeth.

A flitter of motion moving down the hall caught her attention. She jumped. *Holy shit.*

Toothbrush in hand, she slowly peered out through the bathroom doorway. "He-he-hello?"

A burst of wind gushed through the house. Crap. She

hadn't left any doors or windows open. Someone was inside.

Ohmygod. Find a weapon.

She looked at the toothbrush in her hand. *What are you going to do with that? Give the intruder minty breath?* She threw it into the sink and slid open a small drawer in her vanity, where she kept a pair of stainless steel scissors.

Hand violently trembling, she made her way down the hall toward the living room. "I have a ... knife! So you'd better run."

Is that the best you can do? Really?

"Fast," she added.

Dork.

She repeated the phrase in Spanish for good measure anyway.

She glanced around the corner and quickly peeked at the living room and entryway. Her front door creaked as a gentle breeze nudged it completely open.

Strange. Her purse remained on the small hand-carved wooden bench in the entryway. Why would someone break in but leave her purse? Her car keys were right there, too.

Oh no. Whoever was inside the house didn't want her valuables. So then what could they possibly be after?

She gasped. *I better get the hell out of here!* She bolted to the door, grabbing her keys and purse. She ran to her car and got inside, but when she tried the engine, nothing happened.

"You've got to be kidding me!" She tried again.

Ohmygod. Okay. Think, think, think. She could open the gate and run for help, but her neighbors' homes were gated in the front and it was still completely dark out. It might take forever to get one of them to wake up and let her in. Many weren't even around this time of year.

She could try to find Luis, but he didn't patrol the road. He stuck to the backs of the homes where break-ins were more likely.

Okay. She'd have to make a run for it. She'd go around the side of her house, through the garden, and down to the beach. The intruder wouldn't even see her. She grabbed her purse and took a breath before pushing open the car door and sprinting to the left side of her house. She slowed right before getting to her sitting area under the large palm tree; she didn't want to run into any chairs or potted plants.

Panting quietly, trying to ignore the frantic thumps inside her chest, she cautiously skirted around the tree.

"Aaa-chew!"

She froze. *Babyjesusholycowohlord.* Had someone just sneezed on the back of her neck? Ewww. And...*Shit, shit, shit.*

"Aaa-chew!"

She covered her mouth to keep from screaming. The intruder was right behind her.

Oh, infernum. He couldn't believe he'd done that. She must've had plumeria in her garden. He was allergic to those. Yes, deities had allergies. For example, it was a well-known fact that Belch, the God of Intoxication and Wine, couldn't eat gluten, though it didn't stop him. And the stupid bastard didn't even have to eat. Then there was Akna, Goddess of Fertility; she couldn't eat shellfish. She also had an aversion to garlic, undercooked meat, and anything spicy. Similar to a pregnant human female. As for him, it was plumeria. "Aaa-chew!"

Deities all mighty. He stilled and held his breath. He hoped she didn't run. With her luck, she'd end up tripping on a pebble and breaking her neck.

"I can't see you, but I know you're there," she said between several heavy breaths. "And whatever you think you're getting from me, you won't. I'll die before I let you rape me."

Rape her? Bloody hell! "I'm not going to touch you. Not like that, anyway. But if you run..." Though his vision rivaled that of any nocturnal beast, he could barely make her out in the dark but saw she remained motionless, her back to him.

Poor woman must be terrified. What a complete asshole. He was supposed to protect her, but instead ended up terrorizing her.

Or killing her. Or letting her be taken out by a bee while you jerk off. Idiot.

"And if I do run. What are you going to do?" she challenged.

"You do not want to get hurt, do you? Accidents happen all the time." *Oh, hell. That had come out all wrong.* It had sounded like a threat.

"Why do you want to hurt me? What have I done?" she asked bitterly.

This was not going well. "I do not wish to harm you; I simply want to talk."

"Like hell you do." Something hard and fast knocked him over the head. He fell to his knees.

Six

Ashli heard a loud gong when the shovel made contact. From the sound of the intruder's deep groan and his body hitting the ground, it had been a direct hit to the head. "That's right! Nobody messes with the Ashli...the Ashli..." *The Ashli-nator? The Ashli-cutioner? The...Oh. Forget it!* "Nobody messes with me!"

Okay. So now what? She needed to go find Luis or call the police. If she left, he might wake up and escape, only to return another day and carry out his sick, psychotic fantasy.

My belt! She slid it from her waist and gave it a quick tug between her hands. Yes, it was thin but made from strong leather. It would be perfect for tying his hands.

She crouched, feeling for the stranger's arms. Dammit. If only she could see him, but it was still pitch-black. Winter sucked!

Her fingertips encountered warm, bare skin, smooth and tight. *Oh, what a firm pectoral muscle.* Her hands slid farther south over a set of steely, exaggeratedly ripped abs—*wow, are these implants?*—stopping short of where his waistband might be.

Shit. She snatched her hand away. This guy wasn't wearing any clothes! *Pervert! Hurry! Tie him up.*

She sucked in the crisp predawn air and reached for him again. *Okay. Shoulder. Oh! There's another pectoral. Also insanely hard and bulgy. Pervs must have a lot of time on their hands to go to the gym. Bet he has a damned membership to 24-Hour Perv-ness! And don't think about the odd tingles in your fingers. Or how his chest is built like a Greek god.* Because that would then make her the perv. Or stupid and lame. Either way, not good.

But by then, it was too late. An overpowering curiosity had taken hold, urging her hands to stroll. What did he look like? He was a big pervy stalker so his face had to be all contorted and riddled with unsightly scars. Right?

She leaned in, trying to catch a glimpse of any distinctive shadows, but the sun hadn't come up yet and the garden was a pit of darkness.

She slid her fingers to his forehead and worked her way down, expecting Klingon-like ridges or bony protrusions like one of those Sith Lords (yes, she watched way too much sci-fi). What she found, however, was anything but gross or intergalactic. Or pervy.

Smooth, warm cheeks, a thick growth of bristly whiskers on his jaw, a straight nose, and...She swallowed. Soft, full lips. She leaned down again and placed her ear directly above his mouth. His warm breath bathed her cheek. Damn. The man even smelled nice. Fresh and clean like mountain air, but with a hint of something else, the kind of something one might want to smell over and over again. Like homemade pumpkin bread with a hint of spice. *Must be some pervy mouthwash. Holiday-scented Lister-perv!* But still, it smelled really good.

What's the matter with you? This guy just broke into your house, threatened to kill you, and here you are smelling him and exploring his pecs? You're not so bright, are you, Ash? But the impulse to touch him was uncontainable.

How about your impulse to live?

Can I live with him?

Stop it. Get a grip, Ash!

Yes. A grip.

She slid her hand down his arm, which contained yet another enormous, bulging muscle, and found his wrist. She tugged him a few feet—*damn, he's heavy! Must be huge!*—next to the palm tree. She wrapped his arms around the tree and tied his wrists together. The trunk was only about as thick as a basketball, but it was strong enough to hold him in place. For a while anyway.

He groaned loudly, and she stepped back, knocking herself into her garden chair. *Crap.* He was waking up!

He groaned again with a deep, penetrating voice, sending a shock wave of quivers through her trembling body. The sound sparked images of rolling in the sand naked, wrapped in a man's big, strong arms, feeling his heat against her skin. Yes. This had been the other dream she'd repeatedly had. The dream of the faceless man who ravaged her body with his tongue and hands while he pleasured her in ways only possible in—well, dreams—and with a body so male, so perfect that she shuddered each time she thought of him. A cock so large and thick that she melted with . . .

What. Is. The. Matter. With. You? Go get help!

Righto.

She reached out her hands and felt her way toward the beach to find Luis.

"Wait," that deep voice called out. "Do not leave me here."

Oh, shit. He's awake. "You just tried to murder me!"

Dammit, if only she could see him. This was just too scary talking to someone she couldn't see. She'd give anything for a flashlight.

"Gods be damned, woman," he snarled. "I did not try to kill you. I am here to protect you."

Yeah, right. "And I'm Mary. Didn't you notice my little lamb? It actually looks like a giant shovel, but don't let that fool you."

"You think I jest," he said, "but I do not. I am here to save your life."

"Might I ask from what?"

"Yourself, apparently. You cannot deny, Ashli, that death has a thing for you."

Holy crap. How did he know that?

He added, "Haven't you felt it? The nagging sensation that your life is about to end? Perhaps had dreams about it?"

The blood in her veins turned to crushed ice. How could he possibly know that? The only person she'd ever mentioned anything to was her therapist, and she found it highly unlikely that Doctora Hernandez would share her patients' most private thoughts with a pervy stalker with a workout obsession.

"I don't know what sick game you're playing, but whatever," Ashli said. "You can explain yourself to the police. By the way, in Mexico, a fifty-peso bribe can make your prison stay a little extra horrible. I'm throwing down one hundred."

She scrambled through the garden, feeling her way out to the beach, where the first rays of light came into view over the horizon. "Finally!"

She reached the neighbor's property where Luis resided in a tiny guesthouse, and pounded on the door. "Luis! Luis!" He'd likely just gone to bed. *"Despierta!"*

Luis opened the door, groggy with sleep. *"Sí?"*

She explained how she'd caught the intruder, and Luis immediately went for his handcuffs, baton, pepper spray, and flashlight.

"Voy a asegurar que no se escapa la rata. Usted, se queda aca. Entiende?" he said.

Hell, yeah, she was staying put! She wasn't about to go anywhere near her house until the pervy, nudist muscleman was detained.

She nodded and watched Luis charge off toward her house, but only several minutes passed before he returned.

"Señorita Ashli!" Luis wiped his sweaty brow and bent over to catch his breath. *"No hay nadie."*

What? No one? Of course he was there. He had to be. *"Lo dejé amarrado a mi árbol,"* she explained.

Luis looked at her as if she were mad and then assured her he found no man, woman, child, donkey, or otherwise tied to her palm tree.

How could he have already gotten away? *Ugh! That pervyworkoutbastard!* She stormed toward her house, Luis on her tail, but he was right. When she got to her garden, there was no one there. She scratched her head. Now what would she do? The man had gotten away. What if he came back? What if he came after her again?

"I guess it's time for that dog."

Bloody deity infernum! Máax's head throbbed with a pain so severe it reminded him of the time he'd accidentally been stepped on by Cimil's unicorn. Giant fucking thing thought it was some sort of lapdog but weighed the same as an elephant.

So what had that bloody woman hit him with? A garbage truck? No way was that a simple shovel.

In any case, it knocked a few of his marbles loose because he didn't recall freeing himself or making his way inside her house. But he had. In fact, he'd made it to her bed, and now Ashli lay beside him, sound asleep. How long had he been out, and how the hell had she fallen asleep without noticing a very large man in her bed?

Because you're invisible and were lucky enough to pass out on the side of the bed she doesn't use.

Carefully, he edged off the bed, trying not to disturb her. Ashli rolled over and flung her arm over his chest.

Deorum inferorum. Máax sucked in a deep breath.

"You smell so good," she mumbled.

She talks in her sleep? For some reason he found that adorable.

"What cologne is that?" she added.

His natural scent. All gods produced a pleasing aromatic cocktail of pheromones. He supposed it was nature's subtle way of disarming humans, making it less likely for them to freak out and realize they were in the presence of something not quite human.

Ironically, he felt like the one being lulled by Ashli's scent. He'd never smelled a more enticing fragrance:

tropical flowers mixed with a slight hint of those roasted chili peppers from her kitchen and fresh ocean air. Gods, the scent was just as exotic as the woman. Add to that, Ashli seemed to enjoy the ocean, his passion, as much as he did. If he could live his entire existence on the beach, he would. The air, the tropical breeze, the soft sand... there was nothing better than swimming in the waves or surfing when the opportunity arose, though it had been a very long time. *Isn't such a smart idea to surf when you're invisible.* A lone surfboard, carving a wave on its own, looks a bit strange. Nor was it smart to lay next to Ashli, enjoy the warmth of her touch while sniffing her hair, or allow himself to grow extremely aroused. Which he had.

Idiot. What was the point? So he could remind himself what he was missing out on? Once this was all over, which it would be because he never failed, they'd both move on. Him to some cold, dark tomb probably buried somewhere in a remote swamp where no one would find him for a million years. And Ashli—she would find some nice human to spend her mortal days with.

Or perhaps one of your brothers. After all, Cimil prophesied that twenty years from now, Ashli would broker peace between his brethren. That meant she'd meet them all. And Ashli was a catch, not to mention the one person on the planet destined to save them all. How? He had no clue. Yes, clearly the woman had her attributes— sexy as hell attributes—but aside from that, she seemed quite normal. Nevertheless, being savior of the planet would grant her instant celebrity status and boatloads of attention. She'd have men lining up around the block.

He balled his fists, then let go. *All for the best.* Because he didn't want her. *Much.* And he certainly didn't need the distractions; this was one mission he couldn't afford to fail.

He sighed and Ashli flinched. Máax lifted his head, ready to make a mad dash from the room if she woke up, but found himself entranced. Her plump lips and golden skin; her dark lashes, fanning along the crease of her cat-like eyes; her hair a wild mass of thick black curls. He had no idea of her heritage, but never had there been a more seductive female in existence.

His eyes swept down the length of her small athletic frame covered only in a flimsy white sundress. Next to his large body, Ashli appeared more petite than she really was.

An urge to dominate her, to take her right there, sparked.

Or perhaps you'd enjoy the opposite. Yes, he'd enjoy the feel of her lithe, lean figure straddling him, riding his cock.

Hell, man. That's enough, you horny bastard.

"Fuck this," he hissed and slipped quickly from the bed before he did something he regretted. Like kiss her.

Or motorboat her.

You randy bastard.

He needed to go for a swim. Yes, the ocean water would cool him down. The ocean always made him feel better, like being home.

Ashli's eyes flew open when a gust of wind blew through the house. She sat up quickly, her eyes scanning the room, ears listening for any sounds. In the shadows of her mind, she feared the intruder would return. Had he?

She tensed, continuing to listen.

Nothing.

Perhaps she'd dreamed it.

She ran her hands over her tangled curls. With all the commotion this morning, she'd called Fernando to open the café. Then, while Luis handled things with the police, her head had begun spinning from the adrenaline, and she needed a moment to calm down. She'd crawled into bed but clearly dozed off, which was a stupid move considering the situation. She should've been on her guard, sharpening her kitchen knives or rounding up her garden tools. Something.

What if he'd returned while she'd been napping?

You're an idiot, Ash. He's not going to show up in the middle of the day. And it was highly unlikely he'd come right back after he'd escaped only hours ago. That wouldn't be logical. No.

She did, however, need to think about what to do tonight. She couldn't stay in the house alone, could she?

You're not letting some asshole run you from your home, Ash. What if they never catch him? Are you going to stay away forever? She'd need to pay Luis a little extra for a while and have him keep a closer eye on her house. And she'd start asking around immediately if anyone had puppies for adoption. Yes, and she'd stop by the hardware store and buy a couple more shovels.

That bastard comes anywhere near me, he'll get another taste of Mary's lamb! Thank goodness she'd left her giant shovel propped against the palm tree.

She slipped from bed and made her way down the hall, through the living room into her kitchen, feeling groggy as hell. The back door leading to the beach had been left unlocked. Hadn't she locked it? Then she noticed that scent again. It was sweet and spicy; she couldn't put her finger on it. Where the heck was it coming from?

She sniffed her way back into the living room. Chills spread over her body when the smell became stronger with each step closer to her bedroom.

"Santa Maria." She stared at the giant indentation left on her bed next to where she'd been lying. She picked up the pillow and inhaled. The potent scent permeated her brain.

Wow. That smells so amaz—

Wait.

Her heart raced and a surge of icy, cold tingles violently exploded over her body. The dream. This was his smell from the dream.

Unable to hold her own weight, she sat on the bed hugging the pillow.

"Crap." It wasn't a man who'd been in her house. It was ... Death.

He's finally come for you, Ash. Just like you dreamed he would.

Shockingly, a dark, dark piece of her welcomed him.

Seven

~

The moment Máax submersed his body into the tepid, salty waves, that tightness in his chest and that carnal longing eased just enough to allow him to think again.

He didn't know if it was the result of meeting his mate, centuries of near isolation, or being without a visible form, but the strange sensation deep within him seemed to be growing. It was a peculiar ache, like a hunger that only felt sated in the presence of Ashli. He hoped it would abate after this mission was over and his sister washed away any and all memories of Ashli from his mind. After all, undoing the past—well, his past—wasn't exactly feasible, or better said, wasn't what he wanted. Plainly put, if he were given the chance to repeat history, his history, he would. Just like right now. He would still be here trying to save this Ashli woman and the planet from its impending doom simply because it was the right thing to do. And perhaps, because a tiny piece of him believed that following his conscience would lead to salvation.

Some day.

But for now, he felt content knowing that each violation of the sacred laws had been for a worthy cause. For that, he was the outcast. For that, he was the one No One Speaks Of. Even his name was a symbol of his sacrifices. Máax literally meant "Who?" in Mayan. He'd been called it for so long that he sometimes forgot he once had another name: Maat, which meant "truth" or "justice" in Egyptian. They had been the first civilization to truly embrace the concept and named it after him. Of course, Cimil changed the historical records and made Maat a woman. "Truth has to be female because men are lying, cheating pigs!" she'd said. He supposed, at the time, it had something to do with Roberto, but whatever. He was Máax now, the god of ... nothing. Invisible.

He dragged himself from the water and squeezed the saltwater from his long hair. He glanced down at his body and noted a film of fine sand and salt sticking to him. "Hell." He didn't normally swim during the day for this very reason. He hoped no one was watching.

Instantly sensing he was wildly wrong, he scanned the surroundings. "Fuck." There, hiding in the brush was Ashli, her wild mane of long black curls blowing in the wind. She was looking right at him.

Her catlike eyes opened up like two giant hazel-green orbs before she popped up from her hiding place and started running for her life.

Bloody infernum, *with her luck, she's probably going to get run over by an ice cream truck.* He had to catch her before she hurt herself.

He sprinted after her, the powdery-soft, warm sand making it difficult to close the gap quickly. As he came up the steep bank, Ashli came back into view. She reached for her back door, and everything happened in slow motion.

Ashli fell back, her head landing with a loud crack.

"Fuck. Not again!" Máax bolted to her side and crouched down. Blood flowed quickly from a gash on her head. "Dammit, woman. Why the hell do you always run from me?"

He pressed his hand over the wound to stop the flow. He needed to get her to a hospital. *Hell!* He'd need to reconnect her car battery and drive her there himself.

"You're so beautiful," she croaked. "But I changed my mind; I don't want to die. Please don't take me away."

She reached up and touched his cheek. A wave of warmth crashed into him, snatching the breath from his lungs.

He couldn't stop himself from wanting to feel more of her. Strangely, that gnawing hunger deep inside began to simultaneously quell and consume him.

He reached out with his other hand and palmed her cheek. "I am trying to save you, Ashli. Why won't you let me?"

She smiled briefly before her eyes rolled into the back of her head.

Oh, hell.

Owww.

Ashli cracked open her eyes and found a bright white room. *I must be dead.* Well, at least the game of cat and mouse was over. What a relief. And with any luck, she might see her parents again. If she did, she only hoped they wouldn't be upset about her dying.

Her spotty vision began to clear, and she eyed a poster on the wall. It said something about how boiled water is the safest for drinking.

Dumbass. You're in the hospital. Her eyes combed the room.

Yep. This was the small clinic that usually treated tourists for minor cuts and the occasional jellyfish sting. And holy Christ did her head hurt.

She slid her hand to the back of her head and gingerly kneaded the small bandage. A long IV tube hung from her other arm.

What happened?

Ohmygod. Death. Death had been in her house. Then she'd been overpowered by morbid curiosity and went looking for him. Perhaps she even wanted to end the charade. When she'd spotted him swimming in the ocean, she'd been unable to see him clearly, but he'd been so beautiful, so absolutely male that she nearly fainted. She never fainted. Except when she cracked her head open on cement. But then she remembered Death touching her face so tenderly and speaking to her. His slightly accented voice— *European?*—had been the most hypnotic, wholly sensual sound she'd ever heard. Deep and booming, silky and gruff, sexy and terrifying. All in one. Just like the voice of the man who'd been stalking her early this morning.

Gasp. Yes, he'd been the one she hit with that shovel!

Or had it all been a dream?

No. It was real. She'd seen his towering form, dripping with masculinity and ocean water, with her own eyes. She'd smelled his intoxicating, virile scent on her pillow. Death was real. Death was hunting her. Not that she was afraid. Confused, however, yes. Why had he let her live?

In walked the nurse, a small woman with short dark hair. Actually, Ashli recognized her—it was a small town—though the name escaped her.

"Ahh. You are awake," the nurse said with a thick Mexican accent.

"How did I get here?" Ashli asked.

"I have just started my shift, but I am told someone left you out front. No one saw who. Do you remember what happened?"

"No. I mean, yes. I slipped on my patio and hit my head. But I don't know how I got here."

The nurse shrugged. "Must have been your neighbor."

Okay, but why wouldn't they have stayed with her? And besides, both neighbors were gone. They only came for visits during spring break and Christmas. It was January.

Then who?

Ashli gasped. Could it have been...

No. No. Don't even go there!

"Well, the doctor will be by to check on you in a moment. You've got a minor concussion and a nasty cut. He gave you seven stitches."

Ashli instinctively reached for the throbbing spot again.

"Do not worry, Señorita Ashli. I only had to shave off a small patch of your hair. You have so much of it, no one will ever notice."

Ashli petted the bandage. Not that she cared about losing her hair—it had always been like a wild beast of curls with a mind of its own—but she didn't understand what had happened.

"It is maybe a bit funny, Señorita Ashli." The woman chuckled. "I think your hair saved you, acted like a sort of pillow. *No? O sí?*"

Okay. Okay. I have a lot of hair. I get the point. One of Ashli's grandmothers had originally been from Haiti and her great-grandfather was Irish. She couldn't begin to imagine the fun those two had living in a world once so horrifically divided. Her grandmother and mother had also married men from the opposite end of the racial spectrum. Granddad had been Japanese and her father Mexican. Yes, it made for a very interesting gene pool. She felt like a one-woman version of the It's a Small World ride at Disney. But with Death as her copilot.

No. This can't be happening.

That is absolutely right! Which is why as soon as you're able to drive, you're going to see Doctora Hernandez.

It wouldn't be the first time Ashli's dreams and wild imagination had seeped into her reality. The night before the tragic accident that took her parents' lives, she'd dreamt of a giant fuel truck crashing into them. It was why she'd sat on the left side of the car in the backseat. It was also why she'd lived.

But that's where things became so mixed up in her head. Ashli knew it wasn't possible. Premonitions were something only found in books or movies, yet she still blamed herself for her parents' death. If she'd just told them about the dream, maybe things would have ended differently. But she hadn't. And it was for no other reason than she would have felt stupid. Her pride had cost her the lives of those she loved. That's when she began having dark, horrible thoughts about wanting to die. No, she didn't mean suicide. She simply wished to trade places. She wished that she could convince Death to take her instead of them. She obsessed over the thought for months, the words *Take me instead of them. Take me instead of them* repeated in the background of her mind, like a skipping record that relentlessly tormented her day and night. Then, one day, she heard a reply. She'd been setting up the café for the day and stopped to watch the sunrise. It had been one of those rare mornings where the ocean seemed more like a lake—serene, quiet, and calm. And as the sun burst over the horizon, she recalled everything turning to brilliant shades of orange and pink. That's when she heard the voice of her parents. "He is coming for you," they said. Oddly, it hadn't sounded like a warning, but more like a promise of salvation. Ashli knew she needed help.

Over time, Dr. Hernandez, the local psychiatrist, got Ashli to see things more logically. The "premonition" had been nothing more than a coincidence, and Ashli couldn't blame herself for dismissing it as such. But she still couldn't shake the feeling that she'd cheated death, and she began having wild dreams. The man wanting her. Death hunting her. Sometimes, she even saw her parents—they yelled at her for visiting them. Regardless, she still liked seeing them.

But this? This was no dream. Death was real. Even now, she smelled his scent in the air and felt his energy buzzing about the room.

What was she going to do?

You're not afraid of Death, Ashli. No, she really wasn't. In fact, she'd grown irritated by this game.

Ashli watched the nurse leave and then blurted out, "I know you're there. I can smell you." She closed her eyes and tried to keep her nerves steady, expecting to hear that seductive, masculine voice that had such an effect on her.

Silence.

Her eyes snapped open and searched the room. "Cat got your tongue, huh? Okay, well, I just want you to know that I think you are a sick bastard. And I can't wait to get home so I can get in one more good smack. But this time, I'm aiming for your balls. If you have any."

"*Sanctum infernum*, woman," said that oh-so-deep, alluring voice. Despite the anticipation, his timbre still sent goose bumps charging over her skin. And his smell. It was far more scrumptious than any holiday muffin she'd ever had. Why did Death insist on having the sublime voice and scent of an angel of seduction? Seemed so unfair.

"What did I ever do to you?" he added with shock.

Oh, cute. Death is playing the "oh, my pride is so wounded" game. "Do you really need me to answer—"

The nurse appeared in the doorway. "You called, *señorita*?"

"Uh...no. I was just...singing." To prove her point, she moved her feet like windshield wipers beneath the white sheet. *"La cucaracha. La cucaracha...ya no puedo caminar."* Oh, God. I have lost my mind.

The nurse cocked a brow and reached for the door. "The doctor will be right in."

The moment the door shut, a deep chuckle radiated from the corner, next to the green plastic molded chair placed there for visitors.

"What's so funny?" she asked. *I can't believe I'm talking to Death.*

"Nothing," he said all too innocently. "I was simply enjoying your choice of music."

Ugh! "It was the first song that popped into my head— hey, can we quit the chitchat and get this over with?"

Silence.

"What?" she barked. "What are you waiting for?"

The voice emanated from the space immediately to her side. "I do not know what you mean," he said.

Infuriating! Death was playing with her. "Do it already. Okay!" She closed her eyes and braced for the inevitable.

"What in the devil's name are you talking about, woman?"

She opened one eye and then snapped it shut again. "Waiting for you to take me."

"Mmmm…" he said. "As much as I'd enjoy that, because you are a very lovely woman, I do not believe this is the appropriate place. That bed is much too small for a man of my size."

Wha—wha—what? She sat up to berate him, but her brain pulsed with a crippling ache. She grabbed the sides of her head instead.

"Lie back down," the voice commanded. She felt two warm—no, they were actually kind of hot and tingly— hands, one on the front of her chest and the other on the back of her neck. The sensation was elating.

Death touched her and she…liked it? Yeah, she did. She liked his smell and his voice, too. It was almost impossible to explain because she'd never experienced anything like it; being next to him felt like being…

Home.

What's wrong with me?

Maybe she secretly longed for death. *Yes! That had to be it. My soul must be ready to cross over.*

He removed his hands, and she instantly felt the loss. She wanted him to touch her again.

"Okay," she whispered. "I'm ready. I didn't think dying

would be so easy, but I have to admit, you really do make it nice. Must be that voice."

"What the *sanctum infernum* are you speaking about?" he said, his voice gruff.

"Hey, I was just starting to feel okay with this. Stop being such an ass, and kill me already. Especially if you're going to start speaking Latin. It's such an annoying language. Makes you sound like a wannabe wizard."

She felt a small pain on her hand. "Did you just . . . flick me?" she asked.

"Yes. Yes, I did. And the next time you speak to me that way, human, I will be flicking your bare ass with the palm of my extremely large, extremely powerful hand."

Had Death threatened to spank her? *What the hell?* "You just try it. I don't care if you are Death. No one spanks a grown woman. That's totally *machista* and lame."

"Death? I am not Death."

"Oh, sure. Like I'm going to believe anything you say."

"I am incapable of lying. It is not in my nature."

Ashli burst out laughing, which really hurt. *Ouuuuuch!*

"Do not mock me, woman. I speak the truth. Why would I drive you to the hospital if I wanted you to die?"

Good question. "Um. Because you're a sick bastard who's been playing with me for years, stalking me in my slee— Wait. You drove me here?"

"That is correct. And do you have any idea how hard it is for a male of my proportions to drive such a tiny vehicle? I am seven feet in height. I scarcely fit behind your steering wheel. I will also highlight that you should park your car in the shade. My ass is still burning."

Ashli blinked. This wasn't happening. She had to be dreaming this up. "Your . . . uh . . . ass?"

"Well, yes," he said. "Merely because you cannot see me doesn't mean that I do not have an ass. One with feeling."

So why was he complaining about his ass? Unless... She started laughing, rubbing her hands over her face. "Oh, this is juicy. Death is stalking me. And he's a seven-foot-tall naked guy with the voice of an angel and smells like fresh mountain air mixed with holiday baked goods."

"You like my voice?" he said with eager curiosity.

The doctor entered the room, startling Ashli.

"*Buenas tardes*, Ashli." She knew Rubin, aka Dr. Ruiz, because he came by the coffee shop all the time. He was in his late thirties with a lean build and a very charming smile. Her cleaning lady also took care of his house and loved to gossip about all of the random women who showed up, bearing gifts of homemade cookies, cakes, pozole, and tamales. There wasn't a single woman in town who hadn't tried to snag him. Except Ashli, of course. What was the point of dating or falling in love when death loomed over you? Didn't seem practical. Or fair to the guy.

"Hi, Rubin," Ashli said.

"Ashli, lovely to see you as usual." Rubin leaned over her and flashed his penlight in her eyes. "You lost a little blood and have a concussion. I suggest you stay here for the remainder of the afternoon, but you should be fine." He flicked the IV bag with his finger. "Do you have someone to drive you home?"

Ashli shook her head no. *Owwww. Don't do that.*

Rubin glowed with a smile. "Then it would be my pleasure to take you after my shift."

"Are you sure?"

"I've waited a very long time to have the elusive Ashli Rosewood all to myself." He winked.

Strange. It wasn't like Dr. Ruiz to be overtly flirtatious. He had asked her out once on a run, but that was over a year ago. She'd politely declined, making up some excuse, but hadn't really thought much of it. Rubin continued to come by every few days, drink his coffee, and read his paper. Being the sort of man that was more into himself than anyone else, he'd never made an effort. Not that it would have made a difference. She didn't date. But now, he was flirting big-time.

"I will be back to check on you shortly," he said. "Let us know if you need anything for the pain, back rub, candle-lit bubble bath, the key to my house. The numbing shot I gave you will begin to wear off shortly."

"Uh, I'm good?" *And speechless.*

Rubin eyeballed her, grinning like a fiend.

"Really. I'm good," she repeated.

The doctor and his creepy smile exited the room rear end first.

"Slimy bastard is going to get a visit from my foot up his ass. What sort of doctor hits on his patient?" said the deep voice in a tone so stark it made her heart palpitate.

"Sorry?"

"Nothing," he said. "You and I need to talk. I must understand the nature of your comments. Why do you believe that Death has been stalking you?"

This conversation was simply too surreal for words. "I can't do this anymore."

"Do what?" His voice filled the room every time he spoke. Why did it have that strange effect, like his voice flowed right through her and she heard him with her entire body instead of with just her ears?

"This!" she hissed. "I can't keep talking to thin air."

"Of course you can. You are doing it quite well."

It was funny—this man, or whatever he was, spoke with the naivety of child and the authority of a king. He was kind of sweet but a total a-hole at the same time. It was a strange combination. If she was, in fact, losing her mind, she had to give herself a few brownie points for originality.

She sighed.

"Perhaps," he said, "if I were to introduce myself, you might feel more at ease."

Oh, nice. Let's make friends. "Why not?"

"Excellent." She felt the bed sink on one side. The indentation of where he sat was in the shape of an . . . *ass?*

"Are you really naked?" she asked.

"Yes. Did I not say that already? Are your ears not functioning properly?"

A-hole.

"But I suppose it deserves an explanation," he added.

Sweet.

"I will start by explaining that I am a god. An ancient god. And you will do well to heed my every word."

Huh?

"Because I have come here with the sole purpose of saving your life."

Scary.

"What? Why?" she asked.

She heard the faint sound of whiskers being scratched. *Of course, how can he shave if he's invisible?* she thought to herself sarcastically.

"I cannot provide many details," he said, "because I do not have them. However, twenty years from now, you will do something very important for humanity. You will stop the end of the world if you survive, which you will. Because I am here to save you."

Annnnd add crazy. Sweet, crazy, scary a-hole.

She closed her eyes. This was simply all too much.

"What are you doing?" he asked.

"Trying to fall asleep so I can wake back up," she explained.

"Ashli. This is most serious. I assure you. Otherwise, why would I waste my time with you?"

Pompous. Add pompous.

"Oh, trust me. I'm taking this seriously," she said.

She felt his hot breath wash over her face. The bed sank to either side of her head. Was he leaning over her?

"I do not joke, Ashli," he censured her. His hot, sensual scent filled her nostrils. "You will cease your foolish behavior and listen carefully because there is nothing more important than saving you."

Simultaneous explosions of heated thunderbolts and ice-cold shivers exploded over her body. She didn't know why, but she found herself needing to touch him, to make sure he was real. It was ... as if ... she needed it more than the blood in her veins. She felt her heart might actually collapse if she couldn't have proof. Proof he was really, really there.

Cautiously, she reached for him, her breath sticking in her throat. Her palms collided with hot flesh. A man's flesh. She gasped as a jolt of unchaste neediness surged through her. She couldn't pull back. Her hands molded to his face and began to explore. A sculpted jaw covered in

a thick, short beard; sharp cheekbones; soft, thick brows.
She heard his breathing stop. Was he holding it? Did he
feel the same wanton elation? *Ohmygod.* It was amazing,
like nothing she'd ever experienced in her entire life.

Her hands slid just above his ears and found soft hair.
She gingerly glided her fingertips down, down, down,
following the silky strands until she reached their tips,
lingering just above his shoulder. *Skin. Oh, God.* She
wanted to touch every taut inch.

"What are you?" she whispered.

He pulled away, leaving her grasping nothing but air.

She blinked and snapped out of her trance. Had it been
an illusion? *No. Please, no.* She just might die if she discovered that pool of lifesaving water was a mirage.

"Don't go," she begged. She never begged anyone for
anything.

"I am here." His voice sounded irritated, shaken.

"Please, tell me. What are you?"

Máax stood with his back pressed to the wall and stared
down at Ashli, her hands extended in midair as if beckon-
ing him to return.

What happened? He didn't know, but now he was
in a state of what he believed humans referred to as
WTFH. Because he knew damned well that LOVE was
just an acronym for "loss of valuable energy," and love
was exactly what he'd felt. Or was it merely his mate's
bond drawing him in, the Universe's masterful way of
conspiring?

The moment Ashli touched him, his light erupted with
rapturous energy that spiraled and twisted, coalescing

into a single strand of light. He wanted to envelop himself in it and drink from it. Then the strand sieved through his skin, into his veins, and tangled itself around his heart like a boa constrictor capturing its prey. The cord began to elongate, stretching through time, through this world into the next, until it reached the land of dead souls. Ashli. Ashli was there! He witnessed the strand of brilliant light tether itself to Ashli's wrist. He began pulling, exerting every fiber of his being to extract her like a desperate man attempting to salvage his own heart from a pit of hungry vipers. Máax watched in terror as his grip faltered, and the cord slid from his blistering hands. He screamed Ashli's name, mirroring her cries of agony as she dissolved inside a pool of vicious, hungry souls, feeding from her light.

WTFAIGTDN? What the fuck am I going to do now?

And why do I keep speaking to myself in acronyms? They are quite annoying.

Máax's heart raced at a sickening pace, and his chest expanded with one careful breath, the kind of breath a man takes when he's about to pray for a miracle. What had the vision meant? Yes, he understood his role was to save her, but there was something else. The Universe was trying to tell him something.

"What. Are. You?" she repeated.

He felt an unfamiliar lump of doubt in his throat. "I am your mate."

"Sorry?" she said.

He cleared his throat. "You are my . . . match. My soul mate, which I already knew. But what I do not comprehend is why the Universe wants to exterminate you. And she will not quit until she has you."

Some things in life have no explanation. This was one of them. Because when the strange male voice spoke those words, Ashli knew he'd spoken the truth. It was like drinking a glass of cold water from a mountain stream; you recognize the taste of purity, even if you're unable to describe or articulate it. That's how his words felt. There was simply an absence of lies or deceit. Just…truth.

"Oh, God." She sat up slowly, rubbing her forehead. "I always knew I was different, but this is too much."

A warm hand embraced her own and that strange current of electricity once again flowed through her body. Her eyes couldn't help but seek him out.

"Why can't I see you?" she said. She recalled the image of the man coming from the ocean, the outline of his flawless male body glistening in the sun. He was definitely worth seeing.

Ohmygod. The dreams! She'd had them ever since the accident. This man in her dreams had been faceless, he'd done things to her body that left her feeling almost embarrassed but also deliciously weak and sated, and he'd pleasured her in every possible way known to man—errr, woman.

That's him! He's the man from my dreams!

"It is my punishment for breaking a few rules," he explained without emotion. "My mortal shell was taken from me. But I do not want to discuss that now. I must go to see my brethren."

What? He was leaving? "You can't go."

That warm hand, gentle but rough, trailed across her cheek. "I will return as quickly as I can."

"Why do you have to leave?"

"Because the Universe is waiting for any opportunity to take you. I must find out why."

She watched the door open.

"Wait!" But he was already gone. She felt his absence in the air.

She shook her head—*ow, ow, ow*—unable to process the barrage of emotions barreling over her. He was real. He wasn't Death, but an invisible god. He was her soul mate. The Universe wanted to kill her.

This can't be happening. I need meds. "Dr. Ruiz?"

Eight

Like a drippy old faucet, an anxious voice inside Máax's head commenced nagging the moment he walked out of that hospital. "Go back. Go back to her," it said. And while the sensible part of his mind understood this to be the effect of their bond—a bond he was still determined to forget once this mission concluded—his body did not seem to give a rat's ass and protested violently. Leaving her felt like having his atoms busted apart with a crowbar. Not only that, but traveling to a time where Ashli no longer existed felt like traveling to hell. In the future, she was still dead. He had not saved her yet.

Thanks for the reminder, asshole.

Yes, he'd prevented her from dying this time. But what about the next? And the next? That was the conundrum. When he'd originally agreed to this whole thing, he'd assumed that saving Ashli from death was a onetime deal. Humans die all the time in accidents—cars, drowning, falling off a cliff when searching for a secret stash of rare Miss Piggy Pez dispensers.

That was actually Cimil who fell off the cliff.

Right.

Point was, he'd believed, erroneously, that saving Ashli was simply a question of inserting himself at the right place at the right time. Afterward, she'd be free to live a full, healthy, happy existence. Now, after the vision, he understood this was not the case. Death would come for her again and again. But why would the Universe want such a thing?

It can't fucking have her. Especially if she was the key to stopping his brethren from going to war with each other. But he still couldn't figure out how. That was the kicker. By now, he would've expected to see some clue as to why this was her destiny.

He rubbed his brow. *So what's the plan, Máax?*

You must go to Cimil and force her to tell you what she knows. She is hiding something. The vision had something to do with the realm of the dead, and that was Cimil's turf.

But what leverage could he employ? *You'll think of something. Or perhaps you should try to think like Cimil. What would she do?*

She would find your weakness, the thing you desire most, and then make you hop through flame-engulfed hoops until you lost your mind and all sense of hope. Then she'd torture you some more, talk to a bug or two, go shopping for useless used human merchandise, and then you'd get your prize.

Hell. I don't have time for that crap. He'd opt for threatening her.

Planting his bare feet firmly in the sand, he stood over

the buried tablet, focused his thoughts, and watched a small pit the size of a manhole open in the sand. The portal.

Not wanting to walk in on Cimil and Roberto mid-coitus, lest he be forced to remove his own eyeballs, he aimed his arrival a few moments ahead. He stepped inside the portal, successfully landing in the same conference room he'd departed from twenty years into the future. He approached the heavy metal door and cracked it open, listening for any signs of lovemaking. Or in Cimil's case, noises resembling animal fornication.

To his delight, prison riot–like shouting greeted his ears instead. Not to his delight, the foundation began to shimmy and creak all around him.

Splendid. Another earthquake. He wondered what the score was now.

Máax entered the long, sterile-looking hallway—gray paint and fluorescent lights—turned the corner, and immediately spotted Cimil, sitting cross-legged on her cell floor, playing paddleball. Toward the center of the cellblock, a line of vampires attired in black leather and tees stood in formation like an immortal football team, their gazes cold and alert, ready for anything.

Except for that guy. Máax quirked a brow. One of the vampires, a blond on the end, stroked an empty space of air to his side. "There, there, Minky. All will be well."

Cimil's unicorn. How the hell had it gotten inside the prison? Damned beast was as big as a rhino.

Thankfully, his brethren remained inside their glass holding tanks, each in varying states of "pissed as hell" or "freaking the hell out."

Máax had to admit, despite the dire situation and count-down to doom, seeing all thirteen gods jailed, guarded by fucking huge vampires, had some entertainment value. They had even managed to capture the infamous chick magnet Zac Cimi, Bacab of the North (also known as Ix Zacal, the inventor of weaving; Z, Keeper of Tchotchkes; and Kuju, the Yukaghir Spirit God of Food—his specialty happened to be creamy sauces—among many, many other titles and gifts), and most recently titled God of Temptation. Zac had gone into hiding because he also held the honor of being the gods' most wanted. (Not wanted in a sexy way, but in a "you're in a heap of shit" way for trying to steal another god's mate.) While it was common for the deities to have many, many gifts and to be known by many, many names, depending on the culture, "most wanted" was not a title anyone desired. Not even Máax who prided himself on being known as the bad boy of the gods.

Bastard deserves to be locked up. In fact, perhaps they will all benefit from a little reflection time.

Sure he loved them just as a human might love his or her siblings—though the gods were not truly related—but they'd all used Máax in one way or another, taking advantage of his need to see justice served at any cost. Example: There was the time Camaxtli, aka Fate, had Máax travel back to ancient Greece to steal the book of the Oracle of Delphi. Fate had used the book for years to predict the future. Why? A secret. One she made him swear to keep until his grave. Example two: The time Cimil had him steal the book away from Fate so she could give it to some Demilord. Why? Yeah, another secret. The list of manipulations, deceit, and games went on and on. And yet Máax never turned his back on the other gods—not even that lying coward, Fate—when they asked for help. Not even when his suffering became almost too much to bear.

So, yeah, despite the apparent eminent destruction of their world, he found it pretty damned satisfying to see them all incarcerated. Too bad the moment felt ruined by his need to return to Ashli. And the fact that the Universe wanted to kill her.

Oh, well. "Revenge is completely overrated anyway," he muttered.

All heads swiveled in his general direction.

Kinich, ex–God of the Sun, was the first to start yelling at him. "Máax, you will release us from these cells! Immediately!" His long golden-brown hair fell about his face while he pounded his fists into the glass.

Then came the screaming from Ixtab, Ah-Ciliz, Zac, Akna, Acan, K'ak, Votan, and the rest, including his other sister—the one whose name no one ever remembered. Sucked to be the Goddess of Forgetfulness.

Yes, everyone yelled, except Cimil, who looked bored out of her immortal mind. Then she simply held up five fingers. "Rumble, rumble. Ticktock, Invisi-boy!"

Máax knew she meant five earthquakes had now passed and was about to say something else when he noticed one other god oblivious to the chaos: Chaam.

His large frame, draped in a black caftan garment, sagged on his bed. Next to him, his mate Maggie, with long brown hair and wearing a light gray dress, resembled a barnacle clinging to a sinking battleship.

Maggie hiccuped and mopped her tears with Chaam's long black hair.

This is very troubling.

Back off, man, you need to return to Ashli. Whatever troubles him can wait.

Máax's gaze wondered back to Maggie. With her wide

brown eyes and freckled nose, her aura of innocence was just the sort a deity—*him, okay; him!*—couldn't turn away from.

Yes. Yes, you can. Think of Ashli. He had to see her again soon. Perhaps touch her silky, soft lips and get yet another glimpse of that perfect, smooth, round ass or those gorgeous, cocoa-brown breasts with the pink little nip—

Maggie hiccuped once more and then snorted between heart-wrenching sobs.

Hell! Bloody deity hell, hell, hell!

Máax knew this wasn't a detour he could afford, but his nature to ensure a just world drew him right in like a moth to a flame, like a bee to honey, like Cimil to a BOGO sale on pirate costumes. (She'd started some idiotic holiday having to do with pirates. How did a god have time for such frivolous bull crap?)

"Brother?" Máax placed his palms against the glass of Chaam's cell, ignoring the raging voices exploding in all directions. "What is the matter?" *Besides this fucking apocalypse.*

Maggie looked up with wet doe eyes. "Máax! You have to help him. Please tell him! Tell him it's not his fault!"

Chaam didn't bother to lift his drooping head. His long hair hung like a flag of defeat. "Don't defend me, Maggie. Don't do it. Tell the vampires you've relinquished your love for me so they'll set you free. Just...*fucking go*, woman."

"How can you say that?" This time she wiped her tears with the backs of her hands. "After everything we've been through."

It was true. Everyone knew the two had been through

their share of pain and struggles. After meeting Maggie, his one true love, Chaam had been possessed by dark energy, committed a series of heinous atrocities— started breeding like a rabbit with random women and then murdered his female children to use them as some sort of apocalyptic biofuel (yeah, like he said, heinous)— then had been captured and imprisoned inside a real-life "temple of doom." Maggie had also been imprisoned inside one of the tablets. Well, not inside, but in the dimension that existed between everything. Not pretty. Chaam had since been cured, thanks to Máax and their sister Ixtab—but Chaam had a mountain of baggage to deal with.

"Leave! Before I kill you!" Chaam raged and then sank back into his pit of despair.

Maggie hesitated for a moment and then wrapped her arms around Chaam's hunched-over frame as he began to sob.

Saints of yore! Máax moaned in his head. Gods didn't cry. Ever. *This is too much to bear.*

"No, baby." Maggie squared her shoulders. "I won't go. I don't care what you say. I've watched you suffer"— Maggie pointed toward Cimil's cell—"because of that evil…evil cow whore! I'm not leaving you! And I won't rest until I see her pay."

Máax glanced at Cimil, who seemed to be looking at someone nonexistent, and mouthed the words, "Cow whore? What the hell?" She then began singing "Supercalifragilisticexpialidocious" while merrily smacking that paddleball.

Máax groaned. He didn't have time for this fucking drama. He had a crisis to tend to.

"Chaam. Brother. Tell me why you are so distraught," Máax said, already suspecting he knew the answer.

Chaam shook his head with regret, the tears sheeting down his cheeks. "I killed them, my own daughters. I seduced their mothers. I had children with them. Then I slaughtered my own. I am a monster."

Maggie punched Chaam, a man twice her size, in the shoulder. "No! That was Cimil! She made you do it."

"No!" Chaam argued. "If I'd been strong enough, I could've resisted her. I'm weak and evil."

Maggie looked up at Máax, and for a moment he wondered if she could see him. But of course, she could not. "Please help him, Máax. He trusts you. He knows you can't lie. Tell him it's not his fault."

Máax took a deep, satisfying breath. These were the moments he lived for. Setting things right, helping others, serving truth. Yep, made him feel like a complete badass. Of course, he was a badass. Who else could pull off the kind of shit he did? No one. That's why he would be the one to save the world. Okay, Ashli would, but he was her protector. Same thing.

Máax said with a loud voice for all to hear, "It is not your fault, brother. You are not evil. You have done no wrong."

Chaam's head snapped up. "What?"

Yes, Máax had gotten his attention, because everyone knew that Máax did not lie. Ever.

Máax crossed his arms over his chest, not that anyone could see him. Fucking sucked to be invisible. "I have undone every evil act, brother. Your children live on and you are free to enjoy a happy and peaceful life with Maggie, and blah, blah, you're welcome, blah, blah, blah."

Cimil suddenly jumped up and started clapping. "Yippee! Give that man a gold star! Woo!"

Chaam stood, crossed the cell, and looked straight at Máax. Well, straight at his ear. "What is the meaning of this?"

"Brother," Máax said, "why the fuck do you think I made those trips to the past? To prove my badassery cannot be surpassed? I already know that."

Chaam stared, speechless.

"Nice shooting the shit with you, as always, but I must—"

"I don't understand," Chaam said.

"I saved every one of them," Máax admitted. "None have died by your hand, and most are happily living out their lives. And for those whom I could not find a safe home, I brought them forward."

"You mean..." Maggie's words crackled with emotion. "Those women, the Payals who can't remember who they are?"

Máax's patience wore thinner by the second. "Yes." What? Did he have to spell it out? There had been approximately a thousand women of Chaam's descent (called Payals), spanning over the course of eighty or so years, whom Máax had quietly plucked from death's doorstep, relocating them before their fates took a turn for the worse. He'd helped all but two hundred find new lives, safe from Chaam's evil henchmen, the Maaskab. Those two hundred had been severely traumatized, leaving him no choice but to employ the help of his sister, the Goddess of Forgetfulness. The women were now safe, living right there on the Uchben base where they could start anew. Not a perfect ending to their stories, but sometimes perfect wasn't possible.

Maggie wailed and then jumped on Chaam, wrapping her arms around his neck, her legs around his waist. "I told you so, baby. I told you. We were meant to be happy."

Chaam's face whitened with astonishment. "But why? Why did you do it?" he asked Máax.

It had taken Máax the equivalent of one human year, working around the clock to accomplish the task, but what the hell. Not like he had had anything better to do. "'Cause I'm the only one with the balls big enough to pull it off. Why else?" Okay. Maybe he cared a little bit, too, but no one needed to know that.

"But all of those times you traveled back," Chaam said. "You will be punished for breaking our laws."

"Really? No shit. Now if you don't mind," Máax grumbled.

"Thank you, Máax. Thank you," Maggie offered.

Chaam glared at Cimil. "You are not off the hook, Cimil. I still have a score to settle with you."

Roberto moved in front of Cimil's cell, faced Chaam, and crossed his arms. "Over my dead body."

"That, my vampire friend, can be arranged." Chaam's eyes flickered over the faces of every vampire standing guard.

Maggie nudged Chaam. "Will you stop, you arrogant, overgrown manchild? Don't you see what's happened? You can let go of your guilt. You're free—well, sort of— and we're together."

Chaam looked down at Maggie and threaded his fingers through her mahogany-colored hair. "Yes. Yes. Of course. You are right."

"Oh," Máax added. "And brother? Before you thank me again, I'd like to point out that you're now the proud father of two hundred daughters. Good fucking luck with that."

Maggie squealed. "I've always wanted a big family!"

Chaam's lips hardened for several moments, but then he grinned. "So have I, actually."

Sloppy tongues began to fly, and Máax suddenly wished that *they* were invisible. Or that the prison cell had tinted glass, anything to hide what these two looked like they were about to do.

Oh, well. At least they'd stopped talking. Máax could go back to focusing on his own damned carnival-of-crap situation.

Máax's mind drifted to visions of Ashli.

Ashli. Mmmm. Ashli. Gods, why couldn't he control the wanting and lust for a few lousy minutes? It was as if she'd taken over his mind. And his cock.

He leered at Cimil who disco danced to a phantom song in her cell. "Cimil?" Máax warned. "We need to talk. *Now.*"

She ignored him completely.

He walked over and pounded on the glass. Surprisingly, Roberto took a step back, though he remained on his guard.

Good choice, asshole. Máax was in no mood to play Cimi-games. "I know you are hiding something."

She stopped dancing and raised her brows. "I hide nothing!" She covered one side of her mouth and whispered, "Except for the new unicorn tat on my bum. It's a surprise for Roberto." Cimil paused for an accomplished sigh.

Máax was not amused. "Tell me what you really know about Ashli. And do not play stupid, because clearly you have deceived me."

Cimil pointed to herself. "*Moi?* Well, I have been known to lie. But what can I say? That's how I hop." Her disco move transformed into a bunny hop to prove her point.

"This isn't a joke," Máax growled. "She's going to die, and I won't be able to stop it if you don't help me."

"Cimiiiil? What is going on?" asked Roberto who stepped to Máax's side. "I, too, am beginning to suspect there is more going on here than a simple attempt to halt the end of the days."

Máax was surprised by Roberto's suspicious attitude.

Cimil's eye toggled between the floor and Roberto's face. "Okay. You got me." She held up her hands.

"Speak, my evil little turnip," Roberto prodded.

"Well," she said, "I do have another reason for this lockdown. I kinda thought this would be a nice opportunity for a family therapy session."

Roberto visibly fumed. "You locked everyone up for that?"

"Nooo, you locked them up! This was all your idea. Okay. Maaaaybe I planted the idea in your head. But!" She held up her index finger. "When I told you that the gods go to war against each other and destroy the planet, that was true. What I didn't tell you was that we are also carrying massive quantities of baggage. It's time to let it all go and find peace. I mean, whether we all live or die, it would be nice. Don't you think?"

"I think you are lying," Roberto said in an irritated tone.

"Where's the fun in the truth? Hey, got any bad people hanging around? Minky's getting hangry."

"You mean hungry?" Roberto cocked a brow.

"No. Hangry. That's when you're angry because you're

hungry. She needs her afternoon snack. Preferably anyone who wears a mullet."

"Cimil!" Máax barked. "You will cease this conversational detour and tell me what you know about Ashli. Why does the Universe want to kill her?"

Cimil's turquoise eyes glowed with mischief, and her lips curled into a giant smirk. "I have told you; Ashli will be the one to prevent us from fighting each other. She will broker peace if you save her and she is allowed to live out her natural life in her natural habitat. Or Ashli-tat, as I like to call it. If not… well, at least we can all enjoy this family time together."

"There is more. I know you're hiding something," Máax said bluntly and then looked at Roberto who also had the expression of a man trying to figure out a very complex puzzle. "The Universe wants her dead. Why?"

Cimil shrugged. "If I had the answer to every question, do you think I'd be locked in here? Okay. Maybe I would. It's cozy."

Máax slammed his fist against the glass. "I'm not fucking around, Cimil! We've had five earthquakes. Five!"

"He is right, my evil dove," Roberto agreed. "You must tell him what you know."

Cimil crossed her arms and turned away.

"Very well." He was on his own. What was new, really? That was the way it had always been. Máax did everything in his power to save everyone's bacon, and they turned their backs on him in his time of need. Again and again and again.

No more. He was done saving everyone. Except for Ashli.

Now he had no choice but to figure this out on his own.

Something greater was at play. But what? Why would the Universe want her head?

Well, the Universe cannot have her. She is mine. She always will be.

He took a mental step back; his possessive thoughts stunned him.

He already knew he wanted her on her back, in his bed, maybe more, but he'd already settled on the fact he wouldn't continue on this path. However, it seemed with each passing moment, the temptation to fantasize about a different destiny, one with Ashli in it, grew stronger.

Well, he wasn't going to give in, and he had to stop letting this mate garbage cloud his judgment. His one and only task was to stop the apocalypse. Perhaps if he dug deeper and found out what miracle Ashli would perform, what made her special, he'd uncover why the Universe wanted her dead. The two had to be linked.

"I will return shortly," Máax said.

"Wait! No! Let us out!" screamed his brother Kinich who looked very much like himself—long honey-brown hair with streaks of gold, built like a tank, and a deadly look in his turquoise eyes. "If you let us out, we can lift the curse. Make you whole again."

Máax glanced at Cimil, who shook her head and said, "Not until you save Ashli."

Fuck. Only a unanimous vote would reverse his current state and return his powers. Cimil would hold back the final vote.

On my own.

"Remember this moment, Cimil." Máax marched back to the conference room and prepared for another trip to 1993.

Nine

⌒

Two days after release from the hospital

Ashli sat in her living room, curled up with a book and her favorite raspberry tea, trying her hardest to focus on the story. Usually anything with a drafty castle and a warm kilt sucked her in, but today? Not a chance. Her thoughts were fixated on the mysterious man. Why hadn't he returned? What was he really? Where did he come from? Were there others? Where did they live? What did they eat? Did they have powers? And that business about him saying she was his soul mate, but the universe wanted her dead?

How can someone just say those things and then... leave?

Or perhaps she'd imagined the entire thing? Rubin, or Dr. Ruiz, said he'd given her some sort of drug for the pain. And it wasn't unheard of for people to hallucinate after a head injury.

Ashli's stomach did a sickly little polka dance. She didn't want it to be a dream. She wanted the man to be real. The way he made her feel when he touched her was...

Magical.

Magical? Do you know how lame that sounds? We're not talking about a damned unicorn!

But what other way could she describe it? Sexy, delicious, blissful? None of those words came close to the magnificence of what transpired in that hospital room.

There was a loud buzz from the intercom at the front gate.

Ashli sprang from the sofa and looked out the window.

Rubin. She looked down at her clothes, a little yellow sundress, and determined she was presentable enough, and then hit the release switch to the front gate. She opened the front door and watched him approach, carrying a brown paper bag.

He was a lean, nice-looking man, that was for sure, but hallucination or not, he didn't hold a match to...

A guy you can't even see? You do get why that makes you nuts, right?

"I came to check in on you," he said as she closed the door behind him.

"That's really thoughtful, but you didn't have to. I'm fine, I promise." Ashli returned to her cozy white couch. "Other than my head still hurts."

Rubin sat next to her and the scent of fresh pastries filled her nostrils. "I brought you these. Fernando sends his regards."

Ah. Yes. Fernando was holding down the fort. She looked inside the bag and saw her favorite Mexican pastry, conchas. They kind of looked like perky boobs rolled in sugar.

"I stopped by for my morning coffee and didn't see you," said Rubin, with his thick accent, "so I thought I'd come by to check up."

"That was very thoughtful, but I'm sure I'll be fine." Hadn't she just said that?

Rubin scooted closer and slipped a penlight from his pocket. "May I take a look?"

She shrugged. "Sure."

Rubin flickered the light across her pupils. "Looks good." Then he simply stared at her. "Has anyone ever told you that you have the most beautiful eyes? They are a very, very unusual shade of green."

Hitting on her again?

"Thanks. My mom used to say that I have my grand-mother's eyes." She moved back just an inch, and that's when she noticed it. The smell in the air.

He's here. Oh, my . . . I can't say God. That sounds weird. Okay, but he's here! She tried to hold in her excitement. And slight irritation. She wanted to ask where the hell he'd been, or if he had any idea what she'd gone through, wondering if she'd lost her mind. The questions would have to wait until Rubin was gone, which needed to happen ASAP.

Ashli feigned a yawn. "Well, thank you for stopping by, Dr. Ruiz."

Rubin chuckled. "I am Dr. Ruiz now?"

Ashli smiled politely. "I didn't get much sleep last night. I think I'm going to take a nap." *Yawn, yawn, yawn. See how sleepy I am?*

Rubin stood. "I get the hint, but I'm not leaving until you agree to come to my home for dinner."

She just wanted him to go. "Sure. Love to. Sounds good. How's next week?"

A strange energy vibrated through the air. It made the hair on her arms stand up.

"Saturday then," he said. "I will prepare my famous chicken mole," he said proudly. She found it hard to believe he could cook anything. She already knew that his housekeeper prepared most of his meals.

"Mole. Love mole." She smiled and went straight for the door. "Thanks again for stopping by."

Rubin gave her a kiss on the cheek. "Of course, if you need anything, you must promise to call?"

"Absolutely." She smiled sweetly, shut the door behind him, and pushed her back against it, holding her breath. She peeked out the window and watched him disappear out the front gate.

"Dammit! I know you're there," she barked.

No response.

"Why were you gone for so long?" she called out.

Silence.

She shook her head and went to the kitchen. "Unbelievable. Doesn't matter what species, men are the same." She continued her mumbled rant, grabbing a small plate and filling up a glass with milk. She knew he watched her. She felt his eyes all over her body, and she sensed that weird, angry vibe in the air. Why did he insist on torturing her like this? "Like I care what a stupid invisible guy thinks anyway. He doesn't even wear underwear. What kind of guy walks around naked—"

"My condition," he interrupted, "is not a power. I cannot transfer it to other objects. Wearing clothes only terrifies people."

Ashli turned her head toward the voice. "I knew it! I knew you were there. By the way, spying is completely rude."

"That man, you want him?" asked that deep, seductive male voice, filled with irritation.

Is that all he had to say?

"Nice," she sneered and went outside to her patio. She sat at her tiny table, where she often loved to read or eat breakfast while marveling at the jewel-colored waves. She took a giant bite of her pastry. The sugar on the top was always her favorite part.

Suddenly, a chunk of bread caught in her throat. She sprang from her seat and attempted to cough it out, but the air in her lungs simply wasn't passing.

She clasped her throat.

"Dammit all to bloody deity hell, woman!" Two large arms wrapped around her stomach.

One thrust.

Two thrusts.

With the third, the chunk of bread flew from her mouth, landing in the sand.

The arms released her, and Ashli leaned forward to catch her breath.

"Soup. You will only eat soup from now on," he roared. "Do you hear me?"

He was angry? She'd almost died. Again!

"Oh my God. I can't take this." She wobbled into the kitchen in search of a glass of water.

"I am taking you away from here," he said, following closely behind her. "Somewhere without oceans, cement patios, bees, and anything else that might be deadly."

Ashli turned toward the sound of the voice. "You can't be serious."

"Why the hell not?"

"You really think the universe wants me dead?" The logic of that defied everything she understood to be true in the world, despite the eerie evidence.

"How else do you explain that you have died at least twice since I found you and almost died twice more?"

"Whoa—whoa—whoooa. What?" She set down her glass of water on the countertop. "What do you mean, I died? Twice?"

Máax had not originally intended to reveal that little tidbit of information to Ashli, but now, he saw no other way to inspire the obedience he required to protect her. After all, he no longer had powers, so compelling was not an option.

Máax cleared his throat, wishing Ashli could see his face; it would make it easier for her to discern the importance of what he was about to say. "A few days from now, you are stung by a bee, right here in your kitchen. You do not receive your medicine in time, and you die. A few days after that, you run from me and are hit by a bus."

Ashli's curls fell over her lovely, sweet, and confused face. "I don't understand. You're saying I die twice? In the future? That's not even possible."

"Of course it is possible. I do not lie."

Her head snapped up and focused on something in his direction. Gods, he wished their eyes could meet, and she could see what was inside his.

"And you know this how?" she asked, her hands trembling.

"Each time you have died, I come back to you a few days earlier to when you are still alive."

"Oh, hey. Thanks. Makes tons of sense."

"You are making fun, I see. However, I assure you, I tell the truth. My first trip to meet you is ten days from now. This is when you are hit by the bus. My second trip is in approximately three days from now. This is when I fail to save you from the bee. My third visit to you was a few days ago, when you hit me with the shovel. So as you see, this is why we must leave now. I must take you somewhere safe until your life is squarely on a new path, one where you are destined to live."

"Okay." Ashli took a deep breath and bobbed her head. "But I'm not leaving here."

Máax's anger spiked. Why did she need to argue this point? "Because you have a date with the doctor?"

Ashli huffed, "You're joking, right?"

"I do not joke."

She rolled her eyes. "'Kay, buddy. Whatever."

"My name is Máax, not Buddy."

She smiled as if trying not to laugh. "Máax. It's a nice name."

"Not really, but it is a story for another day. In the meantime, you will answer my question."

"Listen to you. You're like a robot. Are all gods so stiff? Christ, I can't believe I'm having this conversation."

"I am very ancient, Ashli. I simply do not see the need to add hyperbole to my speech or inflection to my voice. It will do little to impact the situation. A situation, I might add, that is dire, yet you refuse to take seriously. But I assure you, there is nothing more serious than this. I must keep you alive so that you can fulfill your destiny, which is why you need to come clean. What are you hiding?"

"Hiding? Me? Like what?"

"You're the key to stopping the apocalypse. There has to be a reason why—your family history, special abilities, something. And do not lie to me; I will know."

Ashli rolled her eyes. "You can't seriously believe I can stop the end of the world? That's absurd."

"I couldn't agree more."

"Wow. You're a real charmer."

"Yes. I am. It comes with the territory. Now stop avoiding the question, woman."

She threw up her hands. "Listen to yourself. Do you honestly think I have a clue what you're talking about? Or that if I did, I'd lie about it? I hate liars. Dishonesty is for cowards and criminals."

"And you have no idea why the Universe wishes to extinguish you?"

"Ohmygod! No!"

Fantastic. This was like trying to steer an oil tanker through a maze of icebergs while blindfolded. At night. Alone. While doing tequila shots and hopping on one foot. "Then I have no choice but to take you somewhere safe. You will pack your things immediately."

She stifled a chuckle and then released a frustrated breath. "What makes you think I'm safer somewhere else? If my number's up, it's up."

Fucking hell! Why did she not understand? That was not how the Universe functioned. Survival of the fittest. You fought or perished. Nothing was handed to anyone. It was a brutal, brutal world that required an iron constitution, conviction, and determination. Without those, you'd be overrun by the will of many. Drowned by their competing agendas.

He growled. "If you are not willing to fight for your

existence, then I will. I will not allow you to take such a complacent approach."

"So you're a superhero, Máax? You think you can stop the planet from spinning, change the order of the seasons, stop time?" she asked.

"But of course. I am a deity." Had he not said this already? What was the matter with this woman? "However, this does not signify that I do not encounter my fair share of challenges. Such is life. Complications are to be expected. For example, I cannot be allowed to encounter myself. It would be very destructive for the order of the Universe, which is yet another reason we should leave."

She grabbed a pen off the counter and marked a giant *X* on her puppy calendar. "Okay, then."

"What is the meaning of that?" Did she want to play tic-tac-toe?

"Today is the day I've heard it all," she explained.

Oh. Good. Because tic-tac-toe was his competitive Achilles' heel. Once he started, he couldn't stop until he won. "In actuality, you have not 'heard it all.' You haven't begun to scratch the surface of my world; however, that will have to wait. We must leave."

"You don't actually expect me to pick up and go? Who'll take care of the café? Fernando's new; he can't run the place by himself."

"This is why I did not return to you immediately. I have made arrangements for your café and home to be looked after for as long as you are away."

"By whom?" she said bitterly.

"We call them Uchben," he explained. "They are our human allies and manage our affairs in this realm."

She laughed and put another *X* on her calendar. "Sure. Why not?"

She was mocking him. And sparking an urge in him to draw a circle on her calendar. "Do you truly find it hard to believe?"

"I can't just let some strangers take over my life, Máax."

"Then we shall stop by your café, and you will meet our most valued Uchben soldiers: Brutus and his men. Then they will no longer be strangers. I have also arranged for the Uchben to take us to my brother's home in Arizona. It is the safest place I know. There is a large Uchben encampment a few kilometers away, along with our private hospital, underground bunker, and 24/7 security."

She frowned and rubbed her temples. "I'm not going."

"Of course you are; I told you so." Was her hearing impaired by the head injury?

She gasped. "You can't expect me to uproot and leave behind everything I love because you mistakenly believe I'll save the world someday. Or because you tell me to. This. Is. My. Home."

"And I. Am. A. Deity. I am never mistaken, and it is my job to tell you what to do." *Ridiculous woman. Does she not understand the order of the Universe?*

"I will say this once and once only"—she lifted her index finger in the air for emphasis—"I don't care if you're the pope who's got a magical lottery wand powered by unicorns, you don't rule me."

Infuriating woman! What importance do Minky and the ruler of the Catholics have to any of this? He took a step toward her, barely resisting the urge to shake her by the shoulders and spank her silly. "You are a human.

Hu. Man. Simple. Mortal. Naive. I am a god. Immortal. Ancient. Wise."

"You're an ass. That's what you are." The smoldering fury in her hazel eyes caused him to take a step back and check for any shovels. Coast was clear.

"You call me an ass, yet you are the one fighting to stay inside this hovel. It doesn't even have air-conditioning."

"This *hovel* was built by my parents. I love this hovel!"

"It is still just a home. A material thing that can be replaced like any other. Your life, on the other hand, cannot."

"I'm. Not. Leaving."

He sighed. This conversation wasn't going according to plan. Perhaps if he explained his superior rationale, she'd understand why his plan was best. "Ashli, can we please cut the crap?"

"Finally! A word I understand! Crap. Which you're totally full of." She crossed her arms and leaned her weight on one foot, causing her hip to jut out. He couldn't help but note how her feisty, defiant nature made him hot under the collar. Metaphorically speaking. The fire in her hazel eyes, her heaving chest, the blush on her outraged cheeks were enough to make his cock turn into a sold brick.

Sonofabitch. He stepped back, not wanting to poke her with the fucking thing. He glared down at his throbbing erection. Not that he could see it. *Really? Can you not wait until we are somewhere private?* Though he could not leave her again to take care of business. With his luck, a 747 packing piranhas would crash into her house and take her out.

Dammit. He needed to calm her down. He needed her to cease this exasperating—okay...stimulating—behavior lest he be forced to bend her over the kitchen counter and fuck her like a mindless beast, possessed by lust.

Breathe, breathe, breathe. You will not think of mounting her like a randy little dog. You are a god. Divine. Above your physical needs.

Tell that to your raging erection.

"Ashli," he said in a forced calm, "I merely wish to provide the optimal circumstances for your survival." Without her, the world was doomed. She had to see that.

"Poke my eye."

"Sorry?"

"Poke it," she said. "My eye."

With what? Because surely, she can't mean what I think she means. "Care to elaborate?"

"I'd prefer that over listening to the stick up your ass talk to me."

"Grrrr..." He was a deity. Not to be defied or trifled with. Why would she insult him? "You cannot see me, so I will tell you that at this very moment, I am looking at you in such a way that would convey utter fury. You are insolent, ungrateful, and rude. I cannot, for the life of me, understand why the Universe thought to pair us. But I will tell you this: your unappreciative, peasantlike attitude only affirms that I've made the appropriate decision to have all memory of you wiped from my mind once I have saved you."

Ashli's eyes opened wide and then narrowed into tight little slits. "What did you just say, Casper?"

"I know not who this Casper fellow is, but *I* am more suited to be mated with a festering pile of cow dung than to you. I plan to save you, then have you forever removed from my mind."

"Couldn't agree with you more! Festering pile of shit would be perfect for you!"

"No," he clarified. "*Better* than you. A festering pile of dung is *better* than you because it doesn't waste its time with silly, irrational attachments to houses when the fate of all life hangs in the balance."

I cannot believe I just said that. I am an idiot.

Her eyes went from anger to something resembling wounded, and his heart instantly retreated from its self-righteous rage. Why had he said that? Yes, he'd meant it—well, sort of; the woman wasn't without her jaw-dropping, attractive qualities, to be sure—but that didn't mean he had to hurt her feelings. After all, she was his mate. It was his job to make her realize how special she was and to make her feel adored.

Perhaps it is you who is beneath the dung. Yes, you belong in a dungeon for unworthy dung.

Shut up, you idiot.

Her gaze dropped to the floor. "I see."

"What I meant to say was—"

"Don't." She held out her hand. "I get it. No need to explain. You win. I can't fight anymore. I don't have the strength." Ashli sighed exasperatedly and turned toward her bedroom.

Fantastic job, asshole. "Ashli, you must listen—"

"Will he mind?" She stopped with her back to him.

"Will who mind?"

"Your brother?" she asked solemnly. "Will he mind us barging in?"

So she'd given in and seen he was right. *Winning!* He hit pause on his ego's victory lap and noticed something odd. *Funny, the victory feels more like a loss.* Why was that? Could it be because his winning the argument had been at the expense of her feelings? He didn't quite know.

"In this particular juncture of history, he and my other brothers and sisters are currently trapped inside several cenotes a few hours from here."

She looked toward him from over her shoulder. "Should I ask why you don't free them?"

"I, too, am with them—the version of me that exists in this time—but we will be freed in about nineteen years." He chuckled. "Ironically, twenty years into the future, they are locked away again but inside glass jail cells. I sense a theme emerging."

Ashli glared for a moment and then shook her head.

"It is a long story," Máax explained, "but I'm sure it will all work out in the end." *Perhaps.*

"Whatever. I'll go pack." She disappeared down the hallway, punctuating her annoyance by slamming her bedroom door.

Fury, confusion, denial, and sadness churned inside Ashli's heart like a temperamental time bomb, ready to burst in her chest. Was the world really going to end? How? And why did he believe she'd be the one to stop it?

Completely ridiculous! There was nothing special about her other than she'd been right about death chasing her. And that those dreams of hers weren't dreams at all. She really had died. Or was about to die?

Ohmygod. This is depressing.

She sank down on the edge of her unmade bed, trying to catch her grip. But what shocked her most was how wounded she felt. That invisible being in her living room had said he couldn't stand her. He'd compared her to a pile of poop and went so far as to say she was beneath it.

What a complete jerk! Arrogant, pompous, a-hole extraordinaire! And yet, a stupid little part of her actually felt wounded. Yes! Wounded. Like a child on a playground who'd been told she had cooties or had bad breath by the cute boy.

She cupped her hand in front of her face and sampled her breath. Still smelled like raspberry tea.

She chuckled at herself. *Oh my God. You're better than him. Who cares what he thinks? That's right. In fact, I'm glad he'll be out of my life for good once this is all over. The dude is transparent and the biggest Cro-Mag to walk the planet since… well, the Cro-Mag!* Though she knew damned well he was a god and had the body to prove it, which brought her to the next set of unsavory thoughts. She still felt drawn to him. Yep. Genuinely—*gulp!*—fascinated by the entire unfathomable mess.

Gods actually exist. Gods actually exist. "Gods actually exist," she repeated aloud.

Who would have thought? Now she had so many new questions. Not only about Máax, but about the others, too. How old were they? Where did they come from? Couldn't one of them speak to Death and just tell him, her, or it to go away? Were all of the male gods as sexy and mysterious as that invisible, card-carrying member of the club-toting club; that manpig; that testosterone-spewing, tank-sized male in the other room? *He is not, and I repeat,* not *sexy and mysterious. Nor does his smell drive you crazy. And you do not have fantasies of him climbing into your bed at night, feeling that warm, solid co…*

Ashli! Stop that!

But for three long years, she'd had those erotic dreams of the faceless man. The way he held her against him, their naked skin pressed together, the weight of his large body moving between her thighs and his thick, hard—

Gah! What is wrong with me?

But were those dreams premonitions, too?

Wait. Hadn't she just established that *he* was beneath *her*? Hell, the "guy" had just shown his true col—okay, not colors—but the guy was a complete miscreant! So why had her mind made this lame-girl U-turn and meandered back to pining for him without her permission?

Strange. That was so unlike her. The urge to want him, despite her not wanting him, felt overpowering, as if someone else was in the driver's seat. Maybe it had something to do with this mate thing that Máax had mentioned? But then the connection couldn't be that strong, could it?

Ashli's heart returned to an erratic beat. He'd said he was going to erase her from his mind. Maybe the connection between them was more than just a subtle, annoying attraction. Truthfully, she'd been feeling strange from the moment they'd met. She felt all weird and tingly. Maybe when he'd said "soul mate," he'd meant it as the true meaning of the word.

I'm in serious trouble. Maybe she'd ask to have him erased from her mind, too, once this was all over.

"Over can't come soon enough," she mumbled.

Ten

⌒

After the strange, uncomfortable walk to her café with the pretentious invisible man—uh, deity—on her heels, Ashli didn't know what to expect when she arrived.

More weirdness, she guessed. Of course. What else? This entire situation was an insanity apple covered in insanity caramel. On an insanity stick.

Apocalypse! Yeah, right. And there was no way in hell she was any sort of savior of the planet. She ran a café.

Okay, but a few days ago, you would have said that the existence of gods or that Death was really after you was crazy.

Crap. Could there be any truth to what Máax had said?

At least it was late morning and the rush of vacationing caffeine addicts would be over. She wouldn't have to worry about having an epic freak-out in front of a ton of customers. The thought of a bunch of soldiers running her café and of her leaving it behind for an indefinite period of time did not sit well. The café was a piece of her family's history, a cherished, beloved heirloom.

She approached the first small bend in the beachfront road, the one that skirted the edge of the eco-resort next door to her café, and noted something odd: a crowd. All female. Right in front of her shop. Given this was low season for tourists, it was normal to see a few random people strolling down the narrow dirt road, but not a crowd.

Was someone famous in town? *Maybe Spin Doctors, Meat Loaf*—gasp!—*Nirvana?*

She approached, realizing the crowd was really a line flowing from her café into the street. She squeezed her way past the eager, chatting women through the front door.

Huhhh?

A team of six men—enormous, frigging smokin' hot, unshaven men, wearing cutoffs and well-fitted tees—were busing tables, washing dishes, and sweeping the floor. The drool practically flowed from the women's mouths as they gawked and *ooh-ahed*, waiting for their turn to order something from the largest man, with cropped brown hair and stunning green eyes, who stood behind the register beside Fernando. Ashli had never seen so many sexually ravenous women, nor had she seen so many people inside her tiny café.

Speechless, Ashli also stared at the burly men. The white aprons they wore, the ones with the café's logo—a tiny, fluffy cloud that said "Cielito Lindo"—looked more like doilies pasted on their massive chests. *It looks like my café was taken over by Chippendales.* And at any moment, the men would burst out into a choreographed dance where they'd reveal that those cutoffs were seamed with Velcro.

Fernando looked up and spotted Ashli. "*Caray*, Ashli. Where have you been?"

She made her way to the register only to be stopped by a short little lady in a neon-orange beach dress. "Excuse me, but the line is back there." She scowled.

Ashli glimpsed at the mob of glaring female beach-goers. They looked like they might drag her outside and beat her with their flip-flops.

"Uhhh…sorry ladies," Ashli said apologetically. "I just need this guy for a moment. But I'll leave the big one right where he is." Ashli pointed to Fernando. "Can I talk to you outside?"

"Yes, please," he replied and quickly followed her toward the back patio, out to the beach.

She knew Fernando was about to start asking all sorts of questions, but what would she say? The truth was completely out of the question. *Death is stalking me. An annoying, arrogant, rude, handsome, sexy god, who smells like heaven and is completely transparent, was sent from the future to prevent me from dying, so I can save the planet someday—not that I believe it. Oh, and I'm supposedly his "mate," whatever that means, but he finds me beneath him and plans to have me wiped from his memory. That bothers me. I don't know why. I'm stupid.*

"From the way you're walking, I'm guessing your head is better?" Fernando said, catching up and walking beside her.

The wind suddenly picked up, blowing her wild curls over her face. *Oh, good. Maybe then he won't see the panic in my eyes.*

"Fine. I'm fine," she said, trying to mask her nervousness. "But I need to leave for a while. It's a…family emergency."

Fernando grabbed her elbow and stopped her. "Ashli, are you in trouble?" he whispered. "Who are these men? And why do I get the feeling that they are not really your cousins."

Is that what they'd told him?

"They're distant cousins. I barely know them."

"Why don't they speak?" he asked. "Well, one does—that guy behind the register with me, Brutus. But the others haven't said a word. It's really weird."

Ashli felt a poke in the small of her back. She yelped.

Máax. What a knave!

"Are you okay?" Fernando looked at her with curiosity.

"Ummm...yeah. I have this *annoying* cough. So, so, so *annoying*. I wish it would *go away*." She felt a tiny pinch on her bottom, causing her to yelp again.

Ohmygod. What a jerk!

Fernando probably thought her marbles were going to show up on the back of a milk carton.

She coughed again, trying to mimic that yelp. "See. Totally annoying. Not funny. Not at all."

Then she felt something that nearly sent her spinning with her fist, but she resisted. Máax had placed his hand on her ass. And left it there.

"Darn it! Don't you just hate those?" Ashi swatted a nonexistent no-see-um and turned, using her body to shield the view of her elbow jabbing into Máax's chest.

Máax grunted on impact, and she made certain to flash a satisfied little smile before coughing again, this time with a deep voice—*hack, hack, hack*—to mask Máax's groan.

"Damn pests!" she said. "Don't you just want to squish them with your bare hands?"

Fernando stared. "Are you sure your head injury is better?"

Nope! "I have to go, Fernando." She stepped to the side, but the hand returned to her ass. Did he think this was funny? "Oh! And don't worry about my cousins," she added. "They're the quiet type but totally harmless. I'll call you every day and check in on things. Okay?"

"Uh...Okay." He gave her another look, this one saying that he thought she was completely full of shit.

Smart guy!

She gave him a hug, and they headed back toward the café. Once inside, the tallest of the men stopped and stared for a moment before pasting on an exaggerated smile. "Ashli. My dear cousin. Say hello to Uncle Máax for us. We hope he recovers from his head cold."

Ashli smiled back uncomfortably. "Thanks. I'll let him know, Brutus."

She pushed her way through the anxious female crowd and headed outside. A black SUV with tinted windows immediately pulled up, and Máax ushered her toward it. Their ride, she presumed.

Just then, a scraggly-looking older man wearing a worn straw hat and a grungy shirt stepped between her and the vehicle. *"Ya viene el fin del mundo! Arrepiéntanse ahora."* He shoved a flier in her face.

The end of the world is coming. Repent now. Jeez, thanks.

"Uhhh. *Gracias*?" She took the piece of paper and waited for the man to move from her path, which he did not.

"Ya viene el fin del mundo! Arrepiéntanse ahora," the man repeated, a wild look in his eyes. What did he want?

"All right. That's about enough," Máax blurted out. "I get the point, but you're certainly not helping my confidence here."

Unable to see anyone, the man stumbled back and fell on his ass.

"Máax," Ashli chastised.

"Oh. He had it coming. Trust me," Máax replied as the man scurried away, flashing frantic glances over his shoulder. "*Así es!*" Máax barked at the fleeing man. "This fucking world ain't over until I say it's fucking over! You got that?"

"Wow. Nice. Real nice, Máax," she grumbled and hopped inside the awaiting SUV, feeling the large, annoying, transparent deity sneak in one final grope of her ass as he slid in beside her.

The moment the door closed, she swung with her hand, and it landed with a loud slap.

"Ouch!" Máax hollered. "What the *infernum* was that for?"

Ashli rubbed her stinging palm. "Don't ever do that again, you giant perv!"

"What? My hand slipped."

"Oh, right. Just like it slipped when I was talking to Fernando?" she argued.

"I was simply trying to get your attention," he grumbled. "You were spending too much time with that male."

"That was what? A minute?" Ashli responded.

"Sir?" the driver asked. He was another large man, dressed in a black suit and wearing dark glasses. A man who appeared to be his fashion twin sat in the passenger seat.

"Timothy, did you pick up her things from her house?" Máax asked, ignoring her question.

"Yes, sir," the driver replied.

"And everything else is ready?"

"As you instructed, sir."

"Good. Let's go," Máax said.

Ashli wasn't going to let him off the hook; she didn't appreciate him trying to control her. "Máax, answer me. What do you mean, 'too much time'?"

"A figure of speech, Ashli. My observations were not based on physical time," he clarified.

"Then what?" she asked.

Long pause. "I simply do not approve of how he looks at you."

Was he jealous? Of Fernando? Seriously? The thought made her both excited and annoyed. In any case, given what he'd said earlier, his possessiveness was over-the-top hypocritical. "That's no excuse. Keep your hands off my ass."

"My ass," he retorted.

"What?" She turned her head toward the sound of his voice.

"Technically, you are my mate. That makes it mine."

She rolled her eyes. How dare he! First she was too lowly for him, and now she belonged to him?

"Oh, really?" she asked. "Because if I were to follow your logic, then I could argue that you are my mate, and therefore, your hand belongs to me. In which case, as owner of your hand, I forbid your hand from touching my ass." She paused. "Or your..." Did gods actually pleasure themselves?

Well, he may be a god, but he's also male.

"I forbid your hand from ever touching your mandy bar," she said smugly.

"Mandy bar?" he questioned.

Quiet chuckles erupted from the men in the front. She ignored them.

"Ugh! Yes. Your ... you know." She flashed a glance down at the black leather seat to where his groin would be.

Máax and the men burst out laughing.

"You are quite amusing." Máax chuckled. "I believe it is called a penis. Can you not say the word?"

She narrowed her eyes. "Well—I-I ... I can say it. Penis. There. I said it!"

He continued laughing to himself. "Mandy bar." He sighed with one last chuckle.

She swatted his arm. "Oh, stop it. My mother didn't raise me to be vulgar."

"Very well. But if you are going to give mine a name, it should be a shlong-a-saurus or a dong-zilla, not *man-dee-bar*."

The men began to roar.

She gasped with disbelief. "Wha— Ohmygod." He was so full of himself. "I'm sure your ka-junk-a-junk is more like a gherkin-saurus or willy-pop."

More roaring from the front seat.

"Really now?" he replied, then grabbed her hand, slapped it right over his groin.

"Jesus." She snapped her hand back from the colossal, dormant anaconda between his legs. "You didn't have to go there."

"Oh, but I did," he said smugly. "When it comes to such important matters, I want there being no doubt in your mind of my superiority." He leaned in and whispered in her ear, "All eleven inches of it."

"Eleven inches?" she whispered. She had to admit, that

was impressive. Not that she'd let him know it. Or know about the mental image that suddenly popped in her mind of them lying naked in bed together, him slowly sliding himself between her legs.

Away, lusty thoughts! Away!

"Too bad," she said in a shaky voice filled with false conviction, "you're creepy and invisible. Must be frustrating when women scream and run the other way."

The men stopped laughing, and there was a long silence.

"You, Ashli, are the only woman I've ever chased or had any interest in chasing," he said in a very cold tone.

Why had he said that? Did he really mean it? She was the only one?

She suddenly felt twisted inside. Like she was somehow special.

Wait! He completely treated you like dirt. Now he's flattering you a little, and you're ready to jump on him?

"Well," she said, "too bad then that you'll never catch me; I happen to run very fast. And for the record, though I don't date, I'm pretty sure I'd stay away from any guy who thinks I'm inferior to a pile of poop."

Máax went silent again for several moments. "Yes. Well, that was uncalled for, and I'm sorry for saying it. But I assure you, it was only an attempt on my part to convince myself to stop . . ." His voice trailed off.

"Stop what?"

"Wanting something I cannot catch," he replied.

Ashli's thoughts spun in dizzying, pathetic circles while the black SUV charged down the highway toward the

Cancún airport. She couldn't deny Máax's words left her feeling more confused than ever. She didn't want to like him, but she couldn't help herself; there was simply something about him she found irresistible—besides that body. And that smell. And his voice. Ugh! He was downright magnetic.

How can this be happening? How could she have such strong emotions for a bossy, strange, nonhuman male she'd just met?

Odd, to say the least. Especially when one took into consideration that she was an emotional iceberg—cold, hard, and drifting at sea all alone.

Okay, now you're being a bit dramatic. Yeah, she was. Truthfully, though, she found it extremely difficult to feel attached to anyone or anything besides her memories after losing her parents. Even now, as she sat calmly in the truck gazing out the window at the thick, green foliage of the jungle, a tiny emotional tug-of-war had broken out inside her heart. She didn't want to leave her home. It felt like being torn away from her parents all over again. God, what she wouldn't do to see them just one last time. Perhaps if she'd had the chance to say good-bye she would've let go by now.

She sighed and then glanced in Máax's direction. What she wouldn't give to see his face. What emotions were in his eyes? Indifference? Concern? Lust?

Affection. That was the emotion radiating from the mysterious man to her side. But she couldn't actually feel his emotions, could she?

She focused on the sensation once again. Yes, something was definitely there. She could almost touch it.

Fascinating. The man was like a supernatural force, pulling her in, taking over her mind. Maybe that's how

they'd gone from loathing each other to irritated to…
well, she didn't know what state they were in now, but it
wasn't loathing. It was somewhere in between irritated
and wanting. Getting on a plane with him and going away
together suddenly sounded pleasant.

Whoa. Am I really leaving? The anxiety returned. *And
I'm getting on a plane?*

"Máax?" She turned her head toward him, wishing she
could see him. Was he looking at her? Out the window?
At the road? Would she ever get used to being with someone invisible?

His hand slipped onto her leg and rested there. "Yes?"

She couldn't help but notice its warmth and how it
instantly sent sensual tingles through her body. *Don't
help the noticing! Send the noticing away!*

Righto.

"If Death is hunting me, why are we getting on a
plane?" she asked.

"It is currently the fastest mode of transportation,"
he replied frankly. Then he mumbled something that
sounded like "no alliance with vampires in 1993."

"Sorry?" she asked.

"Nothing."

"But haven't you seen any of those movies?" Because
she had. She'd seen the ones where monsters wing surfed
and ate the plane's engines. She'd also seen the ones
where the systems failed for no apparent reason.

"No. I do not watch movies," Máax replied. "I find real
life to be excitement enough; however, I believe our flight
on the Sukhoi Su-80 will be free of any drama or movie
grade action. It is the world's safest turboprop, and fur-
thermore, Death is not after the *other* passengers."

"You're looking right at me, aren't you?" she asked.

"Yes."

God, this not being able to see him thing was getting on her nerves. "So you're trying to say that he only wants me?"

"Death is an it, a cosmic force, a part of the Universe's never-ending quest to seek balance, not a he. But yes. *It* only wants you."

Yaaay. Thanks for the clarification. "Explain to me again why you think leaving would stop it."

He patted her leg. "I do not believe it will stop until it finds another way to restore balance. Such is the way of the Universe. But as I already mentioned, my brother's home is near a rather large encampment of Uchben, our human allies. I will have much better luck keeping you safe if I have unlimited support. In addition, staying here only increases the odds that I might overlap with myself, something that must be avoided. I prefer not to take the risk. But I assure you, you are safer on that plane than in your own—"

A loud beep sounded, and the man in the passenger seat dug a flip phone from his blazer. "Yeah?" He listened. "I see. Thank you." He closed the phone. "Sir, we have a problem," he said without turning around.

"What?" Máax said.

"Sir, the plane has blown up. We can call for another, but I know you wanted that specific model, and the nearest one is parked in Italy."

"*Stercore equum.*" Máax blew out a long breath. "What happened?"

"Was anyone hurt?" Ashli asked. "And did you just swear in Latin again, Máax?"

"We don't know, sir," the driver replied to Máax. "But the pilots were having lunch. No one was hurt."

"Maledicta in deos!" he snarled.

"Stop with the Latin! Okay?" She gripped the seat with her hands. "This is really starting to freak me out. The death thing, not the Latin. The Latin's just really weird. Not helping."

She felt his warm, strong hand cover hers, triggering a delicious shiver. An urge to bury her face in his chest and close her eyes enveloped her, but she resisted.

"Do not be alarmed, Ashli," Máax said. "I am a deity. We are accustomed to such unfortunate turns of events."

"Which means?"

"Timothy? Take us to the cabin."

The driver nodded. "Yes, sir."

"Cabin?" Ashli asked.

"There is a small house two hours north of here. It is a remote location, and I've only learned of it today. There is no chance of a future version of me randomly showing up, and you will be safer than at your—"

A loud crack came from the engine, followed by smoke spewing from underneath the hood. *"Cruentum stupri gehenna.* What next?" Máax grumbled.

More wizard talk? Ugh!

"Sir, the engine is overheating. We're only five minutes outside of town. I'm sure we can turn around and make it back."

She couldn't see Máax, but she imagined him making little circles over his temples.

"See?" she said. "This was exactly my point. If what you say about Death hunting me is true, I can't hide. And if I'm going to die, I want to be in my home, in my café, surrounded by memories of the people I love. Oh. And if you swear in Latin one more time, I will scream."

"You are a most peculiar woman."

"Why?" she asked.

"Latin seems to have more of an impact on you than death. Exactly why is that?" he asked.

She gave it a moment of thought, but the answer wasn't something one could answer in a ten-minute car ride. Without a therapist present. And possibly some chocolaty carbs, wine, bread, and cheese. "I'm not sure. I just know running is stupid. Won't solve anything."

There was a long moment of silence.

"Please?" she pleaded. This plan was silly. He had to see that. And taking her away from everything she loved was even sillier.

"I suppose," he grumbled, "I could have the men put out signs—codes only I would understand—so if another version of me were to come upon them, I'd know to turn back."

Ashli smiled. "By 'code,' you mean Latin. Don't you?"

"What the *infernum*, woman, do you have against the mother tongue of all romance languages?"

"Really? Are you that old, you don't know?"

"Fine. It's antiquated. I will grant you that. As for your request to return home, because of the severity of the situation, I will only agree on one condition."

"Yes?" she asked.

"You must obey me. Without question."

That was a very tall order. "I barely know you. I'm not even sure we are really having this conversation or that you exist."

"Timothy."

"Sir?" said the driver.

"Am I real?" Máax asked.

"Yes, sir. Although you are technically banished, and we should not be helping you or speaking to you."

"But I explained the calamitous gravity of situation, and because you know who I am, you are helping me regardless," Máax pointed out.

"Yes, sir."

"And how do you know I can be trusted?" Máax asked.

"You are the God of Truth," the driver said.

"Ah! There you have it, Ashli. Proof that I am real and the God of Truth."

The God of Truth? Wow. Impressive. She happened to be a big fan of his work. Honesty was highly important. But still, the strangeness of it all was . . . well, strange!

She groaned and pinched the bridge of her nose. "But I barely know you."

"Then we will get to know each other," Máax said before telling Timothy to turn around and drive slowly on the shoulder.

But what if she died again? Would she dream about this very moment like she dreamed about those other visits he'd made? None of which had happened yet?

Infernum, this is so freaky. Oh, great! Now I'm speaking Latin.

"And as it just so happens," Máax added, "I do not plan to let you out of my sight, so there will be plenty of time for talking." He gave her hand a squeeze. "Timothy, please activate plan D."

"Plan D?" Ashli asked. "What happened to C?"

"Plan C involved taking you to my private island in Greece. Though it is patrolled by Cimil's unicorn and quite safe, I doubt that we could get you there in one piece."

Unicorn? "You've got to be kidding."

"I do not kid. My first island was destroyed by my sister Cimil. This one isn't as large as Atlantis, but it is still nice."

Atlantis? That was real? "I meant the unicorn, but— Wait, if Atlantis was your island, doesn't that make you . . . What was that Greek god's name? The ocean god." Mythology was not her best subject in college. Yes, lots of cobwebs in that part of her brain.

"Like the other deities, I am known by many names depending on the culture. However, I believe you are referring to Poseidon," he replied dryly. "But I never carried a giant fork. What preposterousness."

Ohmygod. I am not actually having this conversation.

"It was a crude version of a surfboard," he added. "And I didn't carry the damned thing around like a scepter or make oceans gush from the ground with it. I rode waves with it."

A surfing, invisible god? "I have heard it all."

"You have? Because I assure you, the Greeks' version of me and my thirteen brothers and sisters holds no bearing on reality. It was far more insane. That whole naked Olympics thing: Cimil's handiwork."

Okaaaay.

"Cimil?" Ashli asked.

"My sister," he explained. "However, we are not related technically. Deities do not have parents, although I do consider her my family and often wonder why. She is quite insane. Means well, but cannot help trying to blow up the planet."

Eeeesh. For the first time ever, Ashli was grateful for being an only child. On the other hand, it sounded kind of fun to have such a large family. With powers. And immortal. Trying to blow up the planet.

Okay. Maybe not.

"So if you don't have parents how were you born?" she asked.

"We do not really know. Similar to humans, we don't remember our births. We simply recall small fragments of our early years, perhaps as a child might. When we grew older, we learned more and more about who and what we were. But everything we know comes from thousands of years of trial and error. Including the fact that we are bound to the Universe, slated to serve humanity for eternity. Not that there will be an eternity if we don't determine how to keep you alive." He paused. "Are you certain you do not know what it is you are meant to do?"

"The only thing I know is that the cosmos hates me and wants me dead."

"You mustn't take it personally," he said.

Nooo. Why in the world would she take *that* personally? "Well, lucky for me," she said. "I've always tried to focus on being grateful for what I have." And right now, she was grateful for a place to call home. A place filled with memories of her family and as good a place as any to die if that was going to be the case. She just wished that her death didn't mean the end of the world, too. Not that she actually believed it would end.

Okay. Maybe someday. But in twenty years? All because she didn't do something?

"No, woman, you are mistaken," he said, his voice filled with deep conviction. "We fight every step of the godsdamned way, every godsdamned moment, for every godsdamned inch. We never give up. We never given in. Complacency is the devil if there was a devil. Which there is not. There's only Cimil. And her unicorn. And her very powerful vampire ex-pharaoh mate who wouldn't know a smile if it bit him on his cold immortal ass."

"Did you just say 'vampire'?"

"I am nodding."

She was glad he had pointed that out. "Okay. *Now* I've heard everything."

"Once again," he said, "you are mistaken. You've only scratched the surface, I assure you."

What could he possibly mean? Did she even want to know?

"Ah," he said, "we have arrived. I will tell you more once we are inside."

"Oh, goody. Can't wait."

Eleven

Máax had been wrong. Very, very wrong. A first, really. After all, he was a god. And a damned magnanimous one. But ignoring his connection to Ashli, and the accompanying desires and emotions, was not feasible. The hold grew stronger with every passing second. And now, that little thing called logic, which he prided himself on having mastered many millennia ago, had deflated like a punctured life raft. And it didn't seem to matter how much logic he puffed back into the godsdamned thing—*you cannot be with her; you will be entombed for all eternity; it is unfair to both of you to pursue your desire*—logic hissed out of the gaping hole.

Simply put, he wanted her. Quite badly.

Earlier, as they'd stood on the beach while she spoke to that silly Fernando boy, who followed her around like a godsdamned puppy, Máax hadn't been able to resist marveling at her sensual beauty. The way her short white cotton dress hugged the shape of her petite, athletic frame when the wind picked up and how those tiny little straps highlighted her delicate neck and that sun-kissed, cocoa-brown skin made him realize how stunning she truly was. She simply radiated beauty—the timeless sort that could make a man feel lucky every day of his existence.

Then he'd noticed her beautiful hazel eyes shimmering in the sunlight as she'd looked up at Fernando. That had been what triggered his bout of jealousy. He didn't appreciate any other males looking at her. He most certainly didn't appreciate her looking at them.

Hisssss...Adios, logic. Because she was his.

Fucking hell. This bond was turning him into a childish, immature, weak...*No! You are a god. You fear nothing and no one. You need nothing and no one. You never give in to weakness. You never fail.*

Now more than ever, he needed to remind himself of that because the situation had become significantly more challenging. Not that it concerned him. He would prevail. However, the moment the news came in about the plane blowing up, it became obvious that a force much more powerful than he'd realized was determined to hamper him from saving Ashli.

Remain focused and all will be fine.

But you're a fucking mess! He scolded himself. His emotions threatened to get the best of him, his temper was barely in check, and his cock on high alert every two minutes. *Down for fuck sake!*

This was not going well. For the first time in Máax's existence, he began to worry that he might fail a mission. Sadly, it would cost everyone dearly if he did.

When the SUV pulled into her driveway Ashli immediately felt like Dorothy returning to Kansas. Sure, she'd only been gone for about an hour, but...

There's no place like home, no place like home, no place like home. Except that some of Oz had returned with her. Case in point, Mr. Invisible and his trusty pack of men in black.

And Death is hunting you. Don't forget that.

No, she knew she wasn't out of danger, but the Spanish-style cottage was a little slice of heaven. She couldn't imagine living anywhere else. Which was good, because...

"You are not to leave your home for any reason, do you understand me, Ashli? Not for any reason." Máax opened her front door (it flew open all by itself), and the two suited men from the SUV immediately went inside to inspect. She felt like the president.

Yeah. Of Wacky Town.

"But," she protested, "I have to go to the café and—"

She felt Máax's warm, sweet breath bathe her face as he growled right into it. "Not. For. Any. Reason."

"All clear, we'll be outside. The other six guards will be here in five minutes." The two suited men exited the front door and closed it behind them.

"Cuh! We'll see." Obviously, she wasn't going to win this argument. Not that she needed to. They could say anything they liked, but it wouldn't change two facts: she was going to live her life as she always had, and she wasn't afraid of dying.

She headed toward the kitchen to prepare a sandwich

and some iced tea. She opened the fridge and began pulling out bread, cheese, and ham—

"Nope." Máax snatched away the food and shoved them back inside her fridge. "Soup. You will eat soup." Cabinets started opening and shutting. "Where are your canned goods?"

"You're delusional if you think I'm going to stay indoors, eating soup." Not when the most beautiful ocean was right outside her doorstep. And dammit, there were carbs to be had. Lots of comforting carbs!

"This is temporary, woman. Suck it up and quit your complaining."

"How temporary?"

"In a week or so"—Máax rifled through her cabinets, his quest for soup unrelenting—"I will return to the time from where I came. If you are still alive, then we will have succeeded."

"You're joking. You honestly think this will blow over in a week?"

She heard him scratch his stubble. "I admit that I am at a loss as to why the Universe desires your death. I've never seen anything like it; however, this cannot go on indefinitely. Nothing is constant in this world except change, and eventually, the Universe will seek to balance out the scales some other way." He paused and scratched again. "I've also never failed at anything. Ever. You will survive."

Was he saying that to comfort her? Regardless, she couldn't resist liking him for it. More than she should.

"Ugh. The soup is in the pantry." She walked over to pick out her own dang can of lunch. Máax's heavy steps followed. She felt like she had an invisible watchdog on her heels. A really, really large watchdog. *Thump, thump, thump.*

"Exactly how tall are you again?" she asked.

"Seven feet."

"Holy crap. You're huge." She plucked a can of chicken soup from the shelf.

He snickered. "I am a god. We are known for the categorical perfection of our form." He paused. "And quite . . . *large*, as you've seen for yourself."

Had he meant that suggestively?

Does it matter?

According to her libido? No. Because her mind ran with it, pulling together bits and pieces of what she knew about him to create a wickedly delicious man-collage. Piece number one: The time she'd smacked him with a shovel, she'd groped the rippled plains of his upper torso and abs. She remembered how they'd made her sweat, how they made her crave more. Piece number two: The outline of his body when he'd emerged from the ocean. An awe-inspiring tower of rippled muscles with incredibly wide shoulders and thick, bulky arms. Yum. Piece number three: She'd touched his trouser snake—minus the trousers—in the car. Without a doubt, his body was the embodiment of raw, hard masculinity.

Oh, boy. The gorgeous picture of the man in her head instantly triggered a reaction that . . . well, frankly, made her grateful the guy wasn't a mind reader. Her entire body pulsed with involuntary tingles of raw, sensual need. Sweat began to trickle down the small of her back, and the heat began to build in the most private of places, including inside her bra where her hard, tingly nipples pushed outward.

Christ! She'd never felt more frenzied in her entire life. This was insane. After all, she was talking about a guy— okay, not exactly a guy—who was invisible. But maybe that's what turned her on. The mystery. The intrigue. She knew just enough about him to allow her mind a long, long leash. Her mind had created a false image based on her fantasies.

Ah! See. I'm sure he's not nearly as hot as you imagine him to be. All she needed to do was dispel the myth. Yes, that would snub out the smoldering flames immediately. Well, that and perhaps a really, really cold shower.

She pulled a glass from the cupboard and filled it full of iced tea from her fridge. "Want some?" she offered Máax.

"No, thank you. I eat and drink only for *pleasure*." He said that last word with a deliberately slow, deep voice.

P-p-pleasure? She gulped down the entire glass, hoping the frosty liquid might extinguish the scalding hot flame he'd just ignited deep inside her now-fluttering core.

Nope. She set the glass on the counter and turned. "Máax?"

"Yes?" His voice came from directly in front of her, making her jump.

"We're going to have to put a bell on you." She placed her palm over her heart. Then she felt his sweet, hot breath on her face again.

"Why would I do that?" he asked in that low, seductively masculine voice. "Then I couldn't spy on you."

He'd been spying on her? The thought of him watching her was strangely erotic. "E-e-exactly how much spying have you done?" she whispered.

His breath moved to her ear, and the heat from his body penetrated her clothes. He was close. So close.

"As much spying as you've done on me, my little human. Eye for an eye. Peek for a peek," he whispered back.

Gasp! He'd seen her naked?

Her immediate reaction was to become angry, but she found that emotion quickly overridden by that escalating case of raging lust, building deep inside. The urge to throw him against the wall, wrap her legs around his waist, and kiss him with whorish abandon was unbearable. She couldn't help it. She wanted to lose herself in him. She wanted to know what it would be like to give herself to a god, a male so exorbitantly powerful and stratospherically masculine that he might just very well fulfill those fantasies and erotic dreams she'd had repeatedly.

His whiskered jaw brushed against her cheek. "Mmmm... You smell delicious," he said. "I can't seem to get enough."

Uh-oh. Resist! Resist, Ashli. Must...resist...sexy deity...in kitchen. Why did the voice in her head suddenly sound like Captain Kirk battling the Gorn? *Quick. Ask...him...something. Maybe he has bad teeth or a really heinous face like the Gorn.*

"Máax? What—what do you—um—look like?"

He chuckled softly in her ear. "Why do you ask?"

"N-n-no r-reason," she lied.

"Ohhh," he said in that lascivious, deep voice, "I think you have a reason." She felt his soft, warm lips brush across her mouth, triggering a ripple of shivers.

Ohmygod. Was he going to kiss her? She never felt like this before. His smell, his voice—*sighhh*—her man-collage.

"Would you like to touch me?" he whispered. Before she had a chance to reply, he grabbed her hand, giving her a sinful jolt.

"You're not going to make me touch your Slinky again, are you?"

He chuckled softly in her ear. "I assume you mean my penis. But no, not unless you want to. Now, close your eyes." He pulled her hand to his cheek.

A short breath whooshed from her mouth. Touching him electrified her entire sex-starved body. She was beginning to think he might be a narcotic of some sort.

"What do you feel?" he asked.

Roughness. Delicious roughness. His angular jaw was covered with a thick growth of whiskers, and her mind instantly formed another piece for her man-collage. Then he moved her hand over his brow and down his nose. Their strong definition made her think of the classic features of a Roman statue. Then he moved her fingertips to his lips. They were soft and full, the bottom lip just slightly plumper than the top. Another piece of the mosaic.

He was beautiful. Perfect, in fact.

She sighed and dropped her hand.

"Is something the matter?" he asked.

"No."

"Then why do you look upset?"

Dammit. Because I want you. I really want you. She looked down at her feet.

"Ah. I see," he said. "I scent the pheromones dissipating from your skin. But you need not feel ashamed of your desire for me."

"What?" She knew she was blushing. Fire-hydrant red. "I'm not...*desiring* you," she spat out.

"Yes, yes, you are. The sound of your accelerated pulse and tiny beads of sweat are other telltale signs."

Oh, God.

She felt two warm hands, strong and large, grip her shoulders. Shivers snaked their way through her heated body. "I assure you," he whispered in her ear, "if you could see me now, you would witness my *reaction* to you."

Reaction. Reaction. He meant he was aroused.

She couldn't help it, but his words only elevated the biting need pounding away in her body, begging, pleading, screaming for her to do something crazy.

He brushed her hair to one side and placed a soft kiss on her collarbone. She closed her eyes and sucked in a sharp breath. "Why did you do that?" she asked.

"Because I wanted to. And I knew you would like it."

She couldn't lie, so instead she squeezed her eyes shut. This entire thing was that insanity apple on a stick. *Goddammit!* She wanted him. She wanted him so badly it almost hurt. And it was pointless. She was going to die, already had twice, three times if she counted that he'd come to save her from dying from something in the first place.

Panic set in, mimicking the sensation of being trapped in a car, sinking to the bottom of a lake. Months of therapy, dealing with what had happened with her parents, accepting that she had escaped death, flew right out the window. Christ, and she'd worked so hard! She'd learned to accept that death was part of life. That was the keystone to her sanity. Acceptance. With it, she'd learn to be grateful for each day she was given. When her time came, she wouldn't feel afraid or a sense of loss for anything. Nope. She'd be ready to go.

Now this "man" had shown up and made her want something, something that would make her fear dying. Dammit. Why? He'd ruined everything.

"Ashli?" His breath tickled her neck. "Do you remember when I said you were my match? I do not think you understand what it truly means, who you truly are—"

She thrust him away. "Stop! Just stop! Okay? I don't want to hear another word."

"What is the matter?" he asked.

"You need to leave."

"I cannot do that."

"I'm not asking," she barked.

"I'm not negotiating. I will not leave. Not until I know you are safely alive, fulfilling your role in the future."

There he went with the whole "mysterious destiny" bull crap again. "And as for me, for us"—he paused—"never mind."

"I am destined for one thing only: death. You've even admitted it." She turned to leave but ran into a wall of hot, hard muscles. He gripped her by the shoulders.

"I admire your stubbornness," he said. "Truly commendable. However, I am a god. I've been alive for seventy thousand years, give or take a millennia, and I know when I'm right. I also know how to win. You will not die. The Universe will not take you from me."

His possessive words struck her down like a bolt of lightning. She couldn't resist wanting this—whatever "this" was. She wanted to belong to him, a real live god.

He gripped her chin and tilted her head up. She knew he was looking into her eyes. She could feel it.

"Haven't you ever heard of fate, woman? There is nothing stronger. It is an anchor in the ocean of time. Unmovable. And you are mine."

His mouth was on her, hot, demanding, filled with a potent concoction of conviction, arrogance, and need. It didn't matter what her mind told her; her body, heart, and soul jumped into the tiny life raft he'd just offered her.

Her muscles simultaneously relaxed and constricted with his touch, and she opened her mouth to the heat of his tongue and lips. Her hands moved from his smooth, chiseled chest, up his shoulders, seeking that mane of silky, long hair she knew she would find. Her fingers channeled through the soft, thick strands and pulled him toward her. Eyes closed, she saw every detail of this gorgeous man in her mind. Her collage. He was perfect. Waves of caramel-brown hair with red-and-gold highlights that shimmered in the sun. Skin the color of deep amber honey, and eyes like a tropical ocean, a shimmering turquoise, surrounded by a thick fringe of dark brown lashes. And his lips. Full, delicious, succulent.

With her body, she backed him against the wall, savoring his hard frame against her soft curves. She felt like she'd lose her mind if she didn't do something with this pent-up lust. He turned her into an animal.

"You're really not wearing any clothes?" she panted in between heated, wet, desperate kisses.

Instead of answering with words, he took her hand, the one palming his delicious pectoral, and slid it down. She kept her eyes tightly shut, not wanting what they couldn't see to get in the way.

Ripped abs, a delicate dip in his hard stomach where she found his belly button, and then a light dusting of hair, slightly course. Was he really going to place her hand where she thought? And hoped?

Never breaking their wild, hungry kisses, her fingers grazed a thicker patch of curls and then...*Holy, sacred shlong-a-saurus.* She sucked in a sharp breath the moment her fingertips made contact. Hard, velvety, thick.

Máax released a grating groan, the kind that scraped and clawed at a woman's core. That core which now quivered when she realized her hand only made it partially around his manly girth. Her fingers followed the long, hard line of his wickedly large penis, and she wondered when she would reach the tip.

He groaned again, this time so gravelly that she almost orgasmed. *How is that even possible?* It was as if the sound of his voice delved deep inside and enveloped her throbbing, pulsing flesh, rhythmically pushing against her.

This has to be bad. She had absolutely no control over herself when around him. *But feels so good.*

She leaned into him, their lips becoming more demanding and greedy of each other as she pressed him against her stomach. She'd never wanted to do this with a man, but she found herself needing to pleasure him, to hear him call out her name.

She cupped his erection against her abdomen, using her hand to massage him, while their tongues mimicked the rhythm of their bodies working toward the same delicious goal: to make him come. Yes. That's what she wanted. To make him lose his immortal mind. She wanted to drive him crazy with lust. It felt like a primal instinct.

His hands reached for the hem of her dress, and he swiftly pulled the white flowy fabric up over her head, leaving her in just her pale pink bra and panties.

He unhooked the clasp in the front of her bra and stripped it away. She immediately felt his hungry gaze on her breasts, right down the tips of her hardened nipples, as if he touched her with his mind. How did he do that?

"Mmmm," was all he said, but it managed to push her that final inch, well past any point of control.

Ohmygod. Change plans. She wanted him inside her. She wanted him to take her right there in the kitchen and pound her senseless against the wall. She wanted to feel his insanely thick, hard cock push inside her body. She wanted him to use her for his pleasure. She just wanted him. All of him. All to herself. *I'm so in trouble.*

As if reading her thoughts, he spun them both and placed her back to the wall. He gripped her panties and then broke the kiss. She felt him look her over again, perhaps savoring the task of stripping away the last barrier between them.

"You are so...beautiful, Ashli. The most beautiful woman, I've ever seen. Every inch is"—he sucked in a breath—"perfection."

Her breasts were too big for her frame and her hips were too narrow. She'd always hated that about her body, but for a fraction of a second, she saw herself through his eyes. She did feel perfect, like a goddess. A sexy, smart, beautiful goddess.

She smiled but resisted opening her eyes. She knew the image of him in her mind would not be mirrored by her eyes. Her eyes would see nothing. Oh, but he was there. She felt every pulsing ripple, every hard inch. Oh yes, the man was there.

He slowly slid her panties to her ankles, and she kicked them away, leaving her completely bare. She wanted to say something, to tell him how badly she needed him to take her hard with that enormous shaft, but he didn't give her a chance. His mouth returned to her, smothering her moans and groans.

He lifted her against the wall, and she responded helpfully by wrapping her legs around him.

"I want you, Ashli," he whispered in her ear. "I think I wanted you even before I met you."

She responded by placing her hands on either side of his face and kissing him with everything she had.

Mind-bending anticipation overpowered her when his hand reached under her thigh to position himself. She broke the kiss and held her breath, bracing for his penetration. She gasped with pleasure as his thick, heated tip parted her soft skin and began slowly thrusting inside. But the pleasure she'd expected did not come. Instead, it felt...well, really unpleasant—like a hot branding iron on her most intimate of places.

She yelped, and he immediately backed off, allowing her to drop her legs. She pushed him back and doubled over. "What was that?"

"Bloody hell," Máax said, "I forgot about that."

"Forgot about what?" she gasped.

"We are not"—he paused for several awkward moments, catching his breath—"physically compatible."

What? He had to be messing with her. She fought the urge to pass out. She'd never felt anything more painful in her entire life, like she decided to park it on a campfire.

"Deities are not compatible with humans," he said coldly.

Her head snapped up. No, she could not see him, but he sure the hell could see her, and she wanted him to know how peeved she felt. "You've got to be fucking with me."

"I do not fuck," he said. "Or, more appropriately stated, we shall not fuck without the assistance of black jade, a particular material that blunts my powerful energy."

His words felt like a bucket of ice. "B-but didn't you s-say"—she couldn't quite speak right—"that we're... we're...soul mates? Ch-chosen by the universe?"

If he was so certain they were meant to be together, that it was their destiny, then why wouldn't they be able to have sex? That felt counterintuitive, to say the least. *Unless you're being punished. Punished for everything you've ever done wrong.* Including not saving her family.

"Where are you going, woman?" he asked.

Lie. Lie to him. "To my room. And don't bother me. I need space."

He did not say a word.

Twelve

Fuck, fuck, fuck. What was I thinking? Máax stood in Ashli's kitchen bouncing his forehead against the wall. What the *damnatus inferno* just happened?

He'd gone into Ashli's home, intending to have a frank, practical, mature discussion about how he planned to keep her alive, but then found himself swept away by the smell of her sweat-covered skin and by the radiant, sensual heat of her body. He'd even found himself feeling grateful for the bond, imagining that there might be hope for them. He forgot all of the pertinent facts, which might undermine any aspirations of a lasting relationship. Such as, for starters, he had no future. Ergo, *they* had no future.

Yet he wanted her. Truly wanted her. He'd even said she was his. And he'd godsdamned meant it!

Sonofabitch! It's like the damned thing just snuck up and bit me on the ass. He was screwed! And hell, he didn't even care!

He wandered into her living room and sat down, placing his face in his palms. His cock hurt like a *spurius*, and his balls ached like a godsdamned charley horse. Shouldn't deities be immune to this kind of torturous mortal bull crap?

He groaned and leaned back into the couch.

Get a hold of yourself and think with your head.

No, asshole, the other head.

His mind reeled.

All right.

He would simply apologize for his professional indiscretion and explain how it was the bond's fault. He would explain the unfeasibility of a future as a couple and that she'd simply need to trust him about that. In addition, they simply couldn't afford any diversions from the task at hand. Yes, she'd understand. Ashli was mate to the God of Truth and handled truth quite well.

She is so wonderful.

Gaaarrr… Cease your incessant mooning over her!

His massive hard-on wasn't improving matters.

Yes, but the last time he'd left her alone to, um, do his business, she'd died.

Perhaps I will simply check on her first. He walked to her room and knocked on the door. "Are you all right?"

"Go away! I need to be alone!" Ashli screamed.

"Are you certain you will not leave your room or play with anything sharp?"

"Go. Away!"

Yes. She was certain.

He sighed and wandered to the bathroom. Thankfully, Ashli had a large assortment of scented lotions that smelled like her—sweet, lavender, woman. He'd be set in a matter of minutes. He need only think of her hot, sensual body pressing against his, begging him for pleasure.

"Yep. That'll do it."

Two minutes later, Máax had taken the opportunity to indulge in a ten-second shower and clean up while Ashli cooled off in her bedroom. With a clear head—yes, yes, he meant that both ways; he was a completely randy bastard—he was ready to continue the conversation and get things back on track.

"Ashli, we must speak." He knocked lightly on her bedroom door, but heard no reply.

He knocked again. Nothing.

He opened the door and found an empty room. "Oh, hell." A feeling of dread slammed into him. If anything happened to her because he'd once again... *Oh, gods...* He'd never forgiv—

The faint sound of his men screaming grabbed his attention.

Sanctis infernus. He bolted through Ashli's house, to her back door, and out to the beach.

His pulse froze for several horror-filled moments. His men dragged her lifeless body from the waves.

No. No. No. He ran to Ashli as fast as his legs could carry him, shoving the men aside when he reached her. He dropped to his knees and then pulled her into his lap, clearing away the dark, wet hair from her face. Her blue, blue face.

"No!" he wailed.

He placed her flat on her back, partially aware that his men watched as he began administering CPR. "No!" He pushed air from his lungs into hers and watched her chest rise and retreat. He gave her heart several pumps and then blew into her lungs once again. "Breathe. Breathe. Breathe."

Why had she gone swimming? Alone! Why? Oh, gods, this was all his fault.

He placed his ear above her heart. She now wore a red one-piece, and he wondered how she'd snuck past anyone in such a brightly colored suit. He'd kill them all. Each and every man there who'd been given the task of seeing after her safety.

"Sir?" Brutus, who'd been at the café earlier and the leader of this particular Uchben crew, grabbed Máax's shoulder. "She's gone."

Máax dropped his head. He knew Brutus spoke the truth, and in that moment, Máax felt something snap. Fucking snap. The molecules of his light reverberated from the force. It was as if every inch of his being rejected the Universe. He felt repulsed by it, angered by it, embittered by it. This was not a world he wanted to serve or be a part of if Ashli were not a part of it, too. The pain was simply too much.

And just like that, the bonds of the Universe, everything shackling him to an eternity of servitude vanished. Only his connection to Ashli remained. Oh yes. Now he saw everything with such vivid clarity. Ashli had become just as much a part of him as his own heart. No longer was there a separation between their souls. *But then…*

"She can't be dead. Not again." Yes, Máax could go back in time again and start over, but what difference would it make? He couldn't protect her! He'd failed.

"I-I will keep trying," Brutus said remorsefully.

Máax slowly stood, feeling the weight of his sorrow dragging his transparent bones down to hell. He staggered toward her house, holding back a scream so full of despair that it would be felt around the world.

Why couldn't he save her? Why couldn't he keep her alive? It didn't matter what he did, did it? The Universe—Death—was determined to have its way. But why? What had he done to deserve this torment? What had *she* done?

He realized that he would do anything to keep from losing her, to keep her from dying, to keep her safe.

Anything?

Yes, fucking anything.

The unexpected sound of hacking stopped him in his tracks.

He didn't dare breathe or make a single sound, fearing he'd miss the repetition of what he thought he'd heard. He clenched his lids tightly and tilted his head toward the sky. *Please, please, please, let that be what I think it is.*

He turned, feeling the world move in slow motion, counting to three before he opened his eyes.

Máax dropped to his knees at the sight of Ashli coughing violently.

The air whooshed from his lungs, and he dropped his head into his hands. *Thank you. Thank you. Thank you.*

After stripping Ashli of her wet bathing suit and fighting every urge in his male body to touch her, Máax tucked Ashli into her bed and quietly left the room. He'd never felt so full of hope, so in control of his destiny, and so uneasy. Ashli's death had somehow severed his bonds with the Universe, thereby allowing his soul to completely bond with hers. Now he didn't know where he began and where she ended. They were one.

But what did it all mean? And what next? Practically speaking, the situation was not resolved. Ashli was still at risk, which meant the clock continued to tick.

But she is alive.

He smiled to himself and walked to the kitchen. When she awoke, he'd have everything ready for her. Soup, fresh-squeezed juice, flowers, a platinum Visa. He'd indulge her every whim with the exception of solid food, especially bananas. Or a game of tag with a bus. Or a swim in the ocean. Or a beehive. Other than those, however, he'd spoil her rotten, and he'd figure this out. All of it. What mattered was that she lived.

Máax entered the kitchen to find Brutus sitting at Ashli's small table, sipping a cup of tea. Máax was about to speak and thank Brutus for what he'd done, but didn't get the chance.

Brutus spoke, his eyes fixed on his mug. "This is bigger than you and I. You know that, don't you?"

"If you're speaking of saving Ashli, of course I know that; she's everything."

"Good. I'm glad you see that. Because you can't have her," Brutus said coldly, not bothering to look up from his cup.

Máax halted in his tracks. "What?"

Brutus's eyes zeroed right in on Máax. "You heard me. You can't have her. She is far too good for you and far too important to the rest of us."

"Not sure I follow."

Brutus stood from the chair and crossed his arms over his chest. Like most Uchben soldiers, Brutus wore the standard black tee, cargo pants, and boots. His dark hair was short in a military crew cut but Máax knew Brutus's clean-cut exterior was nothing but an illusion. On the inside, the man was like all Uchben—human volcanoes, waiting to erupt and let loose an explosion of deadly force. A razor-thin membrane of control was all that separated men like Brutus from killing, destroying, serving justice. Controlled chaos.

That didn't mean that Máax was afraid or gave a shit what the man said. Ashli was his and no one would ever challenge that.

But is she really yours? Are you now saying you will keep her?

I don't fucking know. The only thing he knew in this moment was that he was grateful as hell she was still alive and that her death had drastically changed something deep within him. He simply needed a little time to figure things out.

"What's gotten into you?"

Brutus stepped around the table, growling, his eyes drilling into Máax's... well, his shoulder.

Brutus narrowed his eyes. "I saved her life, and I'm prepared to continue doing so because that's what the world needs."

Máax chuckled. Had Brutus swallowed too much ocean water saving Ashli? "Are you insinuating that I do not want to save her?"

"You can't stay here in this time. We all know the rules of time travel, and one of you exists already."

This was true. The Máax belonging to this particular moment in time was currently trapped inside a cenote, but he would not be freed for another nineteen years or so. Plenty of time to figure something out. However, there were also future versions of himself scheduled to show up in just a few days. He'd simply need to be careful. Post a few signs for himself outside of Ashli's home and café.

"This is not your concern," Máax said.

Brutus glared. "You plan to take her forward with you?"

"I cannot do that. Cimil believes that Ashli must stay here in order for her destiny to be fulfilled and halt the apocalypse." Wait a second. Máax did not answer to this soldier, nor was he required to tell him the truth.

"So you will leave," Brutus argued. "And when you do, how do you plan to keep her safe?"

"Why do you assume I am leaving?"

Brutus stepped forward, visibly about to explode. Crazy man. What did he think he could do to Máax? Kill him? "I want to protect her."

Well, so did he. He simply had no clue how he might accomplish it. And what the hell had gotten into Brutus?

"Get in line." Máax bellied up to the crazy man who was only a few inches shy of Máax's height.

"Afraid of a little challenge?" Brutus asked.

"I'm a deity. I fear nothing. Not even nudity."

"Then let the woman decide who she chooses to be her guardian." Brutus smiled coldly.

"She will never choose an overgrown monkey over a god."

Brutus lunged.

Thirteen

~

Ashli woke to a head filled with shards of glass and to the sounds of male voices grunting and growling.

Slowly, she sat up in bed. "Christ. What happened?"

She vaguely recalled feeling like her body had been on fire, her emotions completely getting the best of her. She'd wanted Máax. So much so that she'd almost had sex with him up against her kitchen wall. It was quite the shock when he told her they weren't compatible. She'd flown off the handle. Why? She didn't know exactly. Perhaps her deprived body simply needed to blow off steam after receiving the oh-so-disappointing news. Or perhaps it was something else. Maybe her desire for him had been on a much, much deeper level. Máax was the first "person" she'd allowed herself to connect with since her parents' deaths. After being alone for so very long, being with him felt like a vitamin for her malnourished soul. Everything about him felt so inspiriting and so right. She imagined the two of them lying on the beach, laughing and kissing. She saw herself waking up to him twenty years from now. Not the invisible Máax, but the one she saw in her head: thick waves of caramel-brown hair streaked with gold and auburn, a delicious growth of dark stubble, and those perfect lips. She saw his golden-brown skin and hard, rippling muscles. Yes, she saw every detail of this man. And she *sensed*—there was no other word for it—what their lives together would be like. That sensation of bliss, being in love, feeling whole and grateful for every moment. The luckiest woman on the planet. Within the space of a few heartbeats, she saw and felt it all, only to see it evaporate like a phantasm.

Unable to think straight, she'd thrown on her swimsuit and gone down to the beach for a swim. The ocean was always the one place that helped her put everything into perspective. But before she'd made it even twenty feet beyond the shoreline, an enormous wave crashed over her. The undertow drew her down to the rocky ocean bottom. When she opened her eyes again, that man's face, the enormous mercenary-looking dude with the dark cropped hair, hovered over her, smiling as if he'd won some prize. She'd never felt so strange in her entire life. Her body buzzed and tingled as if she was soaking in a tub full of warm, electrified seltzer water. No, it didn't hurt. It felt kind of nice. Even nicer when Máax's strong arms scooped her up and held her tightly to his chest, thanking the Universe for allowing her to live.

Yes, she'd get to live another day. Maybe. But now she wanted a whole mess of days. She wanted the dream, a life with Máax. She couldn't get enough of him or their connection.

The wailing and grumbling continued to echo through her house. She slipped on her red robe and staggered her way toward the disturbance. When she got to the doorway between the kitchen and living room, she saw that enormous man who'd saved her pinned to the floor, his arms and fists flying toward something invisible.

Máax! "What the hell is going on?" she mumbled.

The man froze and looked up at her. He threw Máax off.

"Ashli. You are awake," Máax said. "You should not be up. Please return to your bed, and I will bring you a meal."

"No. I will bring it to her." Brutus scrambled to his feet.

Máax replied, "Over my dead—"

Brutus lunged for Máax, but instead of attacking, he hugged him tightly. Ashli wanted to comment on the situation (Brutus hugging an empty space in front of him), but she was stunned into silence. After all, Máax was naked ... *Awkward!*

"Get the hell off me!" Máax pushed him away. "What's gotten into you?"

Brutus looked like he'd been hit in the head with a stupid branch. "I, uuuh—I don't know, actually. I feel sort of ... strange."

So did she, actually. Then Ashli felt the room spin and her knees giving out. She landed with a crash on her small coffee table.

"Ashli!"

The taste of blood filled her mouth.

"Ashli? Dammit, woman." Máax's hot hands ran over the side of her head and then popped open her mouth.

"Brutus, get me a towel from the kitchen and some ice."

The man returned quickly. Máax placed the plastic bag of ice against her jaw and the towel in her mouth.

It stung like hell. "Owwww."

"Let me take a look." Máax pulled the towel away for a moment and sighed. "You cracked a tooth."

Great. Just what she needed.

⌒

Máax carried Ashli back to her bed and lay her down. In that brief moment, holding her in his arms, he realized this wasn't going to work. If he wanted to keep her alive, he'd have to do something drastic. He'd have to go against Cimil's instructions.

Which means the prophecy will go unfulfilled. But if he did nothing, she'd continue dying over and over again, in which case the prophecy was void anyway. Yes, he had to take action, which meant doing the only thing he could: make the best of it.

He beamed down at Ashli and then kissed the top of her head. "I'll be back in one moment." He pulled a grinning, googly-eyed Brutus into the hallway. What was with this guy? He looked like he'd been smoking something.

"She needs a dentist," Máax whispered.

"There is one in town. I will send for him," Brutus replied all too eager to help.

"Do you not see the complication?" Máax asked.

Brutus rubbed his jaw. "I am not a fan of visiting the dentist, but even for immortals, clean teeth and healthy gums are simply a part of life. I am sure Ashli will survive."

"No, you asshole. They will need to anesthetize her."

Brutus lifted a brow.

"It's another disaster waiting to happen; I am convinced that Death is after her."

"Death? You mean Cimil?" Brutus whispered.

"No. Death is not a deity. It is a force that maintains the fragile balance in the world. The planet can only sustain so many lives at any given time."

Brutus's eyes lit with panic. "Why does it want Ashli?"

"How the hell should I know? I'm a god. But clearly, she is at risk unless we remove the chess piece from the board."

"Meaning?" Brutus asked.

"Ashli cannot stay here. I'm taking her forward."

"Did you not just tell me that Cimil gave you specific instructions to leave Ashli in her own time? Because I think you should leave her here with me. I will brush her hair and paint her toenails. I will call her Princess Sweetie Pie."

Huh? "Brutus, are you on any medication? Medication you may have forgotten to take?" Of course, that couldn't be right; Brutus was immortal, a gift granted by Máax's brother Votan who'd handpicked Brutus to be next in line for Uchben chief. Not only was the soldier tough as nails, but also he never got sick.

Brutus's smiled melted away, and his rigid demeanor returned. "Uhhh, I'm not sure why I said that."

"And I'm not sure what is going on with you, but I do not have time for this awkward frolic through the land of Brutus's disturbingly sweet alter ego. I must get Ashli out of here before something else happens."

"Didn't Cimil tell you," Brutus argued, "that if you remove Ashli from her time that she wouldn't fulfill her destiny of stopping the apocalypse?"

Yes, but he'd have to find another solution. For gods'

sake, it wasn't as if this was their first apocalyptic face-off. Of course, they'd never cut it so close before. Or had mother earth counted down with earthquakes as if this were some New Year's Eve shindig.

Máax straightened his spine. *Doesn't matter.* His mind was made up.

"Brutus, I want you to make sure the Uchben look after her home, café, and any other assets. She is to be given the same treatment as one of the gods. Do you understand? I want our best asset management and investment team—"

"I can protect her. Leave her here with me." Brutus's eyes flickered with frustration.

What had gotten into this man? It was as if Brutus were possessed by a crazy, stupid, asshole.

"Brutus, if you have miraculously developed feelings for her over the course of a few hours, I can only offer my apologies. I am her mate. She will never want another."

Máax returned to Ashli's bedroom with Brutus on his heels. "Ashli, we are leaving." He sat next to her on the bed, pained by his memories of seeing her dead. Yes, he would find a way to make this work.

Still holding the towel to her face, she asked, "Whe aw we gawing?"

"As you're already aware, Death is after you, seeking to balance out the equation," he guessed, but really didn't know what Death wanted. He'd never seen it target an individual in such a way. The entire thing was very, very odd.

"Annn wha?" she asked.

"And I am going to take you forward in time. I can only hope that removing you from the current situation will prompt Death to seek balance elsewhere."

"Woo mean dat he wiw kill someone ews?"

Yes, Death would likely find another person to take her place. But that couldn't be helped. "That someone else will eventually die anyway. You, on the other hand, are meant to live. Forever if I can help it."

Forever.

Yes. That was it! Why had he not thought of the solution before? *Because now your bond with the Universe is severed. You're able to put Ashli first.*

And that he would. For the first time in his existence, Máax would live up to his bad boy reputation, not because he felt compelled by the Universe to serve justice, but because he selfishly wanted something: to give Ashli immortality.

In this time, 1993, it wasn't possible because the cenotes—portals to the realm of the gods—were blocked by the Maaskab's evil magic. (A long, long, long story.) But that little nuisance would be resolved, and the cenotes twenty years into the future worked fine, which meant Máax could take Ashli to his world. He could give her the immortal light of the gods. No dentist, no more spontaneous bee assassinations, no drowning. Of course, that meant he'd have to break two more sacred laws, but hey . . .

YOLO, motherfucker. YOLO.

Ashli tensed.

"What is the matter?" he asked.

"I don wan someone ews to die fow me," she mumbled.

Oh, infernum. Why didn't she understand? "Ashli, I promise that your leaving will not trigger Death to go out and murder someone; it will simply move on to its next target, to a person whose time it is anyway. You save no one by staying here. Please. Let us try my solution."

She glanced out the window, mulling.

"I want you to live," he added. "I want to give you a chance to know happiness." *Even if it's only for a few short months. Damned apocalypse.* "Please trust me; this is the only way. If you stay here, you won't survive another day. I feel it in my immortal bones."

She sighed and then nodded her head in agreement.

"I'm glad," he said, "that you see the logic. Now, it is time for us to leave."

"But wa about my toot?" she asked.

"We will fix your toot—I mean, tooth—when we arrive," he said.

"I don know. Aw you sure it's safe? Everyting is happening so fawst."

"Fast? No." He picked up her free hand and kissed the top. "I realize now that I have waited seventy thousand years for you. It is not fast enough." Gods only knew what Death had in store for her next. A rabid turtle? An angry coconut?

"I don wanna weave hew," Ashli said.

"I'm sorry," Máax said, "but staying is not a choice. We are leaving. Now."

"You heard her, Máax." Brutus's menacing voice sliced through the air like a hot blade. "She doesn't want to go with you."

"Stay out of this, Brutus," Máax warned.

Ashli sat up, still pushing the towel to her mouth. "Why? He saved my wife. I twust him. I want to hear what he has to say." She looked directly at Brutus.

"Tell her the truth, Máax," Brutus pushed. "Tell her what will happen if you take her forward."

Dammit, man. What was his problem? Máax knew he'd figure all this out. Later, of course. And simply because Cimil said that something bad would happen didn't mean it was true. Cimil lied 50 percent of the time. No, generally she didn't lie about prophecies and such, but Máax had always followed his gut. He'd always done what he felt was right and had faith that the Universe would take care of the rest. So far, so good.

Really, man? You're invisible. Powerless. An outcast.

Okay. Fuck the Universe. This was pure selfishness. He wanted to save Ashli because it would make him happy. Yes, let his brethren figure out how to save the world for once. He was through sacrificing everything for them and everyone else. Enough was enough.

"Tell her," Brutus prodded, "what will happen if you take her forward with you."

Ashli blinked expectantly, her gaze toggling between Brutus and Máax's ... well, his neck really. "What will happen?"

The truth nearly bubbled from Máax's lips, but then something clicked. Something a tad sinister.

He'd never lied. Not once in his entire existence. Telling the truth was simply who he was. Even after being stripped of his powers, he'd never so much as tested the waters or second-guessed the value of the truth. The truth—speaking it, exposing it to light, knowing when he was in its absence—was simply who he was. But now, everything hung in the balance. If he did not lie to her, she would stay. She would die. He simply couldn't have that.

So now the filthy, nasty question stared him down, challenging him like an outlaw from the Old West, daring him to reach for his gun. Was he brave enough to pull the trigger? Could he lie, thereby sacrificing himself, the essence of who he truly was, to save her?

Draw.

Máax cleared his throat. "I do not know what Brutus speaks of."

Brutus made a strange sound somewhere between a growl and a gasp. "I can't believe it. You're lying. You just told me that Cimil gave you strict instructions to leave her here."

"Máax? Is it twue?" she asked.

Máax swallowed. "No. Brutus is mistaken. I said no such thing." The lie felt like a tiny burr sticking inside his brain. It had been so easy to tell. Much too easy. But he instantly knew he'd never forget it.

Brutus's jaw dropped. "He—he's lying. I don't fucking believe it."

"But isn't Máax incapable of wying?" Ashli argued.

Brutus ran his hands though his dark, short hair. "Well—well—yes, but . . . ."

Ashli shook her head. "I don't know whath's going on between you thwo, but—"

"Ashli," Máax said, "it is quite simple; you will die if you stay here. If you come with me, I can fix this."

"But wha about my houws? My café?" She continued holding a corner of the towel to her mouth.

"Everything will be waiting for you"—he hoped—"only it will be twenty years into the future. Brutus will see to everything. Isn't that right, Brutus?"

Brutus still looked like he'd been run over by a bus, a giant bus of festering lies. "Yes, but—"

"Okay," Ashli blurted out. "I'll do it."

Brutus snarled. "You're making a mistake, Ashli. Stay here with me. I will ensure your safety."

"I don think anyone can save me if I stay. I wan to go wit Máax. I'm sowwy."

Máax's ego did a little cheer. Not a pom-pom cheer, but a triumphant warrior–like cheer, just to be clear. She wanted to be with him. *She* wanted to be with *him*.

Great. Now what?

You'll have to figure it out.

Damn. What the hell was he doing?

I'm hoping Cimil is wrong about her prophecy.

Fourteen

⌒

Sun setting to her back, Ashli stared out across the lapping sapphire-blue waves, having never felt so petrified in her life. It wasn't the moving ahead a few decades that necessarily bothered her, though that certainly got an award for bizarre and unusual, but the conversation between Brutus and Máax had bumped her anxiety up a few notches. It didn't help that she also continued to feel out of sorts, all tingly and such. Probably a result of almost dying yet again.

So why hadn't Máax proposed his solution to begin with? And if Brutus worked for the gods, then why would he challenge Máax like that? Something didn't sit right. Especially that bit about Brutus becoming so protective. The look of wrath on his face when he'd stormed from her house left her more mystified than ever. What had she done wrong? And why did it bother her? Probably because Brutus had saved her life, and it meant something to her. Just as it meant something that Máax had saved her, too.

Gods, caring about people is so hard. She almost cared too much.

"Are you ready, Ashli?" Máax's warm, rough hand covered hers, jarring her from her uneasy contemplation. "Come." He positioned her directly under a palm tree that stood a few yards from her back porch. "You must stand directly above the magical tablet I have buried here."

Really? Really? Did he just say "magical tablet"? Maybe he parked it next to his sister's magical unicorn.

Well, consider yourself lucky. At least he's not whipping out the DeLorean and asking you to hold a lightning rod.

"Sure," she replied, "weady as I'll evew be." Damn, her tooth hurt. She hoped there was a good dentist in town twenty years into the future.

"Excellent. I am taking you straight to our cenote about two hundred kilometers from here; I need to make a quick stop."

Whoa. "What? I thought we were staying hew." A few decades into the future, yes, but *here. Here* was important.

"I don't have time to explain; however, I promise we will return to your home after I take care of something."

Her hands trembled. "Máax, I'm not weally weady for all of this. It's too much. Can we just take it one step at a time?"

He grumbled something unintelligible under his breath. Probably more of that annoying Latin. "No. I am sorry, Ashli. Normally, I would default to being a gentleman—Okay, perhaps not—I would probably insist. As I am about to do now."

"Why?" she asked.

"Because there is something important I must do," he

said in a soft, reassuring voice, then gently brushed her cheek. "There is nothing to fear. I promise."

Well, if he said so. Right? After all, the guy *was* the God of Truth. If he said, "Nothing to fear," then he meant it.

But then why did her stomach signal otherwise?

"Time to go." Máax firmly gripped her hand, sending a shock wave of tingles charging through her body. Still, her cold feet seemed unable to move. Before she mustered a protest, the sand beneath her feet began to vibrate and hiss. A dark manhole-sized fissure opened in front of them. She tipped her body forward and peered inside the vertical wind tunnel. It swirled with bits of debris and sand on the surface, but there was no bottom, nothing inside. Just darkness.

Knees shaking, she stumbled back a step. "Maybe this isn't such a goow ideaw."

"I'm sorry, my dear Ashli, but there is no time for further deliberation."

She felt a hard tug on her arm, and then her body fell forward. She yelped when the force of the opening grabbed hold and sucked her in.

"Waaaiiiit." A flash of light momentarily blinded her. She now stood in the jungle at the edge of a dark green pool of water. Speckles of sunlight filtered through the treetops, and a multitude of unseen birds chirped loudly all around her. There had to be hundreds from the sound of it.

"Holy shit." She spun on her heel. "Was that it?"

"Yes. That was it," said the deep, sexy male voice at her side. She felt his rough hands slide down her arms. "However, this next part of the journey will not be so pleasant. Hold your breath." Máax scooped her up in his arms.

"What the hell? Máax!"

"Sorry, love, but it must be done." He hurtled them both toward the dark, murky water.

Lying on a warm, fluffy bed, Ashli awoke in a large, sunny bedroom. She held her breath listening for anything to orient her, but her thumping heart sounded like a loud drum inside her head. An odd, uncomfortable feeling covered her body, as if her limbs had gone to sleep and were just now coming out of that pins-and-needles phase.

Slowly, her eyes swept the room. Not one item looked familiar. A bright red painting of some pre-Hispanic dog hung on the wall next to a large flat thing. A television? The furniture—nightstand, table and chairs in the corner, and the dresser—was that rustic Mexican style she liked, but also unfamiliar.

She looked down the length of her body, relieved to see she wore her favorite white cotton summer dress. Something familiar! But there was also a necklace with a black shiny stone hanging around her neck.

She carefully sat up, wondering if she'd suffered another head injury. She wiggled her toes and wobbled her head between her shoulders. Nope. Everything felt okay.

Her eyes returned to canvassing the room, immediately settling on a picturesque set of doors that led to a balcony overlooking the ocean. It looked like a perfect day outside. Was she at an oceanside spa? The giant bouquet of fresh lavender sitting on the table sure made it smell like it. So how had she gotten here? Where exactly was "here"?

She moved to slip off the bed but was abruptly pulled back. "Ah, you are awake."

She yelped. "Máax? You scared the hell out of me." She looked toward the direction of his voice and noticed the deep indentation of his body right next to her on the bed.

His familiar, electrifying touch slid across her midriff and pulled her the rest of the way down. "My apologies." His lips brushed against her cheek and left a trail of salacious tingles on her skin. "How do you feel?"

She felt…She felt…great, actually. Like she'd had a really long nap after a run on the beach. And lying next to Máax, who caressed her with the entire length of his body, an undoubtedly naked body, had an instant effect. One that fired up the old girlie parts.

Vrroom?

"Relaxed. Except where are we?" She couldn't remember—well, anything really.

"This is your home."

Her home? She propped herself up by the elbows. "This doesn't look like it."

"Ah yes. Well, apparently your little beach house was wiped out ten years ago in a hurricane. It was rebuilt. This house was made with reinforced steel beams running thirty feet into the ground. You also bought the land to both sides permitting us to build something infinitely grander."

Her home was gone? She felt mortified. She'd loved that home. "I lost my house? And I bought land?"

"Well, your Uchben-managed trust purchased it, but yes. And yes, your home is gone. I am sorry. But such is nature. A cruel bitch," he said casually, as if she'd lost her favorite pair of socks.

But this wasn't casual. It was…

Devastating.

"Are you all right, Ashli?" Máax's hand brushed her cheek.

She nodded and sat up again. "Yeah. It's just—wow. It's really gone?"

"We saved your belongings—some, anyway. They've been put into storage further inland, where they'll be safe."

"How do you know all this?" she asked.

"You've been asleep for about a day. The Uchben, including Brutus, have already been here. They debriefed me on everything."

"Brutus? He stayed here the entire time I was away? Shouldn't he be retired by now?"

Máax chuckled. "I may have forgotten to mention that Brutus is one of our elite guards and therefore immortal. But no, he oversees things for us and has had his hands quite full these past years."

"Oh." *How strange.* But of course, why wouldn't Brutus be immortal? He worked for gods and surely that meant many dangerous assignments; they couldn't be worried about him dying all the time. Made sense. On the other hand, living forever sounded—well, like forever. *I think I'd go crazy.* Especially considering the plethora of strangeness that accompanied her life. An eternity of this weirdness might be too much.

"So. You're sure I'm okay?" Why couldn't she remember what happened? Everything was a giant blur after she'd gone into that portal.

"You are perfect," he replied. "Never better. It was only your home that had a little trouble."

"Oh." She needed a moment to digest. For some reason, she thought everything in the future would be exactly the same, just maybe more modern. Twenty years wasn't that much time. Was it?

"Does your new home not please you? Is it not beautiful?" Máax asked.

What could she say? If the rest of the home was as nice as the bedroom, she knew it was gorgeous. The only issue was that it wasn't *her* home. And that people in these parts might confuse her for a telenovela star or a drug lord. Lavish was an overstatement.

Well, she told herself, *you're alive; that's what matters.* And she was with Máax.

"You didn't have to do all this," she said gratefully.

"Of course I did. I want you to be comfortable here."

His lips skimmed hers. Their warmth and inexplicable familiarly melted away the sadness and sense of loss. It was amazing how Máax could do that—heat her up, make her toes tingle, turn her into a raving sex loon with one simple touch. *Squaaaawk!*

A blistering urge to have her hot, lusty way with the god sideswiped her. She wanted to seek comfort in that potent male body—yes, yes, invisible, but she knew exactly what was there—and lose herself in the powerful emotions he triggered. She didn't care that it might not lead anywhere. Like the last time they'd gone at it like frisky little chipmunks in her kitchen, her entire body craved him.

Before she could act on those impulses, she found herself standing, being tugged toward the bathroom.

"They've included every comfort known to womankind: a sauna, jet tub, and champagne bar."

She leaned inside the doorway. Her entire previous beach house could fit inside. "It's incredible. Really, but—"

By the hand, Máax tugged Ashli into the hallway. Raised

ceilings with large skylights above and white tile flooring beneath illuminated every corner with bright, cheery sunlight. Máax dragged her through the rest of the new home complete with six guest rooms, five more baths, a study, one giant living room, and a gourmet chef's kitchen.

How had he planned all this?

"And then there is this..." Máax opened the double doors to her new beachside patio.

What the...? She felt like she'd won the grand prize on a game show. *And look! It's your newww open fire pit and stainless steel outdoor kitchen, Ashli! But wait! There's more! That's right. It'ssss hand-carved furniture! Wild applause.*

"Máax. This is all too much." He'd gone overboard, turning her sweet, charming tropical bungalow into a multimillion-dollar mansion. Not that she wasn't grateful, because she was, but it was all too strange.

"Nothing is too much for you." Máax pulled her into his body. His electrifying hands cupped the back of her head. "I want you to be happy here."

"I didn't come here," she whispered, "for a house. I came because I wanted to live." *And, maybe, to be with you.*

"And live, you shall. For a very, *very* long time—forever, if I can help it."

Her brain tripped and stumbled. "What did you mean by that?"

"Why don't you let me finish showing you the house?" he suggested.

"Máax? What is going—"

Whoa. She suddenly remembered Máax throwing her into that pool of dark green water in the middle of the jungle. "Wait! What happened at the cenote?"

The sound of Máax scratching his thick beard perked up her ears. Why was he thinking so hard about his answer?

"Let us go inside," he finally said.

She swiped for his hand or arm or some piece of him but missed. "No. Tell me now."

Máax was silent. Was he still there?

"Máax?" She waited for several moments.

"Yes," he answered. "I am here."

"What's going on?" Why did she have a bad feeling?

A gust of wind blew her hair over her face. She pushed it back and caught a glimpse of the ocean. Her ocean. At least that hadn't changed. She'd give anything for a swim right now to calm her nerves.

"It is simple," Máax said coldly. "I took you to my realm and filled you with our light. You are immortal now. This is why your eyes are now turquoise. Like mine."

They are? "What? Sorry?" *Did he just say immortal?*

Máax grabbed her hand and placed it over his heart. "I am truly sorry for not telling you, but—"

"Sorry? You're ... sorry? You can't just do that kind of crap without telling a person, Máax."

"Ahhh," he argued, "but I can. I am a god, and by definition, that is our right. We meddle. We make decisions. We use the powers and gifts bestowed upon us by the Universe and Creator to keep humans safe."

He couldn't possibly be serious. Could he? "Okay. But this is my life! You had no right to—"

"Are you saying you are displeased that you will live?" he asked smugly.

She closed her mouth. That wasn't the problem. Not even close!

"Because," he added, "I know you merely pretended

to be comfortable with the notion of death, but I saw the truth. You came here because you wanted to survive. I merely took things a step further and granted you immortality." He paused, giving her a moment to process.

True. She did want to live. He'd given her a glorious glimpse of what life could be like when filled with passion for a man who was so incredible, so powerful and sexy that he made her knees wobble. And he could never die. Ever. He'd never grow old or sick. He would never leave her. That was, if she decided to stay with him, which, at this very moment, was not sounding like a ticket to Happy Ever After Land. How could he make her immortal and not discuss it with her? How?

"So you see," Máax continued, "you made the choice, I simply gave you what you wanted." He said proudly, "And I fixed your tooth."

Conceited, smug, sonofabi—

"I also gave myself something I wanted—well, needed, actually: you." He added, "And your safety as well."

Her fury wavered for a moment but rebounded quickly. It was one thing to want to save her, but treating her like she was ... she was ... not his equal. *Uh-uh.*

"I'm going for a walk." She turned toward the beach. "And you better not follow me."

"You should not be alone," he argued.

Really? Really? "You know, for a deity, you're not very smart." She threw out her arms. "I'm immortal now, remember? I don't need your protection anymore."

She didn't need anyone. Never had. Because she was a survivor. *Uh-huh. That's right.*

Ashli stomped down the beach, anger spouting from her ears. So much had happened so fast that she couldn't quite make it all feel real inside her head. Okay, the anger felt real. Sort of like a wasp break-dancing in her frontal lobe. The hollowness felt real, too. She'd left her home, her café, her life.

Well, you didn't really have much of a life, now did you?
Maybe not, but it was *her* life. And she'd left it all because Máax had convinced her that the future would be a safe place. Then why did she feel more in jeopardy than ever?

Because Máax deceived you. How was that possible? Wasn't he supposed to be the God of Truth?

He made you immortal without telling you, which isn't the same as lying.

Loophole! It's a loophole, and no excuse for not asking you. Stupid god!

As Ashli marched down the shore, the sound of the crashing jewel-colored waves soothing her temper, something caught her eyes. Or should she say a whole lot of somethings?

"Wow." Ashli pivoted on her heel and took in the scenery. Several new eco-resorts, tons of swimmers, enormous houses—the place looked so different. So many more people now. Where had her quaint little Mexican beach town gone?

Her heart sank as one more cherished object simply evaporated into the past, nothing but a memory.

And what the hell is that? Ashli said to herself with disgust, her gaze zeroing in on a foul, two-story structure that looked like Chuck E. Cheese's and Tarzan went out for a wild night of tequila shots and ended up having an illegitimate architectural love child. It was horrendous. Giant plastic palm trees with flashing lights, gaudy jungle murals, and bright red umbrellas with a cartoon drawing of a topless male monkey bearing a six-pack and drinking a cappuccino assaulted her eyes. The cheesiness made her monkey-nauseous. And it was in the exact same spot her café used to be!

No. No. Noooo ... Monkeyccino's? Wh-wha-what? Where had Cielito Lindo's gone?

Despite the urge to monkey-hurl, she couldn't prevent her feet from guiding her body straight for the doors. When she stepped inside, a burst of cool air hit her face, as did the obnoxious decorum, which was equally as "cheesified" as the outside with stuffed monkeys and fake plants hanging from the ceiling, a rope with a swinging Tarzan manikin, and an indoor waterfall. But what shocked her most, besides the place being three times as big as her café had been, were the waiters. Topless Ricky Martin look-alikes with oodles of bulging muscles and ripped abs, wearing surfer shorts, bow ties, and little monkey ears, served coffee to a mass of hungry, giggling women. *Holymotherofmalemonkeystrippers!* What had they done to her café?

The place was packed with tourists, mostly females, sitting around sipping frothy milk shakes.

Ashli glanced at the wall-sized menu above the registers. *One hundred and fifty pesos?* Christ, did the drinks come with a free lap dance and a gold bracelet? That was outrageous!

Was this Fernando's doing? And where was he?

Calm down. Maybe the place was sold. But wouldn't Máax have told her? *Yeah, like he told you about your trip to deityville?*

Ashli strolled past the short line and placed her hands

on the counter next to the register. *"Disculpe, señor. Se encuentra Fernando?"*

The young man with short brown hair—yes, yes, topless and bulging everywhere—wearing a red Monkeyccino's visor stared with a dopey grin, ogling her. "Hi. How are you today, miss?" he said in English. Guess it made sense that employees of a strip café called Monkeyccino's would speak "American."

"I've been better. Thanks. So is he here?"

He continued smiling. "Who?"

"Fernando." What was this guy on?

"Which one? There are five Fernandos," the young man said.

"Five? Five?" She thought about it for a moment. Fernando would be twenty years older now so that would make him... "Well, this Fernando is about thirty-nine. He's worked here for twenty years, maybe?" If he still worked there, that was.

The man grimaced. "You're serious?"

Ashli felt the blood drain from her face into her toes. "Yeah. Why?"

"Señor Fernando died ten years ago," he said apologetically. "In a hurricane. His five sons inherited the café."

Shit. "What? Dead?" And he'd named his five sons after himself? Okay, that was just weird. And slightly narcissistic. But still, poor, poor Fernando. "Are you sure?"

The young man nodded.

Oh no. This was all her fault. Had she stayed around, he would have gone on to be a teacher like he'd planned.

No. Either way, you wouldn't have been there. Had she stayed, she would have died.

Ashli placed her hand over her heart. "Dead. He's

dead." She looked at the young man. "You're sure?" she asked again.

"Yes. I'm sorry."

Ashli bolted for the back door toward the beach. She started running, her tears streaking across her face. It was all gone. Everything and everyone.

I made a mistake coming here. A big one.

Fifteen

~

Máax paced across the tiled living room floor. He'd desperately wanted to follow Ashli, but he'd already pushed things too far. Not only had he lied about the prophecy—and it was only a matter of time before she found out—but he'd also withheld his true intentions: to make her immortal. It was just as good as a lie in his book. And if he followed her now, she'd think him a complete chauvinistic bastard. He couldn't have that. Not when their days together were now numbered. Although, he supposed, they always were. He'd broken so many sacred laws, now including making Ashli immortal without the gods' permission and traveling back to his realm from which he was banished—no regrets, of course—that he'd probably be sentenced to entombment for two eternities. Maybe three. His only means to change that fate would be for the gods to modify their laws regarding mandatory punishment. But that required something nearly impossible: a unanimous vote.

Not likely. The gods never agreed unanimously on anything.

You could always blackmail your brethren. He scowled at himself for merely entertaining the thought. The kind of secrets he kept were the sort that could destroy a person, or deity in this case. And he would never betray an oath or hurt his family simply to save his own skin. The mere thought was repugnant. No. He'd known the fate he'd accepted when he'd broken their most sacred laws. He wouldn't try to wiggle out of it at someone else's expense. That's not the sort of man he was.

Of course, if they didn't stop the apocalypse, none of that really mattered.

Infernum. He sighed. There was no hope of him having a future with Ashli, was there? Well, at least Ashli was out of immediate danger.

"Máax. Where the devil's turd are you?" a deep, familiar male voice called out from the direction of Ashli's kitchen.

Ah, hell. Máax prayed it wasn't who he thought because he'd hoped to have a few days with Ashli, at least.

Máax silently tiptoed closer for a look.

Fucking fantastic. It was Niccolo DiConti, General of the Vampire Army, and two of his biker-looking vampire soldiers.

Of course, what did he expect? The Uchben knew Máax had arrived at Ashli's house with Ashli, which meant everyone knew everything. There were no secrets among the Uchben.

"I know he's here," one of them whispered. "I can smell his overbloated ego."

"Coming from a vampire," Máax said, "I find that remark marginally amusing."

A devious smile flickered over Niccolo's lips. "Ah, Máax. If it isn't my favorite invisible deity." Niccolo's European accent tinged his comment with natural sarcasm. "Don't you look well."

"That joke is as saggy as your thousand-year-old Italian ass. By the way, Cimil's favorite flea market just called and would like you to return their Armani knockoff."

"This is Hugo Boss. My wife says his suits make my ass look centuries younger. Do you really think it looks old?" Niccolo turned, lifted his blazer, and showed Máax the back of his pants.

Oh, gods. He was serious. "What do you want, vampire?" Máax asked.

Niccolo's long dark hair pulled into a ponytail contrasted with his luminescent eyes. Eyes that flickered between apple green and aquamarine like a godsdamned happy meter. Did he have to be so pleased about coming to take Máax away?

"You know very well I'm no longer a vampire; however, it's no skin off my unfanged teeth if you prefer to call me that. I happen to like vampires very much."

The story of how Niccolo ceased to be a vampire was a very, very long one—involved Cimil, say no more—but his wife and coruler, Helena, was a new vampire.

"I repeat, what do you want?" But Máax already suspected the miserable truth.

Niccolo straightened his black tie and then gave his two men a knowing nod that sent them outside. "You and I both know why I'm here; the gods, your brethren and my allies, are calling for your immediate incarceration. And from what I understand, you have a lot of explaining to do."

"I'll explain myself when I'm good and ready, Niccolo. In the meantime, tell my brothers and sisters to . . ." *Oh, what is that expression Cimil uses? Ah!* ". . . Suck it."

Niccolo laughed. "I love these modern phrases. Suck it. Circle twerk. Ear boner. *Carpe noctem.*"

Máax cocked one brow, not that Niccolo noticed. "I see you've been spending excessive amounts of time on UrbanDictionary.com." It was also one of his brethren's favorite places to learn new human phrases.

"Life as an immortal"—Niccolo shrugged—"it's a journey."

"I'm glad you see it that way because I'm going to tell you to fuck off." Máax needed to sort things out with Ashli. Hell, if he was lucky, they might even make up. He'd heard that making up produced the best sex.

Niccolo sighed. "I am taking you, Máax. And the girl. Deal with those apples."

Máax shook his head. Niccolo's use of colloquialisms was always a bit off. Why did he insist on trying to be cool?

Never mind that, man. Think. What are your options? He could take Ashli and run, but his brethren would eventually find him; the gods' connections allowed them to sense each other's presence unless they took measures to block it. Obviously, Máax had no powers so he'd more or less be a sitting duck.

He could fight Niccolo and the vampires, but without his powers, he could not stop the vampires from sifting Ashli or himself away. Basically, it was a no-win situation. That said, he did like the idea of cracking a few skulls.

A fight it is.

Máax punched Niccolo squarely in the jaw, and he went flying across the kitchen, smashing into the cupboards.

Niccolo quickly picked himself off the floor. "Oww. What the hell did you hit me for?" He rubbed his jaw and pouted. Yes, pouted. But in a manly ex-vampire sort of way.

"Like I said," Máax explained cooly, "you're not taking us. Tell my brethren I will come and answer for my actions when I'm ready."

Niccolo's two vampires sifted into the room, hissing for a fight.

"No!" Niccolo held up his hand. "This is between us two duds. Wait outside."

"Dudes. It's dudes," Máax said.

"Whatevers." Niccolo flew toward him, fist cocked, but Máax sidestepped. Niccolo crashed right into the kitchen table. Máax laughed, thinking it would take the large man a moment to rebound, but Niccolo zeroed right in on the sound of Máax's voice and pounced.

Máax fell to the floor and a fist landed right on his cheekbone. His vision twinkled with tiny little stars.

"Son of a bitch." Máax threw Niccolo off and sprang up. Niccolo, too, popped up off the floor and stood with fists ready for action.

Panting, Niccolo said, "I understand your position, Máax; however, I cannot neglect the fact that I have a mate and a daughter who will both cease to exist if the apocalypse isn't derailed. So the sooner you come with me, the sooner we can all figure this out."

Great. Now Máax felt like a veritable douche. "Niccolo, I sympathize, but I'm not leaving with you."

"Then we will take the girl. I'm sure you'll come on your own, then."

Máax's blood fizzed. "Don't you fucking touch her."

"We would never harm her, Máax, but come to your

senses. The end grows nearer with every passing second, and if you've truly derailed our last hope for salvation—"

"Very well. I will come with you, but I want twenty-four hours."

Niccolo scratched his chin, mulling.

"Otherwise," Máax added, "I will continue fighting. And you have to ask yourself how many of your suits and men you're willing to sacrifice for a mere one day of difference."

Niccolo ran his hand over his dark hair and blew out a breath. "I can give you until tonight. Four hours. But that is the best I can do, Máax. Then we will take you to the gods and sort out this shizzle."

Máax cringed. Someone really needed to keep this ex-vampire away from UD.

"Agreed," Máax said. "Now, fuck off."

Niccolo dipped his head—"*Aloha, mi amigo*"—and left out the back door.

Great. Now what? He had four hours to work things out with Ashli, which included coming clean about his lie. But if he didn't set the stage properly, she would never understand, never forgive him.

He turned to start cleaning up the mess they'd made and stubbed his toe on the leg of the kitchen table.

"Ow. *Matrem fututor*." *Gods, I miss clothing. Especially shoes.* Of course, his feet would be getting a long, long rest once his brethren got a hold of him. They would show zero mercy now that they knew he'd brought Ashli forward against Cimil's instruction. Of course, Cimil's prophecy made absolutely no sense. It had been impossible to keep Ashli alive in her time. Cimil's prophecy was useless. Or a trick. *Maybe.*

Yet somehow, he didn't give a damn. Given the opportunity, he'd do it all over again. Sure, he wanted to throw himself at Ashli's feet like a giant sappy mortal and beg for mercy. Not for immortalizing her without her permission, mind you, but for being such a colossal prick. Not that he could help it. After all, he was who he was. A deity. Ergo, prick.

But what was the point to ask forgiveness: (a) He was a god. Gods did not ask for forgiveness. (Yes. Giant pricks, the whole lot of them.) And (b) there was absolutely nothing—not her anger, not his impending punishment, nothing—that could possibly inspire regret for what he'd done. He'd gotten her out of immediate danger.

Great. So I ask again, now what?

He rubbed his unshaved jaw. Damn, he needed a shave. Where was a unicorn when you needed one?

Ashli burst into the kitchen through the back door, tears staining her exquisite face: pert nose, catlike eyes, and a mouth that held one of those permanent pouts. Just looking at her lips made him harder than a diamond wheel.

"Máax! Máax?" she screamed.

He rushed to her side. "*Sanctum sanctorum cacas.* Please don't tell me you almost died again?"

"More Latin? Really?" She wiped the tears from under her eyes, eyes that were once a gorgeous hazel but now had the mark of the gods. Turquoise, just like his. A small price to pay, he supposed.

"Forget it," she said. "Just send me back. Right now! I don't care if I die; I can't stay here."

"Hell no."

Her eyes widened. "What?"

"That was English so I know you understood, but let me repeat it. Hell. No."

Ashli knew that the words coming from her mouth might seem outlandish and rash, but who cared? It was her life, and she didn't want to live it in this place. There was nothing left for her. Nothing but goddamned Monkeyccino's!

"What do you mean, 'Hell. No'?"

"Ashli." Máax's hand slid down her arm. "I realize things are different here, but give it some time, I'm sure—"

"Monkeyccino's? You turned my café into a twig and berries buffet! No. Take me back right now so I can undo it." She found his hand and attempted to tug him toward the door.

"Ashli." He stood firm. And dammit, with his enormous size, making him go anywhere he didn't want to go would be like moving a tree stump with a pair of tweezers.

Maybe he's ticklish. She jabbed for his armpit and missed.

"What are you doing, woman?" he asked as she attempted to locate the strategic spot.

Bingo! She slid her hand under his arm and began wiggling her fingers.

"Ashli? Why are you molesting my underarm? While I admit I enjoy it, the behavior is a bit peculiar."

Ugh! It wasn't working. She dropped her hand. *Of course! Why would gods be ticklish? They were too powerful for that!*

"Ashli?"

She made a little snarl. "You have to take me back."

"I do not want to do that, and even if I did, I cannot. The tablet I use to access the portal in this time is currently located in Arizona."

Grrrrr. "You're lying again, aren't you?"

"Why have you taken up growling?" he asked. "You do realize that is my move, yes?"

"Don't you change subjects, you lying sonofabitch."

"Perhaps I deserved that," he replied, "but I promise you—"

"Prove it." She pointed outside. She wanted to see the truth with her own eyes. Trust was a fragile thing, and he'd broken hers.

"Very well," he grumbled.

They went outside to the spot where he'd buried the tablet twenty years ago. He dug down a few feet and sure enough, nothing.

"I'm certain the tablet washed into the ocean during one of the many hurricanes," he said.

"Then take me to Arizona." She didn't want to stay a moment longer.

"Your request makes absolutely no sense, which means that either you are not telling me everything or you have gone mad. Or you are drunk."

"I'm not drunk. Or mad." Fresh tears welled in her eyes, and she turned away. She didn't want him to see her cry. She was stronger than this.

Okay. No she wasn't, but she really, really wanted to pretend.

"Ashli," Máax said with a sweet, sympathetic boyfriendy kind of voice, "tell me what is troubling you."

"That house," she sniffled, "and that café were the only things I had left of my parents, Máax. And now they're gone. It feels like I lost my family all over again." She turned toward him. "Why didn't you tell me everything would change?"

"If I had known how much they meant to you, I would have explained that things may be different twenty years ahead. But I am unused to thinking that way. After living tens of thousands of years, I no longer attach myself to material things. I barely notice them." Máax's hand cradled her cheek and sparked tingles all over her face. "I am sorry. I did not understand." He pulled her into his body and held her close. That might have felt comforting except for the fact he was buck naked. Somehow those two didn't go together.

She pulled back and cleared away her tears. Máax was silent for several moments, but she heard the faint sound of his beard being scratched. When *would* that man shave?

"I will take you to Arizona on one condition," he said.

"What?" she asked quietly.

"You take a swim with me. And you do more of that thing with your fingers. Okay. Those are two conditions, but so be it. I am a god, and this is my prerogative."

Was he out of his mind? A swim? At a time like this? And he wanted to be tickled? "Hell. No," she said, to use his own words.

He laughed in an arrogant, pleased sort of way.

"I don't see what's so funn—"

Máax pulled her into him and pressed his warm lips against hers. The kiss instantly dissolved her anger. His touch, his smell, the way his velvety, strong lips slid against her mouth made her forget why she'd been angry. Or worried. Or that he'd asked her to tickle him—weird.

Wait a second!

She pulled back and slapped him.

"Ow. What the *diabolus*!" he barked.

"You can't do that kissing thing! It's cheating," she hissed.

Máax laughed with that deep, deep seductive voice. "Perhaps. But can I help that our connection is so powerful, my little time kangaroo?"

Time kangaroo? What the— He pulled her back—*to his naked, naked, hard body...sigh*—once again and seized her mouth. She struggled, but he hung on. Dammit, the man knew it was only a matter of moments before...

Oh, gods, he's so, so delicious. Can't resist.

Why did kissing this man, a man she couldn't see, do this to her? He melted away any spark of resistance and worry, any apprehension and fear, with one lousy kiss. Okay. It wasn't lousy. It was, hands down, the most elating experience of her life. Being touched by Máax was like being touched by a...by a...

A god?

Yes, her god. All hers.

"Please, Ashli," he whispered between kisses.

She slid her hands over the hard swells of his, well, perfectly defined pecs, enjoying the sensation of him. Everything about Máax was so fiercely male. He made her feel feminine and delicate, but strong and sexy. But dammit, the man was so infuriating!

And sinfully male.

And so confusing.

And so heavenly!

And so dangerous. Yes, he was a danger to her soul. He was the kind of man who could blind a woman with his raw masculinity, his control and determination. But how could he be a threat to her when he also felt like her center of gravity? Her home.

"Has anyone ever told you that you're a paradox?" she asked.

"Yes," he replied. "I am a god. Comes with the territory. Are you agreeing to my terms?"

She looked down at her feet. She didn't want to keep fighting with him. It was like constantly trying to swim upstream. Jeez, how did salmon do it?

Because they are swimming toward love, not away from it.

Love? They're fish, Ashli.

Good point. They are swimming toward hot sex.

Ashli, they're fish. They don't have sex.

Good point.

Oh, forget it!

"Yes," she finally said. "But I'm a salmon."

"Sorry?"

"Just swimming," she said. "Nothing more."

She imagined Máax was smiling and that it was a heart-stopping smile. If only she could see him.

"Would you mind if I remove my clothes for our swim? I happen to be partial to skinny dipping."

"Har-har," Ashli laughed. "Sure." Charming bastard.

An hour later, Ashli emerged from the tepid turquoise-green water feeling a little less, well, like a living, breathing roller-coaster ride. She'd swum out farther than she ever had. Was it her new body? It didn't seem to tire at all. She'd even made it to the small sandbar about a kilometer from shore where she'd gone snorkeling many, many times but had always gotten there by boat. And yes, it was still there. Just as it had been yesterday, only yesterday was twenty years ago. Then, from the middle of the ocean, she'd gazed out across the hypnotic, jewel-colored waves and magnificent field of billowing clouds. They were no different than the ones she stared at for hours from her porch. *No. Not everything you adore is gone,* she thought. And on the swim back, she wondered if she hadn't been too hasty in her reaction.

Yeah. Maybe. But why can't I let go of the past? Why? She gazed up at the late afternoon sky peppered with dollops of gold-and-white clouds and savored the warm sand beneath her feet. The final rays of the sun warded away a shiver as the wind picked up.

"Letting go isn't always easy," Máax whispered in her ear as he wrapped her body in a towel.

How did he know what she was thinking?

She looked to her side where the indentations of giant feet marked the sand. "Exactly how do people let go?"

"I'm over here," he said from behind her.

Ashli quickly turned toward the seductive, magnetizing sound of his voice. "You scared me." Then her eyes saw him, the faint outline of his perfect form—stacks of behemoth muscles, broad, strong shoulders, chiseled cheekbones, and that square, masculine jaw. His brows glistened with ocean water, and she saw their shape clearly. They were thick but not too thick. And his lashes were longer and fuller than anything she'd seen on a man. His wet, dripping hair hung past his shoulders. His beard wasn't long, but she could tell he hadn't shaved for several weeks.

Oh. My. Gods. She forced the air back into her lungs. He looked so rugged and wild. So virile. What she could see of him anyway.

Her brain went to work and filled in the missing pieces. His expression came into focus, and she held back a gasp. He was so ethereal, so beautiful, but the look on his strong face was subtly tormented. Gods, he was striking, herculean. Yet he looked...vulnerable. Like he was lost, just waiting for someone to rescue him. To love him.

"My apologies. Perhaps it is time for that bell, after all," he said.

She laughed to mask the depth of emotions crashing into her. Nothing was as it seemed. Was it? Not even Máax.

Ashli continued to stare at that colossal man standing before her, and it felt like she was opening her eyes for the first time, finally seeing everything for what it truly was. Her past. Him. The world. It was a life-changing moment. She realized a future existed, one with endless, magnificent possibilities. The recent changes in her life were proof of that now, weren't they? And she need only dare to dream, to hope, to let go of the past and open her eyes if she wanted her life to change for the better.

Yeah. She'd been too hasty. She wanted to be there. With him. Her god. Everything about it felt right. She could see that now.

So it was settled; she'd be staying. She'd give living in her new home with Máax a try. She'd make it work.

She let out another little laugh; this time, however, it was genuine. Real live joy.

"You should laugh more often, Ashli. It is truly a beautiful laugh." His deep, powerful voice jarred her from her thoughts. "But then again, everything about you is breathtaking. I am quite the lucky deity. The Universe chose well."

She rolled her eyes and smiled up at him. "All right, big guy. You can lay off the charm. I want to tell you—"

"Charm? You think I'm flattering you? Can you not see what I see?"

When it came to her physical appearance, she was remarkably average. And she was certainly no god. But it didn't matter, she was who she was. "Guess I don't, but—"

"You, Ashli"—he pressed his body to hers and brushed her lips with his—"are millions of years of evolutionary perfection. Your mind is sharp and observant. Your will is fierce and determined like a champion steed. Your body is a godsdamned work of art, a seduction machine built for lovemaking, with a powerful god, of course. You have free will, free thought, and a free heart, one designed to give without question or judgment. Your skin and hair and eyes are the result of millions of years of humans selecting that which they loved or, at the very least, desired. So how is it possible that you see yourself as anything other than perfect? You are the most beautiful woman I have ever seen."

"Wow. Well, that was one hell of a speech."

"I speak the truth, Ashli," he added. "You were a magnificent woman, and now you are a magnificent immortal. You will do great things. I feel it in my soul."

How was it possible he saw so much in her? How?

"Thank you." She looked away, feeling a little embarrassed. She wasn't accustomed to someone saying those sorts of words to her. "For everything," she added.

"If you really want to thank me"—Máax's warm hands cradled the sides of her head—"close your eyes. I want you to feel something."

If that something was pressing against her stomach, she already felt it. And heaven on earth, did she want it. And everything attached. Flickers and sparks were firing off all over her damned body.

"I want you to open your mind. I want you to feel our connection."

They could do that? Sounded interesting, but in all honesty, her body ached for another kind of connection. In fact, shouldn't they go inside before someone spotted her shamelessly grinding her wet body against thin air. Or worse! They might see the shimmering outline of an insanely seductive, powerful-looking man with a very, very large erection. "Let's go into the hou—"

His lips were on her, but he kissed her softly, only allowing the tip of his hot tongue to gently glide over her lips. "Relax," he commanded in a gruff voice. "I want there to be no secrets between us. I want to tell you—"

"Shut up and kiss me," she commanded. "A real kiss."

"But I must—"

"Now."

She stood on her tippy-toes and reached for his neck. He bent down to meet her halfway. At first, he kissed her slowly, passionately. But then his scent began to work its way into her lungs. She instantly wanted more. More of his heat, of his touch, of his smell. He was so deliciously sweet and spicy, so male that it weakened her joints. And then something else overpowered her senses. It wasn't a taste or a sound, but an odd feeling. Like she was inside Máax's mind. But not in a way where she could read his thoughts. She knew what was in his heart. It was intoxicating and pure; it felt like being bathed in a warm light filled with love.

Love?

She wasn't sure, but never in a thousand years would she have guessed such a powerful connection between two living beings was possible.

Máax pulled her even closer, molding her to him for more demanding kisses. "I want you, Ashli. Now."

Oh thank gods. She was about ready to start begging. Her body felt like a giant bubbling Crock-Pot of hormones and lust. Tingles and erotic pulses blazed through her. Especially in her most intimate of parts. "But what about the thing that happened last time?"

"Ah yes. That. Though you are now infused with the light of the gods, you are still of the mortal world. I am not. However, the necklace will take care of everything."

She looked down at the pendent around her neck. It was a large shiny black stone that felt strangely light. She'd actually forgotten about it.

"Where'd you get it?"

"Had the Uchben hunt one down the moment we arrived."

"Really?" she asked.

"Really." He scooped her up and carried her inside. Through the kitchen and the living room, up the stairs, and down the long hallway. She noticed how the house still felt foreign, but not in a bad way. Now it felt fresh and new. Máax and she could start a life here. As strange as it sounded, that's what she wanted. Just like she wanted him.

He brought her into the bedroom and laid her down on the bed. "Ashli," he said, "I want you to know that being with you is . . ." His voice trailed off.

"What?" Her eyes searched for his but found nothing. Air. Would she ever get used to this? Not being able to see him?

"Incredible. I won't waste a minute of it."

She felt the same. She couldn't believe she was doing this. Opening her heart to this man, to the possibility of a life with him, leaving behind her past. Everything had happened so fast, but she didn't care. Being with Máax felt right. Yes, like a dream, but right.

His hot hedonistic lips made their way down her bare stomach, sparking an illicit groan. Her body tensed with anticipation. Máax's hands slid around her hips, and she watched him peel down her swimsuit. His mouth moved a bit farther south. Then a bit lower. *Oh my God. Is he going to . . .*

She gasped with pleasure and gripped his damp hair, shutting her eyes tightly.

He rubbed her lower belly with his rough, warm hand. "Just relax, Ashli."

He going to— *Oh!*

His wet, hot tongue thrust inside her heated entrance. A tiny spark of something shot through her delicate flesh, traveled directly into her stomach, and then radiated out. Every part of her body lit with a sensual ache, one she now needed him to address. She wanted to feel his body push inside and—

There, Yes, there! He placed his mouth directly over her pulsing bud and vigorously massaged with the tip of his frenzied tongue. Oh, Lord, she'd never felt anything so wicked, so good. In her mind, she saw Máax's enormous body kneeling between her thighs, his bulging biceps flexing and moving as he held her against his pumping and flicking tongue. The only thing that would make this moment more spectacular would be if she could see him. Really see him. Although her fingertips and skin knew he felt as real as any man. A man who truly enjoyed pleasing a woman.

Máax let out a husky, raw groan and that was enough to send her over the edge.

Ohmygods! She moaned his name while he relentlessly ground his mouth against her, extracting every last exquisite contraction.

Finally, he let up and planted slow, lazy kisses on her inner thigh. She sighed contently.

"I have dreamed of doing that to you, Ashli, just as I have dreamed of what will come next."

And she could only imagine how good he would feel. His heavy body grinding against hers. His enormous cock slowly pushing inside, every thick inch of him a mixture of carnal bliss and primal torment. There was only one thing that could make it better—if she could really see him.

"Oh!" she said, "why didn't I think about this before?" She sat up. "Do me a favor?"

"Did I not just do that?" he said playfully.

"Oh yes. And very, very well. But this will be even better. I promise."

"I am intrigued."

"Good. Wait for me in the bathtub. I'll be back in two minutes."

"Bathtub?" he questioned.

"But don't put any water inside. I'll be right back."

~

Máax had never been with a woman. Ever. And the need to take her was paralyzing. Sure, on the surface, he seemed like a man in control, taking his time with the woman he loved. But underneath? Active volcano. Boom. Ready to blow his top in one seismic explosion.

Where the *diabolus* had Ashli gone?

Máax looked down at the cold tub beneath his feet.

A tub? An empty tub? Maybe she feared his masculine eruption might be messy?

He chuckled. Well, he *was* a god. Of course she would think that. But right now, he was a regular mortal male. Not divine. Not powerful. Just painfully aroused and waiting anxiously for his first time.

Where is she? He looked down toward his throbbing erection. "Don't even think about it. You're not starting the party without her."

But knowing she now wore the black jade necklace and that nothing barred him from sinking between her supple thighs, nothing stood in the way of making her moan over and over again, only made the anticipation that much more intoxicating. Yes, he was drunk with lust. So much so that he had completely forgotten about the impending doom awaiting him.

"Eh-hem." Ashli stood in the doorway, wearing a robe and holding a saucepan. The bathroom was immediately permeated with the smell of . . .

"Hell, woman, you left me here with the world's most painful erection so you could have a snack?"

Her turquoise eyes glowed with mischief. She swiped her finger into the pan and coated it with a golden-brown syrupy liquid. She licked her finger and then her lips. "Oh yeah. And you're the snack."

Sanctis infernus. He gripped his shaft and gave it a tight squeeze. *No, no, no.* He was going to burst, and she hadn't even touched him yet.

Ashli made her way over to the tub. "Are you standing?"

"Y-y-yes." *Now I'm stuttering? Gods, what this woman does to me.*

"Excellent." She hopped up on the flat edge of the tub

and reached forward, feeling her way around the top of his head. "Face me."

He did as she asked. "What do you plan to do with that?"

She lifted the pan over his head. "I want to see you."

She was going to pour that sticky stuff all over him? *Fantastic.*

"I agree," he said, "but only if you slip off your robe first."

"You can have anything you like just as soon as I'm done."

"Anything?" He swallowed.

"Mmmm-hmmm..." She smiled.

"Good, because as soon as you've covered me with that concoction, I plan to take you to that enormous bed out there and fuck you senseless."

She froze, and for a moment he wondered if he'd just been a little too honest. But what could he say? He was still the God of Truth (give or take one or two little lies), and he knew exactly what he wanted: Her. Sweaty, panting, moaning his name as he took her hard. Again and again.

"Twelve," he said slowly in a low voice, "of the hardest, thickest inches you'll ever find."

"I thought you said eleven?"

Ah, she remembers. "Right you are. But in full disclosure, I've never measured. I am more than happy to let you do so if you take off that robe."

"Patience, Máax. I promise you're going to love this."

He already did.

"Close your eyes." Ashli tipped the pan filled with warm caramel topping she'd found in the pantry. She would have gone for chocolate, but she'd only found some ice cream and somehow imagined Máax would not appreciate the coldness given where she intended to put it.

Slowly, the liquid ran down his head, shoulders, and back. She set the pan down and started running her hands slowly over him, massaging his shoulders and then firm, round, hard pecs. The sweet coating was working perfectly, sticking to his skin and giving him a golden-brown hue.

She reached for Máax's face, feeling the rough stubble of his cheeks. The warm, sticky syrup stuck to his jaw and ears.

"That feels surprisingly good," he said.

You just wait.

She hopped into the empty tub and gazed up at her living sculpture. Her god. Her giant caramel apple god.

Yes. Now she could see him. Really, truly see him. She let out a tiny gasp. His face was a vision of perfection just as she'd imagined. If only she could gaze into his eyes.

"You're so...handsome, Máax." But that word was silly. It didn't come close to doing justice. Divine was more like it. She couldn't wait to see the rest.

With eager anticipation, she frantically smothered every inch of his chest and arms. Every new piece she revealed painted a picture far more delicious than the man-collage her imagination had invented.

"Enjoying yourself?" He lifted a brow and smiled.

"Oh yes." And in a few moments, she planned to enjoy much, much more. Especially those lips. Yes, they were as gorgeous and plump looking as they felt. "You are so sexy."

She slid her coated hands a bit lower. This was the part

she had really been waiting for. She carefully spread the mixture over every ripple of his lower abdomen, hesitating only for a moment when she reached his shaft. She dipped her hand back into the pan and recoated it before reaching for his pulsing erection.

Máax released a deep, masculine groan. "Hell, woman. I'm not going to last another second if you move on me like that."

Her insides knotted with tension, tension she wanted him to release.

She glimpsed down, and it nearly took her breath away. It was thicker and longer than she'd seen in her mind. It was magnificent. And as wanton as it sounded, she craved to know what it would feel like pushing inside her. Was it true what they'd said about large men? Was sex better? She'd only been with one other man, and that was back in college. She recognized how unusual it was for a woman of twenty-five to have such a lean track record, but she was always the sort of person who grew attached too easily. That's why over the years she'd learned to be cautious when it came to her heart. After her parents died, cautious turned to an impenetrable wall. No one was getting in if she could help it. That was, until Máax came along. For the first time in a very long time she wanted to let someone in. She felt safe with him, and not just physically, but emotionally. He would never hurt her or lie to her or break her trust. And he would never die.

For the first time ever, Ashli felt no barriers. Emotionally or intimately.

Ashli began stroking him firmly, admiring the view, but then he swiped her hand away. "No. I am not joking, Ashli. I'm about to pop off like a rocket."

Yes. That's what she wanted. She licked her lips and released him.

She kneeled down and started licking off the delicious coating.

"Holy hell, woman. Don't do that."

She slid him between her lips and sucked him in. His hips began pumping his cock into her mouth with vigorous short thrusts. His arousal only seemed to turn her on even more. Could a woman orgasm without being intimately touched? Because she felt like the one who was about to "pop off like a rocket."

She worked her mouth over him, cupping his large balls, which were now beginning to tighten. His primal grunts and groans only urged her to go faster.

"Ashli, you must stop. I-I—"

No way would she stop. This was by far the hottest thing she'd ever experienced.

Finally, Máax let out a throaty, masculine groan, and she tasted him in her mouth. She'd never done this for any man, but she knew she'd just become addicted to him. The taste of his manhood on her tongue, the sound of him being driven over the edge. It was the most erotic thing she'd ever experienced.

Máax's cock pulsed a few more times in her hand, and she looked up at him. She could hear his rapid breath and see his chest heaving.

"I've never...Bloody hell, Ashli. You're amazing."

He quickly lifted her up, placing her on her feet. Gods, he was strong.

"Bed. Now," he said.

"Hate to interrupt, but I fear I must."

Ashli gasped when the deep and unfamiliar voice

rang out from the doorway. The man in a suit had dark shoulder-length hair and turquoise eyes just like hers. He was almost as large as Máax.

"For fuck sake, Niccolo. Turn your back." Máax calmly reached for a towel from the stack by the side of the tub.

The stranger raised one dark brow and sighed, turning around with a deliberate slowness. "But it appears as though you two were doing something worth watching."

"Fuck off, vampire. You're early," Máax growled.

Vampire? Ashli clutched the fabric of her robe and covered any visible flesh.

With his back turned, still standing in the doorway, he replied, "It is officially nighttime, and per our agreement, I'm here to retrieve you and the woman."

"Máax, what's going on? Who's this guy?" Ashli asked.

The man raised his hand and made a tiny wave into the air. "General Niccolo DiConti. Pleased to meet you, Miss Rosewood."

"Nothing to worry about," Máax said, clearly irritated. "He is an old friend of the family." There was a bit of squeaking when Máax stepped from the tub. "You may wait in the living room while we clean up, Niccolo."

"No can do. If I leave, you little bunnies might go at it. I'll be waiting three or four hours. I'll stay right here in the doorway." He flashed a wicked little glance over his shoulder and smiled.

"I am sure Ashli would like to shower," Máax said with a menacing voice. "Would your wife Helena approve of your voyeuristic ways?"

"Downstairs it is." Niccolo disappeared.

"Come, Ashli. Let me get you showered." Máax tugged her toward the large glass-encased stall.

"Excuse me?" She pulled her arm way. She wasn't in the mood for communal bathing; she simply wanted to know what was going on. They'd put their serious discussion on hold only because their lust had gotten the better of them; however, that little moment of blind stupidity was gone. "I'm not going anywhere until you tell me who that man is, why he's here, and why I feel like we're in trouble."

She watched Máax open the stall, turn on the water, and begin rinsing the caramel coating from his skin. "Ashli, I have done many, many things, which require explaining to my brethren. *You*, however, have nothing to fear."

Not that she'd let him go anywhere without her, but something wasn't adding up. "Then why can't I stay here? Why did he say he's here for me, too?" she asked.

Crap. Her brain did a belly flop. "Did you just call that guy a vampire?"

Máax signed exasperatedly. "Niccolo was once the general of the vampire queen's army. Now he and his wife rule the vampires, although he is no longer a vampire himself."

"Okay . . ." The powerful stream of water ricocheted from Máax's hard body and sprayed her face.

"It is much to take in all at once," he admitted, "but you are doing extremely well." His voiced dropped an octave. "Very, very well. In fact, I don't think I've ever seen any female as talented as you."

"There's a man downstairs waiting to haul us both away, and you're talking about what I did to your spicy meat wrap?" Honestly, she couldn't stop thinking about it, either. What was wrong with her?

"It is called a penis, Ashli. And yes, perhaps I was. Why? Is that offensive? Are we not both adults?"

"No, I'm an adult. You're just ancient." She paused for a breath. "Why is he here? What did you do? We are coming back, right?" She vaguely remembered that Máax had said something in the hospital, when they'd officially met, about his current invisible condition being a punishment. He'd never told her what he'd done, but not like they'd had much time to talk. Everything had happened so fast.

Máax turned off the shower and stepped out, dripping all over the floor. The faint outline of his face expressed some level of distress.

"I...I..." Máax rubbed his jaw.

"Máax! Sixty seconds," that man Niccolo's voice echoed from downstairs.

"Dammit," Máax grumbled. "I'll hold them off. See you downstairs. You'll find new clothes and undergarments in the closet."

Oh no. He wasn't sneaking away without answering her questions. "Máax, don't you dare leave without telling me—" She blinked, and he was gone. A trail of little puddles confirmed it.

Sixteen

After a quick shower and rummage through the "Ohmy-god, is this really a closet?" closet, Ashli dressed in a long stretchy red dress, which was a little too tight for her taste, but a far better choice than the lederhosen or giant teddy bear costume she'd found (she definitely needed to ask Máax about that later), and went downstairs to the living room. She nearly tripped on the last step but caught herself on the railing.

There, four men, all incredibly large with pale skin and unusually dark eyes, wearing leather pants and slightly snug tees, huddled around that Niccolo man, quietly talking. They looked like the kind of guys who ate hornets' nests for breakfast. Or maybe knives.

Despite the eighty-degree weather, Ashli shivered in her matching red sandals.

"Máax?" She pushed a few stray locks of wet curls from her eyes.

His voice projected from the stairs behind her. "I am here."

She jumped. "I thought you were waiting down here."

Silence.

"Did you just shrug?" she asked.

"Perhaps," he replied coyly.

She rolled her eyes.

"I merely went to check on you," he explained, "but found the show much too enticing to pass up. Who knew that watching a woman dress could be as sexy as watching her undress? Especially when she puts on a black satin thong and matching bra, handpicked by a deity."

The men in the room all made throaty, hungry, animal-like sounds.

Ummm. Okaaaay.

She shook her head. "You and I are going to have a chat about boundaries. And by the way..." She leaned toward him and whispered, "Are those..." She could hardly bring herself to say the words.

One of the men, thinnish, tall, and handsome with short dark, messy hair and warm brown eyes, pointed to his ear. "We can hear you. Vampire super-hearing. And you must be the notorious Ashli. It is quite an honor." He bowed. "Not every day that a woman convinces a deity to give the entire human race the middle finger. How did you convince Máax to do it?"

"What?" She turned toward Máax—well, to where he last stood, anyway. She really did need to put a bell on him. "What's he talking about?" *Shit.* "And are they really vampires? Blood"—she swallowed—"drinkers?"

An invisible hand stroked her arm from the expected direction. "Nothing to fear, my love. These vampires are good, complete assholes and childish in every way including their addiction to Netflix dramedies and Foosball, but good. They only dine on those with evil souls."

What the heck was Netflix? "Good to know, Máax, but," she whispered, "we need to talk. Why is that vampire calling me notorious and saying you gave everyone the bird? Why do I feel like we are being taken prisoner?"

"Máax," said Niccolo, "we really must leave. So please get your human under control."

Huh? Had he just spoken about her as if she were Máax's pet? "Excuse me, but I don't recall the ceremony making any of you scary big dudes my keeper. And let me remind you, you're in my house. Though it doesn't feel like my house. But I'm told it's mine. So you can all climb a tall tree and go scratch yourselves because I'm not going anywhere until someone tells me what the hell is going on."

Niccolo and his men simply stood there staring, grinning like giddy fools.

These good vampires kind of remind me of clowns with all that smiling. So creepy! "Okay. Out! All of you big, weird, smiling men, errr, vampires whatever-the-*infernum*, just *get out*." Ashli shooed them toward the front door.

"Gentlemen, I'm feeling inexplicably generous; let's give them a moment to talk." Niccolo glanced at her and held up his finger. "A moment. Nothing more. I have the sudden urge to write a love poem for Helena before I get home, and I'm due in five minutes. I promised my daughter Matty I would be home in time for *My Little Pony*."

Huh?

"Oh. Can I watch?" asked the vampire with the kind eyes.

"Sure, Sentin." Niccolo shrugged and headed out the door. "*Winx* is on right after."

The men, errr, vampires, followed Niccolo outside. "I really like that Ashli," one of them said, "she kind of reminds me of Helena."

"Yes," Niccolo agreed. "I think Ashli will get along splendidly with the rest of the girls. And she smells nice, too. Kind of sweet."

Sweet? Who's he calling sweet? She slammed the door behind them and turned toward the loud sighing sound. "Máax? I'm going to give you one chance to come clean. But I warn you, if I find out you withheld anything, you'll never get my trust back again."

The ground rolled violently beneath their feet, and Ashli stumbled to the side. "Crap. What was that?"

"A sign. The end is near."

Máax stared at Ashli, feeling as though his heart might crumble like a high-rise in the big one, to use an apropos metaphor; however, it wasn't because of the earthquake, though that certainly sucked. *It is the lie.*

He wanted to ignore the uncomfortable feeling, but frankly, he'd never experienced anything quite like it. His soul felt tainted. How long would he stand it?

Think, man. You never intended to keep the truth from her, anyway. You merely lied to get her here, to save her life. She will understand. She will forgive you when she hears that you did it out of concern for her well-being. You had no other choice.

Máax took a stiff breath. "Ashli, the truth is—"

"That was earthquake number eight! Sorry, bro!" A

blur of leather pants swooped past him and swiped Ashli away.

"Dammit, Sentin. You fucking idi—" He felt a cool hand clasp his arm.

One moment he stood in Ashli's living room, ready to spill the godly beans, and the next, he stood inside the Uchben prison in the center of the main floor where his brethren yelled from their cells. Rather loudly, he might add. Some hurtled insults at each other, some toward the line of vampires standing guard alongside a rather large contingency of Uchben. That's right, Uchben—the gods' human allies, each one sworn to obey, serve, and protect humankind and the gods.

Oh, boy. This just got unnecessarily more interesting. For whatever reason the Uchben were now assisting in the gods' captivity. Cimil must have convinced them.

Máax quickly surveyed the chaotic scene before him and spotted his beautiful Ashli in her red dress, a wild mess of damp curls pulled into a sexy little knot at the nape of her neck, standing next to Sentin. She did not appear to be afraid, more stunned really. Probably by the sight of his brethren behind enclosed glass. Who could blame her? After all, they were an eccentric lot. His brother K'ak, for example, wore a metallic-silver toga and a two-foot-high silver-and-turquoise headdress depicting intertwining serpents. K'ak still hadn't selected an official deity title, like God of Giant Obnoxious Headdresses, for example, because he didn't have a flagship power, but nevertheless he had many gifts. Such as the ability to chuck lightning bolts, which he currently did at the glass.

Then there was their sister, Colel Cab, the Mistress of Bees. One couldn't help but stare at the enormous living beehive atop her head. Of course, the bees swarmed in her cell, completely obscuring Colel. Then there were the others: Akna, the Goddess of Fertility, so powerful that even rocks couldn't resist multiplying in her presence (the Pet Rock craze of the seventies was all her fault); Acan, the God of Intoxication and Wine, aka Belch, who currently lay facedown on the floor next to a beer keg, the hose sticking from his mouth as he suckled like a babe; and Ixtab, the Goddess of Happiness, once known as the Goddess of Suicide because her gifts of producing happiness depend upon removing one's evil thoughts and redeploying them into another living creature—usually an evil, sick, or dying person—and her incubus slash vampire mate Antonio, aka the Spanish incu-pire. Or was that the vamp-ubus? He couldn't remember. Then there was Camaxtli, the Goddess of the Hunt, aka Fate, who looked like a blonde Wonder Woman carrying bows and arrows in lieu of a lasso; Chaam, God of Male Virility, the master of seduction, with signature nipple-length waves of black hair, and his mate Maggie; Votan, the God of Death and War, aka Guy Santiago (words could not describe what mortal women experienced when their gazes set upon him) and his lovely, pregnant redheaded mate Emma; Zac, the God of Temptation; Ah-Ciliz, the God of Eclipses, aka A.C.; and last but not least, Kinich, ex–God of the Sun, the original golden boy, now vampire—long, long story—and husband to his also-pregnant Penelope, the current keeper of his solar powers and the official leader of the House of Gods, although he and Penelope shared responsibilities.

Yes, they were an immortal zoo. But wasn't every family a collection of odd creatures?

Niccolo and one of his men sifted beside Máax, pushing him back. Máax stumbled and caught himself from falling.

"Would you fucking watch where you land?" Máax growled.

Niccolo's turquoise eyes twinkled before he chuckled. "Sorry, didn't *see* you standing there."

Why did everyone think his transparency was so damned funny? It wasn't. It blew to be invisible.

"Máax! Bad god! Bad!" Cimil's voice screeched through the other gods' roars.

A silence quickly fell over the prison.

Kinich, ex–Sun God and the epitome of all things sunny right down to his skin, hair, and fucking annoying altruistic attitude, placed his palms flat against the glass. His large body eclipsed the petite brunette behind him, Penelope. "Máax, where the hell have you been? Let us the fuck out of here right now. Or so help me gods—"

"I am not the one holding you prisoner," Máax barked. "That said, keeping everyone jailed does seem like the logical solution, albeit a temporary one. Except in my case. Which cell is mine by the way?" Máax was ready to face the consequences of his actions.

"You think we're worried about locking you up?" Cimil rolled her eyes and then pointed straight at Ashli. "As if that matters now! We've had eight earthquakes. Eight! Human cities are about to crumble like a fine, drunken goat cheese! And why don't you try explaining, Máax, what the *hell* Miss 1993 is doing here? The one thing I told you not to do, you did! Now we're all completely screwed. And not in a fabulous orgy kind of way, either!"

"Máax." Ashli's wounded expression pierced his heart from across the room.

Well, time to face the ugly music. This was not how he wanted Ashli to learn the horrible truth. He'd brought her forward in time, rendering Cimil's "cure for the apocalypse" prophecy null and void.

But Ashli cares for you; she will understand.

Or be a thousand times more hurt.

Máax cleared his throat, and all eyes shifted in his general direction. "Before anyone passes judgment, I ask that you hear me out. I realize Cimil believes that in order to halt the apocalypse, I had to leave Ashli in 1993 and allow her to arrive here through the normal course of time, but that simply was not possible. Ashli would not have survived, and I had to save her. She is my mate."

Ashli pushed her way through the crowded room, following the sound of his voice. "Máax? What are you talking about?" The look of hurt in her eyes was almost unbearable.

The entire room instantly fell into a hush, all eyes glued to Ashli.

He swallowed. "I was told, Ashli, that in order for your destiny to be fulfilled, in order to halt the apocalypse, I could not bring you forward in time. Your life needed to play out the normal way without time travel. However, that is the silliest—"

"You lied to me! To me?" Ashli's face turned rage red. "How could you? I trusted you!"

"Máax." Kinich's turquoise eyes flickered from black to a calm pastel blue. "Why have you betrayed us? We're your family. Don't you love us? Because we love you." Grumbles of concurrence erupted from everyone in the prison, including the platoons of Uchben and vampire soldiers. Looked like a godsdamned leather pants convention.

Máax ignored the awkward touchy-feely question from Kinich and instead focused on Ashli. "You would never have survived, Ashli. For whatever reason, the Universe sought to eliminate you. She told me herself in a vision. But I have rectified that now; you are immortal, a gift I was unable to give you in 1993 because the portals to my world were sealed during that time. It's a long story but true."

Cimil tsked in Máax's general direction. "Now you've done it! You've been banished from the realm of the gods. But you went there anyway and made her immortal? Without our blessing? Máax! I'm shocked. Bad god. Bad!"

Why did Máax have the distinct feeling that Cimil was putting on a show? *Because she is a horrible liar.* Yes, she was up to something. Perhaps the entire prophecy thing had been a ploy. Wouldn't surprise him at this point, honestly.

Ashli's gaze fell to the floor. "Is it true that we are all going to die? All because of me?"

"I do not believe so," Máax said. "I believe that—"

"Yes! Yes! It's true!" Cimil squawked. "After earthquake number ten, the gods go to war with each other. Within seven months, we completely destroy the planet."

Ashli flashed a glance over her shoulder at Cimil. "That must be your sister."

"Ashli, do not listen to her. Cimil is not trustworthy," he said.

"Oh"—Ashli poked his chest—"but you are? You lied to me. *Lied.* And aren't you the God of Truth? Aren't you supposed to be incapable of lying?"

"If you'd simply allow me to—"

"No." She held up her hand. "I don't want to hear another word. I should have known better, but it's my own damned fault. I allowed myself to be taken in by you and your—your godly hotness. I'm an idiot." She threw up her hands. "I actually allowed myself to dream this could work, that we could have a life together. And now you're saying that my being here is a death sentence for the entire planet?"

"Not exactly. Prophecies are very difficult to interpre—"

"I want to go back," Ashli said. "And not just to my house, but to my own time. We have to undo this!"

Go back? Yes, he'd made her immortal, but she wasn't indestructible. She was more like a vampire who might live forever as long her body wasn't destroyed. Gods were the only true immortals in existence. "You cannot return to your time." Bottom line, she might be fine. She might not. But why take the risk? What for? They would find another way to stop the clock.

The smell of anger wafted from Ashli's body. Yeah, he had to admit, it turned him on.

Maledicta, is there anything about this woman I don't like?

"You made me immortal, didn't you?" Ashli looked at Cimil. "I'm safe now, right?"

Cimil shrugged. "Your guess is as good as mine. Except on Fridays. My guessing sucks on Fridays. Because that's when I go to happy hour. It's such a distraction when hot wings and onion rings are complimentary with a purchase of a pint. Yanno what I mean?"

The vampires and Uchben soldiers exchanged glances and then nodded and mumbled in agreement.

"See." Cimil grinned.

"Today *is* Friday," said Kinich.

"Oops," Cimil said cheerfully, "I guess the guessing store is closed today. Or not. 'Cause I just guessed."

"Ashli," Máax pleaded. "Do not listen to Cimil. We will find a way to make everything right."

"I hope you are certain about that, brother," Kinich argued. "Because now the prophecy will go unfulfilled, and we are almost out of time. You've gambled with the lives of everyone, including those of our children. By the way, can anyone explain why I have the sudden urge to write a song about puppies and cute little chipmunks? Anyone?"

"Have you all gone mad?" Máax argued. "Have you? We all know by now that Cimil isn't to be trusted. Hell, she doesn't even trust herself half the time. Just ask Roberto."

This was the only perk about being invisible: intelligence gathering. Máax had long ago begun to suspect that Cimil was up to something and began spying on her. Of course, he never could have imagined the shocking truth. Cimil had aided the gods' enemies—those evil Mayan priests, the Maaskab, and evil vampires called Obscuros. She'd also poisoned Chaam with dark energy and used him to do her evil bidding. Again and again, she'd masterminded unspeakable atrocities. But then Máax discovered something else. There was an odd cosmic method to her cataclysmic madness. Yes, when one stepped back— really, really far back—one began to see that those seemingly unconnected, malicious events she'd orchestrated weren't random at all. One might even go as far as saying that Cimil was the yin of the Universe's yin and yang. Good always seemed to blossom from the rubble she left behind. But that did not mean she could be trusted.

Roberto crossed his arms. His dark eyes and the angular planes of his face matched his hard-boiled personality. "It is true. In fact, Cimil is the bringer of the apocalypse."

A collective gasp erupted from everyone inside the prison.

Cimil shrugged. "I'm a complex creature. What can I say?" She looked behind her and stared at the vacant corner of her cell. "I'm not talking to you, Twinkie twat, now am I?"

"Ashli." Máax cautiously took her hand. "I know you are upset, but I want to explain my actions—"

"You've sentenced everyone to death," Kinich challenged. "There is no explaining that."

"What would you have me do?" Máax snarled. "Tell me, brother! Would you shove Penelope and your unborn child into a burning volcano if it meant saving the world?" He paused. "How about you, Niccolo? Would you let Helena, the mother of your child, die for the good of humanity? Or would you fight like hell to find another way to stop the end of days?"

The couples looked at each other, their eyes filled with sadness.

"You are right, brother." Kinich took Penelope's hand. "I would not give her up. I would find another way." His brother Votan and sister Ixtab agreed.

Yes, they understood.

"That is the path I have chosen," Máax added. "There is nothing I will not do for Ashli. Nothing. And I will fight until my last breath to keep her from dying, including in an apocalypse. What I do not understand is why my brethren will not fight by my side when I have sacrificed everything to come to your aid time and time again."

"He is right," Votan, the God of Death and War, said. "He has selflessly put himself in harm's way. Repeatedly. We love you. In fact, I too feel the urge to write a song. But about you, our brother."

One might think that Votan was joking, but he wasn't. What the hell had gotten into everyone?

Must be the apocalyptic vibe in the air messing with everyone's heads.

"This is all wonderful. I'm touched. Truly touched," Ashli fumed. "But I won't be writing any songs in your honor because I want nothing to do with you, Máax. Take me home. This time, I mean it. I was an idiot to trust you. And it's a mistake I'll never make again."

Ashli had never felt so betrayed in her entire life. Ever. From her point of view, she'd done an amazing job rolling with the punches given the circumstances, but this was too much. How could she stay with Máax, knowing he'd lied to her? Lied. Sure, she'd been able to forgive him when he'd withheld information and made her immortal without her permission, but she'd assumed that would never happen again. And technically, it had not been a lie.

But this? It was the textbook definition of a lie, and blatant dishonesty was the one thing she couldn't tolerate. Especially not from a man like Máax who had such a strong emotional grip over her. Extra-especially from a man who claimed to stand for the truth. That made him an extra-special fake.

Worst of all, the lie had brought her forward in time and derailed the prophecy? She didn't know what it meant to break one. Or why her staying in 1993 would have stopped the end of the world. But it was clear that the situation was bad. Really, really bad. And they were almost out of time. Why hadn't he frigging told her?

Oh, giantmonkeycchinoballs! The world is going to end! Ashli gripped her stomach. She was going to hurl. What had she done?

"Take me back," she croaked.

"You cannot mean that, Ashli," Máax argued.

"I can, and I do. Take me back!"

"But we don't know what will happen," he said. "Death might still seek you out."

"I would rather have one more day of a life I loved and trying to fix this mess than spend one more minute here with you, living a life based on a lie. Or worse, living with a god who proclaims to stand by the truth, but is just a weasel."

The entire room tensed. It was as if the cosmos held a breath.

Máax tried to take her hand, but she yanked it away.

He made a little growl. "I understand why you might feel that way; however, if you gave me the opportunity to—"

"What? To treat me like an infant? Make a life-altering decision for me? I've lost everything, Máax. Everything. First my family, and now you've taken away my humanity, my home, not to mention, have you seen my café, Máax? Have you? It's like Starbucks turned into a gigolo and knocked up a baboon!"

"I admit that the Uchben asset team may have overstepped their boundaries. However, their ability to predict consumer trends is flawless. Your café is quite successful. You have over one hundred now."

"What? Ohmygod, do you think any of that matters? We're all going to die!" Her mouth hung open.

"Uh, no. Not really. But you brought it up—"

"I hate what you've done to me. I hate that you've made me some murderer of the human race, not that I even come close to understanding how that's possible. But I hate it, nonetheless. And I hate that for a few hours I got a taste of a damned happy new life; then you snatched it all away. But none of that matters now, because I'm going to fix this. Take me back," she demanded.

Even the vampires in the middle of the room looked uncomfortable.

"Ashli, you are upset. And probably in shock. But we will get through this. All of us will get through this if we pull together."

Was he for real?

"Máax. Didn't you hear me? I want you to take me back."

"I cannot do that." There was a moment of pause. "I *won't* allow you to run away, Ashli. Not from me. Not from this fight. It is time for you to grow up and cease being an emotional hermit who lives in the shadows of the past. We will fix this. Sentin, please take her to Kinich's home. I will be there momentarily."

"Are you kidding me?" He was going to take her against her will?

"I am a god, Ashli, I rarely kid," Máax said.

"I'm a god, and I do it all the time," Cimil said.

"There are many things you do that I would not advise," Roberto pointed out. "Such as lighting your own jail cell on fire."

"One of my best moments, indeed!" Cimil replied.

"You're treating me like your property, Máax," Ashli growled. "Don't you dare do this."

"Sentin. Please take my woma— Ashli."

Son of a bitch. "You're not who I thought you were."

Sentin stepped forward in a blur, and Ashli found herself standing in the middle of a very large bedroom.

Ohmygod! She spun in a circle. "I can't believe this. I hate him."

Sentin laughed. "Gods are known to be a bit overbearing at times," he said with a thick Italian accent. "But they are nothing compared to vampires. By the way, are you single now? I'm digging your whole angry human vibe thing. It's kind of hot."

"What?" Ashli stared up at the tall, lean vampire with dark messy hair and a boyish smile that she wanted to slap right off of his face.

He lifted both brows. "I cook really well, and I'm great with kids. Just ask Niccolo's wife."

Ashli huffed. These people were unbelievable.

Seventeen

~

As soon as Ashli left, the heated debate reignited. Only it wasn't a debate; it was more like a frantic screaming match among the gods, vampires, and Uchben over what to do next.

As for Máax, he paced the cement floor of the cell-block, trying to understand what had transpired. How could things have gone so very, very wrong? Not only had the apocalyptic situation escalated to DEFCON 1, which was bad, but Ashli also hated him. That had to be a first in the world of mates, didn't it?

You had this coming.

"Fuck!" He punched the glass in front of Cimil. "Fucking hell!" He had to fix this. But how?

Cimil, who now wore pink shorts and a gold blouse with a pink unicorn on the front, sat cross-legged on her cot, scrunching her face into a tiny pale ball. "They don't actually do that in hell. And come to think of it, hell is a fictitious place. Unless you want to count waiting in line at the DMV, then hell yeah! Totally there with ya. But they don't fornicate there, either. Except on Talk Like a Pirate Day. Mark it on your calendar. September nineteenth. Arrr."

Fucking Cimil.

"Cimil. I'm going to ask you a question," Máax fumed. "And I warn you, the next words that come from your mouth had better be the godsdamned truth."

"The godsdamned truth." She cackled and then buffed her nails on the front of her shirt. "Oh, I'm on fire today! Not literally, but figurat—"

"Cimil!" he screamed, then looked at one of the vampire guards—not that the guard knew Máax was looking at him. "Open this cell right now. I'm going to snap her neck."

"I think not." Roberto stepped in toward Máax.

"Jeez." Cimil rolled her eyes. "Since when did you become King Poopie-Doo of the party, Máax? I was just kidding."

Máax had had enough. "Cimil, so help me—"

"I already know what you are going to ask; a dead little birdy told me. Can we stop the apocalypse? No. Well, maybe. I don't know. According to my last vision, Ashli is in present day and in her forties when she stops the apocalypse, meaning she did not jump through the portal to get here."

"Okay. Fine. Ashli is immortal now. So what do we do?" Máax asked.

"Hello! I told you not to introduce any additional variables because then we wouldn't know what to do. Voilà! Here we are. As clueless as a teenage girl on prom night!"

"It doesn't make any sense," he grumbled. Cimil said that Ashli needed to live out her life normally. But he was certain, dead certain, that Ashli would not have survived.

"Hmmm." Cimil jostled her head from side to side. "Yes, perhaps my snark was outdated. According to a very reliable source, *Vampire Diaries*, the females of this day and age are quite experienced by the time they get to prom." She began tapping the side of her mouth. "Hmmm...I need a new snark. Clueless as a unicorn in a skateboard shop—"

"Cimil. Focus. Are you certain about what you saw in your vision? Because I promise, Ashli would not have lived another day had I not interfered," he said.

"Yes, I told you Ashli was not twentysomething in my vision. She was much, much older." Cimil sighed with fake sympathy. "But none of that matters now. You've brought her here. You made her immortal. You altered everything. And, yes! Before you ask, we are still on a path of destruction. That's the one thing I know for sure. Oh! And here comes...."

The structure shook with staggering turbulence for four long seconds. The steel beams inside the walls groaned and creaked.

"Number nine," Cimil said to the now deathly silent room of immortals.

"Son of a bitch." Máax scratched the thick growth of whiskers on his jaw. "There has to be another way to fix everything."

Cimil stood and began playing with her cell phone. "Your guess is as good as mine, except on Fridays—"

"Cimil, can you not be serious, even for a moment?" he grumbled. "Especially given the situation?"

"Nope." Cimil shoved the phone down the front of her shorts.

"What in gods' name are you doing, Cimil?" Máax scowled.

"Yes, what are you doing?" Roberto asked.

"I'm taking a selfie of my privates. It's called a privie. Here, want to see?" She held up the phone.

"No!" Máax turned away. "What the hell is wrong with you?"

"Mmmm..." Roberto groaned lightly. "I like."

"Put the phone away, or I will come in there and beat you with it." Máax was truly close to losing it.

"There! All gone!" She returned her phone to her pants and held up her empty hands. "So, where were we?" Cimil once again glanced over her shoulder toward the empty corner of her cell. "No one asked you, crazy coolots!"

Impossible. She is impossible.

"Cimil, what if we sent Ashli back?" Not that he would allow that, but it was an answer he needed to know.

Her index finger shot up. "Ah! Now, there's an interesting idea. Would the Universe accept Ashli as an offering? A tragedy for our triumph. A yin for a yang. Let me think that through. You've fallen in love with her so if she were to die," Cimil mumbled to herself, "it would be a true romantic tragedy, old-school style. Like big Romeo and Little J." Cimil tapped the side of her face. "Little J was *Gossip Girl*, wasn't she? Sorry, I meant J.Lo."

"That is not what I meant," Máax said.

"Oh, good." Cimil snorted. "I was gonna say...I mean, what kind of asshole would suggest sacrificing his mate like that?" Cimil shrugged. "Not sure what will happen if you take her back."

"Has anyone ever told you that you're the worst prophet the world has ever known?"

Cimil rolled her eyes. "The world is not over yet so there's still time for me to come in second." Her cell phone began to squawk like an irate chicken. "Hold that thought." She held up her index finger and dug down into the front of her shorts. She pressed the talk button and held it to her ear. "Yo."

Disgusting, he thought, knowing where that phone had just been.

Cimil turned her back and began pacing the length of her tiny cell. "Uh-huh. Uh-huh. Corner office, huh? With a view of downtown LA?" Pause. "Oh. And underground parking? And day care one block away? I'll take it!" She turned, shoved the phone back down her pants, and sighed happily. "So! Where were we?"

"Nowhere," Máax groaned.

"Ah yes! Nowhere is precisely where you are. So may I suggest that you focus on feeling grateful for what you've got instead of not. What else is there to do now? And look at the bright side. At least this way, you're not going on trial. You're free to live until doomsday. Unless we magically find a way out of this, in which case you and I are completely hosed. Because we've been naughty." She smiled and stared at the floor. "Really, really naughty. Yessss. I should be punished. Gods, I love being me." She froze for several moments, convulsed, and then picked up her paddleball from her bed. "Which is why I'm going to enjoy whatever time we have left."

"No. You're going to help me fix this mess and stop the end."

"Nope," Cimil replied. "I'm going to throw a giant

party. We're going out with a bang. And lots of banging! It's going to be fornication fabulous."

"You can't be serious," he said.

"Do you have any idea how many times I've gone through this doomsday hullabaloo? Any at all? Six thousand seven hundred and two. I steer us clear of one disaster only to find we're on a collision course with another. It's apocalyptic Whac-A-Mole. I'm pooped! It's time to say thank you to the Universe and celebrate the lives we've had. And hump like feral lemurs. 'Cause I like to move it, move it."

"Of course we can hump like strange little animals"—Roberto appeared next to Máax—"if that is your wish, my little apocalyptic lollipop. But you do not mean the part about giving up. You love saving the world from the brink of extinction. It is your favorite pastime aside from garage sale hunting."

"Yah. Not so much. Gettin' old. In fact, I'm officially retiring as of this moment." She sat down on her cot and began typing into her phone. "Look. See! I tweeted it, and that makes it official!" She held up her phone. "Now for the party announcement."

"You're not leaving that cell, Cimil. Because we are not giving up," Máax said sternly. "Not on this world. Not on Ashli. And there certainly won't be any parties."

Cimil tilted her head, raised her cell phone, and tapped the screen. "Not according to the almighty tweet. The party's on, baby. On!"

"Over my dead, invisible body."

"All those in favor of giving up on this futile effort to stop the apocalypse and enjoy the time we have left, raise their hands!" she screamed.

"I don't give a shit about your voting." Máax looked around the prison. Everyone had their hands up, exceptions being those with mates. "No. Uh-uh. No one leaves here until we figure out a solution." Máax was losing his patience.

"Let us out! Let us out! Let us out!" The chant started with Cimil but quickly spread to Máax's other brethren. The entire underground prison shook beneath his feet as a hurricane began to rage inside of his sister Ixtab's cell (she involuntarily created bad weather when upset). Her mate, Antonio, pressed himself into the corner of the cell, attempting to calm her down to no avail. The rest of the deities screamed or pounded away on the thick glass. Meanwhile, fifty or so vampires and Uchben scrambled, preparing for some sort of offensive.

"Tell them to back down, Cimil! This instant! Or no more Minky visits!" Roberto roared.

"You wouldn't dare!" she yelled back. "'Cause I'll take away your Cimi-treats! Forever!" Cimil turned, bent over, and began shaking her rear. "No more for you, Roberto!"

"Cimil. Stop this instant!" Máax knocked loudly on the glass.

"Ain't gonna happen!" Cimil popped up and began clapping rhythmically. "Party. Party. Party."

Unbelievable.

Máax glanced over at Niccolo and the other soldiers who were preparing to detonate smoke bombs. He assumed those were what they'd used to knock out the gods during their summit meeting. Quite effective, yes, but putting his brethren to sleep would solve nothing. "Ain't gonna happen. Party, party, party!" The chanting continued.

Máax took a deep breath, attempting to vanquish his fury and find a rational solution, but there was no getting around it. Not this time.

"Enough! I hope you're all planning to live like hunted animals once you get out." Máax's livid voice echoed off the cement walls of the cavernous structure. "Because I promise, I'll spare no one on Team Cimil from my wrath. No one!" He may not have his divine powers, but he still had strength. And he was invisible. It completely freaked their shit out.

From the thirteen holding cells, his brothers and sisters stared with wide turquoise eyes. It was the first time—well, ever really—that he'd seen them quiet.

Yeah. That's what I thought. "I don't care how many times I have to say this, but let's get one thing straight: this fucking world ain't over until I fucking say it's over."

"Hey! You stole my ain't. That's my word of the day!" Cimil whined.

"Shut up!" Máax said.

Cimil crossed her arms. "You can scream all you like, but I know what I saw, Máax. I see us fighting. I see the end. It's completely pointless to try to stop it now. Game over! Party on!"

"And exactly who did you see fighting?" he seethed.

"Well"—Cimil scratched the corner of her mouth—"the vision merely showed me bits and pieces—kind of like 'Chat Stew.' Joel is my backup mate BTW should Roberto ever perish. So meaty."

Roberto growled.

"What pieces did you see, Cimil?" Máax questioned impatiently.

"Well." She tapped her cheek. "I see the vampires

fighting the Uchben, and I see the gods with mates fighting the gods without."

Oh, vomica *no.* "We wouldn't all happen to be inside a prison, would we?"

Cimil gasped and her eyes lit up, but she didn't reply.

"Cimiiiil?" Roberto warned.

Her mouth crinkled to one side. "Maybe?"

"Gods dammit, Cimil!" Máax screamed. "You mean to tell us that this entire time, your vision showed you this exact scenario playing out? This very scenario you've created? Did you ever stop to think that you were driving the apocalypse, Oh Bringer of the Apocalypse? Did you?"

She shrugged. "Oopsies?"

Máax hung his head. "We should've known better than to listen to you. Roberto, set them all free."

Roberto looked crushed. "Oh, my love guppy of destruction, is this true? And I helped you?"

Máax glanced at the large, ancient vampire and frankly felt a little bad for him. Women were so damned complicated; he felt his pain. "Roberto, she's the Goddess of the Underworld, the Bringer of the Apocalypse. Even when she wants to do the right thing, she cannot."

"Let them free," Roberto commanded his men in a melancholy tone.

The men quickly unlocked the cells and released the gods and four mates, Emma, Penelope, Maggie, and Antonio, who'd been holed up with their significant others.

Everyone gathered in the center of the cellblock, exchanging glances.

Cimil looked from side to side. "Dammit! This doesn't make any sense! You're all free, and there's no change. We're still going to die!"

Everyone threw up their hands and grumbled miserable thoughts.

"How do you know that?" Not like they could trust her visions anyway.

She murmured, "The dead don't lie. Except on leap day. That's not today. I checked."

For once, Máax saw the plain truth in Cimil's eyes, and she was just as heartbroken as everyone else. And though no one else caught it, Máax noticed Cimil rubbing her hand gingerly over her lower stomach.

Oh, saints. Cimil is pregnant? This just couldn't be. Máax's heart felt heavy and saturated, as if filled with lead. But if she were pregnant, then why was she advocating so strongly for throwing a party and giving up?

Perhaps she is not giving up at all. Quote, I am a complex creature, unquote. Was Cimil trying in her own way to fight the end? Yes, she loved parties, but she loved a happy ending more than anything in the world. It was her one saving grace. Even after she'd destroyed Chaam, she knew exactly how to save him. She'd personally given Máax the list of each and every woman who'd died, including where to find them prior to their deaths.

"Máax, I'm sorry." Cimil sighed. "I really thought I was helping."

"So what do we do now?" Niccolo asked Roberto. It was a damned good question. "The ship's going to sink, and we have no clue as to why."

Máax glanced at Cimil's tormented face, and his gut told him to roll with it. Somehow, goodness always managed to blossom from the wreckage of her wake.

"I suggest," Máax said, "we do what any family might and celebrate our blessings. We throw a party."

Cimil pasted on a smile. "We'll party like it's 1999! Except for Ashli. She skipped that year." Cimil looked at Colel, aka Bees. "Get your ass to Walmart. We've got decorating to do."

"I cannot believe I'm agreeing to this." But even Máax knew that sometimes, when all appeared hopeless, one simply needed to have faith.

Immediately after Máax had that flirty, young-looking vampire deposit Ashli in a room, the shocking events came crashing down. Being hunted by Death, the trip through time, becoming immortal, losing her home, Monkeyccino's—*cringe*—vampires, gods, and the now-eminent apocalypse, which could have been avoided had she not traveled forward in time. But that was the irony of it all. Now that she'd had time to breathe, she saw the truth and knew in her heart Máax had been right; she wouldn't have lived much longer had she stayed in 1993. Her dreams and near-death misses were proof of that.

So perhaps Máax really had done the only thing he could to save her. She just wished he'd spoken with her first instead of lying, and more importantly, she wished his choice to bring her forward hadn't meant derailing all hope for mankind.

Bummer.

Nevertheless, Ashli was determined to find a way through this and pull herself together. Of course, her version of being "together" reminded her of a Rice Krispies Treat, bits and pieces stuck together with artificially sweetened goo.

Until Máax came along, she reminded herself.

He'd offered glimpses of what it felt like to be alive again. To not feel, well, gooey and patched together. That was the other epiphany she'd had. She realized that she'd physically walked away from that car accident so many years ago; however, her inner chutzpah had not. Sure, she still walked and talked and breathed like a living person, but that's as far as it went. She'd completely closed herself off from the world. What had Máax called her? An emotional hermit who lived in the past. Well, he was right. And she didn't want to be that person anymore. If the world was truly about to end, she wanted to leave it feeling like she'd conquered her demons. But how?

You need to embrace life and take this new chance you've been given, even if it's a short one, she decided. Not that it meant she'd forgiven Máax.

There was a knock.

Boy, were the people around this parts friendly. In the last ten minutes alone, she'd had seven visitors.

Jeez. Ashli cracked open the door and peered into the hallway. A man with sandy-blond hair, medium height and build, wearing leather pants, stared down at her, grinning from ear to ear, flashing some major fang.

Another vampire? "Yes?" she asked, trying to hide her confusion.

"Just wanting to make sure you're all right."

"Yep." She smiled. *Awkward.*

"And wondering if you need anything?" he asked.

"Oh. Thanks, but no. I'm great," she replied.

He stared.

Weird. "Okay then." She began to close the door. "Nice to meet—"

"Do women prefer flowers or chocolate? I met a

woman, and I'd like to ask her out, but I'm not sure which she'll prefer."

Seriously? "Uhhh ... I really don't know. Maybe just ask her?" Ashli tried to close the door, but he stuck his foot in the opening.

"I can sift," he said.

"Um. Cool."

"If you help me, I can get you anything from any-where," he added.

Getting weirder. "That's really generous, but I really don't think I can. Good luck." She closed the door and scratched her head. Was this normal behavior in this world?

There was yet another knock at the door. She opened it. "Listen, I really don't need ..." There was no one.

"Máax?"

She waited for a reply. If he was there, he wasn't saying anything. Ashli then noticed a card and rectangular box wrapped in shimmery red paper on the floor. She picked it up and closed the door, locking it behind her.

The card was an invitation for a party tomorrow evening. *A costume party? For the end of the world?*

Your driver will pick you up at eight o'clock. I hope you like the dress.

Yours Forever,
Máax

Ashli opened the box. "Funny, Máax. Real funny."

Eighteen

⌒

Ashli's limo pulled up behind a long line of other flashy vehicles to the red carpet, where svelte men in crisp tuxedos lined the walkways and giant floodlights speared the desert night sky. It felt like a lavish Hollywood movie premiere until she noticed the crowd pouring inside. Unicorns, clowns, genies, kings, and queens, the costumes were elaborate and outrageous.

Great. I'm underdressed.

Ashli thanked her driver as an usher opened the door, and she made her way inside the grandiose ballroom. The dimly lit interior pulsed with loud music and flashing lights. Giant twenty-foot-high golden statues of several gods illuminated every corner. The ceiling was a radiant spectacle of thousands of sparkling white lights arranged into constellations and...

Googly-eyed unicorns?

There had to be at least a thousand people toasting, dancing, and laughing.

Flabbergasted, Ashli stepped aside and gawked at the river of people flowing by. Or fountain of people? Yes, a man dressed as a fountain, complete with running water spouting from the top of his head and a giant round basin to catch the flow, floated by right next to another woman riding a very tall ... well, she didn't know really, because there wasn't actually anything there.

"Hello, Ashli. Welcome to the end of days party. What do you think?" Ashli looked up at two tall women. One wore a gold crown and short white dress, the other a giant—and she meant *giant*—beehive atop her head.

Ashli busted out laughing. "Oh! I get it. It's a beehive hairdo. That costume is hysterica..." The beehive woman looked like she just might reach down and rip off Ashli's eyebrows. "What? What did I say?"

The woman in white narrowed her eyes and poked an angry finger at Ashli's chest. "That's not a costume, you little twa..." She pulled back the offending finger and looked at the beehive lady. "Hey. Are you in the mood to write a poem? Or maybe braid each other's hair?"

"Yeah. Actually, I am." Beehive lady gave her little head a shake. Amazingly the hive stayed in place.

"Let's go find Kinich and Votan," said the woman in white. "They have long hair. Maybe they'll want to join us." She turned her attention back to Ashli. "As you for... we'll let your little insult slide. But just this once."

What was with these two? And why was everyone so into poetry, writing songs, and braiding hair?

A strong hand gripped Ashli's arm. "Ashli," said Máax in an amused tone. "I see you've met my sisters, Camax-tli, also known as Fate, and Colel, Mistress of Bees, who happens to have a hive living on her head."

Ashli yanked her arm away. "That one poked me."

Máax leaned in. "Just ignore them. They're jealous because they pale in comparison to your beauty."

Then Ashli noticed something truly strange. Shocking, really. She was talking to Máax. Yes, Máax, an actual person whom she could see, standing right in front of her. His skin and hair had been painted gold. He wore sunglasses and a white toga. Ashli could see every bulging, rippling muscle shimmer as he moved. He was magnificent. And huge. Somehow he'd seemed smaller that day in the tub, but standing next to him made her feel like a toy Yorkie next to a pit bull. Only he did not look like a dog, but a god. A real-life god. And delicious. Those bare, broad, square shoulders that tapered into a tight waist; those thick, strong arms. *Sigh.* He was a sight of perfection. Every last inch. Was that gold paint edible? Had he painted his mandy bar, too?

"You look, um, amazing," she said.

He looked down at his body. "Thank you. The idea came from you, actually. I cannot stop thinking about your special caramel body treatment."

Caramel. Yes. She couldn't stop thinking about that, either.

You're an idiot! Look at you, pining for him. And appreciating. And thinking dirty, dirty thoughts about that mouth of his and the way it had kissed her. Or the way she'd kissed him back. Or how when she was around him, she became completely wild for him. Or when she'd pleasured him, he'd groaned in a voice so primal and masculine that she'd almost tumbled over the edge. Or the way he moved against her body and—

"Ashli? Did you hear what I said?" Máax asked.

Oh, had he been talking while she'd just snorkeled to the bottom of the gutter?

"I advise you to steer clear of those two sisters of mine. Or any of my brethren for that matter." He rubbed his forehead, causing a bit of paint to streak just above his brow. "Thank the gods you're immortal now."

Immortal. Immortal. Still doesn't feel real when I say it. Immooortal. Immooortal. Nope.

He leaned in close and whispered in her ear, "By the way, that toga looks stunning on you. I may have to remove my costume so that others do not mistake my toga for a pup tent."

His scent, so sweet and addictive, overwhelmed her senses.

"And your hair, I love it loose and wild like this." He rubbed a lock between his fingers and then slid his hand across her cheek. "You are so lovely, Ashli. Every inch of you."

Standing next to him, seeing him with her very own eyes, hearing him whisper those tempting words was too much. He was a seduction machine.

"Hey. Looking good, Máax." The deep male voice came from behind Ashli.

Máax glanced over Ashli's shoulder. "Andrus. Tommaso." He dipped his head, grinning. "Amusing costumes, gentlemen."

Ashli turned her head to see who stood behind her, but when her eyes registered the two large men wearing loincloths, their nearly bare bodies and hair caked in dried mud, she yelped. *Ohmygod.*

"Ashli." Máax chuckled. "Andrus and Tommaso are dressed as Maaskab, an evil sect of Mayan priests."

Ashli pieced together a half smile. No doubt the other half was a look of disgust. Both men wore necklaces made of plastic fingers and had fake blood smeared on their faces.

"See, Tommaso," Andrus said. "I told you. The ladies weren't going to be into this. Now I'm not going to get laid. It's my first night off in six months. Do you know how hard it is to find qualified stand-ins when the gods throw a party?"

Tommaso rolled his eyes. "You're such a fucking wuss, Andrus. Come on, I saw a couple Payals over by the hors d'oeuvre table eyeing our Scabby thongs."

"I am not a wuss; I am a lethal assassin." Andrus punched Tommaso in the shoulder.

"You're a fucking nanny, Andrus. Now shut the hell up and let's get hammered. By the way…" Tommaso tilted his head to one side and turned stone-cold serious. "Have I ever told you that I really love you, man? Not in a gay way, not that there's anything wrong with that. But like a brother. Fuck—why did I just say that?" Tommaso glanced at Máax and Ashli. "I gotta get a drink. Nice meeting you, Ashli."

"Uhhh…" Andrus shrugged his brows and watched Tommaso scurry away before turning back to Ashli. "I guess I'll go join him. See what's wrong. Nice to meet you, Ashli…" His voice trailed off, and his eyes locked on Ashli.

Okay. Awkward. She glanced at Máax, then back at the man.

"Enjoy the party, Andrus," Máax said, politely shooing him away.

Andrus shook his head, snapping out of his distraction. "Yeah. Thanks." He disappeared into the crowd.

"That was interesting," Máax mumbled.

Ashli turned her attention back to Máax, who began rattling away some story about Andrus being hopelessly in love with another man's wife—that Niccolo guy?—and caretaker to his daughter. Honestly, Ashli wasn't really listening. How could she?

She sighed at the deeply chiseled muscles, the ripples of his partially exposed abs, the thick, strong thighs jutting out from below the hem of his almost too short toga, a toga that barely covered him and reminded her of what was underneath. *Mandy bar!* It was a part of him she remembered touching and tasting and enjoying. She'd never felt so free and uninhibited with a man. She'd never felt so needy for one, either.

Have you forgotten about his other fine traits? Like being a liar?

Yes, but even you can admit, it wasn't with malicious intent.

"Hi, Máax." Twin petite blondes with sparkle-covered skin and wearing flimsy white negligees smiled lustily at him.

"Where have you been hiding yourself? You naughty, naughty boy," the one on the left said in a saucy voice.

Ashli felt the urge to punch her.

Máax smiled stiffly. "Hello, ladies, may I introduce you to Ashli, my mate. Does she not look lovely tonight?"

The two perky-boobed women looked at Ashli. "Is this the mortal who dumped you?" the one on the right asked. "Doesn't look like much to me. Kinda plain."

"I hear from the vampires," said the other one, "that she couldn't, you know, please him so she tried to run away. Is that true, Máax? Because we know how to handle a god."

I'm gonna punch them both! Right in their perky little boobs!

"Ladies." Máax scowled. "We both know that is untrue—"

"I'm sorry," Ashli interrupted, her fists clenched. "Who the hell are you—"

"Let me handle this, Ashli," Máax said, cutting her off. "You're still new to everything."

Incredible! He's incredible, she thought bitterly. *I had this!* Why did he insist on being so, so, so *condescending.* Ugh!

"I dumped him," Ashli said, "because he's a liar. And he's all yours, ladies." Ashli turned away and began pushing through the cocktail-sipping crowd. "I'm going to find the ladies' room."

Can't please him? Can't please him? Had he really been telling people—uhh, vampires—that?

"Ashli!" Máax called, but she needed to get away from him before she got sucked in again. His voice, his smell, his mere presence acted like a giant amplifier for her emotions. And those two disgusting…What the hell were they?

"They're sex fairies!" Máax screamed. "You can't believe a word they say!"

She kept walking. "Sex fairies?" she mumbled. "Well, just great!" Sex fairies were publically shaming her bedroom skills while hitting on Máax.

Maybe you're not ready for this. Maybe it's too much.

No. You can do this. Just take a breath. She fought the tiny voices in her head, urging her to run back to her room. Or to 1993. But she was determined to leave her old, emotional hermit–like ways behind and enjoy what little time she had left.

She found the ladies' room near the corner of the packed convention hall and pushed the door. "Sex fairies. Really?" Who ever heard of such a lame species? Probably some man had invented them.

She walked over to the sink and stared herself down in the mirror. "You are not going to cry. Not. Not. Not. Do you hear me?"

"Hello, Ashli. Nice to finally meet you. You have no idea how long we've waited."

Ashli looked into the mirror, but there was no one there. She turned quickly and saw a blonde with a bob and a brunette with short hair, both about her age. They wore black-and-white-striped referee outfits, whistle necklaces, and...

"Holly crap! Are those ummm..."

"Wings," said the petite blonde and the shorter of the two. She reached out her hand. "I'm Anne, by the way, and this is my associate, Jess."

Ashli shook hands with Anne but immediately snapped hers away when she noticed an odd tingle. Who were these two? They looked harmless enough, like sweet Midwestern sorority sisters. Except for the referee outfits and frigging enormous white, fluffy wings that sparkled like luminescent diamonds. "Are they..."

"Real? Yes," replied the brunette, Jess. "But we can talk about that later. Right now, we need to chat. And it's *muy importante*. One might even say that you were born for this. *El gran momento!* So time to listen-listen. 'Kay?"

Ashli wasn't really sure she was having this conversation. Perhaps she'd slipped on the floor on the way into the bathroom? She flipped a glance over her shoulder at the mirror behind her. Crap! Still empty. But when she looked directly in front of her, the two women were as plain as day.

What the hell? "You can't be real."

"Come on," said Anne, "by now you should be all broken in. You've met deities—an invisible one at that—vampires, you've been sifted through time, and you've met Cimil's unicorn."

"I met a unicorn?" She didn't remember meeting any unicorn.

The blonde, Anne, smiled. "Uh…yeah. Minky's been hiding out in your room since you arrived. Apocalypses make her nervous. Didn't you notice?"

Ashli shook her head no.

"Minky is mostly harmless, except when she gets in a cuddly mood."

"Huh?" *Okay. Now I know I've gone off the deep end.* She turned to escape but encountered a third woman standing against the door. She was extremely tall, especially compared to Ashli's five feet and one inch of vertical presence. This woman didn't wear a referee outfit, however, but instead had on a bunny costume sorta. Black satin short shorts, platform shoes, a teeny tiny tank top, and pink fluffy bunny ears that matched her giant fluffy wings. And a lit cigar. That was sorta bunny. Right?

"Who are you?" Ashli asked, hoping and praying that the woman would not reply with, "The Easter Bunny." Because, yeah, that would be the final straw.

"She's Nicole," replied Anne, who stood so close behind Ashli that her entire body now tingled.

"Our boss," added Jess.

"Friends call me Nick." Ashli watched in awe as the cigar-smoking bunny puffed out a giant ball of smoke that formed a heart, which evaporated into thin air. "Hiya."

"But I ... I ..." *Screw this happily living out your final days bull crap. It's probably overrated anyway.* "Can I leave, please?" She wondered if she could talk one of those vampires into opening the portal and returning her to 1993.

"You," Anne said, "may go just as soon as you listen."

There's no place like home. There's no place like home. Ohmygod, heeeelp.

The bunny lady lifted a brow. "Really? Really? You went Oz on us?"

They can hear my thoughts?

Bunny lady looked at Anne and Jess. "Wow. This is the chosen one? Thank heavens she doesn't have to do anything complicated or we'd all be shopping for a new Universe for sure."

Ashli's mouth fell open. Then she snapped it shut, closed her eyes, and took a breath, waiting a moment before she reopened them. *Dammit. They're still there!*

"Aaaand she's back. Great." Jess removed the whistle hanging around her neck and placed it over Ashli's head. "All you need to do is remember that when the trouble starts, blow that whistle—it's the only help you're getting from us. It's up to you to stop them. Understand?"

Not even. "Blow the whistle and stop them?" *Who? From doing what?* "Can you be a little more specific? 'Cause I'd really love to know what the hell you're talking about."

The three women exchanged glances. "Did you just say 'hell' to a group of angels?" they replied in unison.

Ashli sighed. Why did everything have to be so strange? She ran her hands over her face. "I need to get out of here." Maybe she'd hit her head getting out of the limo.

"No," Anne said. "You need to stay."

"Give her the whammy already," said Jess. "Belch is making pousse-cafés, and I'm not missing out this time. I hear the flame is twelve inches high."

"Fine." Anne stepped forward, and Ashli stepped back. "Listen, Ash. I'll make it short and sweet. Once upon a time, many thousands of years ago, humans were created. And angels—hello, that's us, if you were wondering— were created to keep watch over humans. The Creator is too busy running the cosmos and all, so she's gotta have help. Yunno? But it didn't take long for the Creator to see we weren't exactly cut out for the job. Not because we don't rock, but because humans are flawed. We are not. Anywing, we stopped being relevant because we find it hard to relate, because we don't understand what it's like to be flawed. Yada yada.

"So the Creator decided to bridge the gap by creating the gods—flawed, quirky, and well, downright child-ish at times. Great plan, except there's another problem. Humans evolve. Rather quickly. Which means the gods, too, are fast becoming obsolete. Irrelevant. I mean, really. When's the last time you saw a new monument built to those clowns? Anywing, the Creator was about to throw in the towel, but *we* threw down a challenge instead. We saw potential in the gods. So we made a bet; if we could prove the gods capable of evolving, the Creator would let us keep the planet.

"Fast-forward to present day. Some of the gods have made progress—learning humility, how to love and share their power—but it's not enough. They must all prove they're capable of real change or we all die; the Creator's going to scrap the whole terrarium and start over again."

"What? Scrap? Why? Creator?" Ashli said, holding back an epic meltdown.

"Wow. Ain't she full o' them big ol' words," said the bunny thug or whatever her name was.

"Why are you telling me all this?" Ashli muttered.

"Because," Anne said, "sometimes it just takes one person to turn the tides. One simple act. One simple gesture. But it must be out of love."

"Every ocean starts with one drop of water," added Jess.

"So tonight," Anne continued, "when the time comes, you will blow that whistle and do your thing."

"Huh?" Ashli didn't quite understand.

"And you will forget"—Anne snapped her fingers—"that we ever had this conversation, but you will remember what you must do."

"Okay. I will forget. And remember. But are you really..." Her voiced tapered off, and Ashli stood in the bathroom, staring at herself in the mirror.

What am I doing here? I need a drink!

Ashli wandered out into the party to find a cocktail for her unsteady nerves. She'd been there all of four minutes and had already been threatened by a beekeeper, fended off Máax's seductive package, been insulted by sex fairies, and then been accosted by...

Hmmm. That's strange. I can't remember. What was she about to do?

Find a supersized dirty martini, remember? Hopefully one that didn't contain anything otherworldly. Just good, old-fashioned vodka or gin. Or both. Hell. Didn't matter.

She stood on her tiptoes trying to spot the bar. *There!* A long line of people gathered around an elevated counter. Behind it stood a man who wore nothing but a giant wine barrel with a strap over each shoulder.

She made her way over and watched as he lined up ten glasses and proceeded to pour various multicolored liquids into them like a cocktail assembly line. The tenth glass he lifted to his mouth and gulped it down while people helped themselves to the full glasses. He repeated the task three more times before Ashli moved to the front of the line. The man, tall and rather good-looking, though clearly inebriated and in dire need of a comb, stopped his drink slinging and looked straight at her.

"Coming right up," he said and began mixing a dirty martini with blue cheese olives. Just the way she liked it.

"But how did you know that's what I wanted?" she asked as he placed the jumbo-sized martini glass right in front of her.

"He's Belch, the God of Wine and Intoxication," said a male voice at her side.

"Brutus. Ohmygod. Hi."

"It's been a long time." He hugged her, but did not let go.

Okay there, big boy. She wiggled loose. "Feels like a few days to me."

"Twenty years," Brutus said with regret. "Twenty long years."

Oh no. Poor guy. Changing subjects.

"So." She glanced back at the bartender. "Is he really the god of alcohol?"

"The nammme's Acan," the bartender slurred and winked at her.

Sure. They have a deity for bees, why not beer, too?

Did they have a deity for clearance sales, as well? How about bacon and eggs? Those were important, right?

Ashli simply stared as he whipped up another batch of drinks, then lit them on fire. *Wow.*

"So. You enjoying the party?" Brutus asked.

"It's a party to celebrate the end of the world," she replied. "So, I'm not sure exactly."

"Drink," Acan slurred from behind the bar. "It will make you feel betewww." He winked again before moving his attention to the next person in line, a man with a three-foot-tall, silver-and-jade headdress with a serpent eating some corn. She felt compelled to comment, but then noticed his turquoise eyes and long silvery hair cascading down to his ankles.

Another deity. Actually, this one she remembered from the prison. He'd been throwing lightning bolts inside his cell.

Ashli stepped back a few feet, plucked the olive from her enormous martini glass, and threw back her drink. *Wow.* It was the best dang martini she'd ever had.

Without saying a word, the deity from behind the bar placed another in front of her. Wow. He knew she'd need two? Now those were some awesome powers.

She reached for it greedily. "Thank you."

The man bobbed his head and poured more drinks, which he again lit on fire. This time the flames reached two feet in height. The crowd applauded and then scooped them up.

"He's pretty impressive," she said to Brutus, who she now realized wore no costume. "Are you working?"

Brutus nodded yes. "Someone's got to keep the order. My men tend to get pretty wound up when the game gets to the final round."

Ashli sipped her second drink. "Game?"

"Yes. It's a tradition. The annual Uchben play-offs. We skipped last year's. Too much going on and Cimil was AWOL—she usually organizes the event—but we normally get together once a year, celebrate, and have a friendly game between the two teams: mortals versus immortals. The mortals always win because they have better reflexes; drives Cimil mad."

"Okay. I was about to say that I'd seen it all, heard it all, but somehow I just know that only means it's about to get weirder." Ashli began scanning the crowd, wondering where Máax was. No, she didn't want to talk to him, but she wanted to look at him. She couldn't help it. He was his own force of nature. Irresistible, sexy, and so over-the-top masculine that she couldn't stop wanting him even though she knew he'd only end up hurting her again.

Brutus grinned. "Weird is a good word for it. You are catching on to the way of our world, I see."

Ashli shrugged. "What's left of it, anyway."

"There are never any guarantees in life, Ashli. You of all people know that."

She shrugged. "How can you be so calm about all this? I look at this room filled with people who are all going to die because of me." *Wow.* Where had that come from?

"No, Ashli. None of this is your fault."

She gave it a moment of thought but still came to the same conclusion: It was her fault. If only she could have stayed in 1993 and found a way to survive.

She glanced over at a group of women standing next to them, laughing and hugging. One held an adorable little girl in her arms dressed as a ladybug with fangs.

Ashli's heart sank a little further.

Brutus squeezed her shoulder. "I know what you're thinking, but if you asked, they wouldn't blame you either so neither should you."

"I wish there was a way to fix this."

Brutus took a deep breath. "Perhaps there is. But you won't solve it tonight." His cell phone beeped, and he slid it from his pocket to read the message. "It's time. The final round. I better get over to the table before Cimil hurts someone. Come, you can watch."

Ashli glanced over her shoulder, feeling Máax's eyes on her, but with the dim lighting and extra-tall crowd, it was hard to spot anything beyond what was directly in front of her. She followed Brutus's hulking form through the mob of partygoers, which became denser as they neared the sound of Cimil's cackle.

"That's right, bitches. We're gonna win! I'm not letting the world end without that fucking trophy. It's mine!" Cimil's cackle turned into a strange howl.

Ashli peeked between Brutus and another large man. The people around the table either booed or cheered.

At the table, Cimil stood across from the mean blonde lady from earlier. *Fate?* An older gentleman wearing a Catholic priest's outfit stood next to Cimil, and across from him was a woman about Ashli's size with long dark hair, dressed as a clown.

"Wait a second," Ashli said loudly, trying to be heard above the noise of the cheering, "are they playing ..."

"Hungry Hungry Hippos," Brutus finished her sentence.

Okaaaay. Yes, grown adults and seventy-thousand-year-old beings were facing off to a fierce game of Hungry Hungry Hippos. Seemed a little inappropriate given the horrific situation facing them all. But then again, they were at a party to celebrate the end. Piling on the inappropriate seemed par for the course.

"The last play-off was Barrel of Monkeys. It is a different game every year," Máax said from behind Ashli.

Máax... Oh, great, just what she needed. Another whiff of her Kryptonite for all intelligent thought. Her body immediately reacted to him, heating up ten degrees. Hotter in other places.

Máax and Brutus exchanged alpha male glances and then nodded at each other.

"So why is there so much security?" Ashli asked.

"Cimil takes it quite seriously," Máax replied. "The mortals win every year and not for lack of trying on our part. It seems we fall short on intuitive capability and hand-eye coordination when compared to humans. And of course, we're not allowed to use any powers."

Cimil stood in front of her little station, furiously flicking the lever, gobbling up the plastic marbles bouncing around in the center of the game. "Yes! Two more and we win!"

"Over my dead body!" yelled the priest, who apparently took the game just as seriously. "We've got the big man on our side!"

"Stuff it, Xavier. You're not taking that trophy!" Fate barked, her hips twisting back and forth while she worked the flapping hippo mouth.

Ashli couldn't believe her eyes. Once again, she had the urge to say that now, yes, now, she'd seen it all, but now she simply knew better.

Suddenly, Cimil pointed at something up on the ceiling. "Ohmygod. Look!"

The crowd's gaze zeroed in on something above them,

but Ashli didn't look away. She didn't know why. Maybe she was still in shock that actual, real live gods were playing a priest and clown? But her eyes remained glued to Cimil.

Cimil's attention then went back to the game, and she flicked two more times, threw up her arms, and began screaming, "Boom! Fishedo! Victory is ours! The gods finally win!"

Fate ran around the table and began hopping up and down with Cimil; the two looked like rabid prairie dogs.

Furious, the priest pounded his fist down on the table. "You cheated, Cimil! You and your tricks. You grabbed an extra ball when no one was looking."

Cimil's turquoise eyes lit up. "I beg your pardon. We won fair and square."

"Like hell you did, Cimil," said the woman in the clown suit. "We demand a rematch."

"No. We won. Deal with it," Fate howled.

The four broke out shouting, and Ashli noticed the crowd beginning to grow uneasy. Brutus's men closed in on the fighting four; it looked like Cimil was about to punch the priest. But suddenly, the priest reached out and smacked Cimil across the face. The room fell into a horrified hush.

Ashli felt herself being tugged back. It was Máax pulling her away. "This is going to get ugly."

That large, scary vampire dude that had been guarding Cimil's prison cell stepped between Cimil and the priest. "No one touches my woman."

"You call that lying, thieving, cheating whore a woman?"

"Did I just hear that priest call Cimil a whore?" Ashli whispered in disbelief.

"Yes," Máax replied, "but he's not really a priest. He's an ex-priest and has a thing for her. Sour grapes."

Well, sour grapes are about to get squashed into sour wine.

The vampire reached down and grabbed the man by his neck. Brutus's men descended on the vampire quickly, trying to break the two up, but apparently the multitude of vampires in the room did not appreciate anyone touching Cimil's man. The vampires grabbed Brutus's soldiers and flung them across the room like tiny rag dolls. Apparently, the gods did not appreciate *that* one bit because they stepped in and attacked the vampires. It looked like the immortal version of a WWF match, bodies flying everywhere, fists moving so quickly she saw nothing but hazy streaks.

"Leave, Ashli. Run!" Máax commanded her.

Ashli was about to obey when she glanced down at her chest. "Well, it's worth a try." She grabbed for her whistle, but something large slammed into her body, sending her flying a good fifty feet. She landed on her back with a thud, the wind instantly sucked from her chest.

"I told you! Watch where you fucking sift! I'll fucking tear your head off, Sentin!" she heard Máax roar.

Can't breathe. Can't breathe. Oh, gods, can't breathe. Not only had the wind been knocked out of her, but she couldn't seem to move. "Máax," she managed to grind out in a pathetic little whimper. "Máaaaax."

But the room had erupted into an all-out brawl. Bodies flew so quickly from one side of the room to the other that they looked more like shooting stars. Grunts and screams layered over the loud dance music.

She looked up and saw a man hovering over her. His

long dreads hung around his face like a curtain of black snakes. At first, she thought it was that Andrus guy, but when the lights pulsed, she caught a glimpse of his face. The man's eyes were bloody-red pits, and his face was covered in mud or something dark. Real blood? The smell of putrid, rotting flesh instantly hit her. It filled her lungs and triggered her gag reflex.

Holyrefereebunnyangels! Save me. Why had she thought that? Ashli screamed, but no one paid any attention.

The creature smiled and a drop of his saliva dribbled from his mouth, hitting her on the cheek.

Ew. Ew. Ew.

The large creature effortlessly plucked her from the floor by the shoulders as if she were a wet rag. "You are pretty. You will give me many strong babies." The monster's voice sounded like a strange symphony of tortured souls screaming in agony.

Whatthefuck?

The monster reached one large, crusty hand around her neck and began petting her cheek. "My little love strumpet."

What? No! "Help!" Why was no one noticing?

Because they're too darn busy fighting over a game of Hungry Hungry Hippos! Idiots!

Ashli struggled beneath the monster's icy grip; meanwhile, he dragged her toward the door.

"No. Let me go!" She clawed at his fingers, but this only made him cackle with joy.

"First, I'm going to"—the monster made a sickly slurping sound between words—"eat your juicy little legs so you cannot run away."

What? My legs? Dear Lord! She tried reaching for her

whistle, but the monster ripped it away and threw it to the floor.

"You wiggle too much," he grumbled. "Me no like wiggly humans. Bad for my back." The monster thumped her over the head with something hard, and she fell to the floor. The twinkling ceiling lights momentarily faded to black, but when her vision rebounded, she wished it hadn't. The monster held a large blackened machete. He raised the weapon into the air, and in that moment, knowing she was about to die, or at the very least lose her "juicy little legs," the only thing she wanted was Máax. To see him one last time. Her gaze flashed to the mess of brawling immortals in search of her god, but what she found was simply too horrific to bear. Vampires were ripping out the Uchben's throats. The gods were decapitating the vampires. Blood, so much blood.

The ground began to shake with violent tremors. *Ten. Number ten.*

"Máax…" she gasped as she felt the monster's blade come down on her flesh.

───

The sound of explosions and screaming penetrated Ashli's mind, kicking her awake and immediately sending her into a panic attack. *Oh, shit! The monster!* She sprang to her feet and swiveled on her heels, hands defensively extended.

It took several moments to realize her legs remained intact and she was nowhere near that thing. Instead, she was inside a giant movie theater. Empty, dark, and creepy as hell. The sound of screaming once again grabbed her attention. She glanced at the screen horrified by the violence playing out. It looked like a clip from *Saving Private Ryan*, only set in a modern city. New York perhaps? Dead bodies, bloody and dismembered, lay over heaps of rubble. Buildings crumbled atop people fleeing with small children from whatever chased them.

Ashli held her hands to her mouth. What was happening?

"Nice. Isn't it?"

Ashli gasped.

A petite blonde wearing a referee outfit sat next to the spot where Ashli stood.

"Who the hell are you?"

"I'm Anne, but—"

"Where am I? And where did you come from?"

The woman rolled her eyes. That's when Ashli noticed the woman's wings. "And are those—"

"Wings? Yeah. But that's not important right now." She jerked her head toward the screen. "See that movie?"

Ashli nodded slowly.

"Well, it's not a movie. It's a glimpse of the future."

"Wow! That drink was so awesome!" Another woman, also with wings, appeared right out of thin air next to Anne.

Ohmygod.

The brunette waved. "Hiya, Ashli. Boy, you just cost me five cappuccinos."

Ashli lifted a brow. "Sorry?"

"I bet Anne that you wouldn't need a dry run, but she was right. You so blew it."

Anne sighed. "I'm always right, Jess. Get over it."

Ashli wasn't sure if she should run, faint, or cry. Maybe all three?

"So true, my friend. So true." The brunette, Jess, turned

toward Ashli. "Look. You get one shot. One. Otherwise, that"—she pointed to the screen as a young man's head was removed; his blood spurted in the air—"is our future."

Ashli didn't understand any of this.

"You have to fight, Ashli. Fight hard. You have it in you to turn the tides. So don't mess this up." Jess snapped her fingers. "Oh! And you will forget we ever had this conversation."

"But I don't understand. I was at that party and some monster grabbed me. Then I was here and—"

"We're already breaking the rules by intervening. We can't give you any more help or the Creator will say we welched on the bet. Then it's game over. So now it's time to get out there and make it happen."

"But I don't know what—" Ashli blinked and found herself lying on the floor, that decrepit, horrifying monster standing over her, drool trickling from his mouth.

Ew, ew, ew!

She screamed for Máax, but he was somewhere among the ocean of tangled, brawling bodies. She was on her own.

But then something Máax once told her played through her head: "We fight every step of the godsdamned way, every godsdamned moment, for every godsdamned inch. We never give up. We never give in."

That's right, Ash. Never give in. Her entire body filled with strength from some unknown place deep inside.

"Let me go," she croaked. She dug her nails into the monster's finger and then felt a burst of tingles.

The pulsing lights flickered across the monster's face. Euphoric. He looked utterly euphoric.

"Ashli!" Máax's sweet, sweet voice filled the air. He tackled the monster, and both men fell to the ground. Ashli watched as Máax pummeled the monster into unconsciousness. She stumbled back, gripping her throat.

Máax sprang up and scrambled to Ashli. "Oh, gods," Máax's warm, husky frame enveloped her. "Are you okay?"

She glanced down at the creature. He had a giant shit-eating grin glued to his face. "What is that?"

"That was a fucking Maaskab. How the hell did he get in here? And why in the devil's name is it so happy?"

The mob riot continued to rage all around them. The pulsing beat of the music and flashing lights made it look like some bizarre interpretive dance-off. Not one person noticed what had just happened.

"I am so sorry, Ashli. Please forgive me for leaving you unprotected." Máax ran his hand down her back and pressed her cheek to his bare chest. "Are you sure you're all right?"

She pushed back a bit to touch her neck. "Yeah. I'm fine."

"Thank the gods, I made you immortal," he said.

"He said he wanted to eat my legs. I'm not sure that would've helped."

Another body whizzed by, bumping into them. Suddenly, images of this scene turning into a bloodbath flooded her mind. Was it a premonition? Similar to the dream she'd had right before her parents died? She didn't know, but dammit, this time she wasn't about to sit idly by and do nothing.

"For deities' sake," Máax groaned. "I need to stop this fight."

"No. *I* need to stop it." Again, Ashli remembered the whistle, and somehow she knew she needed to blow it. She spun in a circle, looking down at the ground. The monster had torn it off her neck, but it couldn't have gone far.

"What are you looking for?" Máax asked.

She caught a glimpse of the chain sticking out from beneath the monster's immobile body.

Ewww. Don't be a coward.

She reached down, pulled the whistle free, and dangled it in the air. "I'm looking for this."

"A whistle?" Máax said, clearly questioning her sanity.

She blew and once again felt a strange sensation pulse through her body and radiate out. Everyone froze in their tracks and the music stopped.

Suddenly, the entire crowd—deities, vampires, and Uchben soldiers—began laughing and toasting each other as if the knock-down, drag-out fight had never occurred.

She stared at the damned whistle in shock. How had she known to use it? And how the hell had it worked? "Ashli, where'd you get that?" Máax asked, astonished.

She shrugged. "Not really sure."

"Guess we can figure that out later. I think we're under attack." Máax cleared his throat. "Has anyone noticed my friend here?" he yelled, but everyone was too busy enjoying themselves.

Once again, Ashli blew the whistle to get their attention. "Hey!" All eyes were on Ashli. She pointed to the floor.

No one seemed all too shocked except for Brutus who pushed through the crowd.

"Shit." Brutus pulled a radio from his belt and directed all Uchben to their posts. "Everyone, please make your way to the back of the hall toward the elevators and stairs. You'll be safe in the underground shelter."

"Wait!" Cimil pushed her way forward. "I'm not letting one crusty little Scab rob me of my long-awaited victory."

"Cimil," Máax argued. "That is not important. The Maaskab are here. We must get our guests to safety."

She rolled her eyes. "That Scab is an army of one, bonehead. Roberto and his vampires exterminated the Maaskab over a week ago. You didn't think we'd lock up all the gods and let the Scabs have free rein, did you? I mean, I'm crazy, but not craaaazy."

Roberto appeared at her side. "It is true. We are amazaballs," he said stiffly. "Only a few got away, but we planned to hunt them later. Possibly for Easter. The older vampires are bored with eggs."

The crowd cheered and applauded wildly. Ashli guessed it was for the news of the Maaskab being exterminated, not for their creepy Easter plans.

Cimil took a bow. "There'll be time for lavishing me with ridiculous amounts of praise and gifts later. But for the moment, you may all show your gratitude by giving me my trophy!"

"You cheated." The man in the priest outfit stepped out of the crowd.

Ashli cleared her throat. "Everyone. Um . . . I saw the whole thing, and Cimil didn't cheat. I mean, yes, she made everyone look away, but she didn't grab any balls."

Cimil's tall vampire gloated. "In the last ten minutes, you mean."

"Uh—yeah. Sure," Ashli said.

"See! I won. The girl says so." Cimil flipped the priest the bird.

"Perhaps," the priest argued, "you did not steal any balls, but the momentary distraction gave you the advantage. You still cheated."

Mumbles of agreement erupted from the crowd.

Cimil sighed. "Okay. Perhaps my move was bit unsportsmanlike. I concede. We will have a rematch. By the way, does anyone else have the urge to perform an interpretive dance depicting the beauty of springtime? Or perhaps write a flowery haiku?"

A bunch of people raised their hands.

Cimil fell to the floor like a bag of wet cement, completely unconscious. Her vampire dropped to his knees. "Sweetheart? Sweetheart?" He gently slapped her cheeks and then placed his ear over her heart. "Cimil?"

Cimil grumbled and then slowly opened her eyes.

The vampire smiled with relief. "What happened, my love?"

Cimil sat up and rubbed her temples. "I don't know."

He helped Cimil to her feet. "Let's go find somewhere for you to lie down." The vampire walked the wobbly Cimil toward the exit.

"Wait." Cimil gripped his arm to steady herself. Her head whipped from side to side. "Other me?" She held her breath and listened. "Other me?" Cimil looked at her vampire. "Ohmygods, Roberto, she's gone! She's gone! We did it! We did it! We stopped the apocalypse!" Her two index fingers shot up in the air. "Victory, baby! Twice in one day!" Cimil started doing a strange two-fingered kind of disco dance.

"You no longer see her? At all?" the vampire asked.

"What's going on, Máax?" Ashli whispered.

"Your guess is as good as mine," he replied, just as

astonished as everyone else witnessing the spectacle. "Except on Wednesdays when my guessing is nearly infallible."

Cimil turned toward everyone. "It's over! It's over!"

Máax stepped forward. "Cimil?"

"The apocalypse isn't coming!" she sang out. "My dead self from the future has finally disappeared! It means that we are all going to live."

Máax shook his head. "You had a dead self from the future? And the apocalypse is over?"

"Yes!" Cimil clapped excitedly, hopping like a crazy cricket. "The Universe works in mysterious ways, my brother. Of course, if I had held the tournament last year as scheduled, we probably could have avoided this whole thing, but I forgot to put the event on my calendar—got tied up with that *Love Boat* marathon." Cimil sighed happily. "But now, all is right in the world again. And you may all go on to have your babies, get married, and live long, happy lives."

"What is she talking about?" Ashli stared at Cimil as did everyone else.

"I have no idea," Máax said. "Cimil, please tell us this isn't another one of your stupid jokes."

"Uh-uh. I'm serious as a stripper on a pole."

Everyone in the room grumbled.

"You're trying to tell us," Máax said, "that each of us has gone to hell and back, through months of torment and battles, sacrifices and worry, only to find out that this was the pivotal moment?"

Cimil grinned. "Sure. Why not?"

Groans and boos erupted in the ballroom.

Máax looked like he might actually take her head.

"You knew this was the answer the entire time, didn't you? And you lied about Ashli. You were playing me."

Cimil grinned. "You'll never know. But you had the time of your life, and don't even try denying it!"

More boos filled the room, and party snacks flew at Cimil's head.

She ducked and dodged. "What? Derailing an apocalypse is like an orgasm or finding a garage sale. You don't argue when they happen! You just say, 'Thank you.' Or you say"—she looked directly at Ashli and winked—"'Thank you, Ashli.'"

Was Cimil serious? Putting a stop to that spat had been Ashli's big moment? It all just seemed so...trivial.

Ashli looked up at Máax. "Is it really over? Just like that?"

"I believe so." Máax nodded cautiously. "However, after all of the drama and angst, it feels like we're missing a big bloody battle or a near miss with an A-bomb."

"Nope. I'm good. Drama and angst are completely overrated." She was about to tell Máax about her vision, but decided it wasn't important.

"Well, I suppose there's always next apocalypse," Máax said.

Ashli blinked. "How often do they happen?"

"Often enough, according to Cimil. But we don't usually cut it so close," he replied.

"Oh, goody. And I'm immortal so I get to do it again."

Immooooortal. Immooooortal. Nope. Still doesn't feel real.

"Hey. Put 'er there, Ash!" A blonde woman dressed as a referee angel held out her fist.

"Do I know you?" Ashli asked.

"Nope. This is just a random, congratulatory fist bump." She wiggled her fist, urging Ashli to take part.

"Uh. Okay." Ashli obliged, and the woman grinned, then disappeared into the crowd.

"That was weird. I could swear I've met her before," Ashli said to Máax who simply shrugged.

"This calls for drinks," slurred Belch.

The crowd buzzed with jubilation, everyone exchanging hugs and high fives. Except for Cimil—Ashli caught a glimpse of her being carried away by her vampire. They were mauling each other's lips.

"Cimil?" Máax's deep voice boomed across the room. "Where the hell do you think you're going? I'm not done with you."

"Neither am I." One of Máax's brothers, a really, really big man with long blue-black hair and shoulders the width of a tank, stepped forward. If looks could kill.

Her vampire set her down and then stepped in front of her. "Back off, Votan. I've got five hundred vampires here."

Votan, who was about as tall as Máax, was the sort of deity that made a person tremble just looking at him. "I've got ten thousand Uchben on base, two minutes from here."

Oh no. They were all going to fight again? *This is too much!*

"I have an army of fifty thousand who can sift here in one second," the vampire replied, his dark eyes flickering with lethal rage.

"Dammit." Ashli threw down her giant glass. "Enough! Can't we just have a moment of happiness? Just one? I thought I'd sentenced the entire planet to death. Then some icky monster tried to marry me shotgun style and wanted to eat my legs for the honeymoon. So if you all don't mind, I'd like to party now. No fighting. No negativity. Just party. Can we do that for one night? Please?"

There was a collective mumble of agreement.

"All right, then." Máax cleared his throat. "Everyone, Ashli is correct. We should celebrate. And as for Cimil, I'm sure she is aware that she will have to answer for her crimes and does not plan to run. Isn't that right, Cimil?"

Cimil nodded from behind her large man. "Yep! I'll be there with amazabells on." She snorted. "Get it? Amazabells!"

No one laughed.

Cimil shrugged. "Yes. I'll bring Zac. And don't forget yourself, Máax and Chaam. Ya'll got warrants out, too!"

"What?" Ashli looked at Máax.

Máax grumbled something under his breath. "I will report to prison in the morning. In the meantime, I suggest we all do as my mate has asked. It is time to celebrate. The apocalypse is over. Brutus, get this Scab out of here. Belch, get back to the bar. And you, I forget your name, start the music."

Nineteen

⁓

"Shall we?" Máax held out his hand to Ashli, hoping and praying she might accept. He knew that he had no right to hope for her forgiveness after everything he'd done, but that did not mean he didn't want it, need it. And now, more than ever, he wished he could travel back in time and somehow make things right with her. *No, you fool, you did the right thing. And the proof is standing here before you.*

Yes. Ashli was alive. Alive and safe. The apocalypse was over. It was everything he could ever hope for, and if he ended up entombed for an eternity for repeatedly breaking the gods' sacred laws, then so be it. It was a small price to pay for the woman he loved.

Ashli stared at his hand, her turquoise eyes flickering with conflict.

"Please?" he said. "Just give me this one evening, and then I promise to leave you be." *Forever.*

"What's with the warrant—"

"One evening," Máax insisted. "A few hours of your time, and then I am out of your life for good." He said the words, and while part of him meant them, he knew a much larger piece of him would go insane without her.

"You really mean it?" she asked.

Was that disappointment flickering in her eyes or disbelief?

"Tomorrow I will be imprisoned for my many crimes. And while I'd like to believe my brethren will take mercy on me, I am doubtful. Punishment is mandatory when our laws are broken, regardless of the reason."

"Oh." Ashli looked down at her feet. "How long will you be put away?"

He was tempted to lie and protect her feelings, but that did not feel like the right course of action. "Oh, you know, forever. But let us dance first. Then we may talk all you like."

She hesitated. "I can't handle being around you, Máax. The things you did—"

"You are the one who called a temporary truce among us all this evening, were you not?"

She nodded and pasted on a smile. "Okay."

She slid her hand into his, and he immediately felt that sensation he could not fully articulate with simple words. Her touch felt like being home. It made him feel complete and loved and grateful. It made him acutely aware that he never wanted to let her go.

He dipped his head and kissed the top of her hand, enjoying the feel of her supple skin on his lips, before he led her toward the dance floor in the corner of the giant ballroom. With his overly sensitive hearing, his ears plucked out the whisper from the crowd. The Uchben and vampires, his brethren and their mates, everyone said the same thing: "He's going to be entombed for eternity. It doesn't seem fair."

No, it was not. But who said life was fair?

Dancing with Máax had been a mistake, and Ashli knew it the moment that she took his hand. Her entire body lit up like a naughty lighthouse. And through her torment of wildly mixed emotions, a profound clarity broke through the haze: she still wanted him.

Yes, even after he'd lied to her. Or acted like an arrogant, supercharged Cro-Mag who thought he could get his way simply by speaking.

But when he touched her, she couldn't help feeling something for him. That something was everything. *Stupid jerk!*

Had she meant that for him or for herself?

She didn't know, but when he took her in his arms and began moving her body against him to the sultry rhythm of the music—some sort of sexy, modern mix with a melodic voice and a hint of a country twang—well, she couldn't help but melt.

"What is this music?" she asked.

Máax continued moving, holding her close. "Not sure. But my sister, the Goddess of Forgetfulness, is DJing tonight. Always makes it difficult to determine the song."

"You're joking, right?" She looked at the statuesque woman standing in the glass DJ booth with her long golden hair in pigtail braids, wearing a pair of white go-go boots and metallic-silver micromini with matching top. A young guy with a blue faux hawk, wearing a Club M-Brace T-shirt, stood at her side.

"Joking about what?" Máax asked.

"That your sister, the Goddess of Forgetfulness, is DJing?"

"What are you talking about?"

Ashli laughed. "I get it. She's the one who makes everyone forget? You're funny."

"I am?"

"You are joking, right?"

"About what?" Máax looked down at her with his sunglasses-covered eyes.

"About your sister, the Goddess of Forgetfulness." Máax still looked confused. "Oh, never mind." Suddenly, Ashli forgot what she was talking about and lapsed into a state of bliss. Touching Máax felt so damned good. Seeing him was even better.

"So, my dear Ashli, now that all is set right in the world. What do you plan to do with the rest of your life?"

Damned good question.

"I'm not really sure," she said. "Guess I haven't had a lot of time to think it through." Before they had been kidnapped by vampires from her new home in Tulum, she'd been hoping to start a new life with Máax. She'd been hoping they might live happily ever after, free from the past.

Uh. Yay. Good luck with that. You'll be having nightmares for the next century. Especially about that horrible monster. She still couldn't believe that had happened. Why had he chosen her out of everyone there? How had she managed to fend him off?

Put it on the list of disturbing things to figure out.

"You'll have all the time in the world now. Not to mention, you have plenty of people here to guide you in the ways of immortality."

Immortal. Immortal. Immortaaaal. Nope. "I guess, but I can't stay here, sponging off your brother."

Máax chuckled. "Sponging? Is that what you call being at my brother's home?"

"I guess."

"You're a guest, Ashli. You can stay as long as you like. Kinich wants for nothing. Like all gods, he has enough money to buy a small country, perhaps two. So do you, for that matter."

Ashli knew her mouth hung open like a complete fool. "I'm not some charity case, Máax. You can't give me money."

Again he laughed. "Give? Give you money? I promise you, my dear Ashli, that the money in your name has nothing to do with me, barring the fact that I asked our best Uchben investor to manage your account. And trust me when I tell you that he charges a pretty penny. You've been gifted nothing from me."

Ashli nodded, trying to digest. "Exactly how rich am I?"

"Not as wealthy as I; however, I've about a seventy-thousand-year head start."

"You mean, what, like a million dollars?"

He laughed toward the ceiling. "Oh, my dear Ashli, you are so charming."

She slapped him on the shoulder. "Don't make fun of me!"

"I'm not making fun; I am enjoying your innocence, your beautiful sweet, naivety."

Ashli stopped moving. "Máax?"

"What?" He peered down, that charming smile now clearly on display. So, so charming. It boggled the mind.

"Are you capable of answering any question without behaving like a smug dork?"

"Dork?" He laughed.

"Yes . . . dork."

He rubbed his stubbled chin. "I do believe that is the first time I've been called such a name. I find it moderately offensive, but shall let it slide given you are my mate, and I love you more than life itself."

Love. He'd said he loved her more than life itself.

His words hit her panic button. "Don't, Máax." She jerked herself from his warm, comforting grip.

Máax reached for her and pulled her back. "Don't what?" he whispered in her ear. "Don't love you?"

Yes. No. Dammit. Maybe. "You have no right—"

"I have every right. You were born to be mine. And you wish to deny me the right to say how I feel, to speak the truth?"

"You want to talk about the truth, Máax? Do you?" she hissed. "I'm too afraid to be with you. I'm afraid you'll hurt me."

"I know," Máax replied.

"You know?"

He nodded. "Remember? I can feel your emotions. We are bonded. Which is probably the reason we become so volatile when together. But yes, I feel your fear of me. Of everything. What I cannot determine is how to rescue you from it."

"Rescue me? Is that what you really think I need from you?" She couldn't believe him.

"Of course. I am a—"

"May I cut in?"

Both she and Máax stopped dancing and directed their attention to the man standing before them. Brutus. He now wore a tux, and with his cropped dark hair and husky, muscular build, he looked like the kind of man a woman would appreciate for simply making an effort, although the tux was not in his comfort zone.

"Sure, Brutus, I'd love to."

Máax growled.

"Don't." She pinched his arm.

"Did you just pinch me?" Máax scowled.

"Yes. Now back off."

A moment of brisk silence passed before Máax dipped his head. "As you wish. I'll be in the men's room, removing my paint. It is making my skin itch."

"Fine." *The outrage! Rescue me? Fix me? Save me! How about respect me. Treat me as an equal?*

Máax stepped away and Brutus stepped in.

She pasted on a smile and leaned forward. "You do know he's going to kill you for doing that, don't you?"

Brutus wiggled his brows. "It's worth it. Besides, you looked like you were about to detonate. Thought you might need a moment."

Was she that transparent? "Thanks."

For the next few minutes, Ashli danced with Brutus and focused on calming down. That damned volatility again. Máax created a chemical reaction in her brain. Any fear or negative emotions seemed to magnify.

The song was almost over when someone tapped her on the shoulder. "May I cut in?" Sentin stared down at her as if she were a yummy human treat.

Yikes. "Ummm, I guess?"

"One dance, asshole. After that she's mine for the next two songs," Brutus barked.

Sentin laughed, but not in a happy way. "We'll see."

Ashli took Sentin's hand, feeling a bit awkward. The rudeness between these men was a bit much.

He shuffled her away from a glaring Brutus who now stood at the edge of the parquet dance floor.

"I know I'm new to all this," she said, "but are all men so..."

"Manly?" He winked. "No. Just me. Especially in bed."

Okay. She mentally scratched her head during the remainder of the song. By the last note, there was Brutus pulling her away. "My turn."

Sentin grunted in protest, but Brutus ignored him.

Ashli had just about had it. Really, what was with these guys? Why were immortal men such barbarians?

"May I cut in?"

"Me, too!"

Máax's brothers, the drunk bartender and the one with the giant headdress, were standing there, salivating. That guy in the Maaskab outfit, Andrus, was back, too.

What in the world?

"Take a fucking number." Brutus twirled her quickly and smiled.

Ashli stopped moving. "Brutus. What's going on?"

"What?" He shrugged.

"Why is everyone treating me like the last scoop of ice cream?" She felt seriously freaked out now.

Brutus smiled. "Because there's something about you, Ashli. Something wonderful."

She stepped back. Okay. Strange. The pack of rabid men were right there again.

"What do you want?" Brutus growled.

"Her. We want her, so step aside."

"Guys! Please. No more fighting. Just stop."

Brutus's lethal gaze softened. "She's right. My apologies. Sentin, you should dance with her."

"No. No. I am the one who should apologize; I was behaving rudely to all of you. Brutus, you should finish your dance with Ashli, then Andrus, then K'ak, and then Belch."

"No," objected Andrus. "I will go last. I insist. Besides, I really just wanted to ask for some advice. It can wait."

The men began to argue once again about who should go last. What were these guys on?

Ashli felt herself being pulled away the moment that fists started flying.

"Máax?"

"Let us get you out of here." Máax had taken off his gold paint already. How? Had he run through a car wash?

"What's going on? Why are they fighting like that?"

"I have absolutely no idea," he replied.

She followed his lead out to the parking lot. "Where are we going?"

"To a hotel for the evening. From there, I will make some calls and try to figure out the issue before I must turn myself in in the morning."

A hotel? With him?

"Uh-uh. No way." She pulled her hand away.

"I could take you back to Kinich's home, but I suspect that they will be at your door within the hour."

"Maybe I should go home to Mexico," she said.

"If you wish. But not until morning."

Stubborn goat.

"Fine, but you're not staying with me in the room."

"You won't even know I'm there."

Ugh.

Forty minutes later, they pulled into the luxury spa and resort in Sedona. Máax had never stayed there, but he'd asked Penelope, his sister in-law, for a recommendation. His plan was simple. He might not have an eternity to be with Ashli, but he'd settle for one night. One night of holding her. No, it would not be enough, but if that was all he could get, he'd take it.

Ashli shut off the engine. "That was fun. I've never driven a BMW."

"Yes. Kinich has quite the collection of cars, but I selected this one for the tinted windows, given I drove it to the event myself."

"I can see how that might come in handy when one is invisible," she said.

"Or painted in gold."

She snickered. Damn he loved her smile.

She ran her hands over the steering wheel. "So what's the plan?"

"You check in. I will make some phone calls and figure this out. I only wish I had not committed to turn myself in tomorrow."

She sighed. "How long will you be gone?"

"Forever. As I told you earlier."

Her head snapped in his direction. "I thought you were kidding."

"No," he said.

Ashli's beautiful, delicate face turned a pallid shade of mocha. "But what did you do?"

He didn't answer immediately. "I do not wish to lie or conceal the truth, so I simply prefer to say that I did what I felt was right."

"Are they really going to send you away forever?" Ashli appeared to be genuinely distraught, and he had to admit, it made him feel . . . loved.

"The laws are quite clear, and though a unanimous vote can modify the laws, I am certain my sister Fate will block such a move."

"But why?"

"She is angry at us. It is a long story. One I do not care to recount." Honestly, he wished he'd not sworn an oath to keep his sister's secret. The temptation to throw her under the bus and save his own ass was far too great now. But he was determined not to be that sort of man. It was one thing to lie or break a promise to save another, but to save himself? That would make him a selfish, greedy bastard.

Ashli looked out through the windshield, her eyes tearing up. That was the one thing he'd hoped to avoid. In fact, he hadn't thought about it, but what was to become of Ashli once his punishment was handed down? Her bond with him would prevent her from moving on.

Yes, I will ask my other sister to remove Ashli's memories of me. She will have a chance to find some semblance of love. Although it would not come close to the love they could have shared.

As for Máax, he'd already decided that he didn't want to forget Ashli. He would cherish his memories of her for eternity. He would never let her go, he would never move on. He simply didn't want to.

"Will you be put to sleep?" she asked.

"No. I will be awake, but entombed and powerless. But this is not your concern."

"Not my concern," she repeated in a whisper and then pinched the bridge of her nose. "Máax, this is horrible. Why didn't you tell me?"

"Truthfully, it was not important. To me, anyway. I knew this was coming even before I met you. Then, I suppose, I was distracted by saving you and preventing the apocalypse," he paused, "getting you to forgive me for lying."

She sighed. "Are you sure? I mean, there has to be a way to change this."

"You are not so anxious to rid yourself of me, after all?"

She shook her head. "I guess not. But—Christ, Máax. You should've told me."

"Perhaps. But what would it have changed?"

She shrugged. "How can you be so calm?"

"Ashli, have you not learned by now that there are no guarantees? We have this moment, and this moment alone. And in this moment, I am here with the woman I love. Tomorrow brings another battle."

One he knew he'd lose.

He exited the vehicle and opened the driver's side door for Ashli. "Are you all right?"

"No. Not really." She slid from the car, long legs first. He loved the way she looked in her tiny little white toga dress. She was the most beautiful woman in the world. Every damned silky tanned inch of her. Of course the men would want to fight over her. Although that bit back at the party was rather extreme. He had no clue what was going on.

He stepped to the side and closed the door, but instead of walking toward the reception area, she leaned against the car and folded her arms. "This plan is never going to work."

"Of course it will; I have made a reservation under your name. I will follow you to the room."

"No. I mean, you and me sharing a room.

"Why is that?" he asked.

"Because the only thing I can think about is kissing you. While naked."

"I see you still wear the necklace I gave you, so I think that might be arranged."

Ashli shook her head and sighed. Well, of course he would answer that way. *Men.* But didn't he get it? She didn't want to want him. Especially not now. He'd be gone from her life forever, and she seriously doubted she'd ever get over the loss. If she slept with him, it would make it impossible to forget him. Impossible.

You're already in knee-deep. Sleeping with him won't make any difference.

It won't help.

The irony was that as wounded as she felt about what he'd done, she was beginning to see the logic—he had saved her. And now, she understood there was a sacrifice on his part to do so. He'd lied, and it chafed him to do it.

Why did everything need to be so complicated? And heartbreaking? "Are you sure? Absolutely sure they won't let you go?"

"Quite," he replied.

Ohmygods, this is awful. Awful. How can this be happening?

"Do you really love me?" she asked.

"Quite."

Gods, she loved him, too. And now she was going to lose him? Forever? "Then I want one night with you."

She found herself pushed against the side of the black sedan in the dark parking lot. His body was all heat and hardness.

"Are you sure?" he whispered in her ear.

She placed her palms on his smooth, muscular chest. "Yes."

His lips covered hers, and she felt the prickly roughness of his stubble against her mouth, contrasted by the silkiness of his lips and tongue. He took his time kissing the corners of her mouth, softly biting her lower lip, sliding his tongue over hers. But that wouldn't do at all. What she really wanted was hot and hard and explosive.

Knowing he wore not a stitch, she slid her hands down his chest, savoring the rigid currents of his abdomen, until she reached her prize. He was rock hard. She leaned her body into him, massaging gently. He released an exquisitely male groan and then pressed her more firmly against the car, using his entire body to hold her in place. His sultry kiss turned into feverish lust. His breath came hard and heated from his mouth, and his warm hands slid under her dress, gripping her hips.

"Gods, Ashli, what you do to me."

No. What he did to *her*! She was about to show him.

She moved her arms up and around his neck, wanting to feel her breasts against his chest. She wanted to feel everything against him. He grabbed her legs and slid them around his waist. She felt his erection prodding her through the thin fabric of her panties. She was already so close, she could barely stand it.

"What the hell?" a strange voice rang out through the lot behind her.

"Shit." She gasped. It was the security guard.

Máax immediately dropped her legs.

"Lady, I don't know what the hell you were doing there—goddamned strangest thing I've ever seen—but take it somewhere else." The security guard walked around the car to her side.

Ashli heard Máax chuckle lightly in her ear.

Oh, God, this had to be the single most embarrassing moment of her life. Some guy spotted her with her dress hiked up, making out with an invisible man.

"It's a new kind of yoga. The . . . I love myself yoga." She wrapped her arms around herself and pretended to be kissing the air in front of her.

Again, Máax chuckled, but she didn't dare smack him.

"Sure, lady, whatever." The guard waited.

She smiled awkwardly and made her way inside to the reception area and registered. Apparently, Máax had reserved the honeymoon suite.

The moment she had her key in hand, she headed straight for the room. She knew Máax followed closely; his vibe was in the air, buzzing all around her. She slid the keycard into the lock and popped open the door. Máax pushed her inside and slammed the door shut.

She felt his hot mouth over hers and his hands quickly pulling up her dress.

He pushed her against the wall with his body, and in the dark, her mind filled in every blank: how he looked, the expression on his face, the hard lust in his eyes. It was as if she could see him through her senses. He cupped her breasts through her white lace strapless bra and massaged forcefully, grinding himself against her. No. She couldn't wait one second longer. She pushed him back just slightly, unhooked her bra, and kicked off her heels.

Máax quickly slid down her panties and had her up against the wall again. She wrapped her arms around his neck and her legs around his waist.

"Are you ready?" he asked, his voice gruff.

She'd never been so ready. "Yes. Yes. Ohmygod, yes."

He positioned himself at her entrance and thrust forward with one sharp movement, sliding deep inside her. His groan matched her own. His size and length created an erotic mixture of friction and pressure. She could feel every inch of him inside, pulsing and throbbing.

"Ohmygod, you feel incredible," she panted.

He pulled out and thrust his hips sharply forward again, repeating with a savagely brisk rhythm and equally savage grunts. His mouth ravaged her lips and neck and the tops of her breasts, moving at a frantic pace.

"I cannot hold on much longer." His voice was gravelly and sensual.

She had to admit the thought of him coming put her one thrust from tumbling over the edge. She gripped his shoulders firmly and moved her body against his, meeting him thrust for thrust.

Then she felt it happen, that coiling tension concentrated into one single point at her core. Before she could stop, it exploded, releasing crushing waves of wicked, erotic pulses. He leaned forward, pushing his thickset length into her, as deep as her body would allow, triggering another turbulent explosion. He released a loud, throaty groan, his entire body rock solid for several moments while he spilled inside her.

Without releasing her or pulling out, he carried her to the bed and lay her down beneath him. He began pumping himself, sliding with a leisurely rhythm, between her thighs. He showed absolutely no signs of flagging.

"Gods, Ashli, you are so beautiful, so sexy."

She covered his mouth with hers. No. She didn't want to talk. Then she might have to face the fact that being with him this moment was possibly the most rapturous, blissful moment of her life. All mixed with the kind of profound emotional connection only heard of in fairy tales.

Oh, crap. I really, really love him.

Dammit!

She let out slow breath and threaded her fingers into his hair. *There will be time for thinking later, you idiot. Right now, just be with him.*

She rolled him over and straddled him. The only thing missing from this moment was being able to look into his eyes. If only she could see him for real.

"I bet you're the most beautiful man on the planet," she said appreciatively. She felt his hands on her breasts and his hips prompting her to move faster.

"Not nearly as beautiful as you are, and tonight, I intend to worship every single inch over and over again."

"I hope I can keep up." She grinned.

He flipped her onto her back again and slid inside her. "I've never been with another woman, but the seventy-thousand-year wait for you was worth every moment of torture, Ashli. You've already exceeded every expectation."

Seventy thousand years? For her?

He kissed her hard and pushed deep inside, igniting her once again.

The next morning, Máax looked at Ashli's beautiful naked form snuggled next to him. He could not believe how perfect they were together. The way their bodies moved in unison, the way her soft sighs signaled what she liked and when she was ready for more. The way her soft hands pressed into his shoulders or ass when she wanted it hard. She probably had not realized yet that her immortal body was able to do things a human shell could not—go all night with a god, for example. They made love fifteen times, eighteen if he counted bringing her to orgasm with his tongue. Twenty if he counted the two times they'd showered and she had slid him between her soft, juicy lips, sucking him until his eyes literally rolled.

But now that he'd had this taste of her, of her love for him, he knew there was no way he'd settle for letting her go. He could not face the thought of an eternity without her, she without him. There had to be a way.

You know what you must do, then.

Yes. He could make things right for him and Ashli. Maybe. But it meant exposing the secret he'd sworn to keep. Yes, breaking his promise, betraying his sister would make him a liar for a second time in his existence. But so be it. This was no longer about saving his own ass; it was about saving Ashli from immeasurable heartbreak, too. It took last night to make him realize the truth.

He chuckled softly to himself and beamed down at her. *And the human teaches the old god a new trick.*

He wrote her a quick note and deposited it on the pillow next to her. "I will make this right, my love. I promise." He kissed her on the lips and savored their warmth.

"I love you, Máax," Ashli mumbled and then rolled over.

He smiled. "And I love you."

Yes, perhaps the end of the world had been avoided, but things were about to get ugly. He wasn't going down without a fight.

Ashli violently tossed and turned in her sleep. She dreamed of Máax falling into a dark pool of water. Over and over, he screamed, begging for her to save him. She grabbed at piles of ropes, but they were too short or too weak to hold any weight. "Ashli! Ashli! Help me!" he repeatedly yelled.

"No!" Ashli opened her eyes and sat up in the empty, cold bed.

"Máax?" The air in the room lacked his delicious scent and the strange energy that circulated about when he was near.

She slid from the sheets and checked the enormous bathroom—a complete mess from their crazy, wild sex. They'd had fun on the counter, in the shower, in the bath, and on every other surface available to them. It had been a night like no other because Máax had ignited something powerful inside her. A renewed sense of passion for life, something she'd never dreamed possible.

"Máax?" Perhaps he'd gone out for coffee and pastries. She'd bet this place had a really nice café because there was no possible way he'd leave without saying good-bye. Not after last night. Not after they'd finally clicked in a way that left her breathless merely thinking about it. Not after they'd somehow managed to channel all of that emotional intensity between them into the most rapturous, sinful lovemaking that it could only be described as a union of two souls. Transformational.

In fact, she'd already made up her mind to fight for him. Yes. She'd go see that crazy sister of his, Cimil. There had to be a price for this freedom. In her bones, she knew a solution existed, and she wasn't going to let him go down without a fight.

"Máax?"

She sat down on the bed, a cold thought coating her like a sheet of ice. What if he hadn't gone out for coffee? What if he'd already left to turn himself in without saying good-bye?

Had last night simply been a desperate man's attempt to sow his divine oats?

She threw on her clothes, grabbed her purse and heels, and headed out to the parking lot.

"No. Please . . . no." The car was gone. He'd left without saying a word and had even taken the car.

How could I have been so stupid?

Twenty

——

One day later

Why won't they leave me alone? Ashli covered her head with a pillow to block out the voices outside her door, but it did very little. They were so damned loud.

"Has she spoken to anyone yet, Brutus?" asked a woman.

"No. And she will not move from the bed or eat," Brutus replied.

The woman sighed. "What do you expect? Her heart's been broken. Dammit, Guy! What the hell is wrong with you people?"

"We are not people," said a male voice.

"Don't start with me," she said. "You know what I meant. This is lame. Lamer than lame. You need to fix this."

"I cannot, my love." The man's deep voice reminded

her of Máax. "Our laws are constructed in such a way as to avoid any possibility of loopholes. Otherwise, the laws are meaningless; my brethren are much too conniving and devious to not twist them to their advantage."

"My turn to stand guard!" said another male enthusiastically. Was it Sentin?

"I just arrived," said Brutus. "Your turn is tonight. Now leave."

"Why don't you make me—"

"Boys!" responded the woman. "You will both leave; you're acting crazy, and I'm sure the last thing in the world poor Ashli needs is pair of feral puppies lapping at her feet."

"But—"

"Go!" she commanded. "I will call you if she needs anything. You, too, Belch and K'ak!"

Had she really called someone cock? What a very strange name.

That other deep voice boomed right through the door. "You heard Emma, off with you, now. Don't make me ask again."

Grumbles and snarls seeped into her room.

"Oh, thank gods," said the woman, "I thought they'd never leave. What's gotten into them, anyway?"

"Hell if I know," said the deep voice. "But Ashli seems to be a magnet for every eligible bachelor within a ten-mile radius. Luckily, we're out in the desert, otherwise we'd be overrun."

"Something's not right," she said. "I can feel it."

That's exactly how Ashli felt. Add to that, her heart, her soul, her everything. She could barely breathe. How could life be so cruel? She'd finally found a reason to believe in life again, only to have it snatched away. Why had she been so stupid and reckless to fall in love with Máax? Why?

She couldn't go through this again. After her parents died, it was years of hell, simply to get to a place where she could function like a normal human being. Not that she'd ever truly recovered from the loss. But then Máax had given her this tiny glimpse of who she once was, and of a life filled with love. But as quickly as it had come to her, it was gone. She couldn't face that pain again.

There was a soft knock on the door. "Ashli?"

"Go away!"

Ugh! If only she could make things move faster. She just wanted to get the hell away from that place. But after the incident at the hotel with Máax, she'd realized she didn't have ID, credit cards, or money. She'd taken a cab back to this house and borrowed money from one of the guards. Then she asked Sentin to track down her accountant so she could have access to her funds. (And so she could thank him or her for whatever miracle they'd performed with her money over the last twenty years.) Sentin was only too eager to help, of course. In any case, her new life wasn't to be delivered until early evening. The moment it arrived, she'd be out of there.

The door opened. "Hi, Ashli. I know you don't want visitors, but I'm Emma."

How many people slash nonpeople lived there? It was impossible to keep up! "Are you a god, a vampire, or other?" Ashli poked her head out from underneath the pillow to take a peek.

The woman smiled and made a little wave. "Howdy." She had long red hair and bright turquoise eyes. She appeared to be in her midtwenties. "I'm an other...mostly human, though. Oh! I've also taken a trip to the other side, not the dead side, but the god side, thus our matching eyes. And we're both mated to gods; mine is the big guy with the blue-black hair, Votan. But he goes by Guy now."

Ashli had to admit that she was intrigued, but her heavy thoughts didn't make her feel social at the moment. "Not to be rude, but what do you want with me?"

"Well," Emma said, "I'd like to think of us as sisters. And sisters help one and other."

Ugh! Why is everyone trying to be so nice and helpful! "I don't need help. I just need to be alone," Ashli grumbled.

"Ah. I see you're stubborn just like me." Emma grabbed her hand and squeezed. "But you and I are practically family, Ashli. And I am not leaving until you tell me what happened."

"If I tell you, then will you leave?"

"Yes," Emma replied frankly.

"Okay. Fine. He used me, Emma. Used me. He's getting locked away forever, and he doesn't care enough about me, his mate—whatever that really means—to fight. He didn't even have the decency to say good-bye. He just left me there at the hotel. I had to call a cab to get back here."

Emma wrinkled her nose. "Ouch. Are you sure? I mean, I don't know Máax well, but everyone who talks about him says he's the most loyal and noble of the bunch. Not that I would speak badly about Guy, my fiancé, but he's pretty damned sneaky."

"I'm leaving tonight," Ashli mumbled. "If you see Máax, please tell him..."

She was about to say "he's an asshole," but that somehow seemed so juvenile. He'd told her he loved her, used
her for one night, and then disappeared. Letting him
know how badly he'd hurt her would serve no purpose.
"Never mind."

"I wish you'd reconsider," Emma said. "Even if things
don't work out with him, you have people here who want
to get to know you. You're one of us now."

Like those crazy men hovering outside her door? "No.
I want to be alone. Try to forget this ever happened."

"I understand, but if you change your mind, I'll be here
for you." Emma was about to leave but stopped. "I know
it's difficult to trust a complete stranger, let alone befriend
one, but I would have given anything to have someone
help me navigate this strange, strange world. It would
have made my life a whole hell of a lot easier, including
accepting the whole immortality thing."

*Immortal. Immortal. Immortaaaal. Nope. Still not
real.*

"I guess what I'm saying is," Emma added, "once
things shake out with Máax, good or bad, I'll be right here
for you."

"I appreciate it, but I'm not coming back. I just want to
forget all of this. Máax, the gods, everything. I just want
to move on."

Yes. She was going to run away and hide. So what?

Emma smiled. "The Universe has a way of turning
things around. You just have to have faith."

Faith. Faith. Faaaaith. Nope. Not feelin' it.

"Good luck to you, Ashli."

Luck. Not feeling that, either. "Thank you, Emma."

That evening, Ashli didn't look back as the black town

car took her away from that bizarre place. She wasn't sure where she was heading. She didn't want to return to her new home; she had no real family or friends, but it felt good to be completely alone again.

Just the way I like it. Less complicated, no one else to worry about, and— Ashli felt those invisible strings pulling her back to Máax. *No! You're not doing this!*

Okay, she would go as far away as she could and hope that might do the trick. But what if it didn't? What if the bond between them never disappeared? She wouldn't be able to live like this. Ashli held back the tears. *Oh, please, please, please, Universe. Help me get out of this.*

Her mind quickly latched on to thoughts of Máax. How when they'd first met, she'd been suffering from horrible dreams of death and how much she missed her family. But then, there'd been those other dreams, too. The steamy ones of the faceless man who made love to her on the beach, who touched her body as if worshipping a priceless treasure. Now she knew that the man was Máax. He'd been right when he'd told her their connection was something created by the Universe. She felt it now. She supposed she always had, though she simply didn't understand it. That's why losing him felt like her soul was being ripped in two.

I can't take this. I can't.

Now near the Phoenix airport, the car pulled up to a stoplight, and Ashli glanced over at the telephone pole covered with thick layers of multicolored flyers. Her eyes gravitated to a big bold *M.*

Ohmygods. That's it. The answer to her prayers fell right on her lap.

"Excuse me, sir?" she said to the driver. "Can you take me to East Camelback Road?"

Máax paced back and forth across the floor of his cell, wondering why Ashli hadn't come to see him. It had been well over a day since he'd left her and turned himself in.

Perhaps she feels too nervous? He could not blame her. While he could not tell Ashli what was to come, nor did he want to give her false hope, he would do everything possible to change his fate. And hers. He loved her. More than anything. And now he understood that loving her meant not just saving her, but saving himself, too. They were meant to be together. And while this was no revelation, he hadn't really thought things through before. Perhaps it was a tribute to his age—after seventy thousand years, one does become quite jaded—but being with her the other night made him see that he needed to follow his own advice and fight. He'd told her once that complacency was the devil, and he'd been right.

But why hasn't she come? He'd left her a note on the pillow that morning, telling her what he planned to do and that a car would be waiting for her. He'd received confirmation from one of the guards that she'd indeed arrived safely at Kinich's.

Just then Emma passed by, likely en route to see her ex-Maaskab grandmother—a long, long story—in the cellblock over. "Emma!"

"Máax. Hey." She wore a pink baby-doll dress and had her long red hair pulled into a ponytail. She was just starting to show and looked utterly radiant. He could only imagine how Ashli might look if he were ever so lucky to have her carry his child.

"Have you seen Ashli?" he asked. "It's been a day, yet she has not come to visit."

Emma's eyes widened a bit. "Didn't anyone tell you?"

Maledictus inferno. "Tell me what?"

"She left over an hour ago. A complete mess. I tried talking her into staying, but..." Emma sighed. "What the hell did you do, Máax? That girl's heart was shredded like confetti."

"I do not know what you mean."

"You deities never do," she replied.

"Emma, I speak the truth. I have done nothing but send her letters, telling her how much I miss her and love her."

Emma pondered for a moment. "Who did you give the letters to?"

Máax pointed to one of the guards standing in the doorway. "Timothy."

"Timothy? Who did you give Máax's letters to?" Emma asked the guard.

"Brutus, ma'am. He insisted that all communications should pass through him."

Máax felt his blood boil. *I will remove his eyelids for this!*

"Well, that solves that mystery, Máax, but why did you just..." Emma leaned in and whispered, "...Love her and leave her? And taking the car, Máax. Really? So not classy. Frankly, I'm shocked. You don't seem like that womanizing type. I get you're facing an insanely stiff sentence, but that's no excu—"

"I did not 'love her and leave her,' Emma. I left a note and sent a limo for her."

Emma had an uncomfortable, pained look on her face. "Oh no, Máax. She didn't get that note, either."

"Fuck! How is that possible? I left it right on the pillow next to her." He punched the glass wall, and his fist simply bounced off. "Fuck!"

"Calm down, Máax, I'm sure we'll find her so you can explain everything." She turned toward Timothy. "Can I have your radio?" Timothy handed it over. "Hey, guys, this is Emma. I need someone to track down Ashli."

A voice came over the radio almost immediately. "She's here with us. Arrived at Kinich's five minutes ago."

Thank the gods, she has returned. She must have realized I would never do that to her.

"That goddess brought her," said the male voice over the radio.

"What goddess?" Emma asked.

"Sorry, ma'am?" the voice on the other end said.

"You said a goddess brought her in," Emma clarified.

"I did?" the man said.

Emma's face turned pale. "Oh no. Ummm... is Ashli okay?"

"Ms. Rosewood," the man responded, "no longer remembers who she is. Or anything for that matter."

Máax felt the world spinning beneath his heels.

"Thank you," Emma said. "I'll be up to the house in ten. Keep her there."

"There must be some mistake," Máax groaned.

"I don't think so. She told me she wanted to forget you. Forget ever meeting you. I guess she got her wish."

Twenty-One

Ashli stood in the bathroom, staring at the face of a stranger in the mirror. The light brown skin and turquoise eyes seemed familiar somehow, but she had no memory of them.

"Ashli! Oh my gods!" A young redheaded woman, also with turquoise-green eyes, burst into the room.

"Who are you?" Ashli asked.

"Oh, dammit." The redhead looked at the strange, tall lady with blonde pigtails who'd brought her to this house. "What happened?"

The blonde shrugged. "I was sitting at Club M-Brace, going through my playlist for tonight when she walked in, demanding I make her forget Máax. Of course, I knew who she was and told her no, but then she forgot and asked again. Then again." She paused. "And again."

"So you wiped her memory? Really?" the redhead asked.

"I know better. The newly heartbroken are completely

irrational. But then she lost it and jumped me. Little bursts of something flew from her palms and triggered my powers. It was an involuntary reaction."

The redhead's eyes opened wide. "From her hands? Was it painful?"

The blonde shook her head. "It felt good. Really, really good."

"I don't have a clue, but we don't have time for this." The redhead covered her face and groaned. "Oh, gods, what a mess. Can you undo it?"

"I'm the Goddess of Forgetfulness, not the Goddess of Memory Recovery."

"Ashli?" The redhead looked straight at her. "What were you thinking?"

"Am I Ashli?" Honestly, she had no idea.

"Yes!" The redhead sighed loudly. "Oh, Ashli. What have you done?"

"I honestly don't know. So my name is Ashli? Really?"

The previous evening, Emma confirmed Máax's worst fears. But how had Ashli found his sister—what's-her-face—in the first place? What a damned mess. And if he ever got his hands on Brutus, he'd rip that blockhead's arms from his body.

Well, Máax had had enough of this *stercore de bovem* and was ready for his trial this morning. He needed this to be over quickly and to fix things with Ashli, not to mention actually *fix* Ashli. Yes, his freedom was paramount, and come hell or high water, he would get those damned votes to change the laws. He was not going down without a fight, even if it meant betraying one if his own.

Timothy knocked on the glass of Máax's cell. "Ready, sir?"

Máax nodded.

"Sir?"

Right. Timothy couldn't see him. "Yes, Timothy. Ready."

A short walk and elevator ride from the underground prison brought Máax to the Court of the Gods. It looked very much like one might imagine: At the head of the room, fourteen empty marble thrones sat behind a long stone slab table on an elevated platform with neoclassical Roman pillars to either side. An aisle ran the center of the room, between ten rows of stone-carved bench seats, and a solitary wooden chair (for the person on trial) sat toward the front.

Máax took his seat as did Cimil and Zac. They would both go on trial today, too, and they sat behind him in the first row. When Ashli entered, looking her usual ravishing self in a simple black dress, he felt his entire being illuminate. It was such a relief to see her face, to know she was near, even if she did not remember him. He took a deep breath and tried to remain focused; everything rode on his words today.

One of the Uchben guards announced the gods, and the packed room rose to their feet while the deities settled in.

Penelope, who looked like she'd just swallowed Bees' hat, took her seat toward the middle of the long table next to her husband Kinich. She wore plain jeans and a T-shirt, and her dark hair was pulled back into a neat braid. Kinich, who was standard deity size, also wore a no-frills outfit—jeans and a tee. Both looked like they were displeased to be there. Who could blame them? The two had gone through their own turbulence recently. They probably wanted to be at home in bed, enjoying the fact that the end of the world was not coming after all and their baby would be born into a life filled with an eternity of love.

The remaining gods took their places, and Penelope turned on her iPad with a heavy sigh. "I hereby open the proceedings against the deity known as Máax, who has been accused of violating the sacred laws of—dammit!" She threw down her stylus and scowled at Kinich to her side. "This is total bullshit! Why are we doing this? We all know Máax doesn't belong on trial."

Kinich reached for her hand. "Honey, we talked about this already."

"No! I talked this morning. You ignored me."

Kinich scratched his golden scruff. "I merely tried to explain that these are our laws. I created them to protect humans from our abuse of powers."

"Oh, I get it. Your giant bloated man ego doesn't want to admit that you made a mistake, is that it?" she fumed.

Kinich's turquoise eyes shifted to black. "N-n-no, honey. I just..."

"You just what? Want to see Máax disappear forever? All because he saved a few thousand Payal women, tried to stop the apocalypse by rescuing Ashli, and did a bunch of other nice stuff like killing an incubus, saving your sister Ixtab from being stuck inside a portal, and gods know what other selfless crap? Really?"

Kinich gnashed his teeth. "Our laws are—"

"Laws shmaws!" Penelope barked. "We're changing them. This is bull crap!"

"But—"

"But nothing," she interrupted. "You and I lead the

House of Gods; you and I are husband and wife." She cupped his cheek and lovingly gazed into his eyes. "Haven't you learned, baby, that there's nothing we can't do together? We're meant to change the world. And it's time for the gods to evolve."

Máax smiled. Penelope was a gods' send. Such a smart, smart woman. And a perfect match for his brother.

Fate rose from her seat at the end of the table in her belted little dress and white boots, looking like her usual snotty, uptight self. "Well, you need a unanimous vote to change a divine law, and you're not getting mine. Our laws have worked just fine for tens of thousands of years, and I see no need to change them simply because it's convenient."

She is so predictable. Well, here goes.

"Are you sure about that, Fate?" said Máax.

Fate glanced at him or the chair, he wasn't sure. "Of course I am."

"Because," he said, "our laws state that they can only be changed by a unanimous vote of all fourteen deities. You are not a real deity, are you?"

The room collectively gasped, and Fate's face paled. "I-I have no i-i-idea what you mean," she stuttered. Her eyes shifted from side to side.

"Fate?" Penelope said. "What's Máax talking about?"

Sitting behind Máax, Cimil raised her hand. "Ooh. Ooh. I know! Call me. Call me!"

Penelope looked at Cimil, then at Fate. "Fate?" But Fate looked at the floor. "Okay, Cimil... I call on you."

"Did I say something?" Cimil's eyes widened innocently. "I think it was Máax's turn to speak."

Penelope grumbled, "Máax? What's going on?"

"Don't you dare, Máax!" Fate barked.

"Fate is not a deity," he said. "She's a fake."

Ashli watched with fascination as the strange drama unfolded. The redheaded lady, Emma, had insisted she come to this trial this morning. Why? She didn't know. She didn't know a lot of things, actually. But she did know she'd gone off the deep end because this could not be real. The people who sat at the front of the room were a combination of surreal and beautiful, bizarre and scary. The men, all the height of basketball players, were the most gorgeous male specimens she'd ever seen and built like armored tanks. The women were ten times prettier than any Victoria's Secret model, but dressed in everything from summer frocks to beehive hats. The courtroom was also filled with a strange brew of individuals—more large, beautiful men (many in leather pants), soldiers in black who looked like mercenaries, and a few hundred women of all shapes and sizes standing in the back. But what boggled her mind most was how all eyes were glued to an empty chair . . . a chair that spoke.

I must be seeing things. And one might assume that would be enough to win the prize—an extended vacay in a pretty padded room, but oh no. This was like that Magic Bullet infomercial she'd just seen on television this morning. *But wait! That's not all. There's more!*

So what was "more"?

Ashli wanted that chair.

Yes. Wanted. And *not* as in, she wanted it for her dining room or kitchen. Oh no. She wanted it like a woman wanted a man. From the moment it spoke, she ignited and a strange frenzy of lust flooded every inch of her needy, crazy body.

If it's the last thing I do, I will sit on that chair and show it my naked body. Yes, something about the chair's voice engulfed her in a spell of seduction and temptation.

Yep. I've ingested shrooms. If only I could remember why. Drugs are so uncool. Dirty martinis on the other hand... I think I like those.

But regardless, she wanted that damned stinking chair.

The chair spoke again, and she held her breath as did everyone else inside the room, though she suspected it wasn't for the same reason.

"Fate," said the chair, "was born of divine origins, as were we all, but she is not divine, only immortal."

Fate, with her short white skirt, and bows and arrows, pointed at Máax. "Liar!"

Máax laughed with a deep, hearty chuckle. "Fate, this is your chance to come clean. I suggest you do so— perhaps the court will take mercy on you."

Fate's blue-green eyes narrowed. "I have no idea what you mean," she said innocently.

"So be it," he said. "Everyone, Fate cannot see one's fate, guide one toward their fate, or create fate. She has absolutely no powers and never will. She has been faking it all along, lying to everyone." That, in itself, was a punishable crime given that Fate had consulted on thousands of matters during summit meetings over the millennia. They had based many important decisions on her words.

"That's a lie!" Fate stood from her chair.

"Nope! No it's not. Fate is a lying, evil cow." Cimil clapped. "Why do you think I like her so much?"

"Shut up, Cimil!" Fate barked. "You crazy bitch."

Penelope held out her hands. "Whoa. Fate, is this true? You have no powers?"

Fate became very silent, but Cimil chomped at the bit to spill the tattletale beans. So she did. "According to my sources, Fate is a dud. A bad egg. The Universe has rejected her. In fact, she's no more powerful or divine than a regular old human, except that Fate will live forever."

"How do you know this?" Penelope asked.

"Well, that my friends, is the furry little dingleberry all its own, the rotten stench to be revealed shortly as I'm the next batter up. But if you want proof, simply ask Fate to show us her gift."

"That proves nothing!" Fate screamed. "K'ak still awaits his flagship gift. Zac just found his. Not having a gift does not mean I'm not a deity."

"So you admit you've been lying? You have no powers?" Penelope asked.

"I admit nothing. And may I remind you that I'm not the one on trial here. Máax is!" Fate huffed.

"Yes," Penelope agreed, "but for a law that's outdated, unjust, and should be changed."

"Well, you still need fourteen votes to change a sacred law," Fate pointed out, "and the way I see it, you're not getting it. With or without me."

Cimil raised her hand. "Ooh! Ooh! I've got the answer to that one, too!"

Penelope looked at Cimil with extreme apprehension. "Cimil?"

"Ashli is *numero* fourteen!" Cimil clapped wildly.

Now Máax was lost. "Cimil, you're not helping me. In fact, I was planning to leverage our sacred policy, which states that any law found to be impossible to execute or uphold shall be null and void."

Cimil made a pouty face. "But my angle is way sweeter! Come on! Give it a try. If my little romp through the village of Get the Fuck Out or Shut the Door doesn't satisfy your drama tooth, then we can always backpedal. Come on. Don't you want to hear my big news? Dontcha? Dontcha? Huh? Huh?"

"No. Not really," Penelope said.

A cold brick settled in Máax's stomach. What was Cimil up to? What had she meant about Ashli being number fourteen? "All right, Cimil. I'll play. Tell us your news."

"Say please!" Cimil popped her fist on her waist.

"Cimiiiil?" Máax growled.

"Okay! Hold your hookahs!" Cimil hammily cleared her throat. "Máax's bond with the Universe has broken, and his soul has now fully bonded to Ashli. Two lights, one soul. And as we all know from experience, once that occurs, all sorts of fun things happen—did I ever tell you about the time General DiConti was PMSing with Helena?" Cimil slapped her knee, laughing hysterically, tears forming in her eyes. "Oh, gods! He didn't know if he wanted to cry or boink her!" She clutched her belly. "Then there was Kinich who lived inside Penelope's body— Rarrr! Talk about kinky! Then Emma and Votan with their Vulcan mind melding—"

"Cimil. Enough," Máax interrupted. "Get to the point."

Cimil grinned, her turquoise eyes sparkling with giddiness. "From the moment Ashli met you, her light began pulling your power. She is now officially the Goddess of Love as it has always been destined to be."

Impossible. "Why do you think Ashli is the Goddess of Love?"

"Ask Ms. Forget-Me-Yes over there. Ashli popped her good."

All heads swiveled toward the Goddess of Forgetfulness who wore a short metallic-silver tank dress and white go-go boots, her blonde hair in Princess Leia spirals over her ears. "It's true. Ashli hit me with something. It felt pretty good."

"See!" Cimil pointed at him. Or the chair. He wasn't sure. "She inherited your gift of love. And once she learns to use her power correctly—'cause we all know how easily love can go sideways on ya—she's destined to do many great things for humanity. Personally, I'm hoping she can turn Valentine's Day into a global holiday. And rename it hump day. Wednesday doesn't deserve that title."

"But my powers have been taken away; I have none," Máax argued.

Cimil wagged her finger. "Uh-uh-uh. Your powers weren't taken away. We just fixed it so that you couldn't use them, but they remained inside you."

"But I am not the God of Love, I never was. I am the God of Truth," Máax said.

"Really now?" Cimil smiled. "Think carefully, Máax. Was it truth that drove you to come to our rescue over and over and over again? Or break our laws to help us and later take the punishment? Was it truth that got you to take an oath to Fate to keep her lie a secret? No. It was love, Máax, your love of your brethren. Truth was simply another way of expressing your love—being honest, keeping your word, those are all symptoms of love. Once you lost it, you started lying like a fiend."

"A fiend? I lied once," he protested.

"And broke your promise to me!" Fate barked.

"Shut up, Fate," Penelope said. "Or shall we call you, Fake?"

"I'm not a fake, I'm just…" She sighed and sank into her chair. "…Just not like you."

"So it's true," Penelope said.

"I had powers," Fate said, "at the very beginning, but then they vanished. I don't know why. I don't know what I did." She sobbed. "And there you were, all of you, complaining about your lives, how hard it was to be the Goddess of Suicide or the God of Death and War. Wah, wah, wah. You're all a bunch of spoiled rotten deities. You have everything. Some of you even have mates and children on the way." She pointed at Ashli. "And now that little bitch has the gift of love! I hate you all! I wish nothing but death and suffering on all of you!"

Cimil chimed in, "Shouldn't that be suffering and then death? It's really hard to suffer once you're dead."

"Cimil!" Máax screamed. "Be quiet!"

Cimil shrank into her chair, crossing her arms. "I save your ass, and that's the thanks I get?"

Máax turned toward Ashli who looked like she might keel over at any moment. "Ashli? Can you tell us if this is true? Do you have my gift?"

Ashli's gorgeous turquoise eyes seemed to glow against the backdrop of her light brown skin and her wild dark curls flowing past her shoulders. "I-I don't know. I mean, I didn't know that chairs could speak, let alone have magical powers of love."

Máax refrained from laughing. "You think . . . I'm a chair?"

Ashli shrugged. "You're not?"

He stood, walked over to her, and then reached out and touched her hand. Ashli yelped and jumped from her seat, scrambling back. "What the hell was that?"

"Ashli," Penelope said, "that's Máax. He's invisible."

Chest heaving, Ashli's head dropped, and she closed her eyes. Several silent moments passed while everyone waited for her to answer. Did she truly have the gift of love?

Ashli's body began to shake, and she laughed toward the sky. "Well, thank goodness for that. I know I've totally lost it, but I was really freaking out there when everyone said I'd mated with a chair."

Máax gently touched her arm. "No, my love. I am not a chair. A stupid asshole, yes, chair, no. And you are everything to me."

Ashli's eyes shifted from side to side. Clearly this was overwhelming her.

"Penelope," Máax said, "why don't you take a vote now, so that Ashli and I may be on our way."

Penelope looked at the faces stretching down the table. "Sure. Just as soon as Fake is removed to a holding cell."

The Uchben soldiers approached Fate, and she left quietly. Perhaps she had grown tired of hiding. Perhaps she was already plotting her revenge. Who knew? But it was time for the truth to be out. Máax had protected her secret for thousands of years. All because he pitied her, loved her. She was family. Still was. But it was time for Fate to accept her own fate and grow up. Just as it was time for himself and the other deities. But growing up is hard to do when everything is handed to you on a silver platter. The gods, himself included, needed a reason to evolve, a reason to be better. His reason was Ashli.

Penelope sat back down and grinned. "I don't even know where to start."

"Start at the beginning, Penelope," Kinich said lovingly and placed his arm around her shoulders. "We must change the laws, just as you said."

She glowed triumphantly. "Right."

Penelope took a vote to change the rules that governed the modification of their sacred laws. A unanimous vote by all fourteen gods would no longer be required. Ashli was the fourteenth vote to approve this change.

Next, time travel would no longer be banned or a crime, specifically for Máax. He would become their official traveler—the Keeper of Time Travel, although missions would need to be approved by a majority vote.

"And finally, Máax," Penelope said, standing from her chair, smiling with tears in her eyes, "I move to lift any and all punishments that have been cast upon you. Your powers will be restored—whatever remains, obviously—and your physical form returned to you." Penelope looked across the table. "All in favor?"

The gods raised their hands, smiles on every face.

"It is a majority vote." She burst out crying and turned to Kinich.

Máax took a triumphant breath. The air swirled around him, and his body surged with light, power, and strength. It was finally over. He won, and Ashli had saved him. She'd been the key all along.

There is no such thing as an accident. It was all meant to be.

Ashli stared at the chair, her mind spinning with so many questions. For starters, being near this *man* made her feel so safe, as if she were home. And strangely, it didn't bother her one bit that she couldn't remember anything. She felt so full of love. Who was he?

The air kicked up around them, and she expected someone, him, to appear.

Nothing.

"Why can't we see you?" she asked.

"I must return to the cenote for a new body. Will you come with me, Ashli?"

Was he kidding? As weird as it sounded, the only thing keeping her sane right now was him. "Can we bring the chair? I've kind of grown attached to it."

"Uh...sure, my love." An invisible hand reached out and dragged her from the rowdy courtroom. She didn't know where they were heading, but she didn't care. She'd never felt happier. *I think?*

Twenty-Two

⁓

Standing outside of the Court of the Gods under the warm winter sun, Ashli felt relieved to leave the strange place. That scene left her wondering why she would do something so silly as have her memory removed. Clearly, she needed her faculties to deal with...all that. Whatever that was.

And a goddess? Of love? They must be out of their minds. Máax had attempted to explain their world, how powers resided inside a deity but could be transferred from one being to another if they were connected. He told her how she'd changed his life and how they had spent the night together. He apologized a thousand times for leaving her like he had that morning. Not that she was mad, because that would require remembering. However, he said that the moment he realized what he had to do, it couldn't wait. He'd left her in order to expedite the trial, but he never imagined she wouldn't find his note.

"I love you, Ashli. And I will fix this. No matter how long it takes, I will make things right again." He threaded his warm hands through her hair and kissed her hard, sparking erotic images in her mind. Were they her memories or his? Máax explained how their bond allowed them to feel each other's emotions, how it connected their souls for all eternity.

She slid her hands around his waist and enjoyed the warmth of his naked body. She couldn't actually believe the guy just ran around without any clothes.

Nice. How cool was that?

The sound of a man clearing his throat caused Máax to abruptly break the kiss.

"Ah, Sentin. Thank you for volunteering to take us to the cenote," Máax said.

The man wore a dark suit and looked like he had just walked off a modeling runway. She recognized him as one of the men who'd been hanging around outside her bedroom door in the morning.

Sentin beamed down at her. "So. Goddess of Love, huh? Guess that explains why we are all so drawn to you, but I suspect I'd like you regardless."

"Give it up, vampire, she's mine." Máax's voice wasn't angry. More like extremely happy and confident.

The man's eyes looked a little sad. Poor thing.

"Would you like my chair?" Ashli pointed to it. It had seemed wrong to leave it behind, but now it seemed selfish to keep it. After all, she had an actual deity all to herself.

"Uh...sure. Thanks." The man nodded and looked at the empty space next to her. "Take good care of her for us, Máax."

"Always," Máax replied.

"Are you ready, Ashli?" Sentin reached out and latched on to Ashli's arm. Before she could blink, she found herself standing in the middle of the jungle.

"All right," Sentin said. "Here you are. Call if you need anything." The handsome man whisked away a tear and vanished into thin air.

"Wow," Ashli said. "That was amazing."

"Wait until you see this." Máax led Ashli to the edge of a large, dark green pool of water, its sides steep and about ten feet high. "It all began right here. At this very cenote."

She leaned over to get a better look. The hazy water buzzed with a strange energy. She could sense it in her bones. "What started?"

"This is the cenote where my brother, Votan—the first to find his happy ever after—met his mate. And now, we shall have ours."

"So what happens next?" she asked.

"Now I get a new body, and we start our new, happy life together. Wait here." He pecked her on the lips and jumped into the water.

"Wait! Where are you going?" But he was already gone.

Ashli stared at the water expecting Máax to resurface, but several minutes passed. Then five minutes. Ten minutes. Twenty minutes.

"Ohmygod." She paced along the edge of the enormous pool, biting her fingernail. Why hadn't he come out? Why?

She peered over the edge again. Maybe something had gone wrong? Maybe he'd gotten hurt? "Máax? Máax?"

There was no sound apart from the squawking toucans above.

Okay. She could go for help, but she wasn't really sure where to go. She didn't speak Spanish—or did she? She wasn't sure. And they were in some crazy Mexican jungle. She pivoted on her heel and looked around. Dammit. What was she going to do?

A few random pockets of air floated to the surface of the cenote, making a strange *glup, glup* sound. *Oh no. What if he's stuck down there?*

"Oh, gods." She had to help him.

Without giving it any thought, she pinched her nose and jumped. Her body immediately reacted with hard shivers. *Brrr. Cold. Cold. Cold.* She pushed the wet strands from her face, and sucking in a giant breath, she dived straight down into the murky water.

Within a matter of a few feet, the sunlight faded. The air in her lungs immediately felt saturated and heavy. She needed another breath. She started to kick her way back to the surface, but hit her head on a ceiling of solid rock.

Shit! No! The air in her lungs turned to poison. She reached and clawed at the jagged rock, but she was trapped. A scream escaped her mouth, and the water flooded inside her lungs. She fought to gasp and hack, but it was no use.

She. Was. Drowning.

Ashli's mind broke away as if beckoned to some unknown place, a place of comfort and without pain.

Am I dead? Is this what it feels like? Her body or soul—she didn't know—rose from the water into the air. Like a runaway balloon, she floated up through the tree canopy into the crisp February air, higher and higher, disappearing inside a big puffy cloud. Where was she going? She didn't feel afraid or panicked; she felt at peace.

Then a small burst of warm air enveloped her body, and she found herself sitting in the sand, looking out across turquoise waves.

"Oh, for heaven's sake, Ashli, why do you keep coming here? We told you not to come back."

Ashli looked up at the woman with the deeply tanned skin and long, thick black curls much like her own standing next to a man with short dark brown hair. Both wore white linen suits that seemed to flow over their lean bodies.

"Do I know you?" Ashli stood quickly.

The woman and man exchanged glances. "We're your parents. And you are in big trouble, young lady."

Máax had chosen this particular cenote because it was the most powerful of the portals when it came to creating a human form. Unfortunately, that also meant he'd be slammed into his new body. Not that he would know, but he guessed it felt similar to hitting a brick wall at one hundred miles per hour. Most deities avoided this cenote for that very reason, a small price to pay given his urgency to return to Ashli. He needed to find a way to mend her memory, to make things right for her.

With his new human form complete, the cenote spit Máax out into the dark, cold water. He kicked his way to the surface and noticed a form floating facedown.

Ashli?

No!

He reached the water's surface and immediately flipped her onto her back. Her face was bluish as were her lips. "No. No. No."

With her in tow, he swam to the side of the pool and

gripped a small ledge. He heaved and tugged with all his strength, but he was weak and would be for several hours until his new body fully absorbed his light. "Dammit, no. She can't be dead! Ashli!"

Doing his best to balance her body against his in the water, he propped her head in the crook of his arm and began blowing into her mouth. "Wake up! Ashli! Wake up!" Why was this happening? He'd given her the light of the gods, made her immortal. As long as her form wasn't destroyed, she would live forever just as a vampire might. Something wasn't right.

Then he remembered; his powers had been returned to him! Yes, not only had he been the God of Truth—or love, as he'd discovered—but he had many, many other gifts. To name a few: the ability to know when a person lied, to control people's actions with his voice, and to heal the sick, and the ability to enter another's body. He rarely did so—it was really disturbing to walk inside the mind of another—but perhaps he could will Ashli's heart to pump and lungs to move again. He closed his eyes tightly and felt his essence sift inside her. He felt nothing. No sign of Ashli. An empty shell.

He willed her immortal body to work again and soon felt her body warming and breathing on its own, but still no Ashli. Where had her soul gone?

Máax exited her form and stared down at her beautiful face. "Please come back, Ashli. Please?"

There was no response. Horror and despair filled every molecule of his being.

Why, after everything, is this happening? Hadn't he paid his dues to the Universe? Why was he being punished? "Ashli! I command you to return."

Once again, there was no response.

Then I will go back in time and undo this. Yes, he'd get a hold of another tablet and find a way to stop this. Even if he had to again defy his brethren and do so without their permission.

"I will never let you go, Ashli. Never."

Máax positioned Ashli's petite frame over his shoulder and began the arduously slow climb from the water.

Ashli could not believe the insane story she'd heard from these two people claiming to be her parents. It wasn't that she didn't believe them, she simply didn't remember.

They went on to explain that whether she or anyone believed it, the Universe was always there, listening to everyone's innermost thoughts and intentions, helping them shape their lives. Some people focused on hate, fear, or whatever they lacked, and found their lives filled with anger and conflict. Others, who focused on love and gratitude, found their world filled with joy even if they faced life's tragedies. In Ashli's case, she focused on her sense of loss.

Had Ashli's unwillingness to let her parents go really drawn Death to her? It seemed ridiculous that missing them, wanting to see them again, could do that. But according to her parents, Ashli had died. Numerous times, in fact. "So I thought Death was stalking me, but really, I was causing it?"

That was weird.

"It seems fitting," her mother explained, "that you're now the Goddess of Love. Your love for us was so powerful that you were unable to let go and move on."

"I see," Ashli said, nodding her head. "Maybe losing my memory wasn't such a bad thing, then. Was it?"

Her mother brushed her arm. "Perhaps not. But if you ever want it back, all you have to do is ask Máax. He can heal you. He just hasn't figured it out yet."

"Really?" That was ironic. She'd been the key to undoing whatever trouble Máax had been in back in that circus slash courtroom. And now that he had his powers back, he was the key to undoing her problem? The Universe worked in mysterious ways.

"Yes," her mother replied. "Really."

Ashli gave it some thought. Whoever she used to be didn't sound very happy, and maybe this was her second chance. How many people got to have one of those?

Hmmm, perhaps this would remain her little secret for the time being.

"As for us," said her mother, "we'll always be here, watching over you. And playing poker. Did you know the dead've got a game going 24/7? Yesterday, I played Texas Hold 'Em with a gladiator who died in 100 BC. Fascinating."

Okay.

"Now," said her father, his eyes filled with a calming love. "It's time for you, our dear little Ashli, to return before your deity has a meltdown. He must be wondering where you are, and he's waited a long, long time for you."

Part of her wanted to stay and chat a little longer, but she knew they were right; it was time to go. She already felt the pull. To where? She assumed back to the real world, the world of the living. To Máax. That was the other part of their story she found unbelievable; Máax had been sent to save her, to teach her how to live again.

And you almost lost him. Dork!

She hugged her parents tightly. "Good-bye and thank you."

"Until we meet again," said her mother. "But not too soon."

Ashli blinked and felt herself pulled through a dark tunnel. The noise in her ears at first sounded like a low hum, but then grew into an earsplitting roar. But it wasn't an animal; it sounded like a man. A man cursing the heavens and life itself, vowing to do very awful things to everyone.

The sensation of her body returned. It was warm and cold all at once, and she had a piercing headache.

"Hey, could you keep it down?" The blinding light kept her from opening her eyes.

The man stopped screaming. "Ashli?" he whispered. "You—you are back?"

"Yeah. And it hurts like hell," she groaned.

"Thank the heavens!" The man squeezed her so tightly he practically cracked her in half.

"Okay there, big boy." Ashli opened her eyes. She lay on a bed of leaves with her upper torso cradled against Máax's broad, bare chest. "You'll never believe where I was. My parents were there, telling me I kept dying because I wanted to see them. They said you were sent to help me learn to live again."

His smile stretched from ear to ear, and his eyes filled with unspeakable joy. "Did it work?"

"Oh my gods!" She was looking at him! With her own two eyes! "Máax? Is it really you?"

He placed his warm hand on her cheek. "Yes, my dear Ashli. It is I."

The man, with the long wet strands of brownish hair,

staring into her face was a vision of heavenly, sinful masculinity. His golden-brown skin and full lips, his turquoise eyes with thick brown lashes, and his strong jaw were so sensual, so male. But that wasn't what took her breath away. It was the way he looked at her and how it made her feel. Like being complete and loved. Like being at peace and set on fire.

"You are so way hotter than that chair."

He smiled. "Wait until you see the rest."

Máax's lips were on her, and the heat of his kiss didn't just warm her mouth; it shot straight through her center and ignited a crazed, raw hunger.

Máax lay her down beneath him on the bed of leaves and worked up her dress. She gasped as she felt his hand slide between her legs and push her panties aside. When she felt his hard shaft parting her soft flesh, her grip on his shoulders involuntarily tightened, nails digging in.

"Oh, gods, yes," she panted in his ear.

He slowed for a fraction of a moment only to stare into her eyes as he thrust with one brutally sensual stroke, stealing the air from her lungs. She didn't need to see his erection to know he was large. She felt every inch as he slid deep inside. The sensation was so delicious and sweet yet rough just like his kisses. And the way he grabbed her, held her in place, made her feel so, so, so . . . his.

He thrust again with a sharp, claiming motion. Then again. And again. Every movement was frantic and hard, uncontrolled yet deliberate. His tongue eagerly lapped away at hers.

Just a few more seconds, and she wouldn't be able to stop the inevitable. "Ohmygod, Máax. Don't stop. It feels so good."

He stared into her eyes and thrust again. "I want to watch you"—he thrust again—"come for me."

His words were enough to push her over the edge. Her entire body felt like a solid, immovable ball of pulsating, tingling nerves and then…she screamed his name as he pushed himself sharply forward, never breaking his feral gaze. With each pump of his hips she exploded, over and over again, in one relentless current of orgasms until Máax let out a throaty groan.

Finally, he slowed and smiled, planting one lingering, lazy kiss on her lips.

"That was amazing," she said.

He nodded his head yes. "That was only a taste of what you'll be enjoying for eternity."

Lucky, lucky me.

He kissed her again, unhurried and tender. "You're shivering. Let's get you home. I arranged for a helicopter to pick us up near the lake a kilometer or so from here."

She was shivering not from the cold, but from the heat of his touch. "No more vampire rides?"

He frowned. "No. No, I do not want any more vampires hanging around my future wife unless she's helping them get over their commitment issues."

"Did you say 'future wife'? Are we getting married? Did you propose, and I accepted?" She honestly didn't know.

He helped her to her feet. "Yes. Not yet but I will. And yes, you will."

"Oh, really?" she teased. "But I am the Goddess of Love. Not sure I really want to tie myself down." She grinned. "Not until I'm absolutely sure you can please me. After all, eternity is a long, long time to be married to someone."

His beautifully plump lips curved into a devious smile. "Mmmm, I love a challenge."

She looked into his impossibly beautiful eyes. He was almost two feet taller, and his body was a mass of hard, ripped muscles and male perfection. His face was an exotic combination of rough masculinity and fine features, as if he'd been sculpted by the heavens. He was huge and gorgeous. And...

"I love you, Ashli. If I were to cease to exist in this very moment, I'd die a happy man."

His admission was so exhilarating. It made her feel like the most precious person on the planet.

His caramel-brown brows furrowed. "You all right?"

"Oh yeah. Better than all right."

"Good. Because I no longer plan on letting you walk out of this jungle."

"Really now?" She smiled.

He spun her around and released a hot breath in her ear. "You, Ashli, are mine. And I've waited an eternity for you." He gently leaned her forward, and she braced herself on the tree. He slid her damp dress up past her thighs and slid her panties down.

She held back a gasp as he rubbed his thick, rock-hard cock against her sensitive bud, sliding his entire length over her. She was instantly and insanely hot for him again. Every intimate muscle pulsed with ravenous need for his penetration. No, she didn't remember her past, but she felt like she'd waited her entire life for this: to be wanted in such an uninhibited way. "Take me again," she begged.

Máax didn't say a word but drove deep. She winced with pleasure as he began hammering away. She knew the moment he came, it would be the most incredible release ever.

"Harder, Máax. Harder." She held on tight while he pumped with a furious, savage pace. Then he groaned toward the sky and bucked wildly against her, and the moment he flooded her with his liquid heat, she felt a strange sensation. It wasn't simply a mind-blowing physical reaction that infused every muscle in her body with rapturous bursts, it was like the final piece that had been missing finally slid into place. A connection not just of their bodies and souls, but something more, something beyond them both.

The air whooshed from her lungs as he clung to her back, quaking with his release. "Gods, what you do to me, woman," he said.

Ashli wanted to tell him how she felt, but her words faltered. It was so, so magnificent. As if life itself had just begun, a spark from a simple dream.

Ohmygod. She gasped as her brain moved the last piece into place.

Máax pulled out and turned her body toward him. He kissed her again, pushing her back to the tree, cupping and massaging her breast. Once again she felt him hard, needy, and positioning her for another round. "Wait." She pushed back to look into his serene turquoise eyes.

"Yes, my love, what is it?"

"I think you just got me . . . pregnant."

Máax tensed and then pulled away. He stared into her eyes. "Of course I did. I am a god who loves you. And you are the Goddess of Love who loves me. Did you really think we could make love and not bear fruit?"

Hmmm . . . Good point.

"But just to be certain, I think I will make love to you a few dozen times more." He looked up at the sky. "From my calculations, we have another hour before we need to make it to the pickup spot."

Ashli blinked in rapid succession. "A dozen times? In an," she swallowed, "hour?"

"Like I said, I am a god. I was deprived of your body for seventy thousand years." He shrugged. "And what can I say? I'm still male." He smiled sweetly, melting her heart.

"In that case"—she flung her arms around his neck—"I'm here to help."

Epilogue One

⌒

Standing at the head of the table, Penelope rubbed her tiny baby bump and looked down at Kinich who sat calmly in the chair beside her. Like the other ten deities sitting alongside them, he hadn't broken a sweat.

"How can you all be so calm?" she asked.

She was overwhelmed with joy for Máax—justice had been served—but she was nervous as hell about the remaining part of this trial. What came next had been culminating for a lot longer than she'd been alive. And the outcome would change everyone's lives. Everyone's. Like many of the women in this story, she'd been drawn into the crazy, beautiful, miraculous world of the gods by whatever forces existed out there in the Universe. And while she still didn't understand many, many things, she did know they were all connected. Kinich, once the God of the Sun and still the most powerful light in her universe, was now a different kind of immortal. A vampire.

She, through some very odd chain of events, had inherited his powers and his title: Ruler of the House of Gods.

The point? She was connected to the gods. What affected them affected her and vice versa.

Deep breath. Because now, she had to serve justice. Zac and Cimil had done terrible, terrible things. This was not going to be easy.

Kinich, quite possibly the most beautiful male on the planet with his golden-streaked, honey-brown hair and trademark god-sized frame, beamed at her, his eyes flickering from blue to black. "You can do this, my wife." He leaned forward and kissed her belly. "I love you, Penelope, and I cannot wait for this all to be over so we can spend our days making love, preparing for our child to come."

Penelope melted.

She turned toward the room, which was abuzz with commotion.

Please, gods, give me strength.

She rapped her gavel on the desk. "Attention, everyone, I hereby call Zac, the God of Temptation, to answer for his crimes."

Zac stood and moved toward the center of the room.

"Sorry," she said, "Ashli took the chair, so you'll have to stand."

Zac didn't bat an eyelash. "Let's get this shit over with."

Penelope didn't know where to start. Zac had betrayed her in the worst kind of way. He had known he possessed the power of temptation, the power to make a person want something regardless of right or wrong. And with such power came great responsibility as it did with all of the gods. But what Zac did was unforgiveable. At her most vulnerable moment, pregnant, having believed she'd lost

Kinich, Zac used his powers to make her believe she had feelings for him. Then when Kinich turned up and became a vampire—a long, long story—Zac made Kinich crave her blood. He thought she would never love a man, errr, ex-god, err, vampire, who was a threat to her and her unborn baby.

A-hole.

Penelope rapped her gavel on the table. "I hereby open proceedings against Zac, God of Temptation. Zac, you are accused of using your powers on another deity without permission—a violation of a sacred law. What do you have to say for yourself?"

Kinich didn't flinch, but Penelope felt the anger radiate from his body. She knew Kinich wanted him dead. Dead dead. Not deity dead. But killing a deity wasn't possible. In fact, punishment was rather limited: banishment, removal of one's human shell, suspension of powers, and incarceration or entombment.

Zac's turquoise eyes locked on Penelope, and she resisted squirming.

"Zac?" Penelope said. "This is your chance to be heard before we decide the punishment. Don't you have anything to say?"

Dressed in a navy-blue shirt and blue jeans, he squared his shoulders. His messy dark hair fell around his ears. "I have no excuse, Penelope. I love you. I would do anything to keep you safe."

Penelope's blood boiled. "You...love me? *Love!* Is that what you call almost having me and my baby killed, you son of a bitch?"

Her words did nothing to rattle his cage.

"You have a right to be angry," Zac stated calmly, "but

my brother threw you away. He turned his back on you not once, but twice. You deserve better than that."

She couldn't believe him. "So you used your powers to get what you wanted?"

"I used them, yes, but never on you. I only told that asshole brother of mine to give in to his temptations, to be exactly who he was—a selfish, bloodthirsty prick."

Kinich exploded. "I'm going to fucking kill you!"

The Uchben soldiers, who'd been milling about the periphery of the room, quickly stepped in front of Zac, ready for Kinich's pounce.

Zac's eyes remained fixed on Penelope. "I never, ever used my powers on you, Penelope. Not once. Everything you felt for me was real."

Crapola. She didn't know what to say because she had felt something for Zac, but it wasn't love. At least, not the romantic sort. In her darkest hour, he'd been there for her, kept her hair out of the toilet when she had morning sickness, held her when she felt so heartbroken that she didn't know if she'd continue breathing. Kinich had abandoned her. Yes, she now knew why, and given the same choice, same situation, she would have done exactly what Kinich had. Kinich had bartered away his divinity to win a pivotal battle against the Maaskab and free his brother. But that didn't mean her heart hadn't ripped in two.

She sank into her chair and covered her face. "He's right, Kinich. I let him in. You were gone—forever, I thought—and Zac was there for me, for us." She rubbed her stomach.

Kinich nodded, and she knew what he was thinking: it had been his own damned fault. He would never blame her, not given all that he had once done to push her away.

"But that does not excuse using his powers on me," Kinich said quietly. "I could have killed you, Penelope."

She nodded. No, there was no excuse for that.

She wiped her eyes and looked up at Zac. "Do you have anything else to say?"

"Only that I will never stop loving you, Penelope. You are truly the most remarkable, sexy, passionate woman I've ever known."

Kinich growled.

"And I truly regret hurting you," he added. "But what I did pales in comparison to the pain Kinich caused you. Yet you forgave him. I only hope you'll forgive me, too."

She bobbed her head, not in agreement, but to acknowledge she'd heard him. "You may go back to your seat until it's time for sentencing."

Damn, this sucked. And it would only get harder.

She blew out a breath. "I call Cimil, the Goddess of the Underworld."

It took one hour and forty-five minutes to read the charges against Cimil who, by the way, looked utterly pleased with herself. She grinned like a madwoman the entire time in her bright red tango dress that matched her bright red hair, loose and wild, just like her mind.

The charges ranged from heinous to the downright unbelievable. The unjust imprisonment of generations of clowns—she hated their unnatural state of constant happiness—shoplifting *Love Boat* DVDs, tag switching at garage sales, operating a taxi without a permit, unlawful unicorn racing, switching Red Hot candies for suppositories at a retirement home, waterboarding sea turtles (looking for Nessy), spraying "Fucktard" on several ancient Egyptian ruins (she'd been fighting with Roberto that day), creating vampires, including the evil ones, aiding the Maaskab, entrapping her brethren, the invention of SPAM, and . . . well, the extinction of the dinosaurs. Hundreds and thousands of deaths of innocent humans along with millions of creatures.

"What do you have to say for yourself, Cimil?"

The room waited with bated breath.

Cimil shrugged. "Touchdown, baby!"

That was not what Penelope had hoped for. "Really? Touchdown. That's it?"

"What can I say? I'm like those guys who scrape road-kill from the highway or clean out Porta-Potties. I do what I gotta to. And I leave the world a better place. Less stinky. You know."

"But Cimil, that's not an excuse." Penelope had hoped with all her soul that there was some sort of logical explanation. Because despite everything, she liked the batshit crazy goddess. She'd saved Penelope's life once. Not to mention her mother's.

Cimil smiled. "Of course it is. I am the only one powerful enough, smart enough, and with balls big enough to make the hard choices."

Un-frigging-believable. "But people died, Cimil, suffered, because of you. You broke Chaam's soul, used him to murder hundreds of women. You created vampires! And the Maaskab!"

Cimil raised her index finger in the air. "Correction! The Maaskab created vampires. One of those bastard priests plucked out my heart to save Roberto and make him immortal."

The room gasped.

Cimil glowed. "Well, the heart grew back. And I'd like to point out that the priest didn't create evil vampires; he created plain old vampires. Vampires have free will just like humans. Bad apples are the result of an individual's choice. Or hanging with Minky. In any case, their creation was not a crime."

"How about aiding the evil vampires and Maaskab?" Penelope argued.

"Ah! All true!" Cimil replied. "But look at the joy and life that rose from the ashes. The Maaskab brought us their dark magic, the black jade that has enabled us to physically be with humans, to have children, families! Now we have the Payals, the result of Chaam's evil detour, including Emma, the love of our brother Votan's life. As for vampires, they have become our friends, our lovers, and have served as a constant reminder to us all that change is possible. Every disaster, death, challenge, and tragedy we've faced has made us richer, braver, wiser. Because of this, some of us have been able to find eternal love. So had I not played my evil role, we would have gone mad and destroyed the planet."

"I hope you understand," said Kinich, "that when I say this, I mean it. Bullshit! You've already admitted that you can't see the future. I think you got lucky. I think you sought to destroy us all, to terrorize us for your own amusement, and it was by the grace and mercy of the Universe that balance was restored, that good came out of it."

Cimil swiped her hand through the air. "Oh, pashaaaw! Do you not see? That is my role. That's who I am! My job is to burn it all down! Burn it to the ground! So the

Universe can build something new. I *am* winter. I am Sam. I like green eggs and ham."

Roberto moved to Cimil's side. "She speaks the truth, though not about the green eggs, obviously. However, I have witnessed the invisible force that compels her to destroy, even when her intensions are pure. I watched her for thousands of years as she refused to play her role, tried to do the opposite of anything her instincts dictated. It only made things worse, moved us one step closer toward annihilation."

"I don't understand. How do you know all of this?" Penelope asked.

Cimil took an accomplished breath. "The dead exist in a place beyond the confines of time. You all came to me from the future—one that no longer exists—but you, me ... everyone was dead. My own self came to me and has been my constant companion for thousands of years, guiding me, telling how things ended so that I could try to change course. Apparently, that particular version of me was Roberto-less, extremely naughty, and did end the world. Of course, she saw the error of her ways—a testament to my good-hearted nature. She came to help me, put me on another path."

"Is she here now?" Penelope asked.

"No. She's been gone since the party," Cimil said. "But it took me finding my true calling. I was not born to create harmony or peace, I'm much better at creating havoc. Which, ironically, creates harmony and peace. Damned. I do sound batshit crazy."

"Slightly. Are you done?" Penelope said.

"Not quite! I'd like to have the opportunity to highlight all of the good that has come from my actions." Cimil pulled out a scroll that unwound to the floor and rolled four feet in front of her. "Ready? The Super Bowl and anything related to the phrase 'Touchdown, baby.' Speaking of babies, there's your little bun in oven, Penelope. Reminder: Maaskab, black jade, drunken night with Kinich, midgets...say no more. Emma, Guy, and their baby on the way. Vampires, aka our BFFs. Let's not forget that I positioned Niccolo DiConti, the nicest, meanest vampire in the world—besides Roberto—to be in charge of the vampire army along with his sweet wife, Helena. The Uchben, aka our other BFFs (my evil made them necessary, and they've really helped us manage the exploding human population so we can get a day off). Ixtab's mate Antonio: Had I not saved his father, the last remaining incubus, by hiding him in my secret Spanish villa, Antonio would never have been born. And let's face it, Ixtab is a tricky, tricky girl to match up. Ouch! Don't stand too close. Top Ramen, someone had to ensure nourishment for the college-aged human masses. Platform shoes. Disco. Weeble Wobles—they don't fall down. How cool is that? Soap operas. Mojitos. Pig Latin—ix-nayy on the unishment-pay for imil-cey. *American Idol*...so, so evil. Those little umbrellas you put into drinks. Okay, that one was really Minky's idea, but I thought up the part about it being important to protect the little people from the harmful rays of the sun. Tang. The wheel, and..." She sighed. "Our big bright future." Cimil bowed. "Oh! And I'd also like to highlight that I did send Máax into the past to save all of the Payals who will play a very important role in the future (ssshhh, it's a secret) so that Chaam could live a free and happy life with his mate, Maggie."

"Are you done yet?" Penelope asked.

She looked up at the ceiling. "Um...I would once again like to highlight that I orchestrated the demise of evil vampires, and I had Roberto and his men completely wipe out the Maaskab—all part of the master plan. Couldn't have us gods locked up and the bad guys free to roam, now could we? Besides, the Maaskab served their purpose. Now it's time to move on and find newer, shinier, more evil challenges. Bring on round two!" She did a little dance, then abruptly stopped once she noticed no one joined in the celebration. "Fine. Be that way. But as you see, I have undone all my sins and left behind nothing but the good stuff. Kind of like when you boil a chicken to make soup. You pick out all of the bones and those slimy bits of skin, leaving behind the savory broth and juicy meat. Gods, I'm hungry. Must be the baby."

Roberto was suddenly gripping her by the shoulders. "Please tell me you are not joking, Cimil."

She lovingly patted his cheek. "No, my sweet pharaoh. I have kept my promise to you. It will be a little girl. And a little boy. And another little boy. And a girl." She shrugged. "I kinda over did it on the fertility spell with Akna. Whoops!"

Roberto hugged her, and she genuinely looked pleased. It almost made Penelope want to forgive Cimil. She was crazy and wild, but she had pulled off the impossible; she'd created a new future for everyone. She'd probably been the only one insane enough to see the possibilities and take the risks. And if she truly was compelled to do evil, how could they punish her? That was her role. But it also made her dangerous. Or did it?

Damn. So confusing.

Kinich rose from his seat next to Penelope. "Cimil, I

know I speak for us all when I say that we are all grateful for every blessing in our lives." He looked directly at Penelope. "I can't imagine a world without our mates, our friends who have become our family, and for every gift you've helped bestowed upon us. Excluding *American Idol* and SPAM. But I agree with Penelope; the suffering, lies, and games you played seemed to be more than simply playing your role. You enjoyed watching us run through your labyrinth of despair. You reveled in our suffering and enjoyed our pain. I think you could have accomplished much of what you did without enjoying it so damned much. What do you have to say for yourself?"

Cimil grinned, her smile stretching from ear to ear. "Guilty as charged!"

"Tell them you do not mean that, my little sweet-and-sour pork bun. Tell them you are sorry." Roberto looked troubled. That was a first.

"But I cannot, my pharaoh-licious vampire. I do not regret a single moment. And don't you think, given that I was the one condemned to being Ms. Mageddon, there needed to be one teeny tiny consolation? Something in it for me?" She shrugged. "I happen to enjoy watching them squirm."

Penelope didn't know what to do. It was all so complicated. "Cimil? Do you have anything else to say?"

Cimil looked at her and said, "Whatever you decide, I ask only that you take mercy on my unicorn, Minky. She didn't mean to kill everyone inside that male strip club, but the leather thongs really riled her up!"

"Okaaaay." Penelope sighed. "I call a recess so that we may decide sentencing."

"Tootles!" Cimil wiggled her fingers. "Come on, Roberto, I gotta pee like a leprechaun."

"Cimil," said Roberto who followed closely behind her, "why are you so happy? This is very serious." He halted abruptly. "Wait. You've got something planned, don't you?"

She winked. "You'll never know."

Five hours later

The deities filed into the crowded courtroom. Everyone fell into an instant hush as the gods took their seats.

Penelope had lived through the hardest afternoon of her life. She'd wanted to remain objective, but given her personal involvement with both deities, it had not been easy. That said, she'd come to realize the entire situation was one of puts and takes, bitter and sweet, tragedy and joy.

Just like life.

And just like life, one could choose to focus on the ugliness, which some of the deities certainly had, or focus on the good. In the end, people and gods simply chose what they wanted to see, which is why it took them five entire hours to come to a decision.

"Zac and Cimil, please rise before us for sentencing."

The two moved to the middle of the floor.

Penelope took a regret-filled breath. "Zac, we recognize that you were ruled by emotions, and that love can make us do crazy things. But your deceit and betrayal of your brother, and of me, cannot be ignored. I only hope that your punishment helps you see that love isn't about getting what you want at all costs, but giving everything of yourself for the happiness of the other. Love is selfless and hard, but it is never selfish and never justifies risking the life of an innocent child. Zac, for your crimes, we sentence you to banishment. Your powers will be neutralized, and you will live in the human world until we see you've truly learned the meaning of love."

Zac stared straight ahead without the slightest reaction. Penelope wasn't at all surprised. He was too proud to show any sign of weakness.

"Cimil, your acts of cruelty and disregard for the feelings of others are unspeakable. Yet we are also grateful to you for all that you have done for everyone. I hope you fully appreciate how gracious we are being because of this." She paused for a moment. "You are also, hereby, stripped of your powers and sentenced to live in the human world."

Penelope looked at them both. "It seems you both need to learn a lesson about empathy and selflessness. You will remain in the human world until we feel that you've evolved."

Cimil huffed. "That could be forever!"

"Well," Penelope said, "you seem to have a knack for helping others find their mates. And Zac, you desperately need to learn firsthand what real love is. So, in addition to banishment, you will both serve hard time. You are hereby sentenced to help one hundred immortals—your brethren, our vampire friends, the Payals, any immortal—find their soul mates. We hope that putting you in the front lines will help you see the error of your ways."

"This is ridiculous!" Zac barked. "I'm not going to play the role of fucking Cupid!"

"Remove him from the court," Penelope commanded the soldiers.

"The injustice of it all!" Cimil screamed in a southern belle accent. "I've given y'all reason to live! I saved the godsdamned world! And this is how you repay me? I am going to swoon." She pressed the back of her hand to her forehead.

Penelope looked at Roberto. "I suggest you remove Ms. Scarlet O'Ham before we change our minds. And Roberto? Congratulations. I recommend you find a really, really good nanny."

Roberto nodded and scooped up Cimil. He looked utterly relieved, likely because he still got to be with the love of his existence.

Cimil squirmed and flailed her arms, putting on an over-the-top show. She was such a horrible actress. "You Yanks haven't seen the last of me!"

Zac, Cimil, and Roberto and his vampires disappeared from the courtroom.

"Wow. That was intense. And strange." Penelope shook her head.

Kinich took her in his arms. "You did well, my love. And they both will be the better for it."

But it pained her to see Zac suffer even after all that he'd done. However, it was time to move on.

"As for Chaam, based on today's hearing, he is absolved of all wrongdoing. He will not go to trial." She looked at Chaam and Maggie. "We wish you nothing but the best in your life together."

Maggie and Chaam embraced.

"Wait." Emma stood from the second row. "You never said anything about my grandmother. What about her?"

Crap. They'd entirely forgotten about Emma's grand-mother. She'd been abducted by the Maaskab, her brain poisoned with their magic, and ultimately became their leader. She'd since been captured and cured, so they believed, but there was little track record to prove if the dark energy truly left one's system.

Penelope looked at Emma. "I think the best course of action is to keep close tabs on her. Twenty-four-seven surveillance until we know for sure she's no longer a harm to anyone."

"I would like to be her observer." Everyone looked at the older gentleman in the jogging suit. "Isn't that the ex–Catholic priest?" Penelope whispered to Kinich.

"Yes. It most certainly is," he replied.

"Father Xavier, are you sure?" Emma asked.

He smiled. "I am no longer 'father,' but yes, I am sure. I've been spending a lot of time with Gabriela during her recovery. We've grown quite attached." He winked.

Okay. So now, they'd seen it all. The ex-priest had the hots for the ex-ruler of the Maaskab army?

Penelope shrugged. "Sure. Why the hell not?"

Epilogue Two

~~~~~~~~

Eight months later

Máax opened his eyes to the sun shining through the glass doors leading to Ashli's private balcony. A large black-and-white photo of him, bare chested, standing on the beach while holding their new chocolate lab puppy, Poseidon, hung above the bed.

He smiled and shook his head. Ashli had taken up photography again and made him pose almost daily. Holding fruit, surfing, doing laundry, cooking. She said she'd never get over the excitement of being able to see him . . . and that he was not a chair.

Whatever. Anything to make her happy. Because that was exactly what she'd done for him.

Happiness was his for the first time in his existence.

Máax looked down at Ashli's sleeping form, her belly round with their baby. He rubbed her stomach with affection and imagined the beautiful child inside. His child. His wife. For the first time in seventy thousand years, he truly understood what love meant. She'd taught him that. Funny how it took losing that power and giving it to her for that to occur. Of course, Ashli had taught him many things.

After their reunion at the cenote, Máax began sharing his story with her—the years of isolation, the missions he went on to salvage unsalvageable situations (like Chaam's), and his reluctance to truly let anyone be a part of his existence. He also told her about the vision he'd had that day she'd hit her head and how the strand of light that connected them had been like a lifeline to his soul. Of course, Ashli insisted he had been the one to save her from her death wish, but he would never see it that way. She saved him from hell. And now, with her gift of love, she was determined to save others, including weekly counseling sessions for Zac and Cimil who'd opened up an immortal matchmaking service in Los Angeles. Both figured they'd turn it into a business and make some money while they served out their sentences.

Those two were such lost causes, but he loved Ashli all the more for trying to help them.

"Máax." Ashli sighed with contentment and then rolled to her side toward him. "I love you."

He stroked her wild black curls away from her face. "And I love you, Ashli."

"Good." She snuggled closer, burying her face into his chest. "Because." She sighed dreamily. "I'm in labor."

"What?" he pulled away, and her eyes flipped open. "But you're only eight months."

"It's okay, honey. It's normal for women who are having immortal twins. My Uchben doctor said so."

Máax released a sigh of relief. "Thank heavens. Are you certain you are okay?"

"I'm sure." She rolled over and grabbed her cell, punching in a message.

"Who are you texting?" he asked.

She winced and rubbed her belly. "My ride."

A team of four vampires, including Sentin, instantly appeared in their room.

"Your suitcase, my goddess?" said the thin one wearing a beat-up biker jacket and leather pants.

"There." She pointed toward the closet.

The other vampire, a young blond, lifted her from the bed. "My goddess, your room is ready at the Uchben hospital. Are you ready for sifting?"

"Yes." She gripped his arm. "Let's go."

"Ashli!" Máax yelled. "What is going on?"

She winked. "I'm going to have your babies, silly." She looked at Sentin who stood at her side. "Let's move, Sentin."

The other vampire with her suitcase vanished in a flash, and the remaining fourth one, a shorter man with scraggly brown hair, looked at Máax with complete frustration. "Dammit. I wanted to take her! She promised I could cut the cord."

Máax snarled. "Take me to her now!"

"Fine. But you should know that you're a lucky bastard already, so don't even think of stepping in our fun."

What was wrong with these guys? "Take me now, or I will castrate you."

In a flash, Máax was inside a large, brightly lit hospital room, standing at Ashli's side. She'd chosen to give birth in the Uchben hospital near his brother's estate in Arizona, given the children weren't human and the doctors there had years of experience dealing with immortals.

Speaking of immortals. *What the devil?* Groans and screams exploded from every direction. Doctors and nurses scrambled every which way. His brother Guy hovered over a pain-struck Emma stretched across a gurney, her red hair wild about her face. Kinich stood beside another gurney, gripping a screaming Penelope's hand. His sister Ixtab sat hunched over in a chair with Antonio holding her firmly by the shoulders, instructing her to breathe. And last but not least, Cimil screamed at the top of her lungs as Roberto tried to feed her ice chips. Strangely, he wore no clothes. His face was painted like a clown. It was disturbing. But not as disturbing as the howls and agonizing groans coming from the five women.

Máax felt his blood pressure hit the cold tiled floor as he took in the scene before him.

Babygeddon.

Nothing in his entire seventy thousand years of existence had ever prepared him for this.

"Let's get you all settled in." A nurse walked Ashli over to an empty gurney against the wall.

"Ashli, honey," Máax asked, "what is going on? The only thing missing is…"

"Move! She's having a baby! Move the fuck out of the way!" Chaam pushed the wheelchair through the doors into the room.

"Holy crap. I can't believe it." Máax rubbed his face. "Okay. Now the only thing missing is a vampire, a unicorn, and a clown."

"Eh-hem." Sentin stood in the corner with a video

camera. He then pointed to Roberto—naked clown face Roberto.

"Okay, the only thing missing is a unicorn," he corrected.

Sentin pointed toward a window. "Minky's outside. Roberto didn't want her eating the children."

Máax nodded slowly. "Okaaay."

Helena burst through the doors, a panicked look on her face, with Niccolo in tow.

"No. Please don't tell me you're giving birth, too?" Máax croaked.

Helena, a young athletic blonde with sun-bleached hair, rolled her eyes. "Idiot. I'm not due for another six months. I'm here to help the girls."

Niccolo looked at Helena with utter joy. "Really? Matty is going to have a sister?"

Helena nodded yes. "And a brother. I'm having twins, too!"

Niccolo kissed Helena, then looked at Máax. "Man! Are you in for ride. Being a father is better than burnt bread."

Máax cocked a brow. "That's sliced bre—"

Ashli screamed. "It's time!"

The nurse rushed over. "Let's get you to a delivery room."

Oh, gods, this was it. He was going to be a father.

"You okay?" Niccolo smacked him in the arm.

Máax glanced over at Ashli's flushed, smiling face. The light in her eyes glowed with the deepest love the Universe could ever offer. And he'd get to spend an eternity with her. "I'm ready."

THE END!!!!!! (Wink)

Author Note

Hi, all!

Well, you made it to the end of the Accidentally Yours series!! (Disco dance!) If you loved it, I sooo appreciate reviews, e-mails, FB notes, and tweets! (Not from the mean people, however. Because yes, they still suck!) As for you (oh, wonderful nice person that I am sure you are!), I want to thank you for hanging on through all those cliffs and twists and immortal bumps in the road. I hope you enjoyed the series. I hope I got you to laugh when you needed it most.

And for anyone who's still pining for more, well...while some of our gods finally got their Happy Ever Afters, I'm sure you noticed a few did not. But I couldn't leave Cimil and Zac without any work to do, now could I?

Keep an eye out for my new series, Immortal Matchmaker.

Bring on victim number one: Andrus Gray...

Once the most powerful immortal assassin ever to exist, this demigod now spends his days pining for the girl who got away: Helena. Doesn't help that he's also Helena's full-time nanny slash bodyguard. But now that the apocalypse is over and her husband, the vampire general, has returned home for good, it's time to move on. But can Andrus let go of the woman he secretly loves? Cimil, Goddess of the Underworld and owner of Immortal Matchmakers, Inc., knows the solution is finding another. But getting a woman, let alone one Andrus might like, to date this callous, unrefined, coldhearted warrior will prove to be the biggest challenge of her existence. Good thing they're in LA.

When aspiring actress Sadie Townsend finds herself only one week from being thrown out on the street, the call from her agent is like a gift from heaven. The six-figure salary is enough to keep her afloat for a very long time. But when she learns the job is teaching the world's biggest barbarian how to *act* like a gentleman, she wonders if she shouldn't have asked for more. He's vulgar, uncaring, and more rough around the edges than a serrated bread knife. He's also sexy, fierce, and undeniably tormented.

Will Sadie help him overcome his past, or will she find her heart hopelessly entrapped by a man determined to self-destruct?

HAPPY READING, EVERYONE!

Hugs, Mimi

Dr. Antonio Acero is a world-renowned physicist whose life takes a turn for the worst—and the bizarre. In southern Mexico, he finds an ancient Mayan tablet that is said to have magical properties. But when he puts the tablet to use, he discovers that Fate has other plans. And her name is Ixtab.

Please see the next page
for an excerpt from

*Vampires Need
Not... Apply?*

Prologue

⌒

Near Sedona, Arizona. Estate of Kinich Ahau, ex–God of the Sun. New Year's Day

Teetering on the very edge of a long white sofa, Penelope stared up at the oversized, round clock mounted on the wall. In ten minutes, the sun would set and the man they once knew as the God of the Sun would awaken. Changed. She hoped.

Sadly, there'd been a hell of a lot of hoping lately and little good it did her or her two friends, Emma and Helena, sitting patiently at her side. Like Penelope, the other two women had been thrust into this new world—filled with gods, vampires, and other immortal combinations in between—by means of the men they'd fallen in love with.

Bottom line? Not going so great.

Helena, the blonde who held two bags of blood in her

lap, reached for Penelope and smoothed down her frizzy hair. "Don't worry. Kinich will wake up. He will."

Pen nodded. She must look like a mess. Why hadn't she taken the time to at least run a brush through her hair for him? He loved her dark hair. Maybe because she didn't truly believe he'd come back to life. "I don't know what's worse, thinking I've lost him forever or knowing if he wakes up, he'll be something he hates."

Emma chimed in, "He doesn't hate vampires. He hates being immortal."

Pen shrugged. "Guess it really doesn't matter now what he hates." Kinich would either wake up or he wouldn't. If he didn't, she might not have the will to go on without him. Too much had happened. She needed him. She loved him. And most of all, she wanted him to know she was sorry for ever doubting him. He'd given his life to save them all.

Tick.

Another move of the hand.

Tock.

And another.

Nine more minutes.

The doorbell jolted the three women.

"Dammit." Emma, who wore her combat-ready outfit— black cargos and a black tee that made her red hair look like the flame on the tip of a match—marched to the door. "I told everyone not to disturb us."

Penelope knew that would never happen. A few hundred soldiers lurked outside and a handful of deities waited in the kitchen, snacking on cookies; new vampires weren't known to be friendly. But Penelope insisted on having only her closest friends by her side for the moment of truth. Besides, Helena was a new vampire herself—a long story—and knew what to do.

Emma unlocked the dead bolt. "Some idiot probably forgot my orders. I'll send him away—" The door flew open with a cold gust of desert wind and debris. It took a moment for the three women to register who stood in the doorway.

The creature, with long, matted dreads beaded with human teeth, wore nothing more than a loincloth over her soot-covered body.

Christ almighty, it can't be, thought Pen, as the smell of Maaskab—good old-fashioned, supernatural, pre-Hispanic death and darkness—entered her nose.

Before Emma could drop a single f-bomb, the dark priestess raised her hand and blew Emma across the large, open living room, slamming her against the wall.

Helena screamed and rushed to Emma's side.

Paralyzed with fear, Penelope watched helplessly as the Maaskab woman glided into the living room and stood before her, a mere two yards away.

The woman raised her gaunt, grimy finger, complete with overgrown grime-caked fingernail, and pointed directly at Penelope. "Youuuu."

Holy wheat toast. Penelope instinctively stepped back. The woman's voice felt like razor blades inside her ears. Penelope had to think fast. Not only did she fear for her life and for those of her friends, but both she and Emma were pregnant. Helena had a baby daughter. *Think, dammit. Think.*

Penelope considered drawing the power of the sun, an ability she'd recently gained when she had become the interim Sun God—another long story—but releasing that much heat into the room might fry everyone in it.

Grab the monster's arm. Channel it directly into her.

"Youuuu," the Maaskab woman said once again.

"Damn, lady." Penelope covered her ears. "Did you swallow a bucket of rusty nails? That voice...gaaaahh."

The monster grunted. "I come with a message."

"For me?" Penelope took a step forward.

The woman nodded, and her eyes, pits of blackness framed with cherry red, clawed at Penelope's very soul. "It is for you I bring...the message."

Jeez. I get it. You have a message. Penelope took another cautious step toward the treacherous woman. "So what are you waiting for?"

"Pen, get away from her," she heard Emma grumble from behind.

Not on your life. Pen moved another inch. "I'm waiting, old woman. Wow me."

The Maaskab growled.

Another step.

"Don't hurt my grandmother," Emma pleaded.

Grandma? Oh, for Pete's sake. *This* was Emma's grandmother? The one who'd been taken by the Maaskab and turned into their evil leader? They all thought she'd been killed.

Fabulous. Granny's back.

For a fraction of a moment, the woman glanced over Pen's shoulder at Emma.

Another step.

Penelope couldn't let Emma's feelings cloud the situation. Granny was dangerous. Granny was evil. Granny was going down.

"We wish"—the old Maaskab woman ground out her words—"to make an exchange."

Penelope froze. "An exchange?"

The woman nodded slowly. "You will free our king, and we will return your prisoners."

Shit. Free Chaam? The most evil deity ever known? He'd murdered hundreds, perhaps thousands of women, many his own daughters. His sole purpose in life was to destroy every last living creature, except for the Maaskab and his love slaves.

No. They could never let that bastard out.

But what about the prisoners? She debated with herself. In the last battle, the Maaskab had trapped forty of their most loyal vampire soldiers, the God of Death and War, aka Emma's fiancé, and the General of the Vampire Army, aka Helena's husband.

Dammit. Dammit. Crispy-fried dammit! Penelope had to at least consider Granny's proposal. "Why in the world would we agree to let Chaam go?"

"A bunch of pathetic...little...girls...cannot triumph against us," the Maaskab woman hissed. "*You* need the vampires and your precious God of Death and War."

Penelope's brain ran a multitude of scenarios, trying to guess the angle. Apparently, the Maaskab needed Chaam back. But they were willing to give up Niccolo and Guy? Both were powerful warriors, perfectly equipped to kick the Maaskab's asses for good.

No. Something wasn't quite right. "Tell me why you want Chaam," Penelope said.

Another step.

"Because"—Granny flashed an odious grin—"the victory of defeating you will be meaningless without our beloved king to see it. All we do, we do for him."

Ew. Okay.

"You, on the other hand..." She lowered her gravelly voice one octave. "...Do not have a chance without your men. We offer a fair fight in exchange for our king's freedom."

Okay. She could be lying. Perhaps not. Anyone with a brain could see they were three inexperienced young women—yes, filled with passion and purpose and a love of shoes and all things shopping, in the case of Helena and Emma—but they didn't know the first thing about fighting wars. Especially ones that might end in a big hairy apocalypse prophesied to be just eight months away.

Sure, they had powerful, slightly insane, dysfunctional deities and battalions of beefy vampires and human soldiers on their side. However, that was like giving a tank to a kindergartner. Sort of funny in a Sunday comics *Beetle Bailey* kinda way, but not in real life.

"Don't agree to it," Helena pleaded from the flank. "We'll find another way to free them."

"She's right, Pen," Emma whimpered, clearly in pain.

Penelope took another step. They were right; they'd have to find some other way to get the prisoners back. Chaam was too dang dangerous. "And if we refuse?"

The Maaskab woman laughed into the air above, her teeth solid black and the inside of her mouth bright red.

Yum. Nothing like gargling with blood to really freshen your breath.

"Then," Granny said, "we shall kill both men—yes, even your precious Votan; we have the means—and the end of days will begin. It is what Chaam would have wanted."

Granny had conveniently left out the part about killing her and her friends before she departed this room. Why else would the evil Maaskab woman have come in person when an evil note would have done the evil job? Or how about an evil text?

No. Emma's grandmother would kill them if the offer was rejected. She knew it in her gut.

Penelope didn't blink. *No fear. No fear.* The powerful light tingled on the tips of her fingers. She was ready.

"Then you leave us no choice. We agree." Penelope held out her hand. "Shake on it."

The Maaskab woman glanced down at Pen's hand. Pen lunged, grabbed the woman's soot-covered forearm, and opened the floodgates of heat. Evil Granny dropped to her knees, screaming like a witch drowning in a hot, bubbling cauldron.

"No! No!" Emma screamed. "Don't kill her! Don't, Pen!"

Crackers! Penelope released the woman who fell face forward onto the cold Saltillo tile. Steam rose from her naked back and dreadlock-covered skull.

"Grandma? Oh, God, no. Please don't be dead." Emma dropped to her knees beside the eau-de-charred roadkill. "She's still breathing."

The room suddenly filled with Penelope's private guards. They looked like they'd been chewed up and spit out by a large Maaskab blender—tattered, dirty clothes and bloody faces.

That explained what had taken so long; they must've been outside fighting more Maaskab.

The men pointed their rifles at Emma's unconscious grandmother. Zac, God of Who the Hell Knew and Penelope's right hand since she'd been appointed the interim leader of the gods—yes, yes, another long story—blazed into the room, barking orders. "Someone get the Maaskab chained up."

Zac, dressed in his usual black leather pants and tee combo that matched his raven-black hair, turned to Penelope and gazed down at her with his nearly translucent, aquamarine eyes. "Are you all right?"

Penelope nodded. It was the first time in days she'd felt glad to see him. He'd been suffocating her ever since Kinich—

"Oh, gods!" They'd completely forgotten about Kinich! Her eyes flashed up at the clock.

Tick.

Sundown.

A gut-wrenching howl exploded from the other room. Everyone stiffened.

"He's alive!" Pen turned to rush off but felt a hard pull on her arm.

"No. You've had enough danger for one day. I will go." Zac wasn't asking.

Penelope jerked her arm away. "He won't hurt me. I'll be fine. Just stay here and help Emma with her grandmother." She snatched up the two bags of blood from the floor where Helena had dropped them.

"Penelope, I will not tell you again." Zac's eyes filled with anger. Though he was her right hand, he was still a deity and not used to being disobeyed.

"Enough." Penelope held up her finger. "I don't answer to you."

Zac's jealous eyes narrowed for a brief moment before he stiffly dipped his head and then quietly watched her disappear through the doorway.

She rushed down the hallway and paused outside the

bedroom with her palms flat against the hand-carved double doors. The screams had not stopped.

Thank the gods that Kinich, the ex–God of the Sun, was alive. Now they would have a chance to put their lives back together, to undo what never should have been—such as putting her in charge of his brothers and sisters—and she would finally get the chance to tell him how much she loved him, how grateful she was that he'd sacrificed everything to save them, about their baby.

This was their second chance.

She only needed to get him through these first days as a vampire. *And orchestrate a rescue mission for the God of Death and War and the General of the Vampire Army. And deal with the return of Emma's evil granny. And figure out how to stop an impending apocalypse set to occur in eight—yes, eight!—months. And deal with a few hundred women with amnesia they'd rescued from the Maaskab. And manage a herd of insane egocentric, accident-prone deities, with ADHD. And carry a baby. And don't forget squeezing in some time at the gym. Your thighs are getting flabby!*

"See? This Kinich vampire thing should be easy," she assured herself.

She pushed open the door to find Kinich shirtless, writhing on the bed. His muscular legs and arms strained against the silver chains attached to the deity-reinforced frame. He was a large, beautiful man, almost seven feet in height, with shoulders that spanned a distance equal to two widths of her body.

"Kinich!" She rushed to his side. "Are you okay?" She attempted to brush his gold-streaked locks from his face, but he flailed and twisted in agony.

"It burns!" he wailed. "The metal burns."

"I know, honey. I know. But Helena says you need to drink before we can let you go. Full tummy. Happy vamp—"

"Aaahh! Remove them. They burn. Please," he begged. *Oh, saints.*

He would never hurt her. Would he? Of course not.

"Try to hold still." She went to the dresser, pulled open the top drawer, and grabbed the keys.

She rushed to his ankle and undid one leg, then the other.

Kinich stopped moving. He lay there, eyes closed, breathing.

Without hesitation she undid his right arm and then ran to the other side to release the final cuff.

"Are you okay? Kinich?"

Without opening his eyes, he said, "I can smell and hear everything."

Helena had said that blocking out the noise was one of the hardest things a new vampire had to learn. That and curbing their hunger for innocent humans who, she was told, tasted the yummiest. Helena also mentioned to always make sure he was well fed. Full tummy, happy vampire. Just like a normal guy except for the blood obviously.

Penelope deposited herself on the bed next to Kinich with a bag of blood in her hands. "You'll get used to it. I promise. In the meantime, let's get you fed. I have so much to—"

Kinich threw her down, and she landed on her back with a hard thump and the air whooshed from her lungs.

Straddling her, Kinich pinned her wrists to the floor.

His turquoise eyes shifted to hungry black, and fangs protruded from his mouth. "You smell delicious. Like sweet sunshine."

Such a beautiful face, she thought, mesmerized by Kinich's eyes. Once upon a time his skin had glowed golden almost, a vision of elegant masculinity with full lips and sharp cheekbones. But now, now he was refined with an exotic, dangerous male beauty too exquisite for words.

Ex-deity turned mortal, turned vampire. *Hypnotic. He is...hypnotic.*

He lowered his head toward her neck, and her will suddenly snapped back into place. "No! Kinich, no!" She squirmed under his grasp. Without her hands free, she couldn't defend herself. "I'm pregnant."

He stilled and peered into her eyes.

Pain. So much pain. That was all she saw.

"A baby?" he asked.

She nodded cautiously.

Then something cold and deadly flickered in his eyes. His head plunged for her neck, and she braced for the pain of having her neck ripped out.

"Penelope!" Zac sacked Kinich, knocking him to the floor. "Go!" he commanded.

Penelope rolled onto her hands and knees and crawled from the room as it was overrun with several more of Kinich's brethren: the perpetually drunk Acan; the Goddess of the Hunt they called Camaxtli; and the Mistress of Bees they called—oh, who the hell could remember her weird Mayan name?

"Penelope! Penelope!" she heard Kinich scream. "I want to drink her! I must drink her!"

Penelope curled into a ball on the floor in the hallway, unable to stop herself from crying. *This isn't how it's supposed to be. This isn't how it's supposed to be.*

Helena appeared at her side. "Oh, Pen. I'm so sorry. I promise he'll be okay after a few days. He just needs to eat." She helped Penelope sit up. "Let's move you somewhere safe."

Penelope wiped away the streaks of tears from her cheeks and took her friend's hand to stand.

The grunts and screams continued in the other room.

"I can't believe he attacked me, even after I told him." Tears continued to trickle from Penelope's eyes. Why hadn't he stopped? Didn't he love her?

"In his defense, you really do smell yummy. Kind of like Tang."

"Not funny," Penelope responded.

"Sorry." Helena braced Penelope with an arm around her waist and guided her to a bedroom in the other wing of the house.

Helena deposited Penelope on the large bed and turned toward the bathroom. "I'll get you a warm washcloth."

Ironically, Penelope's mind dove straight for a safe haven—that meant away from Kinich and toward her job, which generally provided many meaty distractions, such as impending doom and/or anything having to do with Cimil, the ex–Goddess of the Underworld.

"Wait." Penelope looked up at Helena, who'd become her steady rock of reason these last few weeks. "What happens next?"

Helena paused for a moment. "Like I told you, Kinich needs time to adjust."

Penelope shook her head. "No. I mean, you heard

Emma's grandmother; without Niccolo and Guy, we can't defeat the Maaskab. We have to free our men."

"Well—"

"I know what you're going to say," Pen interrupted. "We can't release Chaam, but—"

"Actually," Helena broke in. "I've been meaning to tell you something."

"What?"

"We've been looking for another way to free them, and I think we found it."

"Found what?" Penelope asked.

"A tablet."

Glossary

Baktun: Twenty cycles of the Mayan calendar equal to 144,000 days or approximately 394 years.

Black Jade: Found only in a particular mine located in southern Mexico, this jade has very special supernatural properties, including the ability to absorb supernatural energy—in particular, god energy. When worn by humans, it is possible for them to have physical contact with a god. If injected, it can make a person addicted to doing bad things. If the jade is fueled with dark energy and then released, it can be used as a weapon. Chaam personally likes using it to polish his teeth.

Book of the Oracle of Delphi: This mystical text from 1400 BC is said to have been created by one of the great oracles at Delphi and can tell the future. As the events in present time change the future, the book's pages magically rewrite themselves. The demigods use this book in Book #2 to figure out when and how to kill the vampire queen. Helena also reads it while they're held captive and learns she must sacrifice her mortality to save Niccolo.

Cenote: Limestone sinkholes connected to a subterranean water system. They are found in Central America and southern Mexico and were once believed by the Mayans to be sacred portals to the afterlife. Such smart humans! They were right. Except cenotes are actually portals to the realm of the gods.

(If you have never seen a cenote, do a quick search on the Internet for "cenote photos," and you'll see how freaking cool they are!)

Demilords: (Spoiler alert for Book #2!) This is a group of immortal badass vampires who've been infused with the light of the gods. They are extremely difficult to kill and hate their jobs (killing Obscuros) almost as much as they hate the gods who control them.

Maaskab: Originally a cult of bloodthirsty Mayan priests who believed in the dark arts. It is rumored they are responsible for bringing down their entire civilization with their obsession for human sacrifices (mainly young female virgins). Once Chaam started making half-human children, he decided all firstborn males would make excellent Maaskab due to their proclivity for evil.

Mocos, Mobscuros, O'Scabbies: Nicknames for when you join Maaskab with Obscuros to create a brand-new malevolent treat.

Obscuros: Evil vampires who do not live by the Pact and who like to dine on innocent humans since they really do taste the best.

The Pact: An agreement between the gods and good vampires that dictates the dos and don'ts. There are many parts to it, but the most important rules are vampires are not allowed to snack on good people (called Forbiddens), they must keep their existence a secret, and they are responsible for keeping any rogue vampires in check.

Payal: Although the gods can take humans to their realm and make them immortal, Payals are the true genetic offspring of the gods but are born mortal, just like their human mothers. Only firstborn children inherit the gods' genes and manifest their traits. If the firstborn happens to be female, she is a Payal. If male, well...then you get something kind of yucky (see definition of Maaskab)!

The Tablet: A Mayan relic made of black jade. It has the power to create portals to other dimensions and to another moment in time.

Uchben: An ancient society of scholars and warriors who serve as the gods' eyes and ears in the human world. They also do the books and manage the gods' earthly assets.

Vamp-ubus, Incu-pire: The saucy combination of an incubus and a vampire.

Character Definitions

The Gods

Although every culture around the world has their own names and beliefs related to beings of worship, there are actually only fourteen gods. And since the gods are able to access the human world only through the portals called cenotes, located in the Yucatán, the Mayans were big fans.

Another fun fact: The gods often refer to each other as brother and sister, but the truth is they are just another species of the Creator and completely unrelated.

Acan—God of Intoxication and Wine: Also known as Belch, Acan has been drunk for a few thousand years. He hopes to someday trade places with Votan because he's tired of his flabby muscles and beer belly.

Ah-Ciliz—God of Solar Eclipses: Called A.C. by his brethren, Ah-Ciliz is generally thought of as the party pooper because of his dark attitude.

Akna—Goddess of Fertility: You either love her or you hate her.

Backlum Chaam—God of Male Virility: He's responsible for discovering black jade, figuring out how to procreate with humans, and kicking off the chain of events that will eventually lead to the Great War.

Camaxtli—Goddess of the Hunt: Also known as Fate (until the end of this novel), Camaxtli holds a special position among the gods, since no one dares challenge her. When Fate has spoken, that's the end of the conversation.

Colel Cab—Mistress of Bees: Because really, where would we all be without the bees?

Goddess of Forgetfulness: Um…Sorry. Still no official name for this infamous deity who spends her evenings DJing and is often referred to as "what's-her-face."

Ixtab—Goddess of Happiness (ex–Goddess of Suicide): Ixtab's once morbid frock used to make children scream. But since finding her soul mate, Antonio Acero, she's now the epitome of all things happy.

K'ak: The history books remember him as K'ak Tiliw Chan Yopaat, ruler of Copán in the 700s AD. King K'ak (pronounced as "cock." Don't you just love that name? Tee-hee-hee…) is one of Cimil's favorite brothers. We're not really sure what he does, but he can throw bolts of lightning.

Kinich Ahau—ex–God of the Sun: Known by many other names, depending on the culture, Kinich likes to go by Nick these days. He's also now a vampire—something he's actually not so bummed about. He is mated to the love of his life, Penelope, the Ruler of the House of Gods.

Máax—the One No One Speaks Of: His name literally means "Who?" Once known as the God of Truth, Máax was banished for repeatedly violating the ban on time travel. The gods stripped his powers, including the ability to take physical form, and banished him to the human realm. Turns out that he will play the role that decides the fate of humanity.

Votan—God of Death and War: Also known as Odin, Wotan, Wodan, God of Drums (he has no idea how the hell he got that title; he hates the drums), and Lord of Multiplication (okay, he is pretty darn good at math so that one makes sense). These days, Votan goes by Guy Santiago (it's a long story—read Book #1), but despite his deadly tendencies, he's all heart. He's now engaged to Emma Keane.

Yum Cimil—Goddess of the Underworld: Also known as Ah-Puch by the Mayans, Mictlantecuhtli (try saying that one ten times) by the Aztec, Grim Reaper by the Europeans, Hades by the Greeks…you get the picture! Despite what people say, Cimil is actually a female, and adores a good bargain (especially garage sales) and the color pink. She's also batshit crazy.

Zac Cimi—Bacab of the North: What the heck is a Bacab? According to the gods' folklore, the Bacabs are the four eldest and most powerful of the gods. Once thought to be the God of Love, we now know differently. Zac is the God of Temptation, and his tempting ways have landed him in very hot water. Because no matter how tempting your brother's mate might be, trying to steal her is wrong.

Not the Gods

Andrus: Ex-Demilord (vampire who's been given the gods' light), now just a demigod after his maker, the vampire queen, died. According to Cimil, his son, who hasn't been born yet, is destined to marry Helena and Niccolo's daughter.

Anne: Don't want to spoil the surprise, but some of you on Facebook definitely guessed right!

Antonio Acero: Our hunky playboy Spaniard who discovers his father was the last surviving incubus. Now a vampire, too, Antonio spends his day spreading happiness around the world with his mate, Ixtab. Oh, Antonio also eats dark energy for lunch. Yum!

Ashli Rosewood: No spoilers here. So I'll just say that she's the final linchpin in our Accidental safari. Watch out, Máax, 'cause here she comes!

Brutus: One of Gabrán's elite Uchben warriors. He doesn't speak much, but that's because he and his team are telepathic. They are also immortal (a gift from the gods) and next in line to be Uchben chiefs.

Emma Keane: A reluctant Payal (a descendant of a deity) who can split a man right down the middle with her bare hands. She is engaged to Votan (aka Guy Santiago) and her grandmother was once the ruler of the Maaskab. What a fun family!

Father Xavier: Once a priest at the Vatican, Xavier is now the Uchben's top scholar and historian. He has a thing for jogging suits, Tyra Banks, and Cimil.

Gabrán: One of the Uchben chiefs and a very close friend of the gods. The chiefs have been given the gods' light and are immortal—a perk of the job.

Gabriela: Emma Keane's grandmother and one of the original Payals. She was brought over to the dark side but cured by Ixtab and no longer leads the Maaskab. Her fate will be determined by the gods at the end of *Accidentally... Over?*

Helena Strauss: Once human, Helena is now a vampire and married to Niccolo DiConti. She has a half-vampire daughter, Matty, who is destined to marry Andrus's son, according to Cimil.

Jess: Just like Anne, I don't want to spoil the surprise, but some of you on Facebook definitely guessed right!

Julie Trudeau: Penelope's mother. Julie is also an ex-angel turned vampire and mated to Viktor.

Mitner: The very first Maaskab and the true creator of the vampire race.

Niccolo DiConti: General of the Vampire Army. Now that the vampire queen is dead, the army remains loyal to him. He shares power with his wife Helena Strauss and has a half-vampire daughter, Matty—a wedding gift from Cimil.

Nick (short for Niccole): (From Book #1, not to be confused with Kinich). Similar to Anne and Jess, I don't want to spoil the surprise, but some of you on Facebook definitely guessed right!

Penelope Trudeau: After inheriting her mate Kinich's power of the sun, Penelope rules the House of the Gods alongside her man.

Philippe: Roberto the Ancient One's evil brother. He is killed by Kinich, thereby exterminating all evil vampires.

Reyna: The dead vampire queen.

Roberto (Narmer): Originally an Egyptian pharaoh, Narmer was one of the six Ancient Ones—the very first vampires. He eventually changed his name to Roberto and moved to Spain—something to do with one of Cimil's little schemes. He now spends his days lovingly undoing Cimil's treachery and taking her unicorn Minky for a ride.

Sentin: One of Niccolo's loyal vampire soldiers. Viktor turned him into a vampire after finding him in a ditch during World War II.

Tommaso: Oh, boy. Where to start. Once an Uchben, Tommaso's mind was poisoned with black jade. He tried to kill Emma, Votan's mate, but redeemed himself by turning into a spy for the gods.

Viktor: Niccolo's right hand and BFF. He's approximately one thousand years old and originally a Viking. He's big. He's blond. He's mated to Penelope's ex-angel mother. He's also Helena's maker.

THE DISH

Where Authors Give You the Inside Scoop

♥ ♥ ♥ ♥ ♥ ♥ ♥ ♥ ♥ ♥ ♥ ♥ ♥ ♥ ♥

From the desk of Marilyn Pappano

Dear Reader,

The first time Jessy Lawrence, the heroine of my newest novel, A LOVE TO CALL HER OWN, opened her mouth, I knew she was going to be one of my favorite Tallgrass characters. She's mouthy, brassy, and bold, but underneath the sass, she's keeping a secret or two that threatens her tenuous hold on herself. She loves her friends fiercely with the kind of loyalty I value. Oh, and she's a redhead, too. I can always relate to another "ginger," lol.

I love characters with faults—like me. Characters who do stupid things, good things, bad things, unforgivable things. Characters whose lives haven't been the easiest, but they still show up; they still do their best. They know too well it might not be good enough, but they try, and that's what matters, right?

Jessy is one of those characters in spades—estranged from her family, alone in the world except for the margarita girls, dealing with widowhood, guilt, low self-esteem, and addiction—but she meets her match in Dalton Smith.

I was plotting the first book in the series, *A Hero to Come Home To*, when it occurred to me that there's a lot of talk about the men who die in war and the wives they leave behind, but people seem not to notice that some of our casualties are women, who also leave behind spouses, fiancés, family whose lives are drastically altered. Seconds behind that thought, an image popped into my head of the margarita club gathered around their table at The Three Amigos, talking their girl talk, when a broad-shouldered, six-foot-plus, smokin' handsome cowboy walked up, Stetson in hand, and quietly announced that his wife had died in the war.

Now, when I started writing the first scene from Dalton's point of view, I knew immediately that scene was never going to happen. Dalton has more grief than just the loss of a wife. He's angry, bitter, has isolated himself, and damn sure isn't going to ask anyone for help. He's not just wounded but broken—my favorite kind of hero.

It's easy to write love stories for perfect characters, or for one who's tortured when the other's not. I tend to gravitate to the challenge of finding the happily-ever-after for two seriously broken people. They deserve love and happiness, but they have to work so hard for it. There are no simple solutions for these people. Jessy finds it hard to get out of bed in the morning; Dalton has reached rock bottom with no one in his life but his horses and cattle. It says a lot about them that they're willing to work, to risk their hearts, to take those scary steps out of their grief and sorrow and guilt and back into their lives.

Oh yeah, and I can't forget to mention my other two favorite characters in A LOVE TO CALL HER OWN: Oz, the handsome Australian shepherd on the cover; and Oliver, a mistreated, distrusting dog of unknown breed.

I love my puppers, both real and fictional, and hope you like them, too.

Happy reading!

Marilyn Pappano

MarilynPappano.net
Twitter @MarilynPappano
Facebook.com/MarilynPappanoFanPage

From the desk of Kristen Ashley

Dear Reader,

In starting to write *Lady Luck*, the book where Chace Keaton was introduced, I was certain Chace was a bad guy. A dirty cop who was complicit in sending a man to jail for a crime he didn't commit.

Color me stunned when Chace showed up at Ty and Lexie's in *Lady Luck* and a totally different character introduced himself to me.

Now, I am often not the white hat–wearing guy type of girl. My boys have to have at least a bit of an edge (and usually way more than a bit).

That's not to say that I don't get drawn in by the boy next door (quite literally, for instance, with Mitch Lawson of *Law Man*). It just always surprises me when I do.

Therefore, it surprised me when Chace drew me in while he was in Lexie and Ty's closet in *Lady Luck*. I knew in that instant that he had to have his own happily-ever-after. And when Faye Goodknight was introduced later in that book, I knew the path to that was going to be a doozy!

Mentally rubbing my hands together with excitement, when I got down to writing BREATHE, I was certain that it was Chace who would sweep me away.

And he did.

But I *adored* writing Faye.

I love writing about complex, flawed characters, watching them build strength from adversity. Or lean on the strength from adversity they've already built in their lives so they can get through dealing with falling in love with a badass, bossy alpha. The exploration of that is always a thing of beauty for me to be involved in.

Faye, however, knew who she was and what she wanted from life. She had a good family. She lived where she wanted to be. She was shy, but that was her nature. She was no pushover. She had a backbone. But that didn't mean she wasn't thoughtful, sensitive, and loving. She had no issues, no hang-ups, or at least nothing major.

And she was a geek girl.

The inspiration for her came from my nieces, both incredibly intelligent, funny, caring and, beautiful—and both total geek girls. I loved the idea of diving into that (being a bit of a geek girl myself), this concept that is considered stereotypically "on the fringe" but is actually an enormous sect of society that is quite proud of their geekdom. And when I published BREATHE, the geek girls came out of the woodwork, loving seeing one of their own land her hot guy.

But also, it was a pleasure seeing Chace, the one who had major issues and hang-ups, find himself sorted out by his geek girl. I loved watching Faye surprise him, hold up the mirror so he could truly see himself, and take the lead into guiding them both into the happily-ever-after they deserved.

This was one of those books of mine where I could have kept writing forever. Just the antics of the kitties Chace gives to his Faye would be worth a chapter!

But alas, I had to let them go.

Luckily, I get to revisit them whenever I want and let fly the warm thoughts I have of the simple, yet extraordinary lives led by a small-town cop and the librarian wife he adores.

Kristen Ashley

♥ ♥ ♥ ♥ ♥ ♥ ♥ ♥ ♥ ♥ ♥ ♥ ♥ ♥ ♥

From the desk of Sandra Hill

Dear Reader,

Many of you have been begging for a new Tante Lulu story.

When I first started writing my Cajun contemporary books back in 2003, I never expected Tante Lulu would touch so many people's hearts and funny bones. Over the years, readers have fallen in love with the wacky old lady (I like to say, Grandma Moses with cleavage). So many of you have said you have a family member just like her; still more have said you wish they did.

Family...that's what my Cajun/Tante Lulu books are all about. And community...the generosity and unconditional love of friends and neighbors. In these turbulent times, isn't that just what we all want?

You should know that SNOW ON THE BAYOU is the ninth book in my Cajun series, which includes: *The Love Potion*; *Tall, Dark, and Cajun*; *The Cajun Cowboy*; *The Red Hot Cajun*; *Pink Jinx*; *Pearl Jinx*; *Wild Jinx*; and *So Into You*. And there are still more Cajun tales to come, I think. Daniel and Aaron LeDeux, and the newly introduced Simone LeDeux. What do you think?

For more information on these and others of my books, visit my website at www.sandrahill.net or my Facebook page at Sandra Hill Author.

As always, I wish you smiles in your reading.

Sandra Hill

♥ ♥ ♥ ♥ ♥ ♥ ♥ ♥ ♥ ♥ ♥ ♥ ♥

From the desk of Mimi Jean Pamfiloff

Dearest Humans,

It's the end of the world. You're an invisible, seventy-thousand-year-old virgin. The Universe wants to snub out the one person you'd like to hook up with. Discuss.

And while you do so, I'd like to take a moment to thank each of you for taking this Accidental journey with me and my insane deities. We've been to Mayan cenotes, pirate ships, jungle battles, cursed pyramids, vampire showdowns, a snappy leather-daddy bar in San Antonio, New York City, Santa Cruz, Giza, Sedona, and we've even been to a beautiful Spanish vineyard with an incubus. Ah. So many fun places with so many fascinating, misunderstood, wacky gods and other immortals. And let's not forget Minky the unicorn, too!

It has truly been a pleasure putting you through the twisty curves, and I hope you enjoy this final piece of the puzzle as Máax, our invisible, bad-boy deity extraordinaire, is taught one final lesson by one very resilient woman who refuses to allow the Universe to dictate her fate.

Because ultimately we make our own way in this world, Hungry Hungry Hippos playoffs included.

Happy reading!

Mimi

P.S.: Hope you like the surprise ending.

♥ ♥ ♥ ♥ ♥ ♥ ♥ ♥ ♥ ♥ ♥ ♥ ♥ ♥ ♥ ♥

From the desk of Karina Halle

Dear Reader,

Morally ambiguous. Duplicitous. Dangerous.

Those words describe not only the cast of characters in my romantic suspense novel SINS & NEEDLES, book one in the Artists Trilogy, but especially the heroine, Ms. Ellie Watt. Though sinfully sexy and utterly suspenseful, it is Ellie's devious nature and con artist profession that makes SINS & NEEDLES one unique and wild ride.

When I first came up with the idea for SINS & NEEDLES, I wanted to write a book that not only touched on some personal issues of mine (physical scarring, bullying, justification), but dealt with a character little seen in modern literature—the antiheroine. Everywhere you look in books these days you see the bad boy, the criminal, the tattooed heartbreaker and ruthless killer. There are always men in these arguably more interesting roles. Where were all the bad girls? Sure, you could read about women in dubious professions, femme fatales, and cold-hearted killers. But when were they ever the main character? When were they ever a heroine you could also sympathize with?

Ellie Watt is definitely one of the most complex and interesting characters I have ever written, particularly as a heroine. On one hand she has all these terrible qualities; on the other she's just a vulnerable, damaged person trying to survive the only way she knows how. You despise Ellie and yet you can't help but root for her at the same time.

Her love interest, hot tattoo artist and ex-friend Camden McQueen, says it perfectly when he tells her this: "That is what I thought of you, Ellie. Heartless, reckless, selfish, and cruel... Beautiful, sad, wounded, and lost. A freak, a work of art, a liar, and a lover."

Ellie is all those things, making her a walking contradiction but oh, so human. I think Ellie's humanity is what makes her relatable and brings a sense of realism to a novel that's got plenty of hot sex, car chases, gunplay, murder, and cons. No matter what's going on in the story, through all the many twists and turns, you understand her motives and her actions, no matter how skewed they may be.

Of course, it wouldn't be a romance novel without a love interest. What makes SINS & NEEDLES different is that the love interest isn't her foil—Camden McQueen isn't necessarily a "good" man making a clean living. In fact, he may be as damaged as she is—but he does believe that Ellie can change, let go of her past, and find redemption.

That's easier said than done, of course, for a criminal who has never known any better. And it's hard to escape your past when it's literally chasing you, as is the case with Javier Bernal, Ellie's ex-lover whom she conned six years prior. Now a dangerous drug lord, Javier has been hunting Ellie down, wanting to exact revenge for her misdoings. But sometimes revenge comes in a vice and Javier's appearance in the novel reminds Ellie that she can never escape who she really is, that she may not be redeemable.

For a book that's set in the dry, brown desert of southern California, SINS & NEEDLES is painted in shades of gray. There is no real right and wrong in the novel, and the characters, including Ellie, aren't just good or bad. They're just human, just real, just trying to come to terms with their true selves while living in a world that just wants to screw them over.

I hope you enjoy the ride!

♥ ▪ ▪ ▪ ▪ ▪ ♥ ▪ ▪ ▪ ▪ ▪ ▪ ▪ ▪ ▪

From the desk of Kristen Callihan

Dear Reader,

The first novels I read belonged to my parents. I was a latchkey kid, so while they were at work, I'd poach their paperbacks. Robert Ludlum, Danielle Steel, Jean M. Auel. I read these authors because my parents did. And it was quite the varied education. I developed a taste for action, adventure, sexy love stories, and historical settings.

But it wasn't until I spent a summer at the beach during high school that I began to pick out books for myself. Of course, being completely ignorant of what I might actually want to read on my own, I helped myself to the beach house's library. The first two books I chose were Mario Puzo's *The Godfather* (yes, I actually read the book before seeing the movie) and Anne Rice's *Interview with the Vampire*.

Those two books taught me about the antihero, that a character could do bad things, make the wrong decisions, and still be compelling. We might still want them to succeed. But why? Maybe because we share in their pain. Or maybe it's because they care, passionately, whether it's the desire for discovering the deeper meaning of life or saving the family business.

In EVERNIGHT, Will Thorne is a bit of an antihero. We meet him attempting to murder the heroine. And he makes no apologies for it, at least not at first. He is also a blood drinker, sensual, wicked, and in love with life and beauty.

Thinking on it now, I realize that the books I've read have, in some shape or form, made me into the author

I am today. So perhaps, instead of the old adage "You are what you eat," it really ought to be: "You are what you read."

♥ ♥ ♥ ♥ ♥ ♥ ♥ ♥ ♥ ♥ ♥ ♥ ♥ ♥ ♥

From the desk of Laura Drake

Dear Reader,

Hard to believe that SWEET ON YOU is the third book in my Sweet on a Cowboy series set in the world of professional bull riding. The first two, *The Sweet Spot* and *Nothing Sweeter*, involved the life and loves of stock contractors—the ranchers who supply bucking bulls to the circuit. But I couldn't go without writing the story of a bull rider, one of the crazy men who pit themselves against an animal many times stronger and with a much worse attitude.

To introduce you to Katya Smith, the heroine of SWEET ON YOU, I thought I'd share with you her list of life lessons:

1. Remember what your Gypsy grandmother said: Gifts sometimes come in strange wrappings.
2. The good-looking ones aren't *always* assholes.
3. Cowboys aren't the only ones who need a massage. Sometimes bulls do, too.

4. Don't ever forget: You're a soldier. And no one messes with the U.S. military.
5. A goat rodeo has nothing to do with men riding goats.
6. "Courage is being scared to death—and saddling up anyway." —John Wayne
7. Cowgirl hats fit more than just cowgirls.
8. The decision of living in the present or going back to the past is easy once you decide which one you're willing to die for.

I hope you enjoy Katya and Cam's story as much as I enjoyed writing it. And watch for the cameos by JB Denny and Bree and Max Jameson from the first two books!

♥ ♥ ♥ ♥ ♥ ♥ ♥ ♥ ♥ ♥ ♥ ♥ ♥ ♥ ♥ ♥

From the desk of Anna Campbell

Dear Reader,

I love books about Mr. Cool, Calm, and Collected finding himself all at sea once he falls in love. Which means I've been champing at the bit to write Camden Rothermere's story in WHAT A DUKE DARES.

The Duke of Sedgemoor is a man who is always in control. He never lets messy emotion get in the way of a rational decision. He's the voice of wisdom. He's the one who sorts things out. He's the one with his finger on the pulse.

And that's just the way he likes it.

Sadly for Cam, once his own pulse starts racing under wayward Penelope Thorne's influence, all traces of composure and detachment evaporate under a blast of sensual heat. Which *isn't* just the way he likes it!

Pen Thorne was such fun to write, too. She's loved Cam since she was a girl, but she's smart enough to know it's hopeless. So what happens when scandal forces them to marry? It's the classic immovable object and irresistible force scenario. Pen is such a vibrant, passionate, headstrong presence that Cam hasn't got a chance. Although he puts up a pretty good fight!

Another part of WHAT A DUKE DARES that I really enjoyed writing was the secondary romance involving Pen's rakish brother Harry and innocent Sophie Fairbrother. There's a real touch of Romeo and Juliet about this couple. I hadn't written two love stories in one book before and the contrasting trajectories throw each relationship into high relief. As a reader, I always like to get two romances for the price of one.

If you'd like to know more about WHAT A DUKE DARES and the other books in the Sons of Sin series—*Seven Nights in a Rogue's Bed*, *Days of Rakes and Roses*, and *A Rake's Midnight Kiss*—please check out my website: http://annacampbell.info/books.html.

Happy reading—and may all your dukes be daring!

Best wishes,

Anna Campbell